YANKEE DOODLES IN BLACK HATS

YANKEE DOODLES IN BLACK HATS

Volume II

THE SATTERFIELD SAGA

THE STORY GENES WOULD TELL IF THEY COULD ONLY TALK

Robert L. Skidmore

Indy**Publish**

YANKEE DOODLES IN BLACK HATS

Copyright © 2001 by Robert L. Skidmore

Published in the United States by IndyPublish.com
McLean, Virginia

ISBN 1-58827-012-2 (hard cover)
ISBN 1-58827-001-7 (paperback)
ISBN 1-58827-007-6 (Gemstar e-book)

Dedication

For Margaret and Tad,
to whom I owe everything good in my life.

Chapter 1
Virginia
Summer 1774

James Satterfield, owner and publisher of the *Alexandria Herald*, felt the rivulets of sweat course down his back while droplets formed on his brow as he stared at his half empty cup of strong Ceylonese tea. Despite the fact that his two companions were discussing a draft of a paper that he had written for presentation at Alexandria's town meeting in two days, James was uncomfortable, bored and lost in his own thoughts. The three men sat on the back verandah of George Washington's spacious country home. In the near distance, the Potomac River, almost a mile wide at this point, rushed its burden of cool mountain waters through the steaming July heat towards the waiting Chesapeake Bay and the Atlantic Ocean. A salt-water merchant ship, heavily laden with hogsheads of tobacco, rode the strong tidal current and light wind southward. Normally, James would have admired the graceful three-masted ship's passage. The owner of a small Alexandria boatyard, James had a professional landsman's interest in ships, but the steaming July mid-day heat, heavy with humidity, and George Mason's turgid discourse, which James had heard several times before, dulled James' attention.

James respected the two Georges, Washington and Mason. They were friends, neighbors, mentors and colleagues. James, just two months short of his forty-first birthday, had known Washington for almost thirty years, Mason for almost as long. James still had vivid memories—not all of which were pleasant—of the time that the woodsman James Genn had a led a surveying party that included James, his twin brother John, George William Fairfax and George Washington to the headwaters of the Potomac on an assignment for Lord Fairfax. The Satterfield twins had been fourteen at the time and George Washington only two years older. James had often pondered the fact that he had returned with a strong dislike for the wilderness and a fear of the wild Indians they had encountered while both John and Washington had developed a deep fascination and love for the west with its untamed inhabitants, animal and human.

James picked up the delicate porcelain cup and sipped the bitter, lukewarm liquid. James did not particularly like tea, but he accepted it as part of the social ritual of the Virginia planter society that he frequented. James pondered the oddity that the brew that resulted from steeping the leaves of a weed in water could be the focal point of a dispute that threatened to erupt into war. As an involved politician and newspaperman, James recognized that tea leaves were simply symbolic not causal. The ways of man intrigued the introspective James. Virginians raised tobacco leaf, rolled it cylindrically and stuffed it into one thousand pound casks, called hogsheads, that they shipped to England where the containers were opened and the leaf unwrapped then rerolled into cigars which the cultured English set afire and inhaled.

In turn, the plantation owners of Ceylon grew their weed bushes, picked their leaves and shipped them to England packed in square boxes. Again the containers were opened, the leaves chopped into fragments and sold to English gentry who soaked the leaves in water which they then drank. The planters, the merchants, and the ship owners grew rich from all the burning and steeping. The leaves were so important to the small island that stood at the hub of the English empire that the Crown had decreed they could only be hauled in English ships and must transit the mother country before they could be sold to others, including sister colonies inhabited by native Englishmen. Of course, when the leaves were transshipped in entrepot England, the Crown's custom collectors took their tolls.

This strange trade was responsible for James' present discomfort. As much as he liked both Georges, James was not sure that he could sit quietly much longer while Mason droned on. James glanced at his friend Washington who sat erectly in his chair looking intently at Mason. Washington at forty-two was a formidable man. The fifteen years since his marriage to the handsome widow Martha Custis, the bestower of an instant fortune and family, had treated Washington kindly. He had prospered as a planter and was now the largest slave owner in Fairfax County and one of the richest men in the colonies. At an early age he had attained fame and honor fighting the French and Indians. Despite the fact that he had decisively lost every battle, he had emerged as a hero.

During his last expedition as an aide to the unlucky and ill selected General Braddock, he had enhanced his reputation by leading the remnants of Braddock's defeated army in a hurried retreat pursued by the blood thirsty French and redmen. Washington and his company of Virginia frontiersmen had conducted themselves with valor, making it possible for the fleeing English army to make its way back to Fort Cumberland. Since then, Washington had concentrated on cultivating his plantation at Mount Vernon and acquiring western land. To assist the latter effort, he had served for fifteen years as a member of the House of Burgesses.

James, who had attended the College of William and Mary and had served as Governor Dinwiddie's clerk, had developed his own taste for power and politics while assisting the Governor as he supported Washington's western escapades.

Both Washington and James had returned to Fairfax County following their youthful experiences. The years had brought them closer together. His father-in-law, Ethelburt Randolph, eventually chose James to replace him in the Burgesses, and James inherited the Randolph position in the Washington/Mason/Randolph triumvirate. The three men over the years had come to represent the people and power of the rapidly growing Fairfax area of the Northern Neck of Virginia.

Mason, older, educated, and well read, initially provided the intellectual leadership. Washington, silent, strong and a heavy investor in western lands, lent the respect engendered by his brief military career. James, younger, bright and a fledgling newspaper publisher—he had started the first weekly to be printed in Fairfax County—initially performed as the implementer of the group. He worked behind the scenes as much as possible, letting the two Georges do the front work for the group. The three schemed together as equals; as time passed, James' role had become more pronounced as the older Mason gradually stepped back and let James assume more and more of the burden of serving as the group's innovator.

"Do you see something in that teacup that we don't?" Mason interrupted James' reverie. "Or are we boring you?"

"I've heard some of these inspiring thoughts before," James smiled. He looked at Washington who nodded in agreement. The taciturn Washington spoke seldom, even in the company of friends like Mason and James. "I was just thinking how odd it is that something as undistinguished as this brew," James held up his cup to emphasize his point, "is responsible for so much discord."

"It's not really the tea's fault," Mason laughed.

"I know," James agreed, "but it's still true."

James did not have to explain his point. The two Georges knew well what James meant. The issue was simple materialism despite the rhetoric. Nine short days before last Christmas a group of Sam Adam's Sons of Liberty had dressed up as Indians and good-naturedly tossed 342 chests of tea into Boston Harbor, an act that instantly brewed a tempest that now threatened to involve all the colonies in war. The three Virginians agreed with Adam's motives but not necessarily his actions. Lord North, the English Prime Minister, had been merely pushing legislation to help out his friends in the East India Company who because of their own blunders had some seventeen million pounds of unsold tea leaves on their hands and faced bankruptcy.

Influential company members had persuaded North he could solve a major problem for himself as well as help the company with one simple action. Instead of requiring the company to transship its tea via England, the company should be permitted to send the tea directly to the American colonies. There, the government could collect a three pence tax on each pound of tea, which the company sold directly to merchants who in turn retailed to customers. The only persons to be hurt would be the middlemen in the colonies and England who had previously purchased the tea from the company in London then resold it to the colonists.

Lord North in his naiveté had calculated that nobody important cared about middlemen except they themselves. The Government would get its taxes from customs in the colonies instead of in England. At the same time, North could solve a political problem. In 1770 the hated Townshend Acts had been repealed, negating the taxation without representation issue with the exception of a continuing tax on tea. The colonists had ignored the tax on tea and bought their supplies from tea smugglers, hurting both the Crown and the Company. By pushing through his new proposal in 1773, Lord North reasoned he could help the East India Company and collect tea taxes from the colonists in a painless fashion. To his surprise, the action immediately raised the colonists' ire. To the taxation without representation issue was added the charge of government sponsored monopoly. New England merchants turned to the bullyboys of the Sons of Liberty and the result was the Christmas season tea party.

"I think James' draft of the resolves covers the situation just fine," Washington finally spoke. "Let's take it as is to Alexandria tomorrow and let our friends go over it before the Tuesday meeting."

Mason, who had just been getting started with his commentary, looked abruptly at his two friends. Noting the amused expressions on their faces and recognizing that they were deliberately taunting him by pulling him up short, he laughed in agreement.

"All right. I'll save my comments for tomorrow," Mason agreed.

"It's not as if the thoughts are new to you," James laughed. Mason had virtually dictated most of the draft. All three recognized that Mason was the political thinker of the group.

"Then, if there is no objection, I'll take my leave and hurry over to Eastwind." James set his teacup on the table in front of him as he spoke. The two Georges nodded agreement. Washington rose to bid his friend farewell while the older Mason remained seated.

Both Georges were aware of James' somewhat unusual lifestyle. After her father's stroke and death some four years before, James' wife Vivian, a strong and self-reliant lady, had chosen to reside at the Randolph family plantation, her childhood home, and oversee the enterprise with its five thousand acres and sixty slaves. Since the death of her brother during General Braddock's campaign against the French and Indians some nineteen years previously, Vivian remained Ethelburt Randolph's sole heir. James' life centered on Alexandria and Williamsburg; he admired the sheer physical beauty of Eastwind, but he came from small farmer stock with roots in the Short Hills of what was now Loudoun County, and he did not approve of slavery or the plantation way of life that required ownership of others in order to survive. James had declined to move to Eastwind, and Vivian had been unwilling to give up her childhood home. Still deeply in love and committed to each other and their son Jason, James and Vivian had worked out their own compromise. Vivian lived at Eastwind and managed the plantation. She visited James in Alexandria for short stays whenever plantation demands permitted. This meant she spent longer periods in Alexandria during the winter and remained at Eastwind during the spring and summer months. James lived in his town house in Alexandria and edited the Alexandria *Herald* and supervised his small shipyard on the river. He usually put the *Herald*, a weekly, to bed on Thursday afternoon and rode the fifteen miles to Eastwind where he would remain until Sunday afternoon when he would return to Alexandria.

Frequently, the press of business or politics interfered, but James visited Eastwind as often as he could. During James' extended absences from Alexandria such as his trips to Williamsburg to attend the sessions of the House of Burgesses, Corney Goodenough managed the *Herald* for James. Corney, short for Cornelius, had been the Satterfield tutor in the Short Hills before moving to Alexandria and opening his academy for young men after his indentured contract to James' father, Tom Satterfield, had expired. The tall, slender Goodenough and James had subsequently become close friends and colleagues in Alexandria. The sharp-witted schoolteacher had evolved into James' adviser and alter ego. Together, they had made the *Herald* not only the first newspaper in northern Virginia but one of the most respected small town publications in the colonies. Their incisive commentary shaped the views of thoughtful residents in Virginia and the middle colonies.

Because of the late afternoon heat, James slowed his mount from a leisurely canter to a walk as he approached Eastwind. From a distance, he discerned Vivian and several friends dispersed leisurely about Eastwind's broad front porch. The mansion faced the east and attempted to capture any breezes that happened to track up the Chesapeake and Potomac. Although he never voiced the opinion to Vivian, James frequently thought that Ethelburt Randolph had not shown much imagination when he had named his plantation Eastwind.

James waved as he drew near the verandah, and he had no trouble seeing Vivian raise her hand in casual reply. Most of the women, including Vivian, wore short sleeved, long white gowns decorated with bright ribbons and marked by bare shoulders and dipping necklines. White female skin seemed their most prominent feature. Most of the men had shed their dark suit coats and lounged about in white shirts with long sleeves and ruffled fronts. The number of guests did not surprise James. It was common practice for the owners of the relatively isolated plantations to visit each other and stay for several days at a time. James did not particularly like most of Eastwind's social circle—they were Vivian's friends from childhood and from a different culture than James had encountered in the Short Hills—but he accepted them and they tolerated him, barely.

Mason, Washington and their political friends in Williamsburg—the colony's leadership elite—were members of Virginia's aristocracy as were Vivian's friends and relatives, but those of the leadership elite looked beyond the plantation culture to the challenge of business, politics, and the acquisition of more wealth. The people who sat on Eastwind's verandah, to James at least, were the softer members of the aristocracy who were content with enjoying what they had inherited and not the least interested in life beyond the borders of their plantations. They tended to look down upon the hustling Masons and Washingtons and ignored the small farmers and yeomen of James' caste.

James stopped his horse near the verandah steps and handed the reins to the smartly dressed slave who stood waiting. James knew the house slave would lead the horse around Eastwind to the rear where it would be given to a field hand who would take it to the stables and rub it down.

"Welcome home, Mr. James," the house slave greeted James with a smile. The Africans liked their absentee master and treated him with respect. They appreciated the fact that James acknowledged them as individual human beings and not merely as chattel whose purpose in life was to see to his comfort.

"Thank you, Joseph," James replied. "It's such a hot afternoon I would appreciate it if you would make sure my friend here gets a good drink and a long rubdown after he cools off." James handed the reins to the still smiling slave.

"Certainly, Mr. James. I sure will."

James turned and climbed the stairs to the verandah. Vivian waited at the top. James took her in his arms and kissed her deeply. He had not seen her in two weeks.

"It's been too long, honey," James spoke first. "I promise I'll be back Thursday. "

"That means you're leaving tomorrow." She knew their separations were more her fault than James'. "I'm sorry too," she continued. "I just can't get away from Eastwind in July. There's always some problem."

"I know," James agreed sincerely.

"How's Jason?" Vivian asked, disappointed that their only son had not accompanied his father. Jason, now seventeen, lived with his father in Alexandria. He had left Eastwind with Vivian's full agreement four years earlier in order to attend Corney Goodenough's Academy. She had hoped he would follow his father's footsteps to William and Mary this year, but Jason's disinterest in books and total devotion to his father's shipyard had led her to acquiesce to Jason's demand that he be allowed to work a year before attending college. James only very reluctantly and with much disappointment accepted his friend Goodenough and Vivian's appeal on Jason's request.

"He's working on his boat. Where else? He hopes to have it in the water imminently."

Vivian shook her head wryly but nodded in understanding. Jason had been working on his two masted sloop for six months. The small boat, no more than fifty feet in length and ten feet in breadth, was designed to sail in the Chesapeake Bay, and, if Jason had his way, to explore the ocean coastal waters south of Virginia. Jason had confided to Vivian that he planned to reach the West Indies next summer, but he had not divulged this adventurous dream to his father yet. Vivian had not broached the confidence because she knew it would worry James, but she did not feel guilty keeping her son's secret. It worried her too, but she doubted it would ever come to pass. The situation in Massachusetts appeared to be ready to disrupt all their plans. Vivian was unusual for her sex and class; she followed political developments as avidly as her husband, and her sharp mind was every bit as incisive as his in divining the probable future course of events.

James stepped back and paused to study his wife. To James she was even lovelier at forty than she had been as a twenty-year-old. The active plantation life with long hours in the saddle had assisted in keeping her figure. Her dark hair had retained its luster and the deeper smile lines around her mouth and light wrinkles radiating from her eyes merely enhanced her appearance. Vivian accepted her husband's adoring scrutiny for a few seconds then stepped back. She spun towards her guests, keeping James' hand tightly and affectionately grasped in hers.

"Come," she ordered with a smile. "Greet our guests."

James for the first time turned towards the waiting group, which had quietly watched James' arrival. Most failed to understand why Vivian had married so far beneath her and waited patiently for this unorthodox marriage to fail. James was bright enough and had apparently made his way in the world, but he still had not been born into their class.

James was pleased to note that Bryan Fairfax and his wife Jane and Richard Randolph and his wife Remmie were among the assembled group. James tolerated most of Vivian's friends but genuinely liked the Fairfaxes and Richard Randolphs. Bryan Fairfax was the social lion of the group. He was a brother of Washington's friend George William Fairfax who had accompanied the Satterfield twins and James Genn on the survey of Fairfax lands at the headwaiters of the Potomac, and he was a son of Colonel William Fairfax, the cousin of Lord Fairfax who owned most of northern Virginia in his proprietorship. Richard Randolph ranked at the lower end of the social scale, being a distant cousin of Vivian's from a lesser branch of the far-flung Randolph family. Richard, or Richie as he was known, owned a small plantation along the Potomac River about twenty miles south of the Occoquan River. An owner of only twenty slaves, he was accepted in social circles primarily because of his name and distant relationship with the influential Randolphs.

"Welcome to your own house, James, even if you're a virtual stranger here," Bryan Fairfax laughed. "We've enjoyed your munificent hospitality, particularly your Madeiras and spiced rum.

"Bryan," James replied with a smile. "It's a pleasure to be here," he mimicked Bryan's joshing tone. James shook Bryan's hand vigorously and noted Ritchie Randolph approaching.

"And it's good to see you again," James spoke sincerely, offering his hand to the younger man. Randolph was a tall, slender thirty-year-old who wore his dark hair cropped short despite the current styles. His face was deeply tanned from long hours working in the fields besides his slaves. "How is this year's crop," James asked. His question was serious, not merely a pleasantry. Many of the northern Virginia plantation owners had already shifted from the soil destroying weed tobacco to grains, but Randolph had persisted in his effort to produce a superior money earning tobacco leaf.

"Not as well as I hoped," the young Randolph replied. "Maybe I should have shifted to grains this year," he continued with the worry evident in his voice. "I tried to build up some of my best fields by letting them lie fallow for a year and dusting them good with lime as some of our scientific farmers have recommended, but I'm afraid it didn't help. This year's leaf looks even smaller."

"I'm sorry to hear that, Ritchie," James said, not quite sure what he could say to alleviate his friend's concern. James looked at Bryan Fairfax who had been following the conversation. Bryan and his brother had switched from tobacco to wheat and other grains the previous year.

"I'm afraid you're fighting a losing battle, Ritchie," Fairfax entered the conversation. Both James and Ritchie looked at the portly, younger Fairfax and waited for him to continue. They both knew that the Fairfaxes with all their land and wealth and under the stern direction of Bryan's grand uncle Lord Fairfax had studied the issue of switching crops closely. "We would have liked to stick with tobacco. It's a bigger money crop," Fairfax said, his thin lips compressed in a tight smile. "But tobacco is just too hard on the land. Our wheat this year is much smaller than that of the Germans and Quakers in Loudoun who have never grown tobacco. I'm afraid our small farmer friends have been right all along."

Both James and Ritchie Randolph nodded in agreement. "I'll have to give up tobacco next year. How have you kept your Africans busy?" Ritchie asked Fairfax, referring to the fact that tobacco was a labor-intensive crop that required many expensive slaves to cultivate while wheat was less demanding.

"We haven't solved that problem yet," Fairfax replied. "We may have to go into milling and other small industry like our friend Washington," he began but was interrupted by a sarcastic male voice.

"Well look who's here, our delinquent host."

James could not restrain the disgusted glance he offered to his friends Bryan and Ritchie who nodded in agreement as the loud voiced Elizah Bayley approached. Bayley, a large bully of a man over six feet four inches tall and at least two hundred and fifty pounds, was one of James' least favorite people. Unfortunately, in James' opinion, Bayley's wife Elizabet was a close childhood friend of Vivian's. Elizabet's parents owned a small plantation a few miles to the south of Eastwind and the two girls had been constant playmates, each having spent a large portion of their childhood visiting the other's family home. They had shared thoughts and dreams and were still as close as two individuals of the same sex could be. Elizabet had been a skinny, unattractive child with a long English nose and thin, stringy hair. She had a sickly disposition and seldom was without a runny cold that caused her prominent nose to drip and turn a scarlet red. The malady continued into adulthood. Elizah Bayley, the son of an alcoholic Alexandria merchant, had been her only suitor. Since the marriage, Bayley had moved into the small plantation house of Elizabet's parents and adopted the easy life of a non-working wastrel. Normally, James succeeded in avoiding Elizah's presence and left the socializing to Vivian and Elizabet, the childhood friends. Rarely did the two men meet; today, Elizah, anticipating James would be absent from Eastwind, had accompanied his wife on a day visit to Eastwind to socialize with other more welcome Satterfield guests.

"Good afternoon, Elizah," James forced himself to be civil despite the fact he knew from long experience that Bayley would soon have something insulting to say. In anticipation, James refrained from offering his hand in welcome. James noticed Elizabet Bayley sitting on the far side of the verandah watching her bearish husband with concerned eyes. James smiled and waved assurance to Elizabet who he genuinely liked. Despite the burden of her boorish husband, Elizabet had maintained her kindly personality. She would do anything in her limited power to assist friends and acquaintances. She was known to be one of the more considerate plantation wives who treated her slaves, field as well as house servants, with humanity and kindness.

"What's good about it?" Bayley demanded belligerently. "The English need to be taught a lesson. We should pack all the lobsterbacks in boxes and ship them back to England."

Embarrassed by the provocative tone that was designed to insult James' friends Bryan and Ritchie, James stared at Bayley.

"Let's skip the politics for the afternoon," James said curtly and moved past the belligerent Bayley. "I assume we'll all be able to discuss the matter calmly at the town meeting in Alexandria Tuesday."

"I wouldn't miss it," Bayley spoke loudly to James' back. After speaking, he turned to address Fairfax and Ritchie Randolph, but the two had already moved to the far side of the verandah, leaving Bayley standing alone. He set his empty punch glass on the silver tray held by the impassive house slave and grabbed a full glass. "Too bad the Satterfields can't afford something better than this horse piss," he grumbled at the expressionless slave who ignored the large man and moved towards other guests.

After about an hour of socializing with the other guests, James was able to rejoin Bryan Fairfax and Ritchie Randolph in a far corner of the verandah.

"I was sorry to hear that you withdrew from last week's election," James spoke sincerely to Bryan Fairfax. "We could have enjoyed the sessions in Williamsburg."

"I felt I had to," Bryan said frankly. "After talking the matter over with George," he referred to Washington, "I decided my views were too different from our friends and neighbors to give me an honest chance at election."

"I know," James observed. Fairfax had the advantage of his name and high status in the county but was known to be more sympathetic to the English position than most of his neighbors. Fairfax counseled moderation not threats, and appeals to the Crown for relief not violence. Ritchie Randolph shared Bryan Fairfax's views but was less outspoken about them. James feared that if events came to a showdown that Bryan Fairfax would join his brother George William Fairfax in London. George and Sally had returned to the family estates in England the previous year. James was less sure about Ritchie who was softer in his views.

"Will you be joining us at the town meeting to consider the resolves the county should send to next month's meeting in Williamsburg?" Governor Dunmore in a pique had dissolved the most recent House of Burgesses. Hence, last week's election for a new House of Burgesses wherein James and George Washington had been elected to represent Fairfax.

The old House, however, in a rump session in the Apollo Room of the Raleigh Tavern in Williamsburg after Dunmore had dissolved them had called for representatives from the counties to meet in Williamsburg in August independent of the Crown to discuss matters. Each county would select two representatives and empower them to present the views of their respective county populations. The Tuesday meeting in Alexandria was intended to select Fairfax's representatives and propose a position paper for them. James' draft of Mason's views, which he had just met with Washington and Mason to discuss, would serve as the basis for the Fairfax Resolves.

"I haven't made up my mind about that yet, James," Fairfax said. "I don't want to get in a public debate with my friends over such an important and volatile issue. I've been thinking about simply sending a letter containing my views. I can be more dispassionate that way."

"I understand," James said, and he did. Fairfax was an honest and sincere man. He did not stand alone among his class in his sympathy and regard for England. He simply found it incomprehensible that Englishmen in the colonies, even those two generations removed from the mother country, could turn on "home" as he considered England. The more aggressive of those who shared Fairfax's views, though not Bryan himself, believed Washington and Mason and others of like opinions were traitors to the class for siding with the Massachusetts rabble against the Crown and Parliament.

"We welcome your presence if you change your mind," James sincerely advised his friend. "We will guarantee an opportunity for you to have your say. Though, I admit you may not find yourself popular. Feelings are running high in Alexandria, and some of the hot heads in the Sons of Liberty are making threats."

"I know that," Bryan responded. "They don't frighten me, but I am not interested in lowering myself to their level."

James nodded in agreement. He noted that Ritchie Randolph had simply listened to the conversation without comment. James looked at Ritchie, inviting his contribution, but the sallow-faced young man shook his head and remained silent. Pausing to change the subject, James looked towards his other guests for inspiration. Across the verandah, Elizah Bayley was haranguing a group of wives on his views about what should be done to those traitors to the colonial cause who favored England.

James was discomfited to hear Bayley repeatedly use the words "tar and feathers" in a threatening manner.

Chapter 2
Alexandria
July 1774

On Monday morning July 18th, James joined the two Georges and other prominent members of the Fairfax gentry in a rump meeting to discuss the paper James had drafted which incorporated most of Mason's ideas. The county leaders accepted the draft with only minor changes designed to flag the amender's status rather than change the substance of the text in any dramatic fashion. At the morning conference, James joined Washington and Mason in explaining the intent of the "Resolves" as they were now identified. Following the morning session, James had excused himself and returned to the offices of the Alexandria *Herald* where he shared a light meal of salty ham sandwiches with Corney Goodenough. Afterwards, James and Corney walked through the heavy July heat and humidity to Market Square where the county meeting of freeholders would formally consider the "Resolves."

"Jason tells me that he expects to launch his boat this afternoon," Corney said.

"That's what he said this morning. He and some of the men worked all weekend getting the finishing touches on it. They had trouble smoothing the copper sheets on the hull that Jason believes will cut down on barnacles and improve speed," James said.

"Speed's what it's all about," Corney declared.

"Speed and stealth." James was not sure he approved of Jason's preoccupation with building a small coastal schooner whose purpose would be to run English blockades. "Jason insists that there'll be a big market for small, fast ships able to avoid British men-of-war and hide in the bay inlets and up the rivers."

"He may be right," Corney nodded his head, "but I suspect Jason enjoys the challenge of building a fast boat as much as making money."

"And sailing it," Jason agreed, "and that's what worries me. Things don't look good up north, and those men-of-war carry eighteen pounders. I don't like the idea of Jason getting involved."

"How does Vivian feel?"

"It shouldn't surprise me, but it does. Most mothers would worry about their sons getting involved but not Vivian. She even talks about going along."

"And she might," Corney laughed. "That's one tough lady."

"I should know," James said sourly.

The two men turned the corner and approached the already gathered crowd of townsmen and small farmers who filled Market Square. Most of the county's young men, those who would be expected to form the army if the Americans went to war, noisily filled the square creating a din with their loud, bragging voices. James noted the familiar faces of small farmers and their families from back-country Fairfax and Loudoun. James and Corney pushed their way though the noisy crowd to the open front door of the Court House where the planters and prosperous Alexandria merchants, the county's gentry, had collected. Although any free white male landowner of twenty-one years of age could vote in elections and meetings such as this, the farmers and small tradesmen generally followed the lead of the big planters and the gentry. James, the son of a Piedmont farmer, and Corney, an ex-indentured servant, had worked their way upwards and were now considered members of the privileged classes. Neither had forgotten his humble origins, however, and each dealt as an equal with planter and farmer alike.

The main hall of the Court House was almost filled when James and Corney entered. Several of the milling crowd called words of welcome to the new arrivals. George Washington, George Mason, William Ramsay, John Carlyle, Dr. James Craik and several other town notables, all of whom had participated in the morning meeting, sat in a row on a small dais in front of the room. Mason, noting James and Corney enter, gestured for them to join the group in the front of the room. James, who preferred to work behind the scenes, shook his head side to side negatively, and Mason, who understood James' idiosyncrasies, turned to continue his whispered consultation with Washington.

James noted that Bryan Fairfax was conspicuously absent. Bryan Fairfax, along with his sister Sara, were the only members of the famous family still resident in the county that bears their name. Lord Fairfax, now elderly, lived on his plantation, Greenway Court, near Winchester. His cousin, Colonel William Fairfax who had administered the large grant on the proprietor's behalf, was dead. His son, George William Fairfax, Bryan's half brother and George Washington's close friend, had packed up his family including his wife Sally, Washington's Platonic paramour, and resettled to England. George William had returned home to manage the family's extensive estates. He did not agree with his colonial friends and colleagues in their growing estrangement from the Crown and Parliament, but he had based his decision to move on personal not political reasons. At George William and Sally's request, George Washington, whose plantation, Mount Vernon was located a short distance from the Fairfax home at Belvoir, was occupied with arranging an auction to sell the Fairfax possessions. James wondered how the taciturn Washington felt about selling off the possessions of Sally Fairfax. James knew that George as a young man had fallen deeply in love with the vivacious wife of his friend. Washington had never confided in James, but he had found it impossible to conceal the fact he was smitten with the flirtatious Sally. Washington was too strait laced and stiff to violate his friend's trust, but his love for Sally was a common secret. Even Martha, who George had married five years previously, was aware of the deep friendship between George and Sally.

Bryan shared his family's loyalty to England and the Crown, but unlike his half brother he was not ready to give up the role of mediator. He had considered running for the Burgesses in the last election for the seat James now held, but he had withdrawn recognizing that his views were more moderate than those of his Fairfax constituency. Time and events had passed Bryan by. Bryan wanted the colonists to continue to appeal to the Crown to abolish the oppressive new laws without bluster or threats or punitive counter-actions such as non-import and non-export bans. James had expected Bryan to appear at this meeting to advocate his moderate views. His absence denied the opposition to the Resolves a persuasive spokesman.

"I don't see Bryan, do you?" James whispered to Corney Goodenough.

"No, and I think he's wise not to be here," Corney replied. "Some of the hotheads in the taverns have been threatening public whippings and tar and feathers for the Tories."

"I hope it doesn't come to that."

"Don't mislead yourself, James. Feelings are running high. You tend to intellectualize things too much. The time has passed for appeals to King George the Third. We've tried all that. Look at what his minions are doing to Boston."

James merely nodded agreement. The topic had been talked to death. People were ready to support Boston with action. The word "war" had begun to appear in every day conversation along with the charge "if they can do it to Boston, they can do it to us." The threat, bluff or not, made James even more concerned about Jason and his boat. At least it would not carry guns, James consoled himself, but he knew that possession of such a craft would lead inevitably to its use.

Last year he had been concerned about Jason's infatuation with Lily West, daughter of John West, and the possibility that Jason might impetuously marry the beautiful Scottish girl with green eyes and red hair and not pursue his education at William and Mary or Harvard that James thought imperative. Then, Jason had become preoccupied with the idea of building a fast schooner. Now, Jason busied himself with Lily and building his damned boat, leaving no time for family or studies. Every time Jason tried to raise the subject, Jason evaded the issue by noting that James' twin brother John and younger brother Will had never gone to college.

Corney Goodenough's tutoring had been sufficient for them, and Jason, who had attended Corney's Academy for two years, argued the same applied to him. James had trouble with this logic because he could not respond without disparaging his brothers. Since he respected John and Will and did not consider

himself better than them, James had reached an impasse with Jason. John, a frontiersman to the core of his being, lived in western Virginia with his growing family including a son of Jason's age, Eli, who Jason worshipped. Eli, the very image
of his father John, was about four inches taller than Jason. Despite his flaming red
hair and hazel eyes, Eli was a child of the forest. At nineteen, he was already
emulating his father and acquiring fame as a relentless and unforgiving Indian
fighter. When his mind shifted from reverie to the present, James decided to visit
the shipyard and watch Jason launch his boat. With luck, it would hit a rock and
sink.

At the morning conference, the county leaders had unanimously chosen
William Ramsay to preside over the Court House meeting. As the builder of the
first house in Alexandria, the prominent merchant was widely respected by all
strata of Fairfax society. Ramsay rose, called the meeting to order and introduced
George Mason, the county's intellectual, to present the Resolves which the county delegates, yet to be selected, would carry to the meeting in Williamsburg.
Mason, as agreed, first read the draft of the Resolves. At James' insistence, the
fact that he had drafted the document was not revealed. The Resolves were simply presented as a compilation of the views of the county leadership. Mason's
droning presentation soon lost James' attention. He was after all intimately
acquainted with each and every word

George Mason was a brilliant and creative thinker, particularly in the field of
basic human rights, but he was a lackluster speaker. James looked around the
room watching the reaction of the listeners. He saw an African dressed in the fin-
ery of a house servant obsequiously approach Washington and hand him a sealed
envelope. James recognized the slave was one of Bryan Fairfax's house servants.
Washington opened the envelope, read the single sheet of paper, refolded it and
handed it to William Ramsay who sat on his left. In this fashion the letter was
read then passed along to all the notables sitting on the dais. The men read the
letter and passed it on without comment or expression. Later, James learned from
Washington, that his curiosity need not have been piqued. The letter was simply
a last minute effort by Bryan Fairfax to project his moderate views in his absence
at the meeting. Since the leaders were intimately familiar with Bryan's position,
and had rejected it, they read his note, then disregarded it.

When Mason finished, the assembled crowd broke into a rousing cheer and
on Ramsay's motion passed the "Fairfax Resolves" unanimously by voice vote.
Given the strong feeling that made the crowd almost belligerent, any loyalists
who may have opposed the Resolves kept quiet, probably fearing a hostile physical reaction.

James did not consider the Resolves particularly noteworthy but was pleased
that they were of sufficient quality as not to embarrass Fairfax's representatives
to the Virginia convention. He anticipated that others in Virginia's counties were
preparing similar messages to be carried to Williamsburg. Certainly young Tom
Jefferson was doing the same in Albemarle County. In the short period they had

served together in the Burgesses, James, like most others, had grown to respect the smart young man with the incisive mind and glib pen.

The Fairfax Resolves as adopted consisted of twenty-four separate resolutions. James had tried to keep each resolution succinct, beginning with the word "Resolved" and proceeding with a minimum of verbiage to the heart of each issue. He began with one of George Mason's favorite preoccupations:

Resolved that Virginia is not a conquered country; its settlers were conquerors who brought their own rights with them; they are not natives subject to the wills of others.

James had continued by noting the Virginians' right to be governed by their own elected representatives who led a people who possessed the natural rights of mankind. One resolution denied the authority of Parliament in America and referred to the premeditated design of the British Ministry to impose an arbitrary government on the colonials. James called for the convocation of a congress consisting of deputies from all the colonies who would be charged to prepare a plan for a defense of the colonies and their common rights.

One resolution that had been added by the county leaders troubled James slightly even though he agreed with its intent. It called for the publication of a list of names of those who violated the non-importation association and the identification of those so listed as traitors. Since James anticipated he would be expected to print the list in the *Herald*, he worried about the impact on his subscribers. After all a number of his advertisers and readers would undoubtedly be identified as violators. James personally knew of several Alexandria merchants who sold prohibited goods, primarily because they met the demands of prominent customers, some of whom were sincere patriots who could not bring themselves to make the sacrifices demanded by their political beliefs. Others were planter friends, like the Fairfaxes and Ritchie Randolph, who advocated moderation and compromise with the Crown.

James had swallowed hard when he drafted at Washington and Mason's insistence the final resolution which noted that if there were no redress in response to their petitions there could only be one final appeal, war.

After the Resolves were approved, Mason nominated George Washington and James to represent the county at the rump session of Burgesses called for the first of August in Williamsburg. Having just been reelected to the Burgesses, both men were logical candidates and were elected by the meeting without opposition.

When the meeting adjourned, James and Corney Goodenough were among the first to depart the Court House. They were surrounded by excited townsmen and countrymen, mixed, all talking in loud voices, most pleased with their afternoon's work. Across the square a squad of shabbily dressed militiamen drilled to the beat of two drummer boys and the shrill piping of two fifers. The music gave the setting a martial air prompting many of the milling crowd to shout words of encouragement. The youth of the town watched their friends parade, and many silently resolved to get permission to join the militia and to prepare to fight for liberty and freedom. The high flown words and angry denotation of English misdeeds stirred the emotions of men as they walked in noisy groups towards the City Tavern, the Wild Boar and other Alexandria gathering spots.

"Events are getting people riled up," Corney observed, speaking as much to himself as to James.

"More emotion than reason, I'm afraid," James agreed.

The two friends paused at the edge of Market Square and listened to the conversations that erupted as the crowd of excited men streamed past. Much of the talk centered on speculation as to the identity of Tories, as loyalists who remained supportive of Mother England were called. Most of the names that James and Corney heard cited were those of merchants, doctors, clergymen and planters, all prominent members of the town's gentry. James suspected that if war came, it would change more than the colonies' relation with England. More imminently worrisome to James was the frequent threat to use tar and feathers to teach the traitors a needed lesson.

"Many of our friends have something to worry about," Corney observed as he listened to the prominent names cited. "Some of those being described as Tories surprise me."

"I know for a fact that many are true patriots," James agreed. "It sounds like some of the hotheads are planning to use the troubles as an excuse for evening past grudges."

"I hope not," Corney observed with a shake of his head. "Are you going to join the crowd for an ale?" Corney asked, wiping the sweat from his brow. The late July afternoon sun continued to punish Alexandria.

"An ale would taste good," James agreed, "but I don't want to get involved with our fellow citizens this afternoon. I don't think most are prepared to listen to a voice of reason and moderation. We may in our enthusiasm have overstated the Resolves if this is the kind of public reaction they are going to generate."

"What are you going to do then?" Corney asked. "Go back to the paper?"

"No. I've turned out enough patriotic rhetoric for the day. I think I'll walk down to the river and watch Jason launch his boat."

"I saw it yesterday," Corney said. "Jason was putting on a final coat of paint. If the boat sails as good as it looks, it'll be a fine craft."

"It's rakish. Small, but it looks fast. Jason designed it himself. I'm not sure what use it will be. It's shorter, narrower and has a smaller cargo hold than most schooners. It's really a big sloop, but it has two masts like a schooner. Lots of sail, but it's too small to cross the ocean."

"I don't think that is what Jason has in mind," Corney agreed.

"The normal ocean voyager that we build here in Alexandria is about fifty feet long and fourteen or fifteen feet wide. They run fifty tons and can carry a thousand five hundred tons of cargo. Jason's boat is more a toy. It's exactly thirty feet long and ten feet wide. With his sail locker and crew cabin, he probably would be pushed to carry two tons of cargo at the most. It's simply not economical."

"Jason's aiming for speed," Corney agreed. "He has a lot of sail."

"Almost as much as the large ships. I'm afraid she might be top heavy. It'll probably tip over as soon as its hull hits the water."

"I think I'll come along and watch this," Corney decided.

The two men continued to talk as they walked down the cobblestones of Cameron Street towards Union Street and the Potomac River where the warehouses, sail lofts and shipyards were located. Alexandria over the past twenty years had boomed into a prosperous port. Ocean crossing vessels regularly visited the city to off load cargo and take on board tobacco and grain to carry home for England. Several small shipyards, including James Satterfield's commercial venture, which was the smallest of all, had opened. The two friends, still discussing Jason's boat, turned right on Union Street and crossed Prince Street, which contained the series of excellent homes known as Captains Row. The families of the sea captains who guided the larger ships between England and Virginia occupied most of the houses.

"Non-importation is going to hurt more than the merchants," Corney observed, nodding in the direction of Captains Row.

"And not just them," James agreed. "I imagine I 'll have to close down the boatyard. I have one more order to fill as soon as James gets his boat off the stays."

"I wouldn't be too hasty, James," Corney advised, surprising his friend.

"Why?" James asked. "With non-importation and non-shipment of American goods to England, there will be no need for more ships."

"You might be wrong about that and maybe Jason has the right idea."

James paused and looked at his friend.

"War creates its own needs," Corney explained. "We don't have the capability to manufacture the powder, weapons, uniforms and everything else we will require to fight a war."

"You don't think there will actually be a war?" James shuddered involuntarily at the thought.

"You yourself said there would be in your resolves," Corney replied.

"That was George Mason's idea," James said defensively.

"Well I think he's right. You saw the attitude of our neighbors back at the meeting. They're talking war now."

"That's just talk." James was not sure he believed his own words.

"I hope so. But I don't think so," Corney countered.

The two friends walked silently to the end of Union Street where James' small boatyard, nothing more than two buildings with a slip on each side and a pier extending a short distance into the river that was deep enough to allow ocean crossing ships to anchor along side.

The thought of war worried James. He had heard enough tales about the French and Indian War from his twin brother John to know that war with the English would not be the joyride that the throngs at the meeting appeared to think it would be. James at forty-one with no military experience knew he would be too old to fight, but he worried about his son Jason being drawn to his death.

James defended the patriot position and their Massachusetts brothers in his news-paper, but he prayed a compromise could be found that would avoid the impos-sible situation of having Englishmen fighting Englishmen. Pride and profit, and taxes and principles could all be compromised and should be, James reasoned.

James was in a dark mood when he approached the slip at the end of the street where Jason and several workmen stood admiring the pretty two masted mini-schooner that rose above them. James had to admit that the boat was a beautiful creature. Jason had carefully painted it a rich bluish gray, a pale slate tone that matched the color of sea and sky blending on the horizon on a cloudy day. Jason had purchased two sets of sails, one the usual dull canvas white, and one set dyed to match the color of his ship. Jason explained that he wanted to blend the ship into the horizon and make it as invisible as possible to English war-ships and other predators such as pirates and privateers. Jason over James' mis-givings, most unspoken but conveyed through lack of enthusiasm for the project, had from the beginning deliberately set out to build a prototypical blockade run-ner. Jason with the confidence of youth predicted there would be a market for fast coastal smugglers, but he did not disturb his father's peace of mind by offering this opinion often in James' presence.

"Hi dad, Corney," Jason greeted the two friends as they approached. He noted but ignored the sour expression on his father's face because he mistakenly assumed his ship caused it. "Isn't she a beauty?" Jason asked, unwilling to let his enthusiasm and excitement be diminished by his father. The two were close and were able to understand without passion each other's views.

Corney and James paused and studied the spotless gray ship as it stood proudly on the ways. It indeed was beautiful. James, proud of his son's creative efforts, had to smile in appreciation despite his misgivings.

"That's the prettiest ship I've ever seen," Corney enthused and meant it. "I like the long straight lines."

"She'll be fast," James agreed as he studied the vessel's trim hull."

"Hard to see on the horizon and impossible to overhaul," Jason observed, let-ting the awe at what he had six workmen had created creep into his tone.

"The 'Ghost'll be the fastest ship on the Bay," one of the workmen observed.

"The 'Ghost'. Is that what you have named her?" James asked, turning towards his son. He wasn't sure he approved.

"Yep, the 'Gray Ghost'. So fast the English will not be able to tell if she's been there or not. They'll think they've seen a ghost," Jason said. He pointed toward the bowsprit of the boat that hung some twenty feet over James' head.

James looked up and noticed the simple letters "The Gray Ghost" that had been painted in a slightly darker gray on the boat's bow.

"An appropriate name," Corney agreed. "Not very literary, but appropriate." Corney, always the pedant, would have preferred a more evocative name, but agreed with Jason who he treated like a favorite nephew. He had known the young man since his birth and had played a leading role in training Jason's inci-sive mind.

James studied his son while he continued to admire the "Ghost." Jason's bright green Satterfield eyes sparkled with pleasure. James was again struck by the irony of fate that gave Jason his father's twin John's brilliant gem green eyes while James' eyes were a softer hazel green. Hazel eyes were common in the Satterfield family but the star-crossed sons had the bright emerald green. Every time a Satterfield son, particularly a twin, appeared with the bright green eyes, the possessor seemed to be ordained for extraordinary accomplishment. Jason was not a Satterfield twin, but all the same James wondered what the hard green eyes would mean to Jason's future.

John, James' twin, had the bright green eyes with the flinty white specks when aroused, and John had become a frontiersman of heroic proportions. James, on the other hand, had the hazel eyes that marked the family intellectual. Fate had intervened in the creation of the next generation bestowing the bright green eyes on James' son Jason and giving the hazel eyes to John's son, Eli. Though only cousins and neither a twin, the two boys still had remarkably similar appearances. All who saw them together immediately assumed they were brothers.

While his father stared at the "Ghost" and was lost in his silent reverie about the Satterfield family eyes, Jason blinked his and made his decision.

"All right. Let's free the 'Ghost'. See if she'll float or is merely pretty."

"Let's do 'er," One of the workmen called in reply.

The four shipyard workers took their previously agreed upon positions. Two pushed a long boat from the shore. One manned the oars while the other played out the thick hemp rope that was tied on one end to the "Ghost's" stern. The rower maneuvered the long boat about thirty feet out into the river and then called.

"Let 'er rip."

Jason walked around to The "Ghost's" bow and retrieved a second hemp hawser.

"Can we help?" James asked.

"Thought you would never ask," Jason said with a smile. He held the heavy rope taut in his left hand and brushed a lock of his light colored, near blond hair out of his eyes. His green eyes flashed with excitement. "You can help me with this line," Jason called. "We'll cut the chocks, play out the rope and let her free in the river. After she decides whether she likes the water enough to float on her own, we can maneuver her with the lines around to the dock. I'll tie her up there. Let her sit overnight to see how watertight she is then tomorrow if all is well I'll take her out for a maiden test."

James patted the copper sheathing on the schooner's bottom for luck, then joined Corney and Jason on the bowline. Jason stepped out to the side, looked along the V shaped wood incline that would carry the boat from the shore to the water. He took a deep breath, patted the "Ghost's" side for luck, and called to the two workmen who stood waiting with large sledges near the chocks at the boat's stern.

"OK. Knock her free," he called.

Corney, Jason and James backed slowly up the beach pulling the bowline taut. From past experience they knew the boat could behave unexpectedly. When released from the chocks, it might stubbornly remain in place and require considerable effort to free her; or, she might respond to the freedom and rush down the guiding stays and smash into the deep water carrying anything in her path. All three men held their breath in anticipation as the workmen with the sledges turned to the chocks. To their surprise, the chocks required only a single blow. Jason had carefully coated the slip with axle grease, and it did its job. The "Ghost" when freed silently slipped easily into the water pulling Jason, James and Corney to the water's edge.

The "Ghost's" stern sank deep into the water, as if testing it, then joyously bounced upward. The "Ghost" immediately pulled itself erect and floated proudly between its bow and stern lines. The workman in the boat began rowing while his companion slowly tightened the line. The "Ghost's" momentum from the slip, along with the pull from the rowboat, carried it out into the slow, near shore current. Jason, his father and Corney, still holding the bow line but paying it out slowly, worked their way along the shore and up on the pier. They walked the rope along the some fifteen feet to the point where the dock crossed itself with a T, which provided space to fasten the boat to shore. Jason and his helpers slowly tugged on the bow line as they backed towards the end of the dock. Jason wrapped the line around the large pole that rose some ten feet out of the water to mark the end of the pier. Using the pole as a fulcrum, the three men backed up pulling the rope around the pole and aligned the responsive boat along the end of the dock.

Jason released his hold of the rope while Corney and James now joined by the two workmen who had hammered the chocks pulled the" Ghost" into its docking nest. Jason placed large coils of ropes as bumpers between the dock and the gently bouncing craft. Jason climbed a rope ladder that hung from the "Ghost's" bow. Once on board, he ran along the narrow deck to the stern, retrieved the line from the man in the long boat and tossed it to the workmen on the dock. Within five minutes, the "Ghost" was secure to the dock, and James, Corney Goodenough and the workmen had joined Jason on board and excitedly examined every inch of the taut ship.

Chapter 3
Alexandria, Virginia
July 1774

James and Corney stayed aboard the docked "Ghost" until about six o'clock helping Jason and the workmen rig the beautiful, new ship. Jason enthusiastically discussed his plans for testing "Ghost" and training his crew. He estimated that six men could handle the trim craft and had already selected five crewmen from among his friends in Alexandria and classmates at the Academy. All had grown up in Alexandria and had spent their childhood and early youth mastering the waters and currents of the Potomac, first with self made rafts and then with small sailboats that they used to visit the Maryland shore and to explore the Potomac waters from the fall line at the rapids southward. The rocks at the Great Falls marked the point where navigation stopped and the tidal waters surrendered to fresh, mountain water.

Jason with his father's assent, for he also had considerable time and money invested in "Ghost," planned to spend a month test sailing the ship along the Potomac into the Chesapeake Bay. With luck he might reach as far south as Yorktown and the mouth of the bay where it met the Atlantic Ocean. Jason's dreams included exploring the James and York Rivers as well as the Rappahannock, Mattapony and Chickahominy Rivers and any other streams and inlets with a potential for giving haven to patriot vessels fleeing before British men-of-war. Jason, a son of the Potomac as his father had been of the Short Hills, dreamed of a destiny fighting for Virginia's liberty and independence on the water. Most young men of Fairfax and Alexandria turned to the militia in their enthusiasm and excitement, while Jason and his crew eyed the Potomac waters.

For an hour now, Lily West, daughter of John West, a prominent Alexandria merchant, tobacco trader, warehouse owner and town leader—one could hardly name an enterprise that John West did not share in—had sat on a bench on the

"Ghost's" quarter deck and kibitzed Jason and his fellow workers. Lily, an attractive blond with long almost white curls, had flashing blue eyes, bright regular teeth and a sharp tongue. Her teasing advice to Jason kept a smile on James and Corney's lips. Both men shared Jason's affection for the vivacious young lady, only a year Jason's junior, and each silently envied the young man his tender years and handsome visage which gave him the advantage in the pursuit of Lily. She was a girl whose striking appearance and bubbling personality filled any setting that she graced. Lily, an energetic tomboy indifferent to the social inhibitions that rigidly guided the plantation girls, had driven her own chaise to the dock. Neither James nor Corney had missed the large wicker basket that set on the seat of the chaise. Enviously, they observed that the young suitor and his girl planned a picnic on "Ghost" to celebrate its launch. Both men knew they would be welcome, but also recognized their absence would be appreciated.

"Well, Corney, I think it's time you and I were getting back to the paper," Jason said, glancing at the sun which was dropping slowly in the west.

"I do have to set that last letter from Boston," Corney said with a wink belying his words. Most news items in the *Herald* came in the form of letters lifted from newspapers in the other colonies or the *Williamsburg Gazette*. Corney and James selected the items from the newspapers that arrived by coach or ship, then set them in type themselves or gave them to two journeymen African freedmen who were apprenticed to James to learn the printer trade. Many of Vivian's planter circle did not approve of the fact that James had two African apprentices, but their status as freedmen let James indulge his whimsy despite the negative attitudes. In Alexandria itself, most of the tradesmen had come to accept the apprentices as natural employees of the newspaper and gave the matter no thought whatsoever. The Quakers and the small farmers of the Piedmont in Loudoun and northwestern Fairfax disapproved of slavery and thus showed their appreciation for James' gesture by subscribing to the *Herald*.

"I'll agree, if our boss here will release us," James said with a smile, looking at his son while wiping several drops of perspiration from his forehead with a large, white linen handkerchief that he had taken from his pocket. "It sure is hot," he observed.

"You older fellows should not be working so hard in this heat. It's bad for your tired hearts," Jason teased.

Lily folded her fan and tapped the bench beside her in agreement. She too would have to return home soon and wanted some quiet time alone with Jason.

"Maybe we should show the younger set that we aren't as decrepit as they seem to think," Corney leaned against the heavy mainsail he had just finished furling. "I think I could work a little longer, particularly if that basket on the wagon over there has what I think it has."

James smiled at the flash of dismay that crossed Jason's face.

"You're right," James agreed, "but I think this old body needs a taste of that fine English ale at the Grape." James, like most long time Alexandria residents, still referred to City Tavern by its old name, The Sign of the Grape. A cracked, faded sign bearing the outline of a large, plump bunch of purple grapes still hung on the front of the popular tavern where the gentry of Alexandria gathered. The younger set and the more rambunctious and rowdy preferred the Pig over the more sedate Grape.

"Now that's an idea I can buy even though I would prefer to stay here and work on this fine boat," Corney agreed. The two men noticed the broad smiles that returned to the younger couple's faces.

"We might be able to spare a couple chicken sandwiches, if you are interested, and a little German potato salad," Lily offered generously.

"Now don't tempt us young lady," James laughed. "I'm sure the chicken is just fine on that nice white bread your mother bakes, but I've been thinking of that black bread and big country ham at the Grape."

"That sounds pretty good to me too," Corney agreed. "Though," Corney paused before continuing, "that chicken is tempting."

"I'm sure that ham is tasty," Jason offered, anxious now for the two older men to depart as his workers had done earlier. "I think I'll call it a day and leave something for us to do tomorrow. Everything is ready for our test sail."

"OK," Corney agreed as he leaped agilely down to the dock. "She sure is one beautiful ship," Corney said seriously as he patted the "Ghost's" lee planking. "You're confident that copper plating will make her faster?"

"There's a master boatwright in LeHavre that thinks so," Jason replied. "We'll learn tomorrow."

Jason joined Lily on the quarter-deck bench and sat beside her and watched as his father and former tutor rounded the corner of the building. As soon as they were out of sight, he turned toward Lily who had simultaneously turned to face him. She seized his face with both hands and kissed him deeply. In turn, Jason reached around her and pulled her tight against him.

"I thought they would never leave," Lily laughed when she finally leaned back and focused her brilliant blue eyes on Jason. She studied his flashing green eyes and asked a question that frequently had come to mind. "With those green eyes of yours and my blue ones, what color eyes do you think our children will have?"

"One of the boys will have hazel and one green like mine. Satterfield twins always do, and then the girls will have blue eyes like yours," Jason replied confidently.

"Twins," Lily repeated. "What makes you think there will be twins?"

"In every other Satterfield generation twins appear. My father has a twin brother, so we will have twins. No question."

"Will they be smart?"

"The one with hazel eyes will be the intellectual. Like my father. And the one with green eyes...." Jason paused, considering how Lily might react to what he had to say next.

"And green eyes, like yours, will be what?" Lily demanded pertly, pulling Jason's ears as she spoke. Lily could not keep her hands off of Jason.

"He will be.... He will be an adventurer, like my Uncle John."

"Does he have to be an Indian fighter? I don't think I want one of my sons disappearing on the frontier," Lily said seriously.

"No he doesn't have to be an Indian fighter. But he will be an adventurer of some kind. He might even sail fast ships like his father," Jason spoke only half jokingly even though he laughed.

Both young people immediately thought of the possibility of war as mentioned in the Resolves.

"I don't know if I like that," Lily shuddered with concern.

"He will have to follow his inner spirit, Lily. We won't be able to repress him. The Satterfield genes always have their way."

"I hope not," Lily said. "The West genes will have something to say about that. We're tradesmen and merchants and townspeople."

"Are there really sandwiches in that basket?" Jason asked, hoping to change the subject.

He believed that their children would follow their own stars, but he had no doubt that the Satterfield genes would speak. He, like his Uncle John—he had grown up hearing the stories—had always been strong and interested in challenge not books that bored him, and he was not even a Satterfield twin. He knew the green eyed twin curse would reappear in the next generation. He did not tell Lily, but Uncle John was not just an adventurer. His father had told him that John, a creature of the forest, had the cunning and craft of the animals and killed without hesitation. It was a subject the family did not discuss often. John made them all feel secure. They knew that John was always there to protect them when needed. His father had told him that when his brother's sharp eyes began flashing hard sparks someone was sure to die. Jason was a little sorry that his green eyes never sparkled. He wondered what it would feel like.

"You get the basket, and we'll have the first meal on "Ghost," the first of many." Lily could hear the current lapping at the boat's sides. "'Ghost' is a lucky one," Lily continued, believing her own words. "She will always bring us luck. You created her with your own hands."

"I thought of calling her the Beautiful Lily," Jason teased. He had always had a way of charming the other sex.

"I think the "Gray Ghost" is better," Lily observed soberly. "The English will not be able to see her, and she will be fast and wraith like."

"Wraith like? Where did you get such a word?"

"I read books, smarty."

"What kind of books use words like wraith like?"

"My kind. Besides, I borrowed it from your father.

James was a book collector as well as printer. He had large libraries at both Eastwind and his Alexandria town house. James believed books were compendiums of other men's ideas and as such were intended to be shared, which he did with friends and family. He had only two rules—that the books be returned, and that they be treated gently so that others may also enjoy them.

"And I fetch picnic baskets," Jason laughed, jumping up. "What time do you have to be home?"

"Mummy and Daddy know where I am. What kind of trouble could I get into in Alexandria with you?" Lily asked with a flirtatious turn of her head. "I must be home by dusk."

"And so you shall," Jason spoke soberly as he walked towards the chaise to collect the basket.

The shops were still open and the streets of Alexandria filled with promenading residents. Most of the backcountry people who had traveled several hours by horse, wagon and on foot to attend the county freeholders meeting had stayed over and were treating the visit as a festive occasion. The children, town and country alike, chased each other through Market Square while their parents shopped. Their happy voices filled the air. In the distance, James could hear the beat of the drummer boys and the wail of the fifes.

"Sounds like the militia are starting up again," James said to Corney.

"Still at it, more likely," Corney observed. "You're in part to blame, you know," Corney looked seriously at his friend. "Those words in The Resolves were yours, and one of them was war. The boys are all talking about joining the militia and killing lobsterbacks."

"I know, and I'm sorry to hear that. I'm not sure that killing each other is the way to solve our differences."

James noted Corney looking at him skeptically.

"And war wasn't my word. Washington and Mason insisted."

"George Washington insisted? I've never heard silent George insist on anything. He's too shy and polite."

"George can be stubborn when needed. He's shy and knows he's not a good talker but don't let that fool you. Remember he was an Indian fighter and a military officer when he was younger. He commanded the Virginia Regiment. John says that the Virginians following silent George fought back and saved the scalps of Braddock's Englishmen who had turned and run. George buried Braddock's bones in the road so the Indians wouldn't find them. We might find George leading Virginians to battle again."

"I know that," Corney agreed. "Does Washington still harbor military ambitions? He was big on glory and honor as a young man."

"He never says. He's matured into a strong man. He agrees with the Resolves. I suspect that he believes the time for appeals to the Crown is past, and we will have to fight for our rights."

"Do you think it will take long?"

"I don't know. The English are a long way from home and would have trouble sustaining a war, but they are stubborn. Massachusetts is really troubling."

"I'm too old. It's not my nature. I'll do what I can, but I suspect like other old men my war will be with words. It's Jason and his cousin Eli and even my brother John that I worry about."

"John's the same age as you," Corney countered. "If you are too old..."

"John's different," James answered.

"He sure is," Corney agreed with a laugh as the two men entered the Grape.

The large main room was filled with noisy men. James recognized most of the patrons who occupied the handsome walnut tables where they were being served foamy mugs of ale by the tavern's two rushed barmaids, both daughters of the proprietor. Many of the men were red faced and talking loudly. The common subject appeared to be the day's meeting and what the patriots would do to the lobsterbacks and their Tory friends if they did not back down on the closure of Boston port.

"James, Corney, over here," a loud voice called.

James noticed Martin Cockburn, William Ramsey, and Daniel McCarty sitting with several other friends at a large table in the corner of the room. The air in between was blue and heavy with tobacco smoke, and the table was covered with empty and half-filled mugs and plates with the remains of food from the Grape's excellent kitchen. James, when alone while Vivian was at Eastwind, frequently ate his evening meal, supper, at the friendly ordinary. He could not resist the tavern's specialty, salty Virginia ham cured in smoke rooms located behind the main building.

"What are you going to tell those pompous asses in Williamsburg?" The husky Martin Davis asked.

Davis, a blacksmith who leased one of James' Alexandria buildings, weighed almost three hundred pounds. His bulging arms and chest flagged his trade. James felt affection for the blunt but honest man because blacksmithing had been a Satterfield family occupation. The first Satterfield to leave England for the new world, Thomas Satterfield, had been a smith as had been James' grandfather Old Tom and several other Satterfields including James' younger brother Will who ran a smithy in the new town of Leesburg. James recognized that Davis referred to the fact that he and George Washington had been elected to represent Fairfax County at the conference in Williamsburg called by the rump session of the Burgesses after that Governor had arbitrarily prorogued them in an effort to cut off any petitions or demands over the Boston Port Bill.

"Probably George and I will tell them nothing," James began to the sound of Davis' uproarious laughter. James and George's public reticence was common knowledge. "We'll table the Resolves that you gentlemen agreed upon today. They seem to say it all."

"You bet they do," Davis agreed, pausing to stare across the room to a table near the bar where Elizah Bayley, Ellie as he was known to his few friends, sat morosely with two companions. The nattily dressed planters with their ruffled shirts, brightly colored jackets and powdered wigs looked like dandies when one compared their dress to the dark suits and rough clothing of the other patrons.

For a change, James noted, the usually boisterous Bayley sat sourly watching the enthused townspeople.

"Bayley and his crowd don't look too happy," Corney observed, having caught the direction of James' glance.

"They've got no cause," Martin Davis glared at Bayley before chuckling loudly. Davis would like nothing better than to apply his labor acquired muscles to the large but plump, soft planter. Bayley, a bully towards smaller men, discreetly kept his distance from the husky blacksmith despite frequent, deliberate provocation. "They sure was quiet at the meeting," Davis continued.

"On Elizah's behalf I think it should be noted he hates Englishmen," James objected.

"Bayley doesn't like anybody. There is no secret where his friends stand," Davis replied.

"They were quiet at the meeting because they know they are in the minority," James observed. "Speaking out would have done them no good. Everyone knows their views anyway."

"And it might have done them some harm," Davis added, waving to the passing barmaid. "Another round for our representative and the schoolmaster," Davis called. "And don't forget me," Davis laughed. His capacity for ale was infamous. "Some of the boys over at the Pig are talking up a little public demonstration for tonight," the smith referred to the tavern bearing the less than flattering Sign of the Pig. James had always figured the owner was deliberately appealing to the baser elements of Alexandria. If that was his intent, he had succeeded.

"What kind of demonstration?" Corney asked, sipping from his mug and wiping perspiration from his high brow with a soggy handkerchief. Corney was self conscious about his receding hairline that accented the length of his nose.

"A new suit of clothes, the dark kind," Davis laughed uproariously. "I mean the black kind, tar black, decorated with feathers," Davis continued to laugh, spilling some of his ale down the front of his sweat dampened shirt.

Corney and James exchanged concerned glances. James wondered if his words in the Resolve had been too strong and had served only to incite the younger elements. No wonder Elizah Bayley and his friends were minding their manners.

"Do they have anyone specific in mind?" James asked.

"Sure do," the blacksmith replied. "Don't worry, it won't be one of your Misses' fancy planter friends, though some of them deserve it." Davis had caught James' worried look at Bayley.

"That shit Abernathy will have some visitors soon. If he doesn't already." The blacksmith leaned towards James and Corney as he spoke in a lowered voice. "Some of the boys plan on picking him up at his home and marching him down to the river where the tar pot is already heating."

James knew Beverley Abernathy well. A local merchant, Beverley Abernathy was despised by most who did business with him. He always had full shelves in his large shop and made no secret of the fact that he did not support the non-importation agreements. He had long been a target of the committee who watched him closely trying to catch his sources of supply. James knew that many of his friends, even some on the non-importation watch-dog committee, were hypocrites. Their wives and servants purchased the forbidden English wares from Abernathy's, and they enjoyed them in the privacy of their homes at the very time the husbands were talking loudly about making Abernathy pay for his transgressions against his neighbors. Hypocrisy was not an uncommon trait during the current troubled times. James had sipped tea at Mount Vernon while discussing the Resolves with the arch patriots Mason and Washington. James knew that both Washington and Mason, like most of their planter friends, were rushing hogsheads of tobacco to the Alexandria waterfront for shipment to England to beat the non-export agreements they were advocating to punish the English for their treatment of the people of Boston.

"Abernathy," James spoke aloud as he mused. James shared his friends' contempt for the pompous merchant. Abernathy, a slim, stern man with a receding chin and a walrus style mustache was more English than the English. He loudly supported Parliament's closure of Boston port and claimed to be a distant cousin of Lord North. Abernathy made no secret of his intent to abandon the colonies and return to London if war broke out. James knew that Abernathy was quietly selling some choice plots he had acquired over the years. James had bought one of five hundred acres near Occoquan for what he knew was a choice price.

"Yes, Abernathy," Davis repeated.

"I might like to see that myself," Corney observed.

Like James, the mild, intellectual schoolmaster opposed violence against the Tories but saw nothing wrong with a little tar and feathers. Certainly the hot tar was uncomfortable and the public humiliation of being paraded through the streets before one's neighbors was not pleasant, but the tar could be scrubbed off over a short period of a few weeks. At least the physical aspects of the treatment were not long lasting. James, concealing his smile, nodded agreement. The thought crossed his mind that Elizah Bayley, regardless of his political views, might benefit likewise from such a lesson.

"After you finish your mugs, we might stroll down by the river," Davis spoke softly with a conspiratorial tone. "Who knows, the drum and fife boys might offer a martial concert to while away a hot summer evening."

When they finished their mugs, the three men paid their bill and left the tavern. Only two tables occupied by the morose Elijah Bayley and his friends were all that remained of the boisterous crowd. Most had preceded James, Corney and Martin Davis on the walk to the river.

When they reached the foot of Duke Street, they had no difficulty locating the site of the evening's festivities. A large group of Alexandria citizens were gathered at the river's edge at the end of Union Street. James was relieved to note that the noisy throng was some distance upriver from his boatyard. Lily's chaise was no longer in evidence, and James concluded that the young couple had long since departed the area. Despite his approval of the mob's choice of victims, James did not want Jason to get involved.

When the three men arrived on the fringes of the excited crowd, James noted that Davis' predictions had been accurate. A naked Beverley Abernathy stood with his back against a strong sapling and his hands tied together behind him on the opposite side of the tree. Despite his lack of clothing, Abernathy stood imperiously shouting insults and threats at the Sons of Liberty who encircled him. The young men, many of whom James recognized as friends of Jason, stood silently unable to conceal broad smiles of anticipation while one of their number soberly read a long list of charges of transgression against Abernathy. Most dealt with the illicit sale of tea and other forbidden English articles.

"At least the list of charges is well written," Corney observed. "That's one of my former students reading it."

"Good work, schoolteacher," a man standing nearby muttered. Corney glared coldly at the man then decided to ignore him.

When the reader finished his long list of charges, a loud cheer erupted from the mob of some one hundred men.

"Now let's cover that creature's nakedness," one shouted.

The mob roared its agreement.

"I don't like this," James observed to no one, "but that man deserves what he gets."

As James spoke, Abernathy attempted to spit at his tormentors. The mob contemptuously cheered his futile gesture. Two young men began to stir a large pot of maritime tar that hung over a blazing fire. A young man carrying a short pole with a swab of cloth tied to the end approached the bubbling pot. He looked maliciously at the now silent Abernathy and dipped the swab into the steaming tar.

"Cover the indecent man," another shouted. The man, who had spoken, rushed forward, gathered an armful of the clothing that had been torn from the struggling Abernathy and threw it on the fire. "Nobody's going to need these rags," he shouted to loud cheers.

The crowd grew quiet with anticipation as the youth with the dripping swab approached Abernathy. The chinless man, now frightened, pushed back against the sapling and turned his head in disbelief of what was happening to him. Although about forty years of age, Abernathy's body was completely devoid of fat. Bony ribs clearly lined his chest. James could not help staring at the man's long and skinny, flaccid penis. It hung forgotten by its owner from a mass of black body hair.

"Look at that dick," a man standing next to James observed. "He's got at least eight inches."

"It's a skinny thing," another said.

"And dead from disuse," another jeered.

With a smile, the youth with the black swab thrust it against Abernathy's chest and smeared the black mass in swirls. Abernathy screamed, then cursed.

The hot tar ran in little rivers down his sides. One stream approached his penis, disappeared into the mass of black hair, and then, as the crowd watched in anticipation, coursed down the man's penis and dripped from the end. To the mob's surprise, the penis jerked erect and stood out from Abernathy's body pointing defiantly at the crowd. Abernathy continued to scream.

"Jesus," Davis spoke involuntarily. "That thing's a foot long."

Many laughed nervously. The youth with the swab returned to the bubbling tar pot.

"Make sure it's good and hot," one called.

"And cover that obscene thing," another laughed.

Working quickly, the youth with the swab covered the screaming Abernathy from head to foot with the steaming tar. As he worked two other youths approached bearing large bags filled with chicken feathers.

"Hope that's goose down," a toothless man standing next to James called. "Nothing but the finest for Mister Abernathy."

James, in embarrassment, looked about him. Corney and Davis stared straight ahead in open-mouthed amazement. The mob, now excited, shouted encouragement to Abernathy's tormentors, and the drums rolled and fifes shrieked.

As the tar cooled it began to harden. The two youths with feathers emptied their bags over the tar-coated man. The feathers clumped in masses on his head and shoulders and stuck to his face and body. Strangely, with an apparent mind of its own, Abernathy's penis stared erectly straight ahead. It was now thickly coated with tar.

"Cover the traitor's embarrassment," a youth shouted.

"You should have such an embarrassment," another laughed.

Another picked up a mass of feathers and threw them at the offending penis. They covered everything but the smiling head. As the young man bent to retrieve another handful of feathers, a second young man laughed.

"No that's good. Let the thing watch and see what happens to friends of old George the Third." The crowd laughed and cheered.

As the tar cooled, Abernathy stopped screaming. He slumped against the sapling and suffered the total humiliation. Tears streamed over his blackened face from his eyes that had been mercifully left uncoated. Abernathy painfully opened his tar-coated lips with difficulty and moaned loudly.

"Serves the bloody Tory right," someone shouted, and the mob cheered agreement.

Abernathy's tormentors untied the docile man from the sapling, then waited as two strong young men carrying a sturdy pole approached. Two others joined them, and the four men stood with the pole on their shoulders. Others picked up the tar hardened Abernathy and hung him from the pole by tying his wrists and ankles firmly to the pole. Then, with the drums and fifes preceding them, the four men, their pole and the trussed Abernathy marched along Union Street towards Duke Street. The jeering mob followed along behind.

Corney, James and Davis looked at each other. James shook his head and indicated he had seen enough and was going home. Davis waved and ran along behind the mob joining in the loud shouting and braggadocio. James and Corney turned and walked silently home. Each man was lost in his own thoughts.

Chapter 4
Williamsburg/Philadelphia
August/September 1774

James, George Washington and Jackie Custis, Washington's playboy stepson who had left behind a new wife in anticipation of the attractions of the capital's taverns, arrived in Williamsburg on the first of August. Though dusty and hot from the week-long ride that they had traveled many a time over the past fifteen years, George and James paused to chat along the Duke of Gloucester Street with old friends and colleagues. Jackie in his eagerness rode ahead to the Raleigh Tavern where the three men would be staying. James and Vivian still owned the small cottage where they had lived when first married, but a tenant now occupied it. James planned to visit the house to inspect it to ensure that it was being kept up properly. On several occasions he had thought of selling the house, but neither he nor Vivian could bring themselves to part with it. Memories were too strong, and James still had his official ties to Williamsburg, the scene of many pleasant, youthful experiences.

In Williamsburg, James was better known than his taciturn colleague, Washington, whose military exploits and political career had not gone unnoticed. James had attended William and Mary with many of those he encountered en route to the tavern. Others, including most of the colony's political leadership, he had known while serving as Governor Dinwiddie's clerk. Still more, particularly the younger delegates, he had grown close to during service in the Burgesses. Of the latter, James was particularly looking forward to talking with young Tom Jefferson from Albemarle. The two had become close friends, and James valued the younger man's incisive political mind.

"I don't think I have ever seen so many of the colony's leadership in Williamsburg at one time," James said to his companion.

George nodded his head in agreement but was more interested in tracking his young charge Jackie as he hastened ahead of them. Washington said nothing, but James appreciated his companion's serious mien. When the two men finally reined their tired horses in front of the Raleigh Tavern, they found the new proprietor waiting. Even though he had owned the tavern for four years now, James always considered the current proprietor as the new man. He fondly remembered Anthony Hay who had died in 1774. In his mind's eye, Hay and the Raleigh were inseparable. The eager new man, enthused by the influx of business, escorted Washington and James past the bust of the tavern's namesake, Sir Walter Raleigh. Everything was in its proper place, James noted, including the sign that hung in the Apollo Room which expressed the inn's motto: "Hilaritas Sapientiae et Bonae Vitae Proles." "Jollity, the offspring of wisdom and good living."

"Gentlemen," the proprietor gushed, "I have reserved your favorite room."

James detected Washington's frown. While George liked the Raleigh, he seldom stayed there, preferring the solitary solace of a private room in a smaller inn. James on the other hand preferred the Raleigh. It was the center of the town's social life and during sessions of the Burgesses James could always find a table crowded with colleagues discussing the day's events.

"I'm sorry Colonel Washington," the proprietor had also noted George's expression and knew well the solitary man's preferences. "The town is full to the brim, and everyone is being forced to double up."

"What about Jackie?" Washington asked sourly. He was not worried about the young man's comfort, but Martha expected him to monitor and modulate the young man's propensity for drink and self-indulgence.

"Mr. Custis is sharing one of the larger rooms with several other young men," the proprietor said apologetically. He misread Washington's reaction, assuming Washington was concerned about his stepson's lodging. "I assure you, sir," the proprietor continued, "Mr. Custis will find his accommodations satisfactory."

Washington knew that most travelers shared large rooms with others and that private rooms for two men were a luxury that few enjoyed, but he was not pleased at the freedom being offered his young charge. Jackie was just too irresponsible. He had no self-control.

After washing up, Washington and James dined sumptuously in the tavern dining room before joining their colleagues in the crowded Apollo room where the delegates would officially meet. Despite the fact that most attendees had been or were newly elected Burgesses, they could not meet in the Capitol, or any other of Virginia's official buildings, because this session did not have the Governor's sanction. Governor Dunmore had prorogued the last session of the Burgesses in an attempt to head off any official support to the people of Boston. He had yet to set a date for the newly elected Burgesses to convene.

When James entered the Apollo Room, he noticed a copy of the Albemarle County Resolves on a table near the door. He assumed his friend Thomas Jefferson had written them, and he was anxious to discuss his effort in the Fairfax Resolves with his friend and compare them with those of the well-regarded young writer. James asked a friend standing near the doorway if he had seen Jefferson yet. James was deeply disappointed to learn that Jefferson had fell ill with dysentery en route to Williamsburg and had been forced to return home to

Monticello. Colleagues had delivered Jefferson's handiwork, the Albemarle Resolves, and they were tabled near the room entrance for all delegates to peruse. James paused to scan his friend's contribution. He found it much stronger and more critical of the Crown than his and Mason's effort. Comments from others indicated that this was a common view and that though many agreed with Jefferson in his harsh criticisms of His Majesty they were not yet ready to go so far on paper.

Fairfax and Albemarle Counties' resolves were not the only ones submitted. Every county had seen fit to draft their own views on paper. To James' surprise, most delegates sympathized with the Fairfax Resolves, and they became the basis for the delegates' extensive discussions. James and Washington, not renown for their public speaking, let their printed words speak for them. By August 5th a general unanimity of views was reached. The delegates were deadly serious. They spent their time working. When not in session in the Apollo Room, they met at tables in the city's taverns and continued to discuss convention business. Dancing, card playing and the usual socializing were eschewed. Even Washington, who remained a good friend of Governor Dunmore, did not grace the table at the Mansion.

The delegates accepted Philadelphia as the site for the proposed congress of all the colonies scheduled for September 5th, a month away. They elected seven delegates to represent Virginia including Peyton Randolph, the Burgesses Speaker, Richard Henry Lee, Patrick Henry, Richard Bland, Benjamin Harrison, Edmund Pendleton and, to James' delight, George Washington. The selection projected Washington onto a scene much larger than local Virginia politics. James was disappointed that his friend Thomas Jefferson had not been chosen—no doubt his absence due to sickness had worked against him—but for himself James had no desire to assume greater responsibilities. He was content with his life in Alexandria and his family obligations and felt guilty about taking time to participate in Virginia politics in Williamsburg. His early experience with Governor Dinwiddie had whetted his appetite for politics, but for James politics were a pastime not a career.

As expected, on August 6 the meeting instructed the Virginia delegates to agree to the non-importation of British goods and the non-introduction of new slaves after November 1, 1774. James was not surprised when the subject of prohibiting export of goods to England arose. The majority of the attendees were planters like Washington and Mason who had already purchased goods in London using this summer's grain and tobacco crops as surety. If a non-export agreement were approved, these men, like many colonial merchants, would be unable to meet the debts already held by their English factors. Some of the representatives from the western counties who had no crops to export to London and thus had no debts to English banks and merchants strongly advocated a non-export provision. The delegates finally compromised and agreed if the situation was not resolved before August 10, 1775 a non-export ban could be approved. This agreement would at least enable the planters to export this year's crop and pay some of their debts. Next year, if the situation remained critical, they would not face as large a debt problem because the non-importation ban would prevent most of them from placing new orders for personal goods. James recognized the hypocrisy of the compromise but assumed that many would turn to Yankee smugglers for needed commodities.

James smiled inwardly as he realized that Jason might have been wise in anticipating developments when he designed the "Ghost" as a perfect ship for smugglers and blockade runners.

The delegates also accepted the Fairfax Resolves premise that if the problems between the colonies and England were not resolved the ultimate result would be war. Against this awesome possibility, the delegates authorized each county to establish a militia company independent of the Governor. This authorization was made without adequately addressing the subject of funding. The newly recruited militiamen would need uniforms, arms, ammunition and expense money as James and Washington well knew. Both had been deeply involved in Governor Dinwiddie's futile efforts to meet the expenses of the militia and the Virginia Regiment commanded by Washington during the French and Indian War.

The Virginians' decisions in the Apollo Room shocked Governor Dunmore. The rump Burgesses were behaving unconstitutionally, illegally and were clearly beyond the Governor's ability to manage them. As the King's representative, he was expected to control Virginia. Instead, the colonists were not behaving like loyal Englishmen subject to the laws of England. Not only were they refusing to pay taxes and obey duly passed laws, they were holding their own congresses and had agreed to send representatives to a Continental Congress which in all likelihood would become an illegal American parliament. The rebels in the Apollo Room of Raleigh Tavern had shown their arrogance and independence by authorizing the creation of a citizen army beyond the Governor's control. Dunmore recognized that action could easily give reality to the colonials' easy assertion that if the British did not back down war would follow. Dunmore vowed to keep a sharp eye on the colony's supplies of weapons and powder even as he wrote his report to London attempting to minimize the dramatic actions he had just witnessed. After all, his job depended on his ability to control Virginia for the Crown. It would do no good to point out that all the problems originated with actions decreed from London.

James found it amusing that George Washington and Governor Dunmore were aligned on opposite sides of the heated dispute. For several year James had watched while the astute Washington cultivated Dunmore. Their common interests were easily to discern. Washington was heavily invested in western lands, and Dunmore, like several of his predecessors including Dinwiddie, had decided that such speculation had the potential to greatly enhance his personal wealth. Neither man was inhibited by the fact that following the end of the French and Indian War in 1763 the Crown in the interests of peace had issued a decree forbidding settlers to cross the Appalachians.

Dunmore had been greatly disturbed by recent reports that neighboring Pennsylvania was encouraging settlers to move onto land along the Ohio River and occupy land Virginians, including Washington, considered their own. Dunmore, at Washington's urging, had encouraged Virginia settlers to contest the Pennsylvanian incursions. Four mouths previously, Dunmore, upset at violent Shawnee reaction to the virtual invasion of Pennsylvanians and Virginians contesting for land the Indians considered their own, had unsuccessfully asked the Burgesses to allocate funds for a punitive military expedition. The Burgesses' refusal enraged Dunmore who already had his troubles with the Virginian hotheads. As a consequence, Dunmore mounted his own expedition using the western militia companies. James fully appreciated Washington's dilemma. Undoubtedly, if it had not been for events in Boston, James' friend would have been quietly encouraging Dunmore in his western adventures. As it turned out, Dunmore found himself caught between the stubborn Virginians and masters at home who could not understand why their Governor had decided to ignore his instructions and fish in the troubled waters of the west despite the 1763 ban on settlement in the very area Dunmore wanted to invade.

James was not surprised when the rump meeting at the Raleigh concluded that Washington decided to remain in Williamsburg to take care of personal matters relating to his ward Jackie Custis' estate. James knew that Jackie had inherited over 15,000 acres and several Williamsburg lots along with over two hundred slaves. Jackie now owned the estate, having reached age twenty-one, but the cautious Washington still worried about the young man's profligate tendencies. Jackie, who had enjoyed himself to the fullest during their brief stay, had decided to remain on to visit his estates. The disapproving Washington confided to James that he had to stay behind and monitor his stepson until he was ready to return north to rejoin his bride at their plantation located a few miles from Mount Vernon.

After bidding his friend good-by, James rode northward hard. During his first trip southwards as a young man leaving home on his first trip to begin study at William and Mary, James had ridden slowly, studying and admiring the countryside. This time, however, his only interest was covering the distance as quickly as possible. To his surprise he reached Eastwind in five days.

The verandah was empty when James halted in front of the large plantation house. As usual, the house servants had noticed his approaching dust trail, and two were standing by the front portico waiting to take James' tired horse.

"Welcome back, Master James," the immaculate senior house servant spoke. He stood near the verandah far enough away from the tired horse and rider to avoid being coated in dust raised by the pounding hooves. He wore a starched white shirt with ruffles in the front and white pantaloons over glistening black boots. Vivian insisted that the house servants dress properly.

James paused briefly, raising his hat with one hand and wiping sweat streaks in the grime across his forehead with the other. Somehow, he thought ironically, there is something wrong with this arrangement. He should be the one rested and spotless, and the slave should be grimy from work.

"Good day, Joseph. Is the Mistress about?" James glanced at the sun and estimated the time to be about six PM. James, though he could afford a watch like the one carried by Washington, did not own a timepiece. He prided himself on his farm youth's sense of time.

"No suh," the slave replied. "Mistress Vivian is still in the fields making plans for the harvest. She expects to be able to begin cutting the grain next week. She wants to get the crop in and shipped before the politicians ban sending it to London." Joseph discreetly avoided acknowledging that James was one of those politicians. James ignored the barb, knowing the servant was merely making conversation by expressing a remark he had undoubtedly overheard Vivian making.

"Very well," James said dismounting. "Please have someone take care of my horse." James handed the reins to the waiting boy. Protocol required that he speak through Joseph when the gray haired old African was present. Things always ran better that way.

"Massah Will is here," Joseph spoke as James walked towards the house. The news brought a smile to James' face. Will, his brother, lived with his family in Leesburg where he continued the Satterfield family tradition by operating a smithy. Their father, still known as Young Tom despite his advancing age, continued to run the family farm in the Short Hills on the eastern slopes of the Blue Ridges about twenty miles from the new town of Leesburg. Young Tom's wife, James' mother, Agnes, had died the previous year. James' sister Sally and her Quaker husband now lived with Young Tom and shared the work.

As James mounted the stairs to the verandah, Will appeared in the doorway. Will, only four years junior to James and his twin brother John, looked ten years younger. Will stood two inches shorter than the twins, but his thick neck, broad shoulders and muscular arms made him appear the bigger man.

"Hello, big brother," Will spoke with genuine affection. The Satterfields remained a close family despite the distance and time that now separated them.

"Will," James replied seizing his brother in a tight hug. "This is a pleasant surprise."

"I didn't expect to find you here but I thought Vivian would be," Will laughed as they parted.

James led the way along the verandah to two chairs. He turned to Joseph who waited patiently by the door.

"Could you find us something cool to drink?" James asked. "From the spring cellar," he added unnecessarily.

"That sounds good," Will agreed.

"Yessuh," Joseph responded. "The Mistress has two large bottles of tea cooling." Joseph knew because he had just tried a glass himself. He would send one of the maids running to the deep artesian spring behind the house where the kitchen staff stored the food and drink that needed to be kept chilled.

The two brothers sat in the plantation made rocking chairs and looked fond-ly at each other.

"A hot day for a long ride," Will observed.

"Five days, one of my fastest trips," James said. "I wish they would wait to have their meetings in the fall," he continued, looking at the heat and dust spires rising in front of the house.

"How did things go? " Will asked, genuinely interested; James knew his brother was not one for small talk.

The reason Will had unhitched his farm cart in Alexandria and left it in Jason's care and rode his mare to Eastwind was his hope that James might have returned. He had made one of his rare wagon trips from Leesburg to Alexandria to get some needed iron stock for his smithy. The best iron still came from the smelters of England. Virginia had two of its own iron mines, one started by King Carter himself, but the product was not pure, and Will took pride in his work. He preferred to use only the best iron stock for the shoes he made for Loudoun's horses and the farm tools he forged in his smithy. The Loudoun planters were particularly choosy about the shoes for their racehorses. Given talk of the non-importation of English goods, Will was not sure how much longer he would be able to get the better grade iron.

"Non-import of English goods effective November first and non-export to England next summer. The planters want to get this years crop off before they cut off their noses."

"I had better buy what iron I can before the ban goes into effect," Will observed soberly. "Do you have anyplace I can store it if I am able to collect more iron than I can haul this time in my cart?"

"Certainly, Will. I suggest you buy all you can. Everything will be in short supply because this problem is not going to be solved quickly. We have all the room you need here at Eastwind, and I'm sure we also have space at the boatyard. I'd buy quickly before the news of our meeting in Williamsburg spreads. I should be the first here with the news. George stayed on for several days, but there might be travelers along. I have to write a report for the *Herald*, but it won't be out until Thursday."

"Everybody is worried about the possibility, but I better buy my iron before the news gets confirmed," Will looked relieved at the advance word he had got-ten from his brother. "I'll go back this afternoon to Alexandria. I'll buy what I can tonight then finish off tomorrow morning."

"Good idea," James agreed. He looked up as Joseph approached carrying a large pitcher and two gleaming glasses. Both brothers watched as the house slave poured the cool tea.

"Thank you, Joseph," the brothers said almost in unison as they reached for the glasses. They each drank deeply as Joseph returned to the house.

"This will be one of the luxuries we will miss," Will said.

"I won't miss it," James replied. "I don't like the stuff. Clear water is better. I don't know what the English see in it. I think it is mainly for show."

"You're probably right, brother." Will was the more rustic of the two, and he usually deferred to his brother for value judgments. James had always been the family brain while Will, who had difficulty with the book learning, even under Corney Goodenough's patient tutoring, remained the muscle man. "Those Yankee Indians really started something when they dumped the company's tea in the harbor," Will laughed.

"Let's not discuss that," James smiled. "My ears hurt from listening to words about Parliament's perfidy for the past week."

"OK," Will agreed. "I want to discuss something else before Vivian gets here."

James immediately knew what Will had in mind. He had only one secret from his wife.

"I been worrying," Will said, pausing as he pondered over how to begin.

"About old Braddock's gold," James offered. He had been thinking about the same subject. Their brother John had served with Washington during Braddock's ill-fated campaign against the Indians. During the bloody confusion that followed the terrible ambush of the English and colonial troops, John had liberated the mule carrying Braddock's campaign chest filled with British gold. Later, John, Will and James had retrieved the chest from the mountain cave where John had hidden it. The brothers had agreed to divide the money three ways and invest it for future use "by the family." Each of the brothers discreetly purchased land, John in the west where he had settled, Will in Loudoun County and James in the environs of Alexandria. The family was now land rich but except for James money poor.

The Satterfield farm and Will's smithy provided the Loudoun Satterfields with an adequate livelihood; John had no need for money in the mountains where he lived a life based on the land and game from the forests, and James had prospered with his marriage, newspaper and shipyard. Some of the land was leased to tenants in Alexandria and Loudoun, but the income was barely enough to cover small improvements and occasional small purchases.

"War could mean big changes," Will began in his roundabout rural way.

"An opportunity to make big money," James offered.

"Yes, that," Will agreed then waited for James to continue.

"And you have been wondering about what to do. Should we leave our money invested in land?"

"Yes. "

"Do you or Pa need money, Will?" James asked.

"No. I'm just thinking about future generations," Will said. He now had two young boys of his own, and his wife Shirley was pregnant again. "I don't have any needs. And Pa doesn't."

"I've been thinking about the same. I'll probably be able to expand the shipyard, and maybe you can do more at the smithy. Have you thought about making guns."

"I've tried it, James, for my own amusement. I think with help and the right kind of stock I might be able to do it, but I don't need family money for that."

"And I don't for the shipyard. I'll let it grow naturally for Jason. And I'm sure John doesn't need money in the mountains. I would like to talk with him about it though. I sure miss him. We haven't seen him for three years."

"Me too," Will agreed. "Young Eli must be about Jason's size, grown young men. Maybe, with his new wife, John's started a family again, and we have some more nephews and nieces." John's first wife had died some five years ago and John had married the widow of another mountain man. None of the family had met the new wife.

James sipped the cool tea as he thought about Will's words. Finally, he spoke.

"You know Will, when we started this family legacy thing, we agreed to secretly invest the gold in land figuring each of us could buy parcels without attracting attention. You and me bought farms from families who decided to move west or elsewhere, and John bought mountain land. We've done well. We've got over 20,000 acres among us, me in small parcels around here and Alexandria, you in farms in Loudoun and John in big tracts of forest land. Whatever happens with England during the next few years, I figure land will remain our best investment. We could maybe make more money if we invested in goods and war supplies, but I think we should plan for the long run good of the family and stay with the land. Even get more when and if we can."

Will paused before commenting. "That's the same conclusion I reached," Will nodded his head. "But I thought we should discuss things in case you thought something different. You were always the smarter."

"Only in book learning, Will. You know that."

Will nodded acknowledgment.

"I'm sure John will agree, but you're right. We should discuss it with him. I hope he comes to visit. He's overdue."

"Agree," Will rose to his feet. "Let's leave things as they stand until we see John."

James moved and stood by his brother.

"I best be getting back to Alexandria and take care of my iron," Will said as he moved towards the steps.

"I wish you could stay and have dinner with Vivian and myself. I'm riding into Alexandria tomorrow, but I understand; iron comes first."

"Give Vivian my best and tell her I'll stay next time. You and her owe us a visit."

"I know. I hope to get out to the farm and see Pa and Sally this fall. I'll stop in Leesburg."

"Do that. I'll probably see you tomorrow if you come in. I want to take a ride on that boat of Jason's after I get my iron moved. It's the prettiest boat I've ever seen."

"Designed it himself," James noted proudly. "I haven't had a ride on it myself. It worries me though..."

Will paused and waited for his brother to continue. The family was close and what concerned one concerned the others.

"I mean I'm a little afraid of what he might try to do with it."

"You mean with the English?"

"More likely against the English. He designed it to be a smuggler or a blockade runner."

"He's got one of those Satterfield genes. Like John," Will shook his head with a smile.

"Fortunately, only one of them. He doesn't appear to have John's killer instinct." James paused; the family seldom mentioned John's activities on the frontier.

James looked fondly at his brother. Of the three males, Will was the steadiest, always strong, fair and ready to help a family member. He's the rock of the family, James thought. James embraced his brother then walked with him to retrieve his horse from the stables behind the house.

Lieutenant John Andre of the 7th Foot, a Guards Regiment, debarked from His Majesty's ship, the "St. George", in Philadelphia on September 4th, the very same day that George Washington and his traveling companions, Patrick Henry and Edmund Pendleton, arrived in the Quaker city to attend the First Continental Congress. At the time, neither Andre nor Washington knew of the other. Andre, whose father, a Huguenot, had fled his native France years earlier to escape the persecution of the French Protestants by a vengeful government, had had an easy childhood. His father had worked his way from a second floor London flat over a counting room to a comfortable house in the suburb of Clapton. Young Andre attended schools in Switzerland where he mastered French and German and returned home at the age of seventeen to become a London merchant like his successful father. Not content with trade, Andre purchased his army commission with his inheritance when his father died at an early age. After military training in Germany, young Andre was en route to Quebec to join his regiment. Believing that service abroad would enhance his advancement prospects, Andre eagerly faced his future. An attractive young man, Andre retained the polish and social skills acquiring during his Swiss schooling and possessed a journeyman's talent as an artist.

Lieutenant Andre hurried quickly from the Philadelphia dockside to the central police station where the men of the Royal Irish Regiment served on police duty. Philadelphia with its crossing broad avenues was unlike any European city Andre had seen. He was conscious of the angry glances of local citizens as he passed. John proudly wore the uniform of the Seventh Foot with its bright red coat and scarlet sash. At the police station a red faced English sergeant advised him not to tarry alone on the streets. The locals were agitated over Parliament's action in closing the Port of Boston and representatives from all the colonies were meeting in illegal assembly to consider how to respond. Upon the sergeant's recommendation, Andre walked a few short blocks to the City Tavern, which was considered one of the finest in Philadelphia. To the finely attired young officer's dismay, the tavern was filled with delegates attempting to decide where to meet.

"Young man," the tavern keeper advised Andre, "You best stay someplace else. You won't find that fine uniform welcome here today."

Andre in his uncertainty decided to ask the man if he could recommend another tavern in the vicinity. He was not comfortable on the streets in the town's obviously hostile atmosphere. Some had noticed his uniform and discreetly glanced away, but others had stared meanly. Before he could speak, the tavern keeper turned away and warmly greeted a tall colonial wearing a sober black suit. The material was wrinkled and dusty, but the man's wig had been freshly powdered.

"Good morning, colonel, welcome. Will you be staying with us for your visit?" The keeper's tone was cordial, almost effusive.

"I'm not sure, Mr. Peabody," the stranger replied politely. "I arrived yesterday and spent the night with Doctor Loring, but I will need other quarters."

"We would be honored to have you stay with us. I've kept your usual room reserved since I learned of your expected arrival."

"Do you know where the congress will be meeting?"

"No sir. It hasn't been decided yet. Some say the State House and some the carpenters hall. There's some kind of political dispute. Some of the delegates are discussing the matter now in the main room with Mr. Adams and the Massachusetts delegation."

"Thank you," the tall stranger answered with a soft, slurring accent that was strange to Andre's ear. "If I may, Mr. Peabody, I will let you know about the room as soon as I learn where we will meet."

"Fine sir," the inn keeper replied and watched the tall stranger depart. He turned and acted surprised that Andre was still there.

"Who was that?" Andre asked, impressed by the stranger's demeanor and erect posture.

"That was Colonel Washington, from Virginia," the inn keeper responded, "but as I said, we have no room for you. I suggest you return to your ship or go to your barracks."

Andre, not wanting to stay in such a hostile atmosphere, decided to return to the "St. George." It was scheduled to depart the next day for New York and Boston en route to Canada. The heavy atmosphere made him uncomfortable, and he was glad the regiment was stationed in Quebec and not the lower colonies.

Chapter 5
Alexandria/London
Autumn/Winter 1775

James, dressed in a heavy hunting shirt and wearing his favorite raccoon skin hat, a present from his twin brother John, stood on the front porch of his Alexandria house and watched the snow fall. Although snow in December was not that unusual, a thick, heavy snowfall such as this with its accumulation of nearly a foot in a matter of hours was uncommon. James had always enjoyed heavy snows during his youth in the Short Hills and continued to find comfort in the beauty and solitude that enveloped the countryside as nature draped its glistening shrouds over Alexandria. Inside, Vivian and Jason chattered as they sat in front of the roaring fireplace sipping chocolate. James had intended to fetch another log from the supply in the sheltered lee of the porch, but the beauty of the night had seized him. He was not even conscious of the slight chill that crept through his heavy clothes as he pondered the events of the past three months.

He had returned from the Williamsburg meeting in August to devote himself to the forming of the Fairfax County Independent Militia Company as decreed by the rump session of the Burgesses. Normally, George Washington would have taken the lead in this martial effort, but George had departed almost immediately for Philadelphia to serve as one of Virginia's seven delegates to the First Continental Congress. In his absence, the burden had fallen on James who by nature was not attracted to military matters. A county meeting on September 21st had authorized the formation of the company and approved James' recommendations for a uniform. James had relied on Vivian to select attractive colors, keeping in mind Washington's preferences for dark blue with brightly hued sashes. James assumed Washington would take responsibility for the company upon his return, thus deferred to his tastes.

Each member of the company was to have a good firelock weapon, a bayonet, cartridge box and tomahawk. Some of the excited youth who had enlisted had some of the required objects, but few had all. Gunpowder, lead and flints were in particular short supply. Washington, who had returned in early

November, had promised to do what he could to make up the shortfalls, but he had yet to act. Enthusiasm had begun to flag with the advent of cold weather, but Colonel Lewis' surprising easy victory over the Indians in the west at Point Pleasant near the junction of the Kanawha and Ohio Rivers regenerated the martial spirit. The victory marked a successful conclusion to one of the most decisive campaigns the Virginians had fought against the savages. Washington was particularly pleased because he had extensive land holdings in the area. With the bitterness over events in Boston, Governor Dunmore did not get the credit he deserved for having mounted the expedition despite lack of support from the Burgesses.

Washington had reported that the First Continental Congress had been a success, though he confided to Mason and James that after six weeks of talk the Congress had ended up doing little more than restate what James had incorporated in the Fairfax Resolves. The Congress had forcefully declared it's support for the people of Boston, promising to meet force with force if necessary, had approved a non-importation of English goods agreement setting the date for December 1 instead of November 1, 1774, and had promulgated the non-export of colonial goods to England effective September 10th instead of August 10th, 1775. Before adjourning, the delegates had approved the call for a Second Continental Congress to meet on May 10th, 1775. George had opined that if nothing else the delegates from the different countries, as the colonies called themselves, had gotten to know each other and had set a time frame for certain specific actions.

At home, some of James' worse fears had been realized. Jason, true to his adventurous spirit, had not been content to explore the Potomac and Chesapeake in the "Ghost." In early October with Vivian's full support and James' reluctant approval, Jason and a crew of five friends had loaded the "Ghost" with Satterfield and Eastwind grain and sailed boldly for the French islands in the West Indies. The colonial non-import association did not forbid trade with the French, but English law forbade it. Jason in effect had embarked on a career of smuggler. James had passed a very uneasy six weeks during Jason's absence. It had been with considerable relief that James had watched Jason's triumphant return only seven days earlier.

The "Ghost" had apparently performed magnificently. Two ships of the line that Jason assumed were English men-of-war had been sighted on the horizon, but the "Ghost's" speed and ability to blend with the horizon—Jason's scheme of painting the hull and masts gray and obtaining tinted sails had worked like a charm—and had enabled the novice smugglers to escape. Jason still shuddered at the thought of his son losing his ship and being impressed for life as member of an English crew. In any case, "Ghost's" hold had been filled with French sugar and rum from the island of Martinique. The rum had been well received; many plantations, including those of Mason and Washington and Eastwind, as well as taverns and private homes in Alexandria, Leesburg and the Short Hills, now had kegs of the new light rum to fortify residents against the cold.

Finally growing aware of the cold, Jason seized two large logs from the porch and returned to the warm house.

"What took you so long?" Vivian demanded. "We were about to come looking for you."

"The snow is still falling. It's so beautiful I just had to watch it."

"That's what I told her," Jason laughed. The young man sat in a rocker near the fire bouncing his stocking feet up and down as he shook cooking popcorn over the flames.

"That smells good," James observed as he circled James and carried his logs to the hearth. Jason held the popper away from the flames as James dropped a fresh log on the fire. I'll bring in enough wood for the night as soon as I finish this," Jason offered.

"Do that," Vivian ordered before James could speak.

James particularly enjoyed the snug family evenings in his Alexandria house. Vivian had moved to town for the winter in early November. She would stay until April when the time came to begin working the fields at Eastwind. She tried to visit Eastwind at least once a week to ensure that it was running adequately in her absence, but she spent most of her time in town. Jason, too, appeared to have settled into family life again, at least for a while. He was already talking about another trip to Martinique, but he seemed content to spend the cold, icy winter days on land. "Ghost" was back on the slip at the shipyard, and Jason was busily recaulking and painting. Lily had also reentered his life, and Jason spent a goodly portion of his time visiting at the West household.

While the Satterfields enjoyed their winter respite, events in London picked up momentum. By December 1774, reports describing General Gage's problems in Boston and the arrogant acts of the rebels who had presumptuously met in an illegal congress reached the English capital. The Fleet Street moguls used large headlines to proclaim that the American colonies were on the verge of rebellion. Now, the rebels had imposed illegally a non-importation of English goods embargo and had proclaimed their intent to likewise stop exports to the mother country. In addition, the rebels not only refused to pay taxes but also were denying the Crown and Parliament's right to impose them. Most Englishmen had trouble understanding why they should send troops to the colonies to defend them from the French and Indians while the settlers refused to pay their just share.

The Crown's ministers were infuriated and confused by recent events. They had to maintain Parliament's right to legislate throughout the empire, but at the same time not one wanted to dissipate English wealth and blood in a fight with fellow Englishman on a wild continent thousands of miles from London. The Prime Minister and his colleagues recognized what a difficult task it would be to fight such a war so far from home. None-the-less, they had to respond to the challenge with force; reason had failed. Some concluded the fault must rest with their commander in Boston, General Thomas Gage. They deluded themselves into believing they had given the man virtually everything he needed and, yet, the troubles had continued to magnify. Now, the colonies seemed to be uniting behind the Massachusetts troublemakers. Lord North remained convinced that a majority of the colonists, particularly in the middle colonies and the south, continued to support the Crown, but because of Gage's indecision, the troublemakers led by Samuel and John Adams seemed to be winning support. North, a fat jovial politician who preferred compromise to force, faced a growing number in his own cabinet who advocated teaching the colonials a lesson for all time.

The latest dispatches from Gage cited the need for more troops. King George III, determined to uphold his Parliament's sovereignty, ordered his Prime Minister to respond. Finally, North was forced to act. In typical fashion, he gave Gage only half of what he was asking for—the General had requested twenty thousand more troops—while he undercut the General's authority by deciding to dispatch three new major generals who could fight the battles if the commander would not. North ordered Gage to arrest the rebel leaders and impose martial law if necessary. Major General William Howe, Major General Henry Clinton, and Major General John Burgoyne, sensing an opportunity for extraordinary career advancement, eagerly accepted the challenge.

Major General William Howe, slated to become Gage's deputy, sprang from an impressive family. His grandfather had been a member of Parliament and his father a royal governor in Barbados. William Howe, forty-five years of age and a professional soldier, had also served as a Member of Parliament. During the French and Indian war, he had commanded what was described as the best battalion in America. He had distinguished himself in the battle for Quebec and displayed a personal courage that made him popular with his men. When selected to help the hapless General Gage, he was considered by his peers to be at the top of his profession. The selection was not an act of fate; William Howe, also a politician as his long parliamentary career demonstrated, decided for himself to contest for the Boston assignment. Howe let a few friends know he would not be adverse to the assignment and enlisted the support of his even more illustrious brother, Admiral Richard Lord Howe. The brothers had worked hard to gain their military eminence, but family connections helped. Their mother, an illegitimate daughter of George I, was an influential member of English society. Being the grandsons of a King, legitimate or not, did not hurt the brothers.

A cold, bone chilling London rain pelted the roof of Major General William Howe's hansom as it pulled up to the front door of his brother's London house. Even though he sat inside protected from the rain, unlike the soaked and muttering driver who had negotiated the winding cobbled streets from the Parliament building, Howe still shivered from the damp. He knew Boston would be even colder, but the knowledge he was about to share with his brother kept William smiling with self satisfied inner pleasure. He and his brother had maneuvered for over two months for this day, and nothing, not fog nor rain nor chill was going to keep the Howes from enjoying this small victory, the first step in what the they envisaged would be an empire saving success that would propel them both to the top ranks of government.

"Watch your step, General," the dripping driver cautioned as he helped Howe descend from his carriage. "They're bloody slippery."

Howe nodded and concentrated on the steps, ignoring the driver's proffered hand while accepting the obvious advice.

"I'll be about an hour," Howe said. "You can take the team to the stable and rub them dry. I'll send word to you when I want the team out front." His brother's large stable was located in the mews behind the spacious mansion.

General Howe hurried up the steep steps to the mansion's thick front door. Before he could reach for the brass knocker, the door opened and his brother's manservant, an old family retainer who had previously served the Governor, their father, greeted him.

"Good afternoon, William." The old man still treated the General like the young boy he had once been. The old man's haughty but paternal affection for both brothers was sincere and evident.

"Good Afternoon, Horatio," General Howe reciprocated. He paused in the entranceway to shake the rain from his cape before handing it to the old man. "Everything changes but this miserable English weather," he complained.

"The Lord...," Horatio paused remembering who he was speaking to before continuing. "Your brother is in the library."

Major General Howe nodded and walked down the long, dark hallway lined with familiar family portraits. This had once been his home. It might still be but for the simple fact his brother Richard was older and had succeeded to the family title and had inherited the mansion when their older brother had died. Much to William's envy, Richard became the Fourth Viscount in the family line. Despite the inevitable jealousy, the younger brother worshipped his brother, the Admiral. Richard had proved himself on the decks of English men-of-war fighting for Crown and career and had enhanced considerably the family's military reputation, not an inconsequential achievement since even their deceased older brother had been a distinguished general. Admiral Richard Lord Howe now presided as patriarchal family leader; it had been Richard, in fact, who had arranged for William's election to Parliament. Both brothers sagely realized that ambitious military men must maintain a concurrent career as a politician if they wished to advance to the forefront of the senior ranks.

"Welcome, brother," Lord Howe boomed. He stood facing the door with his back to the blazing fire.

"Richard," William responded.

"Bloody English weather," Lord Howe commiserated. "Join me by the fire. A whiskey?"

"Of course, with a dash of water, as usual."

The Admiral nodded at Horatio who had been waiting at the doorway to the library.

William noted that the room was musty. He glanced at the book-lined walls. Most were deteriorating from age, not use. The Admiral was a socializer and a man of action, not a reader.

Richard caught Thomas' glance.

"Father's books are starting to rot," he observed. "Like the old man's bones. "

Thomas, not offended, nodded in agreement. Their father, the second Viscount, had been a cold and disagreeable man, soured by his inability to match his own father's success. Their grandfather had earned the family their first position in the Irish peerage.

Joseph served two small glasses brimming with the dark whiskey, then departed quietly. Thomas sniffed the Irish double malt then took a deep drink.

Noting his brother's satisfaction, Richard laughed. "Why our colleagues poison themselves with the Scottish blends, I don't know."

The General nodded and seated himself in an immense, brown leather chair facing the roaring hearth. The Admiral moved to sit opposite him. The Admiral raised his glass in toast to the portrait of the old gentleman with an unruly white mustache who stared down from his place over the mantle, the family patriarch, their grandfather. William raised his glass, emulating his brother, then smiled with self-satisfaction as he spoke.

"I've just come from Parliament."

"I assumed so," Richard responded. "What's the news? "

"Lord Germain confided that North has finally seen reason and has decided to send me to America to see if I can give Gage some spine."

"Not too much, I hope." Lord Howe rubbed his large nose and pursed his protruding lips in the familiar gesture that indicated he was reacting negatively.

"I'll be Gage's deputy," the General spoke proudly.

"You remember what the family thinks about the mess over there?" Richard used the word "family" but meant himself.

William studied his older brother before replying. Richard rightfully occupied the position as head of the family, but sometimes he presumed too much. Even their mother, who still frequented the King's Court, sometimes felt so. Nevertheless, William knew he had to humor the Lord.

"Certainly. And as Gage's deputy I will be able to provide you with enough information to undermine his authority until you can get over there and solve this problem." The brothers, despite their differing temperaments, held the same views about the American situation. North and his ministers had over-reacted. Both the general and the admiral advocated moderation and were determined to deflect North's efforts to put down the rebellion with military force. They agreed the colonists may be defying Parliament and denying that august body of politicians its just prerogatives, but the solution to keeping the colonists, who after all were Englishmen, in line did not rest with harsh suppression. The two brothers were experienced professionals and recognized that conducting a bitter internecine war on the enemy's turf across thousands of miles of naturally hostile water infested with Spanish and French fleets was an impossible task. The empire had been built on bluff, cunning and trickery and not the actual clash of iron.

"That may take some time," Sir Richard responded. He continued to stroke his large nose thoughtfully as he contemplated his brother. "But maybe you're right," he finally conceded. "If you provide me with timely reports, undermining the hapless Gage, while preventing him from actually doing anything foolish, I will make good use of them here in London with our friends."

General William Howe nodded soberly as he turned away from Richard's intense gaze. He knew his older brother considered him better suited to command a regiment than an army. The general's fondness for drink, womanizing and the good life were well known. The general's shifting eyes caught on the portrait of the oldest Howe brother, Richard's predecessor as Viscount. Richard followed his younger brother's gaze and nodded.

"He might prove a problem," the Lord referred to the dead older brother whose portrait hung on the sidewall in a place of honor. George Augustus Howe, the Third Viscount, had died a hero's death at Ticonderoga in 1758. The proud Americans had even erected a monument to his memory. "We are going to have to tread a narrow path exploiting Gus' memory while deploying the arms intended to subdue his friends."

"But if we can exploit any goodwill that remains, we just may succeed in under-cutting the Ministry and achieve a peace without bloodshed," the general offered.

Sir Richard nodded his agreement and studied his brother, wondering silently if he really was up to the job they had set for themselves. Guile would be required, and William wore his emotions in plain sight. Sir Richard decided he had to work with what fate offered, brother or not. He would begin by talking with their sister Caroline. She played chess regularly with Benjamin Franklin, the colonial's London representative; Caroline had the guile that William lacked and would arrange an appropriate introduction. Sir Richard smiled to himself as he began to contemplate how he could use Franklin to attain his own objectives. With a little luck, he and William would emerge from the squabble with the colonies with enhanced reputations and who knows what that would mean with their mother's assistance at the Court.

"When do you plan to leave?" Sir Richard asked the general.

"North will announce the appointment next week. I'll make a few calls and indulge in the necessary posturing then sail before the end of the month. Best not to tarry."

"Excellent," Sir Richard agreed.

The two brothers continued to sit before the fire sipping their whiskies, each lost in thoughts of future glory. William was confident he would eventually replace Gage as commander of all His Majesty's ground forces in America. By that time, Sir Richard would have been appointed to command His Majesty's North American Navy and then, between them, they would avoid needless bloodshed, work out a compromise and bring the Americans to heel; then, both brothers would return home covered with glory and honor. William looked up at their grandfather's portrait and for a moment imagined that the old man was smiling approval at his two successful grandchildren.

The weak mid-January sun reflected off the pools of brittle ice surrounding Mount Vernon, but Washington's guests inside were engaged in a heated discussion in the over-warm sitting room. George Mason, Martin Cockburn and several others had attended services at the Pohick Church and then had joined Washington as planned for dinner at Mount Vernon accompanied by extensive talk designed to overcome the legal and logistical problems the county faced. James, a deist at best, had not accompanied the dutiful churchgoer Washington to the Pohick services. James had spent the night with Vivian at Eastwind where she was dutifully making one of her mid-winter appearances to check on her slaves and household. He had timed his arrival at Mount Vernon so that he appeared just as Washington and his other guests were sitting down to the dinner table.

George Mason led the discussion while Washington's house slaves served from the steaming silver platters.

"Gentlemen, as you know," Mason said, "we have a legal problem to overcome if we are going to arm our militia company." Mason paused and looked in deference at George Washington, their host and the county's leading military man. George in early January had attended several of the Fairfax County Independent Militia Company drills in Alexandria and had been dismayed to discover that the eager young men were armed with a few muskets and had no ammunition. When the militiamen paraded proudly around Market Square in Alexandria, most carried tree limbs cut into the approximate length of hunting rifles. As a consequence, Washington had discussed the problem with the other members of the triumvirate, James and Mason, and the three had decided to convene this meeting. As was their custom as county leaders, the three men preferred to have the solution to all problems in hand before they were discussed in public meetings with the populace.

Washington answered Mason's silent inquiry with a nod of his head. George had nothing to say and preferred that Mason and James take the lead despite the fact that the subject at hand was Washington's specialty, military matters.

"Well," Mason cleared his throat and repeated himself. "We have somewhat of a legal problem." Mason glanced uneasily about the room at his neighbors who waited patiently for Mason to continue. James sipped Washington's Madeira—a luxury the colonel preferred and still purchased from the Portuguese Island—and smiled inwardly. He knew Mason enjoyed solving problems and talking about them and was only feigning humility; it was his version of politeness.

"Our representatives to the rump meeting of the Burgesses last August," Mason paused and raised his glass with a smile in toast to James and Washington, "in their wisdom directed that each of Virginia's counties should raise an independent company of militia, independent of the Crown that is. Unfortunately, they failed to provide the means for paying for the company's necessaries like rifles, powder, balls and flints."

"Maybe that oversight was because they did not have the authority to levy a tax to pay for the necessaries," James volunteered.

All present knew precisely why the rump session had failed to levy a tax. Taxation without representation was a rallying cry for opposition to the Crown and Parliament in the current struggle. Since the rump session had no legal authority to tax, had no authority to do anything in reality, it could not have directed the counties to raise money to fund their militia companies without subjecting themselves to the same criticism they directed at the English.

"Yes," Mason harrumped. "We understand that little problem. But where, gentlemen, are we going to get the where-for-all to equip our loyal boys?"

The assembled county leaders quietly occupied themselves with eating Washington's sumptuous food. They knew that Mason always answered his own questions.

"Without prior action by the House of Burgesses, Fairfax County cannot place a formal levy on our titheables to fund the purchase of arms and ammunition," Mason continued. "But," and with this significant word Mason smiled, "we can recommend a contribution of three shillings per each freeman to be used to purchase equipment for the company."

"Who should collect the contribution?" Cockburn asked as he swallowed a large bite of juicy lamb.

"Why I suggest the sheriff or some other appropriate person," Mason responded. "And of course the collector should maintain a list of those who fail to contribute

"And what happens to that list?" Cockburn asked.

"Why it should be turned over to the Committee of Safety," Mason smiled guilelessly.

All present immediately recognized that the Committee of Safety, which enforced the non-importation agreement, would be a most appropriate repository for the list of delinquents. Those gentlemen were responsible for the series of tar and feathering that had kept Alexandria's merchants rigidly in line. An occasional act of arson had also helped.

"I think that's an excellent idea, George," Washington agreed.

With that seal of approbation, all discussion ended and the matter was considered carried. The formality of approving it at a public meeting in Alexandria the next day remained. During the conversation that followed, Washington agreed to use his contacts to place the necessary orders. Mason and Washington volunteered to advance the money for the purchases and would be reimbursed when the sheriff collected the three-shilling levy. James was sure that most of the others present recognized as he did that this was the first known time that a county had arrogated to itself the power to raise money without authority from duly elected bodies. James did not, however, make his observation public. All present later agreed with a second Mason suggestion—all male inhabitants between the age of sixteen and fifty should form themselves into companies of sixty-eight men each and duly elect a captain, two lieutenants, an ensign, four sergeants, four corporals and one drummer. This would, Mason observed, let every citizen contribute to the defense of his liberty while obviating the need for England to maintain a standing army in the colonies.

George Washington, who had found undisciplined militia units with short-term enlistments totally unreliable, did not share his professional views. James, who had no intention of serving in the militia and wasting his time with foolish drills on the Market Square common, also remained quiet. He wondered how he would keep his adventurous son Jason from needlessly sacrificing his time.

Two days later the freedmen of Fairfax County, duly summoned, met at the Alexandria Court House and approved the committee's two proposals, the three shilling levy and the formation of additional militia companies. Once again, the moderates and loyalists attended but said nothing, intimidated by the enthusiasm of the members of the independent company and other rebel hotheads. The county leaders, including James, Mason and Washington, gave the resolutions their blessing, and they passed without objection.

By early February 1775, Washington had ordered rifles from two manufactories in Philadelphia. Obtaining powder proved to be a bigger problem. County inhabitants had enough to meet their hunting needs, but the county, unlike the capital in Williamsburg, did not have a supply in a public armory. Washington soon discovered that the colony's few powder manufactories were busy meeting orders from other nearby counties. To James' dismay, Jason volunteered to make a powder run to Martinique in the "Ghost."

Jason assured his father, Mason and Washington that French contacts that he had made during his fall visit would gladly sell the Virginians powder. The fact that it might be used against their perennial enemy, the English, would only encourage the French to give the colonists a good price. The French reaction was not what worried James. The British men-of-war patrolling the mouth of the Chesapeake opposite Williamsburg and the fleet in the West Indies were what concerned him. Finally, the combined weight of argument offered by Jason, his mother Vivian, Mason and Washington forced James to acquiesce. Then, James decided as insurance for his son's safety, he would sail with him. James was no seaman. It took several more days for Jason and his mother to persuade James to stand down. His place was at his newspaper. News from the north was growing ominous, and it was James' duty to keep the county informed.

Chapter 6
Martinique
April 1775

Jason and Skinny Potts sat in the late afternoon gloom of the seedy waterfront tavern that they called the "Chicken" and dispiritedly sipped at their lukewarm ale. The barmaid, a Creole girl with two missing front teeth, a strong body odor and wild black hair that seldom saw brush or comb stood at the bar and talked with her father, a French sailor who had jumped ship in Martinique many years ago and now scratched out a living in the decrepit waterfront shack that for some reason he had named "Le Coq." A faded sign of a rooster with the less than grandiloquent words "Le Coq" hung on the front of the shack. Consequently, Jason and Potts, like most Englishmen who visited Fort-de-France, called the drab drinking spot, the "Chicken."

"I think I'm getting tired of this place, Jason," Skinny Potts complained to his friend. Potts was a tall, emaciated youth with a gaunt face punctuated by thin lips and a long, aquiline nose. His hair, a faded blond, was long, thin and unruly. Skinny, whose real name was Horace, had briefly attended Corney Goodenough's academy with James. Skinny's father scratched out a living on a rock farm on the slopes of the Blue Ridge not far from Ashby's Gap. After discovering that books did not interest him, he had obtained a job as a carpenter's apprentice at the Satterfield boatyard. Skinny was one of six regular employees. Jason had talked his father into letting Skinny accompany him on the powder run to Martinique in order to learn something about boats.

"I know," Jason agreed. Jason was all too aware of the two coarsely dressed French seamen sitting at a table across the room, the only other patrons of the "Chicken."

"Those two guys are still eyeing us," Jason whispered. "Don't look at them," Jason cautioned as Skinny started to turn to look behind him.

Jason fingered the knife that he wore sheathed to the small of his back under the long Martiniquean shirt. The hunting knife with the initials "JS" carved in the handle had been made by Jason's great grandfather, Old Tom Satterfield, in his smithy near the Satterfield home in the Short Hills. The family had presented the knife to Jason's father James on his sixteenth birthday. An identical knife had been given to James' twin brother John. The knife, one of his father's most prized possessions, had a long history. It had been stolen from James many years ago by an Indian savage named Red Eye who had used it to scalp many innocent settlers on Virginia's western frontier. James' twin John had "reacquired" the knife when he murdered Red Eye during one of his frontier expeditions with George Washington. After giving the matter deep thought, James had presented the knife to Jason just before he had embarked on the current powder running trip to Martinique. The knife nestled in its sheath gave Jason assurance.

"Those two have been watching us and chattering in French for days now," Skinny observed.

"Yeah, and they're beginning to worry me," Jason whispered again.

On board the "Ghost" Jason played the role of ship captain, mainly for the benefit of the other four members of their crew. When he and Skinny were apart, Jason felt he could confide in his friend. The other four, just boys, aged fourteen to sixteen, had been recruited by Jason to learn the sailing life. In all, captain and crew had no more than four months sailing experience on the "Ghost."

"When will your friend Jean deliver the powder?" Skinny asked. "We can't stay here forever."

Jason contemplated his friend and wondered if he could answer truthfully. Skinny was a nervous type who frankly admitted he was not brave. He really did not know the answer to Skinny's question. Jean, the French merchant Jason had met six months before on his first visit to Martinique, was not really a friend. Jason had bought some rum and sugar from the Frenchman. When they had parted, Jean had confided he could provide any supplies that the Americans needed, including powder and balls to blow the hated Englishmen to pieces.

Jason was now learning that the English men-of-war were not the only ones who threatened the "Ghost" and its crew. Fort to Port, Martinique's main port, if it could be called that, had its share of pirates and riffraff who preyed on anything that sailed the islands. Jason recognized that he and his young crew appeared to be easy pickings. The "Ghost" did not carry a single cannon, and the four younger members of the crew were not yet able to grow beards. The "Ghost" had been in port for ten days now, and, during their many hours idling about the port, the boys had attracted much hostile attention. Jason had contacted Jean the first day they anchored the "Ghost" in Port-de-France's harbor. When Jason had explained he wanted sixty barrels of powder—Jason had carefully calculated that "Ghost's" small hold would hold ten rows of six barrels each and that is all—Jean had nodded affirmatively, but Jason noted the middle-aged Frenchman with garlic breath appeared worried. He blinked his brown eyes, scratched his long, straight black hair, and muttered a string of "oui, monsieur, oui, certainments." Jean then explained he would need time to arrange the purchase, took two hundred pounds of Jason's money and disappeared, promising to arrange for the powder shortly. Every day since Jason had visited Jean's small store and had been assured by Jean's Creole wife that her husband was expected back momentarily. Meanwhile, Jason waited and worried.

"Monsieurs desire more?" The barmaid asked in her broken English. She had approached while Jason and Skinny had been whispering about the two mean looking men across the room.

"Do you know those two men?" Skinny asked.

"Mais oui," she replied leaning her stout frame against Skinny. Jason could smell the heavy body odor from across the table. Long black hair protruded from under her armpits. "Tres bads hommes. Zey look and talk about you. Zey wants your money. Best give to me," She laughed loudly.

"Yea, sure," Skinny replied. "Just give us two more mugs."

The barmaid patted Skinny affectionately on the back, seized the two empty mugs, and retreated towards the makeshift bar. Her large bare feet left lines in the sand floor.

"We're going to have to do something soon," Skinny scratched his cheek and looked at Jason with a worried glance.

"I know. You stay here with our friends, and I'll try again with Jean."

"What about your ale?" Skinny asked, nodding towards the bar where the barmaid was filling their dirty mugs with ale and foam from a large keg.

"'Let her bring it. That way those guys will think I'm taking a leak and not follow."

Skinny nodded agreement as Jason rose from his chair. Port-de-France was smaller than Alexandria. It would take Jason only minutes to reach Jean's shop.

The atmosphere inside the "Chicken" had been hot and heavy, but the air outside made even Alexandria's torpid August heat appear mild. The late afternoon sun scorched the small town. The white sand streets, packed hard by the passage of many bare feet, singed Jason's soles through his thick leather boots. He and the crew had shed their linsey-woolsy Virginia clothes and had purchased the sleeveless, multicolored shirts and bulky pants of Martinique. Jason's feet were tender, so he wore his boots, but he was rather proud of the white and gray shirt he had acquired. It was now stained with sweat from the tropical heat, but he still wore it proudly, hoping he looked more like a native. His skin was now turning reddish brown. Like his crew, he had been badly sunburned during their first days at sea, but now the skin had peeled and was gradually adapting to the searing sunrays. The ocean breeze that always seemed to blow helped some, but the sun remained merciless.

Jason was sweating profusely when he reached Jean's shop. He brushed aside the long chains of brightly colored wood beads and entered into the gloom. The shop was one of the largest in Fort-de-France and appeared to contain mainly supplies for the sea going vessels that carried the island's rum and sugar to France. Before his eyes could adjust to the darkness that concealed the shop, a small hand seized Jason's bare arm and pulled him forward.

"Ahh, Jason, I'm so glad you came. I have a message from Jean for you." Jean's wife Marie, who Jason estimated to be at least twenty years Jean's junior, was an attractive girl who spoke a passable English.

After the initial start, Jason allowed himself a sigh of relief and followed the dark haired Marie to the back of the shop where she handed Jason a folded sheet of paper and began whispering again.

"Jean has your cargo, but for your sake he prefers not to bring it your boat. You are being watched."

"I know," Jason responded. Only his intrinsic politeness kept him from blurting that he would have to be blind not to notice the unkempt Frenchmen who had been watching the "Ghost" as well as Jason and his crew when ashore.

"Zey are badmen," whispered Marie. "Pirates from Guadeloupe. Zey like to steal Englishmen's boats."

"I'm afraid they are getting tired of waiting," Jason confided.

"Zey wait for you to buy cargo, then zey will jump on you as soon as you leave ze harbor."

"We have no guns, so we have to outrun them," Jason said. "Where is Jean and my cargo? When will he bring it to me? Tonight?" Jason nervously asked several questions before Marie could organize her answers in English.

"'E iz wid our plantation and az your cargo dere."

"Where is the plantation?"

"Ze paper shows you," Marie whispered.

Jason unfolded the wrinkled sheet Marie had handed him and found the rough outline of Martinique. Only two locations were noted, Fort to Port on the Caribbean side and a dot marked Le Robert in a bay on the Atlantic coast almost directly across the island from the port where the "Ghost" was now anchored.

"How long will it take me to sail there?" Jason asked.

"I don't know. Maybe... . " Marie paused before continuing. "Maybe six hours."

"I'll sail tonight and be there before daybreak," Jason spoke with more assurance than he felt. "How will I find Jean?"

"Ze plantation is on the outer tip of the bay. You must be vari careful. Zere are many islands, just rocks, hard to see at night. Jean will light two fires on the shore to guide you."

"How will he know I'm coming?"

"I vill send a message to 'im ... now."

"Then I will leave immediately. Thank you, Marie. I'll see you next trip."

"I 'ope so, Jason. Be careful."

Jason turned and hurried from the shop. As he approached the "Chicken" with its faded picture of a Coq, Jason paused to make sure nothing had changed. He could see the "Ghost" floating at anchor about fifty feet off shore. Two of his crew were moving about the small quarter-deck on the "Ghost's" stern. He glanced at the shore and saw that the small rowboat that the "Ghost" carried to serve as a means for the crew to reach land from an offshore anchor nestled in the sand where he and Skinny had left it. All seemed in order. Just before entering the "Chicken," Jason paused to nervously reassure himself that his knife remained in its sheath at the small of his back. Jason was not an expert knife thrower like his uncle John or even his father, but as a child he had practiced throwing the old hunting knife his father had given him when he reached age ten. Jason had never mastered the art of the overhand throw. His knife always struck wrong end to more often than not. He was reasonably accurate throwing underhand so that the knife did not rotate in flight. In any case he was more concerned about losing his family heirloom than using it, even though it did give him a degree of assurance.

When Jason entered the "Chicken," he noticed the barmaid standing at her usual place behind the bar. She was staring in the direction of the table that Jason had occupied with Skinny. His sudden entrance caused a blur of motion as one of the French toughs rose from a kneeling position near the overturned table that had been occupied by Skinny when Jason had left barely ten minutes previously.

Jason immediately saw his friend sprawled on his back with the second Frenchman sitting spread legged on his chest holding a knife to Skinny's throat.

"Ahh, ze ami," the Frenchman who had leaped to his feet uttered as he turned towards Jason.

"Stop. Let him go," Jason shouted, his voice wavering.

The Frenchman laughed as he walked slowly towards Jason, holding his knife menacingly in front of him. Without thinking, Jason grabbed his knife from the sheath at his back, crouched, and threw the knife underhanded as hard as he could at the Frenchman. Jason doubted he would hit the man in a vital spot but hoped it might alarm him long enough for Jason to try something else.

The knife, perfectly balanced and made with an artisan's care for perfection, flew straight into the Frenchman chest. It struck him point first and buried itself deeply in the man's upper stomach just under the rib cage. The Frenchman dropped to the floor. Jason stared as blood began to stream from around the blade. Bubbles of red froth oozed from the man's mouth. The man sucked in air trying to get a breath, but without success. His loud gasps filled the room and were followed by short wheezes.

The second Frenchman who still sat on Skinny's chest stared with wide eyes at his companion as he lay on the floor with his hands grasped around Jason's knife as it protruded from his bleeding chest. Jason turned, grabbed one of the "Chicken's" handmade chairs and smashed it on a table. It shattered. Jason grasped a chair leg in his hand and pounded it against the tabletop until he freed the chair remnants from the leg. He turned and raised the club over his head. The second Frenchman shouted in fright, rolled off Skinny's chest and crawled crab like to the far wall where he rose and leaned back. Jason continued to threaten with the club. The man turned and ran from the front door, dropping his knife in the fright of his departure.

Jason turned back towards Skinny who had pulled himself into a sitting position about five feet from the sprawled, dying Frenchman on the floor.

"Christ, Jason, where did you learn to throw a knife like that?" Skinny rubbed his throat.

"What happened?" Jason demanded, still holding the chair leg and stepping wide around the Frenchman whose gasping had stopped.

"I didn't do anything," Skinny began defensively.

"I know that. Why did they jump you?"

Jason's legs began to tremble, so he sat down, still watching the dying Frenchman on the floor. The man's body jerked sporadically. Jason did not really care what provoked the Frenchmen into jumping Skinny. It was only a matter of time until they tried something. Jason simply was asking questions until he got his composure back.

"After you left, I just sat there minding my own business. After about ten minutes and you didn't come back, those two came over and jumped me. They wanted to know where you had gone. I told them I didn't have much money. They could have what I had, but they were more interested in you."

"Not me. The 'Ghost,'" Jason said as he shook his head trying to clear it.

Jason stood, cautiously bent over the Frenchman and grasped his knife handle. It was lodged tightly in the Frenchman. Jason finally was forced to place his boot on the man's chest near the wound and pushed down while he pulled on the knife. With a sucking sound it came free, followed by a gush of dark, red blood. Jason carefully wiped the blade on the Frenchman's pants then replaced his knife in its sheath. He turned towards the bar, finally remembering the barmaid. She stood where she had been when Jason had entered.

"Want more beer?" She asked with her toothless smile.

Jason shook his head negatively. He turned to Skinny who had just climbed to his feet.

"Let's get out of here," Jason ordered and turned towards the door. "That other guy may have friends."

"What about him?" The barmaid called, pointing to the Frenchman sprawled on the floor.

"Let his friend clean him up," Jason called as he ran out the door.

The street in front of the "Chicken" was still deserted. Jason had no idea where the second Frenchman had gone.

"Let's get back to the 'Ghost,'" Jason ordered.

Skinny Potts did not require a second invitation. He ran after Jason as he hurried to their beached skiff.

It required only minutes for the two young men to reach their boat. Jason quickly explained what had happened to the four excited crewmen who waited on board. Following Jason's instructions, they lifted the small rowboat to the "Ghost's" foredeck, secured it, unfurled the jib and both main sails, and weighed anchor. Fortunately, a light breeze enabled them to quickly clear the harbor. Once out in the Caribbean, they caught a stronger ocean wind as Jason who manned the wheel turned the "Ghost" westward towards the dropping sun. He estimated they had about two hours before nightfall. Jason looked back and saw no pursuit. The other ships remained at anchor in the torpor of the late afternoon trop-ical sun. Jason hoped the predators who had been stalking them would believe the fight at the "Chicken" had frightened the boys into fleeing homeward. If the pirates suspected he was circling the island to Le Robert and the French mer-chant's plantation to take on cargo, Jason and his crew would be in serious trou-ble. The pirates could easily overtake them during the several hours required to load their powder.

As time passed and the horizon remained free of sails, Jason began to relax. Skinny and three of the crew gathered near Jason on the quarter-deck; Skinny regaled them with an already enhanced version of their experience ashore. The three younger boys stared at Jason with awe in their eyes. He knew they were impressed by the fact he had killed a man with a knife. Jason was surprised at himself. Now that the excitement had subsided somewhat, he had become calm and suffered no remorse whatever for having killed a man. The fact that the man was attacking Jason and deserved what he got left Jason with a free conscience. He only wished his accurate knife throw had been more than accidental luck. He vowed to practice with the knife when he returned home. He doubted this would be the last time he would need assistance if he continued to be a blockade-runner.

Jason finally turned the wheel over to one of the smaller boys and sat on a bench at the rear of the deck. Skinny and the others out of respect for and maybe fear of his newfound stature left him alone. Jason studied the Martinique shore-line as the "Ghost" with its snapping sails hurried on its way. Martinique was the prettiest island Jason in his limited experience had ever seen. It deserved its rep-utation as the land of flowers. The lush green vegetation that touched the pure white sand beaches was filled with the bright colors of bougainvillea, hibiscus, poinsettias and other flowers that Jason could not begin to name. Coconut palms reached skyward and cast the shade from their fronds over pineapple, papaya and banana fruits that made the island an easy place to live. If it were not for the constant heat, Jason would be tempted to settle in the small paradise the French were creating.

"End of island, ho," Skinny called from the bow in an attempt to sound like an experienced seaman.

"I see it," Jason said. He took back the helm. None of the crew, including Jason himself, knew much about ocean waters. Since this was his second visit to Martinique, Jason considered himself their expert. He turned slightly to port and followed a heading to take the "Ghost" around the end of Martinique into the Atlantic. In the distance he could see Mont Pelee which was reputed to be an extinct volcano. Whatever it was, Pelee rose to an impressive height and domi-nated the end of the island.

A full moon hung in the cloudless sky. Jason could not help staring at the glowing, yellow orb and its background of bright, crystal blue stars. The North Star and the Big Dipper were easily located, and Jason could have guided the "Ghost" by them if needed. In order to save time, he followed Martinique shore-line as he traversed northward along its coast. White sand beaches reflected the moon's soft light, and Jason did not need to worry about stars. The rougher Atlantic tide could be heard whipping into the shore, and Jason, afraid of corral reefs and rock barriers in these unfamiliar waters stayed several hundred yards offshore. Skinny and another crewman sat in the bow and kept watchful eyes on the ocean ahead. All were relieved to be finally free of Fort to Port and its unfriendly waterfront. They had begun to relax when it became apparent they had cleared port without predatory sails in their wake.

About three hours after they had rounded the island's southern tip, Skinny joined Jason on the quarter-deck. He pointed directly ahead at an odd shaped, narrow piece of land that protruded from Martinique at a sharp right angle.

"That looks like the small peninsula on your friend's map. If it is, Le Robert should be located in the second small bay after we round the point."

Jason consulted the piece of paper that Marie had given him so few hours ago.

"I think you're right, Skinny," Jason agreed. "We better come about and get farther out to sea so that we miss that odd shaped creature."

Skinny stared into the haze of the night and studied the peninsula. "It looks like a sea dragon with its backside towards us."

"Coming about," Jason shouted. As soon as he was sure his young crew members were clear, he spun the wheel to bring his ship several degrees to the starboard. He still sailed his new boat carefully. All his previous experience had been in small single masted sloops. The "Ghost's" twin masts each carried full sets of fore and aft sails. Jason had been tempted to install square rigged sails on the front mast copying the slick New England brigantines, but the experienced boatmen at his father's yard had persuaded him to stay with the two fore and aft sail masts. A small jib hung over the bowsprit. When under sail in a fresh wind, the "Ghost" was indeed fast and maneuverable. The fore and aft sails made it more weatherly, letting it sail closer to the wind with less sidewise drift than that encountered by square riggers and their much larger and heavier hulls. The "Ghost" handled easily in narrow channels, an important feature for traversing the Chesapeake Bay and its rivers. In addition to adding to the "Ghost's" speed and adroit handling, fore and aft sails permitted Jason to employ many fewer crewmen.

The "Ghost" with virtually no loss of speed responded to Jason's turn of the wheel. The twin booms swung easily across the deck clearing the quarter-deck and Jason's head by a minimum of two feet. Skinny and the crew had loosened the ropes controlling the heavy booms from their belaying pins and allowed the sails slack line as the boat crossed the eye of the wind and turned away from the land protrusion dead ahead. On Jason's order, they pulled the ropes back through the squeaking lanyards until the groaning canvas was once again filled and the "Ghost" leaned into the sea as it raced along the dragon shaped spine of land.

Jason stayed on course for about fifteen minutes until he was confident he had cleared the land tip. Once again he brought "Ghost" about and headed back towards the moonlit island.

"I'm sure glad we've got a full moon and clear skies for this sail," Skinny spoke softly, attempting to conceal the excitement and tension in his voice. Skinny knew that he and Jason had to keep up a front for the younger members of their crew.

"I wouldn't dare it otherwise," Jason agreed. He was experienced enough to be worried sailing at night close to land in waters he had never before visited.

As soon as they rounded the protruding peninsula, Jason could see the dim outline of two bays.

"I think we are supposed to head for the small cove on the left. Marie said there is a small dock that serves the plantation."

"Think we had better take in some sail and slow down?" Skinny asked, the tension still evident in his voice.

"You're right," Jason agreed, as he became conscious of the speed with which they were sailing along the peninsula. "Take in the foresail and furl it loosely. I want to be able to get under way quickly if we have to."

Skinny hurried forward and assisted the four crewmen in tying the foresail to its boom and mast. When finished, Skinny hurried to the bow and studied the shoreline. Suddenly, at almost the same time as Jason, he spotted two fires burning on the beach. According to Jean's instructions, the small dock would be located between the fires. Jason hoped the water at the dock would be deep enough to carry "Ghost's" shallow drawing hull.

"I see two fires on the beach to our starboard," Skinny called.

"I see them," Jason responded. "Best take in the aft sails," he called. We'll use only the jib to keep her underway." Jason silently prayed that he did not smash into the dock. "I think I'll anchor off shore, and we can use the long boat to work her in to the dock."

"Good idea," Skinny called back. "I'll stand by the jib. When you turn windward we'll drop anchor and lower the jib." Skinny hurried forward.

The brisk wind and tide carried the "Ghost" shoreward faster than Jason anticipated, despite the fact he was using only jib power. Finally, daring to come no closer to the unfamiliar landing, he decided to turn windward.

"Bringing her about," he called to Skinny and the crew. "Drop the jib and lower the anchor."

The craft was now out of Jason's control and at the mercy of the anchor. Jason could hear the breakers smashing the shoreline. It seemed he could almost reach out and touch the two bonfires. By staring hard, he could identify figures appearing on the black mass that had to be the dock. It was no more than forty feet away.

"Jason, Jason, is that you?" Jason heard Jean, the French merchant, call.

"Yes," Jason answered. He sat back on the wood bench and breathed a heavy sigh of relief.

"Magnificent sailing," Jean called. "Stay there and we will guide you to the dock with our long boats."

Magnificent sailing, Jason repeated the French merchant's excited words in his mind. "I'm stupid," he thought. "I'm never going to do anything like that again." Jason was intelligent enough to realize how lucky he had been.

Chapter 7
Northern Virginia
Spring 1775

Political developments that winter and spring evolved in a series of hills and valleys setting a pattern that would continue for the next eight years. A dramatic event would occur in one colony or another. Crown governors would send their sensational reports across the vast Atlantic. Weeks later the news would reach London, shock Parliament, the British people and their leaders, and then their irate response would be dispatched back across the thousands of miles of water. Two months later the strong English reaction would drop upon the colonials who by that time would have forgotten the originating event. The colonial ire over the dated English counter punch would generate another cycle. The situation was out of control. The entire process gave the headlong rush towards war a momentum of its own.

In December 1774, Governor Dunmore had written a vivid report describing the Virginian reaction to the First Continental Congress. He particularly stressed the decision by the illegal meeting to promote the formation of independent militia units and the enforcement of non-importation, non-export agreements. Governor Dunmore's solution was to beat the colonials at their own game; he recommended that London set up a sea blockade and enforce the colonials' own bans; then, he reasoned, wait and see who buckled first. Dunmore based his thesis on the premise that only a few hotheads favored war with England and that as soon as the majority of the people saw the English were determined they would force the firebrands to capitulate. Dunmore sincerely did not understand how badly he misread the situation.

Dunmore's Christmas report arrived in London in early February 1775. The blunt words shocked His Majesty, Lord North and the Parliament. They could not believe that the counties of Virginia were preparing for war by following the unconstitutional Continental Congress' recommendation that they form their militia companies and collect arms and ammunition for battle. The Prime Minister reacted immediately. He ordered the colonial governors to seize all weapons, powder and military supplies collected by the rebels and to arrest their leaders.

Governor Dunmore was not the only person to react to the Continental Congress of last fall. The Congress, just prior to adjourning, had called upon each colony to elect delegates to a second congress to convene in Philadelphia in May 1775. Peyton Randolph, the presiding officer of the House of Burgesses as well as of the First Continental Congress, took this charge seriously. He called on Virginia's counties to send delegates to a convention to be held in Richmond on March 20. By holding the meeting in the small town of Richmond, Randolph reasoned they would be safe from Dunmore's interference. Word of the ministerial order to arrest colonial leaders had already spread.

At the end of February 1775, a county meeting at the Court House in Fairfax elected James Satterfield and George Washington to again represent the county in Richmond.

George and James braved the brisk March winds together and traveled to Richmond. They paused in Dumfries long enough for the ever militant Washington to review the Dumfries Independent Militia Company. James assumed that George still harbored an ambition to once again command the Virginia Regiment. They arrived in Richmond just after their fellow delegates had once again elected Peyton Randolph to preside. James frequently wondered how old Governor Dinwiddie felt about his nemesis from the struggle over the land tax receiving so much honor. James still felt a loyalty and affection for the old governor who had given James his first start in politics by hiring him as his clerk. James and Dinwiddie had worked hard supporting Washington in his battles with the Indians for western lands. James found it ironic that Governor Dunmore, who was becoming a bitter foe of the colonials who he governed, had just won the first major Virginian victory over the Indians at Point Pleasant.

The first few days of the Richmond assembly proceeded mildly enough with some of the latest news hinting at the possibility of compromise. Lord North appeared to be considering the withdrawal of the fleet from Boston. Then, on March twenty-third the western firebrand Patrick Henry rose and submitted a series of resolutions that included several arguments from the Fairfax Resolves. Henry captured everyone's attention, however, when he proposed that Virginia be immediately put in a posture of defense and that a committee be appointed to develop a plan for arming a sufficient number of men for that purpose.

Henry at this point became passionate, and his fiery words froze every delegate in their place. He charged the English with increasing their military might in the colonies with the sole object of enslaving them. Patrick Henry, inspired by the heat of his own emotion and rhetoric, then shouted:

"We must fight!"

Noting a small reaction to these words, Henry surged forward by uttering words that James and posterity would forever have ring in their ears.

"Is life so dear, or peace so sweet, as to be purchased at the price of chains and slavery? Forbid it, Almighty God! I know not what course others may take, but as for me, give me liberty or give me death!"

James, who had begun taking notes for a report on key speeches to be printed in the *Herald*, had copied Henry's words verbatim. He was glad he had because later many would challenge the exact wording of the orator's fiery speech, but James knew for a certainty what had been said.

When Henry finished, he calmly took his chair while his audience sat in stunned silence. After several minutes, a few of the more conservative one by one tried to counter the orator's highly emotional impact by suggesting caution before proceeding, but the impassioned Henry had carried the battle. He was the first appointed to a twelve-man committee whose purpose was to develop a plan to arm a sufficient number of men to defend their country, as many now referred to the colony. George Washington, along with an old military colleague from the west, Adam Stephens, was appointed to the committee. James was pleased at the honors Washington was once again accumulating for Fairfax County, and he made a note to remind himself to stress that point in the next issue of the *Herald*.

The committee worked swiftly and within two days submitted its report calling on each of the counties east of the fall line to raise one or more troops of cavalry, each to consist of thirty men. The poorer counties of the west were asked to furnish one company of rank and file soldiers, sixty-eight each in number. Since paying for the arms was still legally a problem, the plan also authorized each county to follow Fairfax's example and raise a head tax to fund the needed purchases. The proposal easily carried.

The Richmond convention concluded by acknowledging the purpose for which they had been convened. They elected seven men to represent them at the Second Continental Congress in Philadelphia scheduled for May 1775. Of course, the delegate from Fairfax, George Washington, was selected to attend. His name was the second nominated, following only the venerable Speaker, Peyton Randolph.

If James thought the pace en route to Richmond had been fast, he was mistaken for he was hard pressed to keep up with the hurrying Washington on the way back to Fairfax. Washington was a skilled horseman and James only mediocre at best. James throughout his entire life had preferred to travel at a leisurely rate and enjoy the countryside. The trip home from Richmond gave him no such opportunity. James was in Alexandria by the last day of March. He had not paused at Eastwind longer than the few hours required to brief Vivian on the momentous developments. Then, he had hurried on to Alexandria to put out a special edition of the *Herald*

Within days, shocking word of Governor Dunmore's reaction to the illegal meeting in Richmond reached Mount Vernon and Alexandria. Dunmore announced that he had decided to cancel all the western land patents issued under the Proclamation of 1754. The Proclamation had been Dinwiddie's reward to the veterans of Virginia who had fought with Washington in the west against the French and Indians. Washington alone stood to lose over twenty-three thousand acres of western land. The Governor explained that William Crawford, the man who had conducted the survey for the veterans, had failed to qualify himself as provided by law as a surveyor. Despite his disingenuousness, Dunmore's purpose was clear. He intended to punish Washington and his friends for their temerity in illegally calling for the raising of troops to be used against the Crown who the Governor represented.

The Governor's tactic failed. Those like Washington who stood to lose the most continued on their path.

"Dunmore made a mistake if he thinks he can blackmail us," Washington confided to James on one of his frequent visits to Alexandria in April to review the Fairfax Independent Militia Company. "If anything, Dunmore's action will motivate many to advocate rebellion from a government that takes away the rights of its citizens in such a whimsical and arbitrary manner."

James noted that Washington carefully avoided acknowledging base motivation for himself despite the fact that his fortune was heavily invested in western land speculation.

In April, spring gave Fairfax County a gift of the finest weather that nature can offer. The rains were warm and refreshing; the air was balmy and the soft earth raised welcoming arms as if begging for seed. At Eastwind, Gunston Hall, Mount Vernon, and other county plantations, the slaves took to the fields plowing, raking and planting. Fewer tobacco seedlings were set down as most began to hedge their futures with wheat, corn and other grains. Still, tobacco was put into the earth because all recognized this would be the last money crop sent to markets in England before the non exportation ban went into effect in November.

Vivian worked long hours in the fields at Eastwind, determined that this year's crop would be sufficient to carry her family home over the next year whatever happened in the struggle between the colonies and the Crown. James busied himself at the Herald, but he found the opportunity to visit the waterfront several times a day hoping for sight of the returning "Ghost." This was Jason's second visit to Martinique but his first as a smuggler. As a consequence of orders recently received from London, the English fleet had stepped up its surveillance of the lower Bay in an effort to cut off rebel attempts to purchase arms and powder, and this was exactly what Jason was doing.

Before the "Ghost" reappeared in Alexandria, trouble broke out in Williamsburg greatly adding to James' unease. As the story was received in a report to George Washington, on the night of April 21st, between three and four AM, a Captain Collins of the English schooner "Magdalen," accompanied by fifteen marines, appeared before the Williamsburg armory. Acting on Governor Dunmore's orders and driving his wagon, the marines stealthily emptied the armory of all powder, some twenty barrels, and hauled it to be stored on H.M.S.

"Fowey." When the townspeople learned what had happened, they filled the Duke of Gloucester Street and loudly demonstrated in front of the Palace; couriers were dispatched to alert the colony's independent militia units. After hurried consultations, Peyton Randolph delivered a message from the colony's leaders demanding to know why the Governor had acted as he had. In the message Randolph noted that the powder had been collected for the colony's security, that it might be needed in case of a slave uprising and demanded that the people's powder be returned. Randolph unwittingly gave Dunmore a cover for his actions. The Governor replied that he had received reports of a possible nearby slave insurrection and had seized the powder to keep it from falling into the wrong hands. He promised that the people could have their powder on a half-hours notice when truly needed. The dubious response did not satisfy the people of Williamsburg who by that time thronged through the streets demanding action with many labeling the Governor a royal liar.

George Washington and the men of the Fairfax Independent Militia Company received a report from Fredericksburg. The latter's militia company declared its intent to dispatch its cavalry company to Williamsburg on April 29th and invited Alexandria and other towns of Virginia to do likewise. They proposed to recover their powder with force if necessary.

Just as affairs in Virginia were in a state of turmoil over Dunmore's actions, news reached the colony of a bloody clash that had occurred in Massachusetts ten days earlier on April 19th. British infantry had marched on the towns of Lexington and Concord, ten and twenty miles from occupied Boston, in an attempt to seize rebel leaders and powder. The Minutemen and townspeople had resisted. The British had to send a column of reinforcements to rescue their infantry who were besieged by patriots firing from behind rocks and trees. The English lost seventy-three men and the rebels forty-nine, and the fat was in the fire.

As best as James could tell, events were simply snowballing with no real cause. The colonials led by Massachusetts and Virginia had decided to arm themselves for self-defense. Alexandria's own militia unit, acting as urged by James himself in the Fairfax Resolves, had been among the first to organize. The Continental Congress had thought this a good idea and had recommended that all colonies should do likewise. Reports from Dunmore and other governors had alarmed Lord North and his ministers and they had replied with orders to seize colonial powder and rebel leaders. Following these orders, Dunmore in Virginia and General Gates in Boston had acted and enraged colonial passions. At least in Virginia, Dunmore's stealth, acting in the middle of the night against an attainable objective, the local armory, had avoided bloodshed.

James in formulating his editorial policy for the *Herald* was forced to ride the crest. News of the volatile events circulated quickly, creating an insatiable thirst for news. James and Corney had to repeat the stories as they were received from Williamsburg and Boston, and the news was already inflamed and bloody. To James' surprise, the calm Corney lost his dispassion and began writing stories

and contrived letters to the paper demanding justice and action. The *Herald* doubled its circulation in a two week period, and James increased the number of visits he made to the riverside hoping for a sighting of the "Ghost" returning safely
from what had become a fool hearty mission.

By April thirtieth, fourteen troops of militia cavalry, some six hundred men in
all, had rallied to Fredericksburg. Before they could march, a message from
Peyton Randolph in Williamsburg reported that the Governor had promised to
return the powder even though he had yet to say exactly when. Randolph recommended a respite in colonial action to give the Governor time to correct his
wrongdoing. To the militia assembled in Fredericksburg these words sounded
like victory. Chanting "God Save American Liberties," a play on "God Save the
King," the cavalry companies departed Fredericksburg and returned to their
homes.

On May third, Horatio Gates visited Mount Vernon. Gates, who had commanded a company under General Braddock, was an old military colleague of
Washington.   Now retired to Berkeley County where he was a friend of
Washington's brother, Charles, Gates was interested in George's plans for resuming a military career in these troubled times. He was also, not coincidentally, anxious to take up arms again himself. Washington sent James an invitation to join
himself and Gates at Mount Vernon for consultations prior to Washington's next
day departure for the Second Continental Congress in Philadelphia; James reluctantly left his riverside watch.

When he arrived at Mount Vernon just after noon, he to his surprise found
Washington, Gates and two other gentlemen already ensconced on Mount
Vernon's rear verandah. Richard Henry Lee and his brother Thomas Ludwell Lee
had also arrived unexpectedly. The spreading reports of conflict had excited the
leaders of the colony, and most had begun consultations intended to divulge how
each could contribute. Those with military ambitions were the most interested.
Washington was a natural magnet.

After shaking hands with the visitors—James knew them all, the Lees better
than Gates—James joined the discussion. Washington, obviously a little overwhelmed by all the attention and naturally a quiet man, was relieved at James'
arrival. He deferred to James, the newspaperman, to brief the visitors on the most
recent news. James observed that as all knew, events in Williamsburg appeared
to have calmed, but the situation in the north remained tense. All agreed that the
new Congress would undoubtedly receive first hand news from the delegates of
Massachusetts and the north and then would be expected to determine the colonial reaction. Gates and the Lees advocated a forceful response, a military one if
necessary. James was less emotional and hedged his position by noting that much
would depend on the latest reports from the north. He agreed, however, that the
situation was serious.

As the afternoon wore on, Washington detected James' frequent glances at
the river. He knew what was troubling him, but he did not know what he could
do for his friend. Finally, about four o'clock, while Gates and the Lees were

debating possible military retaliations, George excused himself and James, noting that he knew James had to return to Alexandria. When they entered the mansion on their way to the front door, Washington took James by the arm and led him into his study.

"Still no word from Jason?" Washington asked.

"No," James responded with a frown and a shake of his head. "I wish I hadn't let him go on this ill conceived adventure. He's not a seaman, and the situation has deteriorated to the point where it's not worth the risks."

"We will need the powder, James," Washington replied quietly, "but I agree. I wish Jason were not the one at risk."

"I have the money to repay you for your share of the advance," Washington continued, trying to force James to think of something besides his worry. James, Washington and Mason had advanced the money to pay for the local militia company's supplies and weapons. Washington himself had ordered rifles from Philadelphia. Although a three shilling levy had been proposed, the sheriff had been slow collecting it, and the three friends had been forced to advance the money to pay for what was needed. James had covered the costs of the powder Jason was buying in Martinique.

"Has the sheriff already collected the levy?" James knew that despite the fact he was authorized to receive a commission for the collection that the sheriff did not expect to have the money in hand until late summer. James sympathized because the levy had to be collected personally from each freeholder in the county. Since specie was scarce, many would have difficulty meeting their obligation.

"No," Washington replied with a smile. "Mr. Mason got impatient with the sheriff and sent his son off to make the collections." Washington usually referred to George Mason as Mr. Mason in deference to the fact that Mason was seven years older. "I suggested he wait for the sheriff, wondering about the legality of using his son, but you know Mr. Mason. When he decides to do something, he does it. Besides, he saves the sheriff's commission this way. Here is your fifty-two pounds for the powder."

James took the leather bag that Washington offered him. He shook it, listening to the clank of the coins. "I hope this isn't blood money, Jason's."

"Will that cover your costs?"

"Certainly. Jason was planning on buying the county's powder then another ten or fifteen barrels, whatever he can carry safely, to pay for his costs. He hopes to make enough to pay for his boat."

"He'll have no trouble selling the extra powder," Washington said approvingly. As one of the richest men in the colony, he appreciated the power of profit.

"Well, I'd better...." James said as he turned to depart.

"If you can delay a few more minutes... ." Washington caught his arm. "I know you are worried about Jason. I am too, but there is nothing you can do now to help him. He is on his own. Jason will survive. He's as old as John and I were when we went west to fight the Indians. At least, almost as old." Washington paused and looked at his friend.

James nodded and sat in a chair facing George who in turn sat in his favorite chair by his writing desk.

"I'm worried about affairs, James."

James knew he was referring to Massachusetts and the Congress.

"I don't know what will happen in Philadelphia," Washington paused. When James merely nodded his head, Washington continued. "After what happened at Lexington and Concord, I fear the hotter heads will prevail."

"What will you do?" James asked, knowing the answer.

"I have given the matter much thought. I'm an old man now and would like nothing better than to stay here at Mount Vernon and tend my crops. My last ten years with Martha and the children have been my happiest. Despite Patsy." Washington referred to the tragic death of his stepdaughter two years previous.

"But I have my duty." Washington spoke more firmly as he continued. James was his closest friend, and with him George came as close as he could to sharing private thoughts with another man. "I have had military experience. If I am called to lead the Virginia Regiment..." Washington again paused. He obviously found it difficult to talk about personal ambitions.

"George, Virginia will need you and your experience," James interrupted. "I do not know of another man better qualified to command. Not our visitor," James referred to Gates the former professional soldier now on half pay retirement from the British army. "And not his neighbor Charles Lee." Lee was another ambitious former British officer. The idiosyncratic Lee who preferred the company of his pack of dogs to men was a neighbor of Charles Washington and Gates.

Washington nodded agreement at his friend's words. With James he did not adopt a pose of false modesty. "Both are good men, but like Adam Stephens, they have their faults."

"Have you been approached?"

"Only by men looking for positions, not offering," Washington spoke wryly. Already the Lees and Gates and the like were cultivating Washington, clearly assuming he would lead.

"I got along well with the Adamses and others at the first Congress. Maybe, I could work with them..."

"But the Virginia command?"

"I can't advocate for myself. It's not my nature," Washington explained needlessly. "I plan to wear my old uniform every day at the Congress. It will demonstrate where my sentiments lie and remind others I have a military background. As former commander of the Virginia Regiment and a member of the Fairfax militia and an honorary member of other independent companies..." Washington began in embarrassed self-explanation.

"I understand, George, and I think you should wear it. It's a good idea. And...."

"And I have a request to make." George interrupted his friend, something he was normally too polite and reticent to do.

"Yes," James paused, fearing what was to come.

"And if I go, to fight, I mean, I will need you with me." Washington paused and stared hard at his friend.

"I can't, George. I appreciate... ." James began, then hesitated, not knowing what to say. He did not want to go to war. "I'm not a military man. I don't have any experience. Not like you and John," James referred to his twin brother who had fought with Washington in the west, then immediately regretted having brought up John's name.

"I've thought of John. Hard. His services will also be needed," Washington smiled thinly. He involuntarily concealed his bad teeth. "I may have to send for John, but that can wait. He knows the Indians better than any man alive. And knows how to deal with them. The English obviously will be relying on the Six Nations...but that's not what I meant," Washington caught himself. "I'll need you. I know you don't have military experience, that you abhor the thought of killing another person, but I will need someone I can trust. Someone I can talk with, share my concerns, ease the burdens, help me with politics." Washington paused and looked at his friend again. He knew it would not be easy to persuade James to give up Alexandria and join him, but he was content to have taken the first step in what would be a campaign.

James was speechless. Washington had played the strongest card that could be dealt, their friendship. He would have a difficult time turning him down.

"I don't mean wear a uniform. You could be my civilian adviser, something like that, but let's not make a decision now." Washington automatically assumed the role of commander.

"Let's watch events and see what happens. Maybe they won't want an old guy like me."

James saw his friend's eyes cloud over and turned away himself to conceal his own emotion.

"Thank you George," James said noncommittally as he rose. "Just remember, I'm not a military man, and I hope none in my family are either. It's going to be a long struggle, and bloody, and I feel guilty for saying it, but..."

"I know, James," Washington too regained his composure."

"I'll see you when I return." Washington paused, then smiled again to himself. "If not before."

James did not understand what his friend meant, but he decided not to push it. He felt lucky to have escaped his friend's request so easily. Washington was a mild man, but he could be stubborn when his will was confronted.

Chapter 8
Martinique and Beyond
April/May 1775

Jason had insisted that Skinny and the crew go ashore and sleep while he, Jean and his plantation slaves loaded the barrels of powder on board "Ghost." The slaves drove the wagons out onto the dock, lifted the barrels up onto "Ghost's" deck, and then carefully lowered them into the small forward hold. The barrels, kegs really, were stacked five abreast and two deep in the limited cargo space. Jason was delighted when he was able to snugly fit eight rows into the hold, making a total of eighty kegs. On the Frenchman's recommendation, Jason supervised the slaves as they packed palm fronds along the sides and on top to immobilize the cargo as much as possible. Noting that five kegs were left over, Jason had the slaves lash two barrels on the boat's stern at the rear of the quarter-deck. Jean assured Jason the barrels were waterproof. Three additional barrels were taken to the crew cabin below the quarter-deck where they were appropriately lashed. The full cargo crowded the available space, but Jason reasoned it would provide balanced ballast that would be needed if they encountered heavy seas. Jason was anxious to see how the cargo affected the "Ghost's" speed. The previous load of rum and sugar had not appeared to slow "Ghost" at all, but the secret was in the ballast balance, and Jason had not been pursued that time.

Dawn had come and had long passed when the loading was finally finished. The sun was at nine o'clock when the "Ghost" was ready to depart. Skinny and the crew had been too nervous to sleep deeply and were back on board when the wagons pulled away from the dock. Jason, worried about what was happening at Port-de-France, particularly at the "Chicken" where they had hurriedly left behind the bleeding body, was anxious to depart Martinique. The Frenchman also seemed relieved when his work was finally done. They shook hands then embraced nervously. The Frenchman jumped back to the dock. At a nod from Jason, the waiting crew cast off, quickly raised the jib and then the foresail, and "Ghost" pulled away from the dock. Jason had the strange feeling that his boat had been as anxious as its captain and crew to get underway and catch the untrammeled ocean winds in its sails. Within minutes they had the aft sails up, and "Ghost" captured the fresh eastern wind and quickly fled from the bay. When they cleared the promontory of land, Jason hurriedly scanned the southwestern tip of the island. The ocean was clear, and Jason tiredly relaxed at the wheel, finally freed from the fear of pursuit.

After about an hour, he called Skinny to relieve him. He ordered him to sail due north from Martinique, reasoning that any pursuit might assume the novices would head northwest towards the mainland. Jason and two of his young crewmembers retreated to the cabin to sleep. As he closed his weary eyes, Jason acknowledged to himself that he had made a serious error in sailing with such an undermanned crew. Less weight, particularly in crew supplies, meant a faster ship, but under hostile conditions the "Ghost" required an alert crew. Only double the current number of hands would provide adequate watch and rest for all.

Jason had trouble getting to sleep. His mind kept reviewing the exciting events of the past twenty-four hours and worrying about his ship. Navigation was still a problem. Jason knew he could rely on Skinny to stay roughly on a northerly course for about two hours; then, he would drift either to the east or west. East would take them into the depths of the Atlantic and west too near the British islands. Both paths harbored danger. Jason himself was only a novice navigator. During his first voyage to Martinique last fall, he had mastered the principles of Hadley's quadrant. Using the instrument, a competent navigator could determine latitude with a degree of accuracy, but it was of no use in fixing longitude. To set their longitude, the professional ship captains like those in the English fleet used two watches, one set to local time and one to Greenwich time. Knowing the time on board and Greenwich time, the difference in hours could be converted to degrees, an experienced navigator could calculate degrees of longitude east or west of Greenwich. Unfortunately, like many American mariners, Jason did not have this luxury. He did not own even one reliable timepiece, a lack he planned to make up with the profit from this voyage's cargo. In the meantime, he and Skinny had to rely on dead reckoning with the help of the stars at nighttime.

Jason's navigational plan was rudimentary. Sail due north as best he could until he got a good reading on the quadrant which would let him identify a latitude he could follow due west to the colonial coast. Then, using America's numerous bays and coastal rivers as refuge from patrolling English men-of-war, war, "Ghost"could move northward to the Chesapeake Bay and home waters.

Jason had just fallen into a deep sleep when one of the younger crewmembers shook his arm.

"Jason, Jason, wake up. Skinny needs you on the quarter-deck."

Jason, not knowing the nature of the problem, jerked into a nervous awakeness, leaped to his feet and hurried to the wheel to face the emergency. He covered the some fifteen steps quickly, but he felt terrible. His limbs ached, and he had a bitter taste in his mouth. A quick glance upward told him the "Ghost's sails were full. If the wind has not changed, Skinnny is still on course, he reassured himself. A look sternward told him that "Ghost's" wake was ridged and that they were making good time. If anything the beneficial wind had picked up a few knots.

"Jason, we've got trouble," Skinny called as soon as Jason appeared. Skinny did not like the responsibility for decisions. He had a good sense for the sea and sailing, but he did not like final responsibility. He preferred to give his opinion and let Jason decide.

"What's wrong?" Jason demanded, too concerned to take the time to worry about Skinny's sensitivities.

"Look to the stern." Skinny turned and pointed in the direction of Martinique. The island was no longer visible, but the large black sails of a brigantine were. Although it was still some distance away, it appeared to be sailing directly for the "Ghost." Jason could make out that its foremast was square rigged with fore and aft sails on the stern mast, a combination calculated to give the brig maximum speed under most conditions. With fore and aft sails on both masts, Jason had read that he could sail closer to the wind with less sideways slippage and could get greater speed on a windward course than a square rigger could; that is if everything else were equal. If two ships were of the same size and one had more sail, the one with more sail would be faster, but things were never that simple. A larger ship with more crew meant more weight, which slowed the vessel despite the amount of sail aloft. The brig was larger than the "Ghost," and it had more crew; thus it was heavier. On the other hand, it was square rigged and had more sail. How it all balanced out in terms of speed, Jason was not sure.

"A black hull with black sails," Jason observed.

"It looks like that brig that was at Fort-de-France," Skinny spoke loudly, the concern transparent on his drawn face. Both young men knew that the troublemakers in the "Chicken," the Sign of the Coq, had been from the black ship.

"Do you think it's after us?" Skinny asked.

"Sure looks like it," Jason answered. "How long have they been there?"

"I called you as soon as I saw them." Jason recognized that Skinny had not directly answered his question. He assumed his friend was covering the fact that he had not glanced sternward for some time. Jason understood. Skinny had been more worried about sailing "Ghost" than he had been about watching the horizon. Jason noted their only lookout was in the bow. That was Jason's fault for having sailed with such a small crew.

"We've got all the sail up that we can get. If we're going to outrun her, it will depend on "Ghost" now. Better let me take over," Jason said, replacing Skinny at the wheel. They both knew Jason was the better helmsman and could hold the ship tighter to the wind squeezing out a few extra knots of speed. Jason automatically turned the wheel tighter to the wind causing the sails to flap slightly. He eased off but kept as close to the point where the sails reacted as he could.

"Better have Tom move to the stern and keep an eye on that black bastard," Jason ordered, referring the to bow lookout. "We can let the others sleep for now." Until he had an idea of their pursuer's speed, Jason could not estimate how long it would take them to catch "Ghost," if they could.

"As soon as you take care of that, get the quadrant from the cabin so I can get an estimate of our latitude. As soon as he could be sure of clearing the English Indies and of hitting the American coast not the Caribbean, Jason planned to turn due west, depending on the wind. It still appeared to be coming from the northeast. Jason studied the sky, noted the sun rested at about three o'clock. Just the trace of a cloud front clung to the edge of the horizon to the east.

After about two hours of tense sailing, Skinny brought Jason a few pieces of hardtack and a mug of hot tea. Skinny relieved Jason at the wheel. Jason sat on the quarter-deck bench, sipped his tea and gnawed at the hardtack. He stretched his arms and shoulders to relieve the tiredness in the muscles.

"It look's like they're gaining," Skinny observed worriedly after a quick glance over his shoulder.

"I'm afraid so," Jason agreed. He, too, had been watching as the black brigantine steadily narrowed the distance between the two ships.

"Slower than they might hope, however," Jason tried to be optimistic. "If we can hold them off until nightfall, we might be able to lose them in the dark." Jason was now pleased with his choice of tinted sails for more than esthetic reasons. At dusk, "Ghost" might blend into the horizon giving Jason the opportunity to change course without detection by the brig.

"How close do you reckon they would have to get before they could begin firing at us?"

Jason looked at Skinny and tried to conceal the fact that the same thought worried him. One lucky shot hitting the powder barrels in the hold, lashed to the deck, or even in the cabin would immediately vaporize the "Ghost" and its crew into true ethereal beings. Jason began regretting the fact he had so confidently dispersed the powder barrels throughout the ship.

Jason studied the closing brig before answering.

"I imagine they have a couple of eighteen pounders. If so, I guess they might be two thousand yards short right now. I estimate another two hours before... ." Jason did not finish the thought. He did not want to worry his already frightened crew even more. "Then again, in two hours it will be dusk, and maybe if we're lucky that storm front to the east might arrive and hide us." Jason studied the dark clouds that had begun to spread across the horizon in the east, obviously growing closer. He did not have the experience to estimate when they would arrive. Soon, he hoped. At least the seas appeared to have become choppier during the past hour.

Jason after about half an hour of rest replaced Skinny at the helm. The brig continued to draw closer.

"What colors is she flying? Can you make out?" Skinny asked.

Jason did not bother to try.

"It doesn't really matter," Jason replied. "Those pirates fly any flag they want. They keep changing them trying to lull their prey into thinking they're countrymen. If that brig is who we think they are, they know we're Americans and also know we know they're pirates."

"They were a mean bunch," Skinny said, speaking more to himself than Jason.

"And I'm sure they're not happy about their friend at the 'Chicken,'" Jason agreed, referring to the evil looking man he had knifed when he attacked them.

"I'd rather they not catch us," Skinny observed seriously. He had been unable to keep the quaver out of his voice.

"Me either," Jason laughed nervously.

At that moment a flash on the brigantine caught his eye. Seconds later the boom of a canon firing reached the deck of "Ghost."

"Christ they can't be close enough to hit us, can they?" Skinny shouted. The other three members of the crew, excepting the boy manning the watch at the stern, had gathered on the deck and now looked anxiously at Jason.

"I don't think so," Jason spoke with more confidence than he felt. "Probably a test shot."

Like the others, Jason, still holding the wheel firmly, turned stern ward to watch for a splash. Finally, the ball hit the water several hundred yards behind them. They watched helplessly as the ball bounced several times on the water before sinking out of sight.

"I'd say they have another hour of sailing to get close enough to begin to worry us," Jason tried to sound confident. "And by then, we should be able to disappear in the dusk and that storm over there." He pointed to the west with his right hand. "We'll be cutting it close but should make it."

"What happens if one of them balls hit the powder we're carrying?" The youngest crew member, only fourteen, asked, his eyes large with fear.

"Don't ask," Skinny responded, attempting in front of the younger boys to be braver than he felt. "You won't even notice. Poof."

The boy turned and looked at the two kegs lashed on the deck at the stern. "Shouldn't we cut those free and lessen the risk?" He asked.

"I don't think that'll be necessary," Jason spoke with more confidence than he felt. "But it's a good suggestion. We'll wait and see. Keep your knife ready."

Within an hour, the sun set in the west. With a sigh of relief, Jason noted that "Ghost" began to blend into the gray of the dusk. Another cannon shot sent a ball that landed only a scant hundred feet behind the fleeing "Ghost."

"That was close," Skinny said, abandoning his braggadocio.

Jason saw a raindrop splash on the deck. Then, the first gust of the storm's vanguard hit them. The wind shifted from the northeast to east suddenly, heeling "Ghost" over. Jason ordered his crew to their places at the sails and spun the wheel, turning "Ghost" to run before the wind heading almost due west. Within minutes "Ghost" was back on even keel and running fast before the wind. Jason looked back and saw the square rigged sails of the brigantine being turned to catch the wind and aim the pursuers at an angle that would let them intercept "Ghost" to the west. Jason immediately perceived he had to do something or they were lost. He called his young crew to him and gave them his decision. He looked at the sky and the storm behind him.

"In another five minutes it'll be completely dark, and we'll be invisible to them. They'll expect us to continue running due west to the islands and safety, and they'll try to intercept us. Take your places at the sails again. When I shout, be prepared to come about. We'll tack back to the northeast as close to the wind as possible and head for jolly old England. They won't expect that."

"But we don't want to go to England," young Tom protested.

"We won't," Jason reassured him. "That would take us five weeks. We would never make it. Tomorrow, after I get another reading on the quadrant, we'll pick out a friendly latitude and head back to the coast. Our friends," Jason indicated the pirates with a smile he did not feel, "will not know where we went. We're too small a prize for them to chase us far."

"They already have," Skinny observed dryly.

Jason sent his crew to their places. At his shout they pulled their halyards like professional seamen. The booms swung across the deck as Jason turned "Ghost" to the windward. After having brought her too far across the wind, the sails flapped. James adjusted his heading and soon had "Ghost" flying into the storm, wind and darkness. Within minutes he had no idea where his pursuers were and hoped they were facing the same lack of knowledge. With luck, "Ghost's" sudden turn had gone unnoticed and the two craft were now sailing in opposite directions. With each passing minute of silence, except for the shriek of the storm wind, the flapping of taut sails and the groaning of the "Ghost's" ropes and timbers, Jason and his crew grew more confident.

After about three hours of blind sailing guided only by the flap of the wind in the sails, the storm began to abate. For the remainder of the night, Jason and Skinny alternated turns at the wheel. Jason made sure he had the helm when dawn broke. He wanted the first sighting of the other ship if it was still in pursuit. To his immense relief, the sun rose on an empty ocean. They had escaped. Reassured, Jason turned "Ghost" back to what he felt was a northerly tack. He planned to continue in that direction for another twelve hours then turn in a northwesterly direction until they reached a latitude that would carry them safely to the Carolinas.

Five days later "Ghost" reached the coast. Jason was not sure if they were off the Carolinas because the land was unfamiliar. His sightings with the quadrant led him to believe he was about one hundred miles south of the Bay. He was reluctant to land for fear of running into English soldiers. He held a brief meeting with the crew and discussed their situation. The youths, feeling confident now that they had outrun their one pursuer, boldly agreed that their best course was to cautiously continue northward until they reached the Chesapeake Bay. All recognized the Bay entrance would constitute their next risk. The chances were much higher that they would encounter British men-of-war off Norfolk and Hampton.

      Jason carefully kept about a mile offshore as he worked "Ghost" northward. At dawn on the day after they first sighted land, they reached the broad Bay entrance. To their surprise, there was not a sail in sight. Jason boldly set all of "Ghost's" sails and taking advantage of the early dawn gray of an overcast day sailed directly into the Bay's mouth. He later learned that indeed they had been lucky. Usually, the Bay entrance was carefully controlled, but on the day "Ghost" reached the mouth, all British men-of-war had been called to shore by Governor Dunmore to assist him in facing down the rebel reaction to his seizure of powder from the Williamsburg armory.

      Once free of the Bay entrance, Jason sailed under full sail northward towards Alexandria. He carefully charted the coastline as he went, noting river and creek entrances that looked large enough to afford a hiding place to "Ghost" when seeking to evade English patrols.

Chapter 9
Summer 1775
Alexandria, Philadelphia

The "Ghost" and its proud crew docked in Alexandria on May first. Jason's mother and father, Vivian and James waited anxiously on the pier.

Vivian, increasingly concerned about her son's extending absence had spent the weekend in Alexandria. Neither she nor James had raised the subject of Jason, but both were tense and nervous. They had taken turns suggesting long walks, always along paths that afforded them a view of the river southwards. Finally, on Sunday evening, they had just settled down to a light supper and a long spring evening when one of Jason's friends broke the gloom by rushing to the front of the house and shouting:

"'Ghost's' back. She's docking."

He said that and nothing more before rushing off. James stopped eating in mid-bite. He exchanged a long look of relief with his wife, dropped his fork and raced to join Vivian who was already moving towards the door. At the Court House Square, they encountered Lily West who had received the news in the same fashion. Together, the three walked at a rapid pace to the riverfront.

"Jason," Vivian and Lily shouted and waved in unison as they joined the small group gathered to welcome the adventurers home.

"Mom, Lily," Jason called back from the foredeck of the "Ghost" as the last hawser was thrown to the dock.

James carefully studied the boat for signs of damage. He saw the two barrels of powder lashed to the stern. He did not think that was a good idea and made a mental note to later caution Jason about such a dangerous practice. James studied his son as he looked down at the group on the dock. His hair was windblown and bleached almost blond, and his face was raw and sunburned, but he looked healthy even though he had obviously lost a few pounds.

"How did it go, Jason?" One of the onlookers called. James recognized the young man who was a junior officer of the militia. He obviously had a vested interest in Jason's cargo.

"No problem," Jason called back confidently.

"We've got all the powder you'll need to blow the lobsterbacks back to England," Skinny, who had joined Jason at the rail, called with pride evident in his voice.

As James watched, the "Ghost's" young crewmembers leaped to the pier and were greeted by friends and family. James had to smile as he watched the boys swagger with pride.

"I'll be down as soon as I make a final check of the ship," Jason, conscious of his responsibilities as captain, called.

While they waited, Vivian and Lily chatted nervously with Skinny who had now joined the group on the pier. James caught the attention of one of his workers and asked him to arrange to have a guard placed on the "Ghost" to ensure that the cargo was undisturbed until morning when it could be unloaded. The militia officer who had greeted Jason overheard the conversation and interrupted.

"If you wish, I'll have a few of the boys stand guard tonight. The powder is for their use and standing guard will be good experience for them."

James quickly agreed and turned his attention back to the pier. He was dismayed to hear two of the younger crewmembers bragging to friends as they passed.

"... and some pirates chased us off Martinique. We was almost goners. They fired big cannons at us. Jason said they was eighteen pounders. But nobody can catch the "Ghost" or Captain Jason. He sailed into a storm. The "Ghost" turned invisible, and we just escaped with our lives."

The boy's friends listened with rapt attention, but Jason turned back towards the ship and his son with concern. He still could see no signs of damage. James assumed the boys' tales were merely braggadocio, but he hoped that Vivian and Lily did not hear them.

James hurried to rejoin his wife and Jason's girl friend, prepared to reassure them despite his own concern for his son. Neither of the women had heard the boys. They waited for Jason with broad smiles on their faces.

"Jason. Hurry up," Vivian called good-naturedly. "We're all waiting anxiously."

Jason later described the voyage with a casual tone. He did not treat it as high adventure as the young crewman had; he downplayed the danger of the pirate pursuit and omitted any reference to the attack in the seedy waterfront tavern in Port-de-France. Jason had sworn his friend Skinny to silence, so not even the young crewmembers had been told of Jason's use of his knife. Skinny was not proud of his own role in the incident and had no trouble keeping his vow. Jason admitted to his father that he had grossly underestimated the difficulty of blockade running, particularly to such a far away island with an inexperienced crew. James was relieved that Jason seemed in no hurry to repeat the expedition. They unloaded the Fairfax powder, turned it over to the militia captain who was delighted to receive it, and stored Jason's share of the powder at the boatyard until they could arrange to sell it. Ultimately, they made enough profit to pay the cost of building the "Ghost."

Events elsewhere soon occupied both James and Jason. Details of the precipitous events in Massachusetts began to arrive. General Gage, like Governor Dunmore, had taken his orders to seize rebel leaders and their supplies seriously. On April 18th he had dispatched six hundred men under the command of Colonel Francis Smith to apprehend John Hancock and Samuel Adams and to confiscate arms and supplies the rebels were accumulating at Concord. Paul Revere and William Dawes alerted the countryside. The irate Minutemen confronted the English and forced them to retreat. Lord Percy arrived with his rescue force, but the British lost some two hundred and fifty men as they hurried back to Boston under a rain of fire aimed at them from virtually every rock and tree along their road.

These events shocked the Alexandria Satterfields and their neighbors into a frenzy of activity. James anxiously rewrote and printed in the *Herald* every report that reached Alexandria from Boston and Philadelphia where the Second Continental Congress was meeting. In Williamsburg Governor Dunmore decided that the political temperature had cooled sufficiently for him to return to the Governor's mansion. Not long after he had returned to the Palace, Dunmore received another instruction from home. Lord North directed him to convene the Burgesses and to obtain their approval of a conciliatory offer from Parliament. Parliament suggested it would forego taxing the colonies if they would raise sufficient funds to meet military requirements determined by Parliament. Dunmore was not optimistic that the proposed compromise would work—matters had progressed too far for that with shots being fired in the north and blood shed on both sides—but he followed his instructions and called for the Burgesses to meet on June first.

Being required to make another trip to Williamsburg at this difficult time gave James mixed emotions. With Washington in Philadelphia, James was the sole remaining Fairfax delegate, and he had no choice but to attend. The session would be an important one, but James hated to leave Alexandria at that time. Vivian was occupied at Eastwind with the new crops, and Jason was doubly busy at the boatyard. The county, shaken by events in Boston and fearing possible British raids up the Potomac as far as Alexandria itself, had mobilized behind George Mason's leadership and through the Committee of Safety had authorized the purchase of two row galleys outfitted with cannon and three armed cutters, all five to be deployed to protect Alexandria and the colonial traffic on the Potomac. Two other boatyards were given the contracts for the row galleys, one of which was to carry a huge twenty-four pounder and one a sizable eighteen pounder cannon, but the Satterfield yard, thanks to Jason's recent success with the "Ghost," received the order for the three armed cutters. Building the three cutters, which were smaller versions of the "Ghost", taxed the small boatyard to the utmost. Jason began working night and day at the riverside with a work force that quadrupled in size. James was delighted with the fact that the new work so occupied his son that he had no time to consider another smuggling run.

James arrived in Williamsburg to find his colleagues in a belligerent mood. Compromise was the last item on their agenda. Some of the western Burgesses wore hunting shirts with tomahawks on their belts to signify their attitudes. Dunmore tried to be humble in his opening address, but his tone was obscured by delegate reaction to another incident at the armory.

Several rum-fueled young men decided to break into the armory after an evening at the pubs and to arm themselves to better be able to defend their rights. On entering the armory, they triggered a trap that resulted in a musket loaded with shot being fired. Three of the young men were wounded. Public outrage was immediate with the perpetrators labeled as murderers despite the fact that not one of the youths had died. A mob stormed the armory. The Burgesses demanded the keys from the Governor so they could "investigate." An irate Dunmore rejected the request. As tempers continued to fray, the Governor finally requested the Burgesses to convene so he could discuss the incidents and the key in particular. Before the Burgesses met on the morning of June 8, the Governor lost his nerve and with his family fled to the sanctity of H.M.S."Magdalene."

For three weeks the Burgesses continued to meet; the Governor waited on his ship; neither agreed to visit the other. The Burgesses declined to consider North's offer of conciliation, and they deferred the matter to the Congress in Philadelphia. The heated sessions gave James the opportunity to talk with his friend Thomas Jefferson. Peyton Randolph had hurried back to Virginia from Philadelphia to preside over the Burgesses in this troubled time, and Jefferson had been appointed a delegate to the Continental Congress to replace Randolph. The decision to defer the North offer freed Jefferson to travel. During his time in Williamsburg, Jefferson had worked with James to moderate the more radical members' call for action. Richard Bland, for example, had demanded that Governor Dunmore be seized from his ship in the Bay and hung.

Lady Dunmore and their children sailed for England. Her departure inspired the withdrawal of several of the Governor's supporters, and his position in Virginia deteriorated. Finally, the Burgesses realized that nothing was being accomplished; neither they nor the Governor could divine a middle position. The Burgesses adjourned for the last time, ever, as a colonial legislature subject to the Crown, and James hurried home.

Anarchy descended on Williamsburg while government shifted elsewhere. A call went out for another Virginia convention to meet in Richmond on July 17. Meanwhile, in Philadelphia the delegates followed events in the north and made their plans. While Gage huddled in Boston and the armed rebels gathered to surround the city in a state of siege, George Washington calmly attended every session of the Congress in his red and blue uniform, a relic from the French and Indian War. The Congress appointed a committee to propose a plan for obtaining the supplies that would be needed by a colonial defense force. Washington, who by now was considered one of the Congress' most experienced military men, was selected as one of three members. The committee filed its report on June first despite the fact the Congress had not yet figured out how to obtain the money to purchase the supplies.

In Boston the situation simplified. The colonials had to maintain sufficient force to keep the British troops pinned in Boston. To do this, the delegates argued that they required the support of all the colonies. These conclusions led inevitably to recognition of the need of a military commander representative of all colonies, not just New England, who had sufficient stature to rally the volunteer armies. John Adams, the spokesman of the north at the Congress decided that Colonel George Washington was that man. On June 14 John Adams nominated Washington for the post of commander-in-chief and with Sam Adams' assistance overcame a mild opposition from those who favored a New Englander or even a more experienced man, Charles Lee. The final vote the next day was unanimous.

Washington graciously accepted the appointment and pledged to serve without pay, though he remained willing to accept reimbursement for expenses. Congress then selected two major generals and five brigadiers to assist their new commander. Politics, of course, guided the selection progress. Artemas Ward, who then commanded in Boston, and Charles Lee, who was at the time in Philadelphia lobbying for position, were appointed major generals. Horatio Gates, another Virginian, attained one of the brigadier general slots. Washington's hand could be seen behind several of the selections.

Washington wrote letters to Martha, Jackie, James and George Mason that he sent homeward with his horses and carriage. He purchased five new horses and a light phaeton at public expense and prepared to depart for the north. As he prepared, his army occupied Bunker and Breeds Hills, which gave a commanding view of the British forces. The English immediately attempted to drive the rebels from these strategic positions which they were quickly fortifying. After being repulsed twice in two bloody attacks, the English recaptured the hills. Losses were high on both sides, but the rebels claimed a moral victory. On June 23, accompanied by his new staff and recently minted generals, Washington departed Philadelphia for Boston.

In Virginia on July 17, 1775, once again delegates representing the colony's counties assembled in illegal session as a replacement for the Burgesses prorogued by a fretful Governor Dunmore who continued to hide aboard his ship in the Bay. In response to the new commander-in-chief's call for assistance, two Virginia companies marched northward, the first such units to join the cause. One was led by Daniel Morgan of Frederick County and one by Hugh Stephenson of Berkeley.

James and George Mason again represented Fairfax County at a Richmond meeting. Although the session opened with the best of intentions and high spirits, it quickly disintegrated into wrangling over petty subjects. George Mason became so discouraged that he took to his bed for several days. James persistently attended every session, but he too grew dejected. The delegates seemed unable to agree on anything. An old friend, Richard Bland, had to defend himself against scurrilous charges of being a loyalist; an argument broke out over Mason's proposal that the ban on export of goods be moved up from September tenth to August fifth; they argued over the naming of officers for the new army, and they debated the organizing of a government to substitute for the royal one that had fled in the person of Dunmore.

Not until early August, when the delegation of leaders who had been in Philadelphia arrived, did the convention acquire a leadership that molded it to a purpose. Mason and James decided the meeting must address two primary tasks: raise troops to defend Virginia and to assist their friend and new commander-in-chief, George Washington, and secondly, to devise a temporary form of government for the colony. By the time the convention adjourned on August 26th, they had attained modest success. They authorized local election of delegates and the continuance of local governmental bodies. They approved the issuance of paper money to pay their debts and appointed an eleven man Committee of Safety to serve as colony executive when the temporary congress was out of session. To defend the colony, fifteen companies of militia were authorized to assist the newly approved two regiments of regulars that were to be raised. Although not totally satisfied with their work, both James and Mason were exhausted when they finally departed Richmond to return home.

"At least a start was made," James summed up their month's work as the two men headed eastwards for home.

"Barely," Mason reluctantly agreed, "and some possible damage was done."

James nodded in agreement but remained silent because he did not want to encourage Mason to once again express views that James had heard several times recently. Mason was worried about the new executive. He knew men abused power and believed the Committee of Safety's authorities were too poorly defined. Mason was determined that Virginia's next charter contain written provisions that defended the rights of the citizens against governmental abuse. Mason believed the high flown rhetoric that the rebels used to justify their actions.

As soon as he reached Alexandria, James became involved in a series of meetings with county leaders to brief them on the Richmond congress' plans and actions intended to fill the voids of uncertainty created by the troubled times. Most feared anarchy; the planters worried about the rumors of slave uprisings, and the merchants fretted about the restrictions on trade. The militia wanted to know when it would get its arms and powder and how they would match up with the new regular army. James was amazed at the leadership vacuum that the absence of the quiet Washington created. Mason was an intellectual who scorned public responsibility, and much of the burden for solving Alexandria's local problems fell to James. At times, besieged by unsolvable petty problems, James wondered why he had gotten involved in local politics in the first place. Sitting at Dinwiddie's elbow as an observer was one thing, but this chaos was something totally different.

As busy as James was, another worrisome thought remained at the back of his mind. He remembered his last conversation with his friend Washington, particularly his expression of acute need for James' assistance. James knew he had not disabused Washington of the idea, and in the first days after Washington's appointment as commanding general, James feared receipt of a letter from the North that would contain a summons he could not refuse. A week after Washington's appointment, James along with others in Alexandria received a letter from the General, as he was now called. James had opened it with trepidation but found that he need not have worried. Washington's words were few in number and mainly conveyed his concern about the magnitude of the task that had been handed him. Washington sincerely worried that he may not have the experience or capability to handle the heavy responsibilities. Washington, however, pledged to do his best. James recognized that Washington's failure to summon him to assist or to even refer to their conversation was ominous. Given the selfless attitudes adopted by Washington, James pondered how he could now refuse to assist.

By the end of September, James became so busy with local problems, the newspaper and the boatyard, that he began to consider himself the indispensable man. James knew better than that; no man is indispensable, but he went to bed every night so exhausted that he could not sleep. He tossed and turned and searched for solutions and answers to the petty problems he and his fellow citizens faced. At times, when sipping a glass of ale at the tavern with Corney or his son Jason, James was tempted to tell them about Washington's departure plea, but James restrained himself, keeping the confidence, knowing that if he divulged it he would be doing so only to massage his own ego. At such times, he remonstrated with himself. He was running the risk of becoming too self-important. Keeping the secret of Washington's appeal for his assistance to himself made James think more about it. At times, he had to admit that Washington's failure to summon him made him wonder if he had been wrong, if he had professed his disinterest too strongly, if maybe he was really more interested in getting involved in the real action than he had admitted to himself.

Then, on the last day of September, the thunder clapped and the lightning bolt struck. James sat behind his worktable at the *Herald* editing a report from Boston when the door burst open and a dusty, dirt grimed young man appeared and breathlessly shouted:

"Mr. Satterfield, Mr. James Satterfield."

Since he was the only person in the room, and he sat at his table a short ten feet from the door, James wondered why the young man was shouting. The sign out front clearly identified James as the *Herald's* proprietor. James studied the youth. He was dressed in a wrinkled buff and blue uniform. He had a dirt smeared pink sash around his waist and wore a ruffled white shirt that obviously had not been washed in days. He carried a blue tricornered hat in his hand. James assumed he must be one of the newly appointed regular members of a Virginia Regiment with a self-important query from the Committee of Safety. They had become more active of late inquiring about local matters.

"Over here, son," James said with a smile, indulging himself his growing maturity which the passing years were imposing on him, through no fault of his own.

"Mr. James Satterfield?" The youth inquired again, this time speaking in a lower but no less demanding voice.

"Yes, son. I'm Satterfield."

"I'm Ensign Grey, sir, of the Commander-in-Chief's family."

The young man bowed formally at the waist, holding his blue tricorn in his right hand with his left placed over the small saber that he wore on his hip.

James' initial response was to smile at the young man bowing so self-consciously to him, then realization shocked him. This young officer had a message from George Washington, and James knew instantly it contained the summons he had pondered.

"The General sends his regards, sir."

James remained seated and stared at the man who carried his future in his hands. Finally, collecting himself, James rose and extended his hand in welcome.

"Please come in Ensign Grey. Forgive my manners. Will you have a cup of tea? I'm sorry, I have nothing stronger. Maybe... ."

"Tea will be very nice, sir. I've been riding hard for five days. But first, may I give you this?"

The young man took a sealed envelope from an inner pocket where he had been protecting it and offered it to James. James took it from him, recognized George's handwriting on the outside. Only his name, "Mr. James Satterfield," and the city, "Alexandria," appeared on the front. James turned the envelope over and examined the heavy piece of wax that contained the initials "GW" firmly embedded in it.

"With your permission, sir," the young man interrupted James' contemplation. "I will help myself to the tea while you read your dispatch."

James indicated the teapot that set on the table at the rear of the shop near the remains of his recent dinner. The tea and sandwiches had been prepared by his cook, one of the house slaves from Eastwind, and left unattended for James' consumption at his pleasure. When working, James was an indifferent eater and ate only when hunger pangs struck.

"Yes, please," James responded. "I'm sorry the tea may be cool."

"That will be just fine, sir," the young officer spoke politely.

"And help yourself to the sandwiches, ham or cheese, I believe." James knew they were either ham or cheese. He ate the same thing every day.

"Thank you sir."

James noticed the young officer spoke with an odd Yankee accent. He assumed it would be Bostonian. Trust George to take on a local aide. Good politics.

James broke the seal on the message, his first dispatch. He smiled again to himself and read quickly while the young officer busied himself at the back of the shop.

The letter was exactly what James had expected. One paragraph, only three sentences long. The first sentence apologized for inconveniencing James. The second asked him to visit George for only one week at his headquarters outside Boston. The third sentence apologized again and asked James to come immediately. It was signed "Your Friend, George."

That was all his dispatch contained, one brief paragraph. It was James' summons. He sat at his desk and studied the piece of paper. It said exactly what he had dreaded, but now that it had arrived, he felt relief. George had said for only one week, so he was not planning on asking James to enlist as a member of his staff. James decided that George had a personal request, maybe something dealing with Martha or his family, that he wanted James to handle in his absence. Or, perhaps, George had in mind a delicate local political matter for Mason and himself to address. James could think of nothing else.

Certainly, George would not want his military advice. The thought forced James to sit up straight. Maybe, it had something to do with his brother John. Washington had said he might need John's assistance with the Indians. This was possible, James reasoned, but Indians were not Washington's problem now. He faced British regulars. James doubted that John's expertise would be needed for that problem. He relaxed again, concluding the summons had to deal with a personal or political problem. In that case, the visit could be interesting. It would free him from the nagging problems of Alexandria and let him see some of the country while obtaining a first hand look at the situation around Boston. He could write several attention grabbing reports for the *Herald*.

"When do we leave, sir?"

James, shaken from his contemplation, stared at the young officer. He had a sandwich in one hand, a cup of tea in the other, and was chewing with a broad grin on his face.

"Do you know what this contains?" James demanded, a little more harshly than he intended.

"Not specifically, sir," Ensign Grey smiled. "But the General gave me ten days to get here, collect you, and return." He was not bothered by James' gruffness. He had been in the army for six weeks, now, and was used to being treated roughly. Compared to some of the arrogant generals surrounding the Commander-in-Chief, James was polite.

"He asks me to visit him," James spoke more softly. "Do you know what he wants?"

"No sir," Ensign Grey laughed. "The General does not confide in me. He just sends me on errands."

"Please call me James," James asked. He was not accustomed to military etiquette or to being called sir. It made him feel older than he wanted to be.

"Yes, sir, James," the young man responded. "And please call me Eric, or Grey, that's my name, or just hay you. That's how most staff officers, the junior ones anyway, are addressed."

"So you are a member of George's, the General's, staff?" James asked out of politeness. The young man had ridden a long distance to deliver his message. It would not hurt James to show him a little courtesy, no matter how junior he may be.

"Yes, sir. I've been in the army for almost six weeks now. My father's a friend of Mr. Adams, Mr. John Adams the barrister, not the Adams who gives speeches, the one called a rabble-rouser, and he, the lawyer Adams, recommended me to General Washington's staff."

Politics, again, James thought. Poor George. The army reported to a committee of politicians, mostly lawyers. It will be worse than Governor Dinwiddie ever was.

"We will leave in the morning, son," James finally answered the young man's question. It would take that long to arrange for Corney to take over the paper, send a message to Vivian, talk with Jason, and brief colleagues in Alexandria. Fortunately, he need plan on only a two week absence. That would be no worse that going to Williamsburg or Richmond. It would involve a longer trip, but this time he would see a different countryside.

Chapter 10
Boston
October 1775

With Ensign Eric Grey as his guide, James did not have the opportunity to do as much sightseeing as he had hoped on the trip north from Alexandria to Massachusetts. The young officer rode hard with an eagerness that James attributed to his companion's only recently having answered the call to arms. James personally doubted that hours or even days would make much difference in the march of historical imperative; as best as he could tell, neither General Thomas Gage, who commanded the English troops in Boston, nor General George Washington appeared anxious to commence battle, and even if they did, James knew there was little that he could do about it. Eric, as James now addressed his young companion, obviously did not share these sentiments. Eric, traveling under orders to make haste, did so. They changed horses frequently at public expense, a luxury that James did not totally approve of, and reached the outskirts of Cambridge, where Washington had headquartered his army, in under ten days, an achievement that James suspected must be some sort of record.

"We're almost there, Mr. Satterfield," Ensign Grey attempted to cheer his obviously travelworn companion.

At times during the trip, Eric had considered pausing for a day of rest, particularly at Philadelphia and New York where the social life appeared promising, particularly given the abundance of attractive young females promenading along broad avenues, but his orders from the General had been to travel hard and fast and Eric was determined to complete his mission in as attention garnering obedience as he could. His older companion, James, was at least forty-three years of age, and this worried him; Eric did not want the old fellow to die of a heart attack on the General's doorstep. That certainly would blunt a promising career.

"Then, slow down and let me catch my breath before we get there," James spoke firmly as he pulled back the reins and teased his horse to a walk. The animal was a handsome beast, strong and stocky with an easy gait, and James had

already resolved to acquire him for his own stable in return for one of his
favorites he had had to leave behind in Annapolis.

The Massachusetts countryside was in full bloom. James had always considered the Fairfax area of the Northern Neck of Virginia to be the prettiest spot on
the face of the earth in April and October, but he had to admit his limited first
hand experience made him a poor judge. With the exception of occasional forays
to the Maryland shore of the Potomac River, this was James' first trip outside the
colony of Virginia. Even the land he had seen in the western mountains belonged
to his home country, and thus far on this expedition his most prominent observation had been of the rear end of Ensign Eric.

James estimated that the season in New England was a good six weeks in
advance of Virginia. Here, the trees and bushes had already been tinted with
beautiful scarlet and yellow hues while at home the leaves remained green, just
turning brown at the edges as the result of a prolonged drought.

"Eric," James spoke as he reined to a stop. "What kind of tree is that? The one
with the beautiful white bark?" James had observed the tall, slender trees with a
paper-thin silver skin for some time and had vowed to take a seedling back with
him if he could. He did not know if it would grow in Virginia, but it would make
an attractive addition to Eastwind's forests.

"It's called a birch, white birch," Eric answered, totally disinterested in the
names of trees. He was anxious to get to headquarters to learn what he had
missed during his enforced absence. Eric hoped the armies had not clashed without him, because he wanted to earn his glory before the English were driven to
their ships in defeat.

Before James could ask another question, Eric spurred his horse into a canter
and shouted:

"Follow me, Mr. Satterfield, that's Cambridge ahead."

James sighed and followed his guide. James could tell they were close. He
could see the cantonments of Washington's army scattered across the fields on
each side of the dusty road.

"Don't you want to appreciate the colors?" James called through the dust
that his now galloping companion left behind. Ensign Grey either did not hear
him or chose not to admit it. James smiled, then acknowledged to himself that he
did not blame Eric. James was not so old that he did not remember what it was
like to be young and eager.

Cambridge turned out to be an attractive little town, despite the jarring sight
of soldiers everywhere. At least James assumed they were soldiers. He had
always pictured armies as being clad in attractive uniforms like those worn by
George Washington or the English. Here and there, James spotted a new buff and
blue uniform; he assumed these were officers, but the majority was dressed in
homespun clothes. They looked like the ragged members of the Fairfax militia.
They carried weapons of all kinds. James had no trouble identifying the shirtmen; probably from home, he thought. James knew that two companies of
Virginia frontiersmen, one led by Dan Morgan who he had met in Williamsburg,

had quick-marched to join the army. The riflemen wore their distinctive hunting shirts and carried the long frontier rifles that they used with frightening accuracy, a skill acquired from constant battles with the Indians.

"Headquarters used to be on the campus," Ensign Grey slowed as they entered town in order to ride beside his charge.

Now he wants to be my travel guide, James thought wryly. More likely he is showing his prize off to his friends.

"The General stayed in Samuel Langdon's house on Harvard campus when he first got here. Had his headquarters there until he moved to old John Vassall's house. They say the General did not like sharing quarters with Langdon. He's the president of Harvard, you know."

James smiled at the look that appeared suddenly on Eric's face as he realized maybe he shouldn't be gossiping about the General with one of his friends.

Ensign Grey, wearing his dust covered uniform like a badge of honor, dismounted in the front of the large house that he identified as "Headquarters." James, catching the curious glances from the crowds of officers and soldiers who seemed to flow to and from the large building, tried to appear inconspicuous. It was clear from the looks that the staff officers in their new uniforms sent his way that they were curious about the man that one of their number had been sent to escort from Virginia. Grey strode briskly as he mounted the front steps and entered the hallway of what had once been a private home.

"The man who owns this place, John Vassall, is a bloody loyalist," Grey proudly proclaimed to James. "He fled to Boston when we took over Cambridge. Left his house fully furnished for us."

James tried not to smile at his companion's innocence. He knew this fact would make Washington uncomfortable. George would feel guilty taking personal advantage of another man's misfortunes, even a loyalist. James speculated how Grey would react if James informed him that many of George and James' friends in Virginia were loyalists, just like this John Vassall. Grey led James past two guards who stood outside a door at the end of the hall. The guards nodded familiarly at Grey and let them pass. They entered a small room, once a parlor, and encountered a young man wearing captain's epaulets.

"Welcome back, Grey," the captain spoke with a friendly smile. "And I assume this is Mr. Satterfield." It was a statement not a question. "Please go right in. We were alerted that two riders were approaching from the south. The General predicted it would be you. Right on schedule."

Ensign Grey stood aside and indicated James should enter a closed door immediately behind the captain.

"I will be your escort while you are in Cambridge Mr. Satterfield. I will wait for your orders here." James glanced at the young man who had called him James while traveling. Obviously, proximity to headquarters made him nervous and more formal.

James nodded and walked to the door. His friend George had certainly acquired a greatly enhanced stature. James knocked politely on the door and waited.

"Come in," the familiar voice called.

James entered to find Washington sitting behind a large desk in what had once been the mansion's library. The owner's books still lined the wall. They will please, George, James thought.

"James," Washington spoke softly as he smiled. He rose and hurried to shake James' hand and embrace him awkwardly. James noted George still had trouble with expressing emotion.

James studied his friend for signs of strain. He had been at war for almost three months now. He noted Washington had acquired a new uniform. The blue coat with buff trim and gold buttons was open at the front, and it extended to Washington's knees in back. It covered a buff colored vest and trousers tucked into knee high shiny black boots. Only the ruffled collar of Washington's white shirt showed over the vest. A blue sash draped diagonally across the front of his breast.

George, catching James' appraisal of his uniform, fingered the blue sash and laughed nervously.

"Congress insists I wear this blue sash to distinguish me from my staff. I think they were afraid I wouldn't be recognized otherwise."

"I doubt that," James laughed, embarrassed to have been caught staring.

"The members of my family," as his personal staff were designated, "wear identical uniforms, but with pink sashes around the waist. Now that you're here, you're going to have to learn our quaint customs."

George led James to a chair near his desk and resumed his place in the seat behind it.

"It's good seeing you again, James," Washington spoke sincerely.

"And you," replied James in kind.

Washington inquired about Jason and James' family. He had heard from Martha that Jason had returned safely and successfully from his trip to Martinique. James briefed Washington on affairs in Alexandria and gave George letters from Martha and George Mason that he had brought with him. Washington gratefully accepted them, studied the envelopes fondly, and then placed them on the desk before him. After about ten minutes of small talk, Washington to James' relief turned to the business at hand. He was still anxious to learn why his friend had summoned him so peremptorily.

"I know you are anxious to learn why I asked you to come so urgently," Washington began.

James was surprised to find his friend still ill at ease in dealing with people, even himself.

"And I know you are too polite to ask," Washington continued. "I need your help." Noting the serious expression on James' face, he continued. "Now, don't

worry. I'm not going to press you to join the army or come to Cambridge. I need
your help for about ten days, then you can return to watch over things at home."

Washington's words relaxed James, and he leaned back in his chair.

"Some tea?" Washington asked, remembering his obligations as host.

"Please. That would be nice," James answered. He took the tea only to be
polite. He never made an issue over his indifference to the bitter weed brew.

After Washington had summoned an orderly to provide tea, Washington
described his life in Cambridge in order to fill in time until it was served. He
explained that he did not want to be interrupted once he began.

After an orderly served tea, Washington began his explanation without further preamble.

"First, James, I want to request that the purpose of your visit remain a secret
between us. The staff and others will be curious, but I want to keep the subject
between you and me."

"Certainly, George," James agreed. "But before we begin, I have a question.
Do I call you General or George?"

Washington laughed. "Certainly George when we are alone. General will be
better when the staff are about. We have to maintain a front if you don't mind."

"That's what I assumed," James agreed, knowing his friend would appreciate having the protocol arranged.

"As I said before I left Alexandria, I need your help." Washington paused
long enough for James to nod assent, then continued. "I have a simple task for
you, but it is very important to me. You may even find it interesting. I want you
with Ensign Grey's assistance to tour our encampment. I don't mean inspect it.
Merely ride about and talk with the soldiers, the officers, looking and listening.
Then study the English in Boston, from our hilltops of course. You can't go into
the city. And don't get shot."

"That sounds interesting, George," James said when Washington paused for
him to comment. "But what do you want me to look at and listen for?"

"Just study our situation here. Get the facts, then think about them. That's
what I want. Your honest opinion."

Before James could speak, Washington held up his hand.

"I know, James. You are not a military man. I don't want your military views.
I have enough of that. I have more military opinions than I can cope with.
Unfortunately, most just tell me what they think I want to hear or what they want
me to hear. All the officers have grandiose plans for attacking the English and
earning themselves glory in the process. Others are looking for a way to make a
profit."

James sat silently, sipped his tea and nodded, waiting for his friend, the
General, to continue.

"I don't need your views on what I should be doing. I know that. I have to
take this rabble and make them an army. That involves training and discipline. I
have to get them uniforms, guns, powder and food. That requires negotiations
with Congress and the colonies. I have to keep the shirtmen from wasting ammu-

nition by taking useless potshots long distance at the English sentries. And as important as anything else, I have to find myself a group of officers I can trust and rely on. Most here now have little military experience. They are simply local shopkeepers and farmers elected by their neighbors to lead them and that poses problems. It's very democratic, but often the men are not ready to take orders and accept discipline from a man who they know is simply the neighbor next door. But, none of these problems are yours. I know what has to be done."

"But George, what can I do then to help you? You clearly know what has to be accomplished."

"Be patient James. I'm trying to explain," George continued. "I have my own theory about what I have to do here in Boston. About what the English will do, and about what will happen next. I simply want you to study the situation, then think about what is going to happen, and discuss it with me."

"That sounds easy enough," James agreed. "But I don't know what earthly good my opinion will be."

"I need to discuss the situation objectively with someone whose views I trust. I know you will be brutally honest with me, and that's all I want. Will you do it?"

"Certainly, George. You know I will."

"Good. Let's be at it then," George rose. "If you will do me the pleasure of dining at my table, you will get an opportunity to get to know my generals and staff."

James rose and walked towards the door with Washington politely accompanying him.

"And when will we have this talk?" James asked.

"When you are ready. Take your time. Learn the facts, think a while, then we can talk."

James nodded dubious agreement.

"And I calculate you will be ready in a week," George reverted to his role of commander.

James devoted the next seven days to doing exactly what Washington suggested. He met Washington's staff and talked with his generals. A brief conversation with George's deputy, Major General Charles Lee, who James had met twice before at Mount Vernon, reinforced his initial impressions. The man had had previous military experience; at least he constantly told you how much he knew, and he was an eccentric always surrounded by his pack of dogs whose company he preferred to humans. The best James could say for Lee was that he was an oddball who had already earned the contempt of peers and subordinates. James reached this conclusion despite the knowledge that Lee had taken command of New York and was in Cambridge only briefly for a meeting requested by Washington.

Major General Artemis Ward, who had been in command before Washington's appointment and who had been a logical candidate for the commander-in-chief's job, had obviously been hurt by being passed over; he behaved in a correct and polite manner, but he was cold and withdrawn.

Major General Israel Putnam, another of Congress' early appointments, was a square jawed, squat man who kept his own counsel; James to his dismay could not get a handle on the man. John Sullivan, a political general who had been a delegate to both Continental Congresses, impressed him. James suspected that Sullivan's political skills concealed the real man, but he genuinely liked the New Hampshire lawyer. The younger men on the staff particularly impressed James. Henry Knox, a twenty-five year old former Boston bookseller with an interest in artillery and engineering, appeared to be a comer. Likewise, Washington's chief aide, Joseph Reed, a thirty-four year old, was a highly intelligent, artful writer who had the skills to protect the introverted Washington.

James talked with the common soldiers wherever he could. Most were earnest country boys anxious to teach the lobsters a lesson and then return to their farms and families. With dismay, James learned that most of their enlistments would expire on December thirty-first; if the army did not defeat the English before then, Washington would have to recruit and train a new one. James was disappointed in the famed Virginia riflemen; he, like every other Virginian, had been filled with pride when the two companies of shirtmen had shouldered their long rifles and marched quickspeed to help Washington save Boston. Unfortunately, up close those tall, rangy frontiersmen were tough, fierce men, but they were too individualistic to make good foot soldiers. They resisted discipline and tended to act as individuals, inclined to set their own tactic and targets. James did not know how they could be converted into responsive infantry who accepted orders without question.

The eager Ensign Grey remained at James' side throughout the entire week James devoted to his study. Gray escorted James to the front lines to study Boston and the enemy. From the top of Prospect Hill, James saw the redcoated English professional soldiers swarming over Bunker and Breed hills that they had fought so hard to win back from the rebels. He surveyed from a distance the ruins of CharlesTown, the unfortunate village that had been burned to the ground during the June fighting, and he studied the English fortifications on the Boston penin- sula and the Dorchester flats.

By the end of the week, James had a compact picture of the battle scene and its participants. Knowledge of the English, particularly information on their plans and intentions, was lacking. Intelligence clearly was one of the rebel army's shortcomings. They learned much from the steady stream of refugees and desert- ers from Boston, but their knowledge was confined to what had happened. Washington's attempt to isolate Boston and cut off supplies from the land was working, but the English were able to support their forces with their sea bridge of English ships. Washington, however, needed to know what General Thomas Gage and his deputy Major General William Howe were thinking. Howe and two fellow Major Generals, Henry Clinton and John Burgoyne, had arrived in Boston on May 25, 1775, and they provided the cautious Gage a triumvirate of the most competent professionals in the English army. This fact alone made the task for

Washington and his general staff of inexperienced officers and misfits a daunting one.

On Sunday afternoon, six quick days after his arrival, James joined his friend George in his office at headquarters for the discussion that Washington had had him travel so far to share. James was much better informed about Boston and what Washington and the colonies faced than he had been when he arrived. He knew he could now interpret events more clearly for the *Herald's* readership, and he could better represent Fairfax County in the Burgesses, but he did not know what he could do for or even say to his friend George, who had such awesome responsibilities. James enjoyed the relaxed Sunday dinner dominated by the egotistical Lee, but he walked with George afterwards to his office with trepidation. Everything James had learned, Washington obviously knew, only in more detail.

"Well, James, what do you think?" George asked after the two men had settled themselves into chairs located on each side of the fireplace. No fire had been lighted, but the spot was the most intimate in the room. James was amused to note his old friend had read his nervousness and was attempting to put him at ease. George had grown considerably as a man during the past three months. Some men do that under pressure, James assumed.

"I don't know what I can say, George. You are already aware of everything I have seen." James was embarrassed by the shallowness of his words. He was accustomed to being the bright one who shared his ideas with what he had thought was the slower Washington.

"I want your opinions, now, James, not information about what you have seen. Just tell me what you think the English will do next and how I should react."

"I'm not a military man," James protested. "I don't want to be responsible for misleading you."

"I know that James. I already have my views formed. I simply want to hear yours."

"Well,..." James paused to collect his thoughts. "From what I have heard, the English have from eight to ten thousand professional troops in Boston. You probably have twice that many. You have effectively confined-the English to the city of Boston and its immediate environs. If I were General Cage, I would face a dilemma. Lord North is pressuring me to break your army's back. I would know I don't have the troops to do so; you have already proved your men can fight, though maybe unfairly by hiding behind rocks and trees, and I doubt I could defeat you easily. You would probably bend when I attack and retreat into the countryside. I would pursue, but you would avoid a major battle. Before long, my lines of supply would become untenable, and to save my army I would have to retreat to Boston. If Gage can't attack you, and I believe he is professional enough to understand that, he has only two choices. He can stay in Boston or move his army somewhere else. If he stays in Boston, he runs the risk of being starved out. You can cut off resupply by land, thus he has to rely on his ships. England is too far away to make this a viable alternative for the long term, particularly since the other colonies are supporting Massachusetts. Maybe, then, Gage's only alternative is to finally withdraw.

"Unless?" Washington asked.

James thought briefly about Washington's question before answering. "Unless... unless he can entice you into a fixed battle on an open plain where his troops can use their European tactics, experience, and massed firepower to defeat you."

"And if I refuse to be lured into such a battle?"

"Then you can win. But ... ."

"But," George continued James' thought. "Much time will be required. I will have difficulty maintaining an army, and our supporters will lose heart. How much time?"

"If the English are determined, and they are, George, because the prize is large, it could take years." James was surprised at his own words. Like others, he had expected the struggle to be over in months. He was not sure his fellow colonials would have the stamina to fight an extended war. The soldiers had families at home and crops to plant. They could easily lose their will to fight for principles that many felt belonged only to the upper classes anyway. Slogans would not hold them.

"Do we have that much time?" George asked.

"I don't know," James responded honestly.

"And the English. They will fight for years?"

"Yes. We are a long way from England, and the people at home will not see the blood."

"Then back to my original question. Recognizing this, and we must assume Gage and his staff are smart enough to see it, what will Gage do?"

"He will try to entice you to battle under conditions favorable to his troops. If he fails, he will give up Boston."

Washington nodded agreement. "And where will he go?"

Again James pondered Washington's difficult question before answering. He recognized his response could influence the whole outcome of the war. Washington was the commander-in-chief, not just a simple fireside conversationalist.

"He can only go one of two places," James finally answered.

"New York or Philadelphia," Washington continued the thought.

"Exactly," James agreed. "Strategy requires the English to capture our cities, and Boston, New York and Philadelphia are key. From New York, he can move up the Hudson and join forces with an English army marching from Canada. That way he can cut the colonies in half, isolate New England."

"Cut off the head, and the body will die," George nodded.

"The English are right to believe that the strength of the rebel cause is in New England. Many in the middle colonies and the south are loyalists or skeptical about the war."

"And Philadelphia?"

"Philadelphia is the political center of the rebellion. That's where the Congress meets."

"And in Europe you win the war by capturing the enemy's capital," Washington again summarized.

James stared at his friend. Suddenly, everything appeared clear.

"The English will withdraw from Boston and go to New York and try to link up with forces from Canada," James declared with a conviction he now felt.

"And if they do?" Washington asked.

"We do the same thing there that we are doing in Boston. Keep them confined to the city of New York, isolate them with a land siege and prevent a link up with Canada." James suddenly realized he had lost his detachment and was speaking like a member of Washington's staff.

Washington, who intuitively shared the same thought, smiled at his friend's sudden discomfort. James had lost his detachment and was now vulnerable. Washington rose and began to pace. He found he thought better when on his feet. James sat quietly and watched while his friend moved from his desk to the fireplace and back. James respected Washington's immediate need for solitude. He wanted to review the conversation for himself. Suddenly James, who had sunk into his own contemplation about the implications of what he had said, was surprised into attentiveness when Washington abruptly stopped halfway to the desk and pivoted to face James.

"We can do it," Washington declared. "With perseverance we can win."

James was struck by the portent of what had happened. The blood drained from his face, turning it a sickly white.

"Don't be concerned, James," Washington said confidently. "You have simply confirmed what I had already determined. The decision is not yours."

Seeing his friend's confidence, James took a deep breath and relaxed. He had talked so confidently, as if he knew what he was talking about.

"Thank you, James," Washington quickly took three steps and stood besides James' chair with his arm on his shoulder. "You did exactly what I wanted you to do. Reach the right conclusion. We can win," Washington repeated and squeezed James' shoulder tightly. Suddenly, Washington released the pressure and returned to his desk. James felt he could see the emotion of the moment subside as he watched. Washington looked at James and spoke:

"I know you will want to hurry home. You will be able to write many first hand reports for the *Herald* that will help our cause. Leave when you wish. I will miss you and still would like to have you here to help, but I understand."

James visibly relaxed. "I'll leave tomorrow. Thank you George for the opportunity to learn." James rose, anxious to escape from the tension that had filled the General's room. Now, James found himself for the first time thinking of his friend as "the General" and not just his friend George.

"By the way, James," the General called as James approached the door. "You can do one little thing for me on the way home."

James immediately knew he was hooked. The General was not referring to carrying letters home to Martha. They were a given. James waited.

"Since we will be moving to New York in the not distant future, maybe next spring I assume, you may wish to stop there and see if you can line up some friends who might be able to keep us informed on what the British are doing there after they capture it." Washington smiled as warmly at James as he ever had. "After all, you are the one who pointed out that is where our future lies." Noting the total lack of reaction on James' face, Washington continued. "And a stop in Philadelphia might also prove useful. You know most of Virginia's delegates to the Congress, and they will introduce you to others. You might also meet some useful friends now resident in Philadelphia. We might be wrong and the English could move there instead of New York. I understand many of the so called loyalists might have mixed emotions and be willing to work both sides."

James smiled his resignation and defeat. "Will I see you before I leave General? You might have some letters you wish me to carry back to Alexandria, or, some other duties you may wish me to undertake on the way home."

As James was closing the door to the commander-in-chief's office, another thought struck him, and he stuck his head back inside.

"And if you don't object, I'll share this conversation with George Mason. He'll enjoy it."

"Only Mr. Mason," Washington agreed and returned his attention to the paper in front of him, barely able to suppress his pleasure with himself.

Chapter 11
Boston, London
October 1775

Major General William Howe, commanding officer of all of His Majesty's land forces in North America, stood alone at the window of his spacious office in his Boston Headquarters. He was pleased with himself. After his arrival in May as General Gage's deputy, he had concentrated on undermining his superior's position. In private, he counseled Gates to take the very actions that he knew would weaken the general's position in London. Then, by private letter, he fed his brother, Admiral Richard Lord Howe, information about the situation in Boston that ultimately permitted the older Howe to lever the hapless Gage out of his position and to install Major General William Howe as commander.

Howe intended to follow the same strategy as his predecessor. He was determined to avoid meeting his adversary, General Washington, on the field of battle, despite the fact that in August they had received orders either to break the rebel siege in Boston or to capture New York. Howe knew he could not receive reinforcements until January; orders had gone out to British units throughout the empire to send troops to help subdue the Americans, but time was required before they would arrive. Like his brother, he continued to believe the solution to the American problem lay in compromise, not military force. Since General Howe did not have the authority to negotiate a peace, he had to wait while his brother maneuvered in London to obtain the appointment as commander-in chief of all the King's armed forces in America, army and navy, and, concurrently, as commissioner extraordinaire with the authority to negotiate a peace. General Howe intended to prolong the stalemate in Boston until Lord North turned to his brother in desperation.

Gage had lost more than one thousand men in the struggle to retake Bunker Hill, which he should not have lost in the first place. One of Howe's military colleagues had observed bitterly that a few such victories as this would ruin the army. In August the government decided to rely solely on force to settle the problem with the colonials, and General Gage knew this simply was not viable. Howe in his effort to undercut Gage privately proposed the abandonment of Boston and the pursuit of a New York strategy. To the ministry, he hedged by suggesting they concentrate on New York but continue to keep some troops in Boston. Confusion had been important in his duplicitous scheme to undercut Gage. While the generals and other politicians got in line behind the decision to use force, Lord North privately hoped to escape by using military might to bring the colonials to the peace table, not to pound them into submission. He, therefore, behind the scenes continued to pursue the idea of appointing a peace commission. He covered his political backside by describing the commission as a vehicle for imposing peace; he claimed it would have no authority to grant concessions.

General Howe's primary objective, now that he had replaced Gage as commander, was to wait and to enjoy himself. His brother's latest letter had assured him that his most recent plan calling for the New York strategy was well received. Admiral Lord Howe was maneuvering. Both brothers knew that when the Lord got his coveted appointments, they could work well together. For now, Howe was content to tolerate Admiral Graves as commander of the American squadron. While Graves supplied Boston and his brother conspired to replace him, General Howe would spend the winter comfortably in Boston. He had no intention of joining Washington on the field of battle. Howe would let the impatient Johnny Burgoyne harass the rebels with raids along the seacoast, and he would dispatch annoyance patrols to remind the bucolic rebels that British might was still nearby.

Meanwhile, he would indulge himself by entertaining the willing wives of anxious Loyalists who had flocked to Boston seeking refuge from persecution by the rebel hotheads. There were about 6,500 professed loyalists residing in Boston, and all were working hard to make General Howe's stay pleasant. Tonight, for example, he planned to attend the theater and then entertain Elizabeth Loring at his mansion for the first time. The lovely Elizabeth with the bountiful chest, the wife of Joshua Loring, a loyalist who was more concerned about maintaining his fortune than his wife, had made it perfectly clear she was willing to accept the general's overtures. The thought brought a broad smile to Howe's face; Madame Loring had the potential to greatly ease the discomfort of Boston's long winter.

Howe despised the provincial city of Boston. The weather now was pleasant; the trees were quite colorful, but the streets were dirty, filled with hogs rooting in the trash strewn by lazy housewives. He had been told that winters in Boston were horrendous. The thought did not worry him; let Washington and his ragamuffins freeze. Next spring, after his brother arrived, then the Howes would teach them a lesson.

Howe turned away from the window and called to his adjutant:

"Springwater, come here." As he did frequently, Howe wondered where the family had acquired such a preposterous name.

"Yes sir," the eager young man barked as he rushed into the room. He was fully dressed in his immaculate red and white uniform as befitted any young brevet captain lucky enough to serve as the General's aide.

"James," Howe could not bring himself to repeat the man's ridiculous last name. "I'm calling it a day."

"Yes sir." Captain Springwater had arrived from England only three weeks previously, but he had already learned not to ask the General for information about his plans. It did not matter. Springwater knew where Howe would be. He would return to the comfortable mansion he had commandeered for his own use; the owner, a wealthy Bostonian loyalist had gladly given up his home, expecting future returns from the man who would teach the rebels a lesson, and had moved to a lesser mansion. Howe would change his uniform, then join his latest paramour for an evening at the theater. The officers of the Royal Welsh Fusiliers were putting on a play written by one of their own; Springwater who had no mimic abilities of his own looked with scorn at the amateur productions the officers staged to amuse themselves, but the general obviously considered their efforts sufficient to put his companion in the proper mood for a long and amorous night. The general's appreciation of the fair sex was as well known as his fondness for Irish whiskey.

"I'm to be disturbed under no circumstances," Howe ordered. He enjoyed intimidating his young aide.

"No sir," Springwater, standing stiffly at attention, agreed.

"And stop standing at attention when I talk to you. Relax, man," Howe spoke firmly but not unkindly as the nervous aide pulled his chin in tighter and froze his hands, thumbs inward, to the seams of his trousers.

"Yes sir," he replied through tight lips.

"I will be at the theater, then spend a quiet evening at home with friends. But no disturbances, understand." Howe knew he was repeating himself but had learned that the technique had a way of frightening young officers even more. "Who is the headquarters duty officer?" Howe demanded.

"Colonel Abernathy, sir."

Howe smiled his satisfaction. Abernathy was a tired old line officer who would be too drunk by seven to be in a condition to bother the general, no matter what happened. Since armies did not fight at night, Howe expected no problems anyway. The last time they had had trouble was when Washington's ants had marched on to Bunker and Breed Hills and dug their fortifications. They're an army of diggers, Howe thought. He had to give them credit for that. In one night they had built fortifications that it cost Gage almost a thousand good men to overcome. Even if they start digging again, Howe thought, there is nothing he could do at night about it anyway. Let them take another hill and set the damned town on fire with their cannon they had stolen from Ticonderoga. He had received intelligence indicating they planned to try and move them over the mountains. He doubted if they would be successful, but if they were, all the better. Then, he could move south to New York sooner. They could have Boston as far as he was concerned.

Without another word Howe pushed past Captain Springwater and departed. He smiled at the enlisted men and staff officers who jumped to attention as he approached. He enjoyed the short walk to his mansion; every officer and soldier he met snapped sharp salutes in his direction, and Howe briskly returned them, nodding familiarly to each. Howe treated Springwater and his immediate staff badly, but he worked to ensure the loyalty of his troops.

As soon as General Howe departed headquarters, the tension subsided. Captain Springwater wiped the sweat from his brow with the back of his hand, fussily straightened the scarlet sash that identified him as the general's aide, then hurriedly departed headquarters. Unlike the general, he did not take the time to acknowledge the other denizens of the building. He had his own plans, and they involved the daughter of a prominent Bostonian preacher. Despite her stern father and his inhibiting religion, the girl was a real vixen. The thought brought a smile of anticipation to Springwater's face. The general had obviously been worried that Springwater might bother him with duty tonight; fat chance of that, he thought, anticipating how he would finally entice the preacher's daughter to the small rowhouse he had commandeered for his own use. There were decided advantages to being an officer in an occupying army.

In London, Admiral Richard Lord Howe admired himself in the mirror. At forty-eight, he still cut a fine figure in his uniform. He had put on considerable weight around the middle, but his sash and tailored coat concealed his girth. His face was still unwrinkled. Even his large nose seemed to the Lord to be an imposing feature. He wondered if he should again grow a mustache to cut down on the size of his nose and hide his slightly protruding lips but decided against it. The hair would probably be white, and he did not want to advertise his advancing years.

Richard turned away from the mirror, adjusted his sword, retrieved his white gloves from the hall table and marched stiff backed towards the door. His wife was at their country estate, and he was going out unaccompanied and unfettered tonight. Just as well, he thought, because tonight would be a working evening. That was why he was wearing his uniform. As a Member of Parliament as well as a serving naval officer, Lord Howe alternated between his uniform and civilian clothing. He wore what the situation demanded, and tonight he wanted to be at his martial best.

His host would be Sir George Germaine. Howe had been delighted when he received the invitation. He did not particularly like the man, who had disgraced himself with cowardice on the battlefield, but he had persevered and had redeemed himself in a political career that made him one of the most influential men in London despite the fact he was forever excluded from a military career.

At Richard's own suggestion, his brother had written privately from America directly to Germaine providing information, which Germaine used to advance himself and incidentally undermine General Gage. The very day he received the invitation, Lord Richard had learned that Germaine had succeeded in wheedling for himself the coveted post of Colonial Secretary. As such, he would be in the direct line of command to the forces in America, and thus a key man to have as your friend. Undoubtedly, Germaine, astute schemer that he was, recognized the Howe brothers would one day be primary players. William already was.

"Admiral Lord Howe," Germaine greeted Richard when he was escorted by the butler into the Germaine sitting room.

"Lord Germaine," Richard replied. Both men were speaking politely but facetiously. They usually referred to each other as George and Richard.

"So sorry Lady Howe could not be here tonight," Germaine continued the farce.

"To her regret, duty in the country called," Richard replied. He looked about the room and was pleased to note that the other guests were fellow Members of Parliament and a few of Germaine's usual hangers-on. He would be the guest of honor.

"Please make yourself at home, Richard," Germaine invited politely, having noted other guests arriving. "I think you know everybody. You look resplendent in your uniform. If you don't object, I would like to have a few words in private with you later."

"I heard the good news," Richard spoke sincerely. He was confident he and Germaine shared objectives and could work together, despite the man's abysmal past.

"Not a word, please," Germaine glanced to see if anyone could overhear. "Nothing official until at least the first of November. Some of the other players have not been informed."

Richard nodded agreement. He assumed Germaine referred to the current Colonial Secretary who, carrying the burden of the losses in North America, was being shuttled aside.

The two men parted, and Richard dutifully began to work the room. The evening surprisingly was a relaxed one and passed quickly despite the attempts of the light headed dimwit, the wife of a minor Member of Parliament, who loyally attempted to further her career by attempting to nestle her fat thighs against Richard's under the dinner table. Howe was sure his host had selected his dinner companion as a gentle, self-amusing provocation.

After dessert, some kind of unrecognizable pudding was served, the wives returned to the sitting room for coffee and the men adjourned to the library for brandy. Without a word to his other guests, Germaine took Richard by the arm and led him to a room off the library that he used as a private office.

"I hope you don't mind my keeping you from our other guests for a few minutes," Germaine spoke superficially.

Richard Howe smiled and waited for Germaine to get to the real purpose of the invitation.

"When Lord North invited me to take on my new responsibilities, he confided a few of his plans to me," Germaine immediately cut to the heart of the discussion. "May I speak with you confidentially."

Why not, Richard thought, and again nodded agreement.

Germaine poured each a snifter of brandy from a crystal decanter that had been placed on the cluttered desk well in advance of the meeting.

"General William," Germaine began again, referring to Howe's brother, "has been keeping both of us informed of events in Boston. I in turn have briefed the Prime Minister. Despite the current popular trend to think we can force a solution on the rebels, we realize this may not be a viable solution." He paused and waited for Richard to comment.

"I agree," Richard observed, trying to keep Germaine talking.

"One alternative is to send more troops and ships," Germaine continued.

"And we are doing that," Richard agreed.

"And we need effective leadership. We have William with the ground forces, but now... ." Germaine paused to sip his brandy.

"We need to replace that fool Graves," Richard contributed. He recognized immediately Germaine's tactics. He knew his name had been bandied about as one of those in line to succeed Graves, but this did not please him. He had his sights set higher. He would accept the position of admiral commanding His Majesty's navy in North America, but he wanted more. He would be appointed concurrently Commander-in-Chief of all forces, army and navy, in America as well as Peace Commissioner. He would use the armed forces as a club then graciously solve the problem as Peace Commissioner and return home the most successful member of his long family line to have lived.

"That and something else," Germaine said, surprising Richard. "I," Germaine spoke a little pompously, Richard thought, "intend to pursue quietly the possibility of negotiating a peace. Lord North agrees and has authorized me to explore the subject. What do you think?"

"I think it is an excellent idea, but I'm not sure how many others agree," Richard replied. Richard recognized that his clever companion was toying with him. "I'm rather taken with William's latest recommendation that we abandon Boston and capture New York City. His New York strategy appears to have the better chance of military success, which is what most are demanding today." By changing the subject, Richard raised his own cat's paw.

Germaine studied his colleague before replying." I quite agree with the New York strategy. Speaking as our most experienced military man, would you recommend abandoning Boston altogether?"

"William believes we could keep a small force in Boston if the politicians so wish. Washington will undoubtedly follow William to New York to defend the city from us, thus our smaller force would not be threatened, but I don't think we should leave any men behind. It's unsound military tactics to split your forces, and our objective is not holding land. We have to defeat the rebel army, or force them to the peace table."

"I agree exactly," Germaine replied, though he was not sure he did at all. "Who should be our overall commander in America?"

"You of course," Richard tried some obvious flattery, recognizing that such a proposal stood no chance whatever given Germaine's dismal military record.

"Out of the question, old chap," Germaine laughed. Howe sometimes was an obvious, pompous prig. "There's only one man, of course, yourself."

"I'm rather more interested in the peace commissioner job," Richard replied quickly. He was pleased with Germaine's suggestion and was of course willing to undertake both positions, but only both and maybe commander of the fleet also.

"I'm not sure how far North will get with this peace commissioner idea," Germaine replied, recognizing that Howe thirsted for both jobs. He saw the man's sudden puff up of pride. "Most of our colleagues would support a peace commission only if it would hasten a rebel surrender. Not many, other than you and me, are really interested in negotiating a peace."

Richard sipped his brandy and stared with interest at Germaine. Richard knew the man was totally insincere. North might be interested in negotiating a peace; the Prime Minister would do anything to get the unwinnable war off his back, but Germaine, pleased with his ascent to power, was merely playing the game.

Taking Richard's silence as assent, Germaine emptied his glass. "Agreed then. We best join the other guests before they notice we are missing."

Richard almost laughed at Germaine's obviousness. As if the other guests had not observed their host's rudeness in abandoning them to consult with Lord Richard.

"We have much to think about," Richard concluded the conversation in which neither man had committed himself to anything.

Chapter 12
Alexandria
Winter, 1775-76

James followed Washington's instructions and stopped in both New York City and Philadelphia on his way home. The side excursions proved most interesting because James had never visited either city before, and he found the political climate in each different and stimulating. As a consequence, he arrived in Alexandria on November first, three weeks later than he had planned. He found little changed, though Vivian had grown somewhat anxious at the delay, worrying much as James had at Jason's belated return from Martinique. He had much to report to George Mason, Corney, Jason and Vivian and friends, and much he could not, his private conversation with George Washington and his activities in the two major cities for example. The *Herald's* readership anxiously read his series of reports on the situation in Boston, New York and Philadelphia.

In New York he attempted to carry out Washington's mandate to spot for individuals who might prove to be useful sources of information if the battlefield should shift southward as James predicted. To his surprise, the project proved to be one of challenge and interest. Despite his misgivings, James found himself being slowly drawn into personal involvement in the war. He began on the morning of his arrival in New York City by calling on the prominent newspaper proprietors. He talked with James Rivington, printer of Rivington's *Royal Gazette*, Hugh Gaine at the New York *Gazette* and several others. The newspapermen's views conveyed little that was new to James; their biases reflected those of their countrymen. Only one major difference appeared. James had concluded that about one third of the American people remained loyal, some more vocal in their attitudes than others, and one third actively rebel with the remaining third, mostly of the country and yeoman class, taking no position whatsoever. Newspapers tended to reflect the views of their subscribers, but in New York James discovered a surprising number of newspaper proprietors who in private offered what James considered loyalist opinions. Hugh Gaine of the New York *Gazette* was a good example of this type; his newspaper in 1775 carried a lukewarm rebel line, but in private conversation Gaine clearly supported the English. Rivington, who also printed the *Mercury*, made no secret of his Tory bias. The Sons of Liberty had already burned his newspaper out once. All, however, were interested in promoting their own newspapers and agreed to James' proposal that they exchange copies of their publications. Since it was common practice for newspapers to pirate copy from each other, the printers were delighted to send him free copies in exchange for his promise to print the name of their newspapers every time he used one of their articles and at the same time to send them copies of the Virginia *Gazette* and his own Alexandria *Herald*.

The newspapermen were also useful for introductions to New York's prominent leaders, social and political, loyalist and rebel. Unlike the provincial newspapers, the larger publications in New York actually hired a young man or two to serve as information gatherers. At the New York *Gazette*, James encountered a young man whose eager intelligence and knowledge of his native city impressed James. After a day in his company, James privately hired the knowledgeable young man to serve as his guide. His name was York Allen. Now in his early twenties, Allen had lived his entire life on the streets of New York. He appeared to James to know everybody of importance, some favorably, some not. The brash, young man had an irritating manner that emerged when the person he was talking to was not as forthcoming as the eager news collector thought he should be. James was never able to elicit Allen's personal political views; he had apparently decided he could best be a friend to all if he appeared apolitical. Because of his journalistic reputation, Allen had access to all levels of New York society. People in the large city like those in Alexandria liked to see their names in the paper. With York's help, James met as many prominent loyalists as he could.

Andrew Partridge, a merchant who owned one of the biggest general stores in the city, was one of those James encountered his second day in New York. Partridge, who based his political views on the fact that the non-import ban was destroying his business and if continued would render him penniless, struck James as a reasonable man despite his misfortune to be in the wrong business at this critical time. Partridge, a portly well dressed man who any place but New York City would have been labeled a dandy despite his girth, no longer worked in his store; he left the labor to others and busied himself in the counting room that he maintained on the second floor over the large store. James suspected that Partridge's political sentiments really rested with the rebels, but since his clientele were all from New York society and naturally were loyalist, Partridge professed similar views.

On his fourth day, James with York Allen's assistance met a second man of interest, Hyde Pigot, Pastor of the Trinity Anglican Church. A Church of England vicar whose flock were loyalists from the high side of New York's aristocracy, Pigot had no choice but to appear to be a one hundred percent Crown man. Allen, an astute observer by nature and profession, had by that time begun to suspect James' motives. The Virginia newspaperman was interested in meeting loyalists, but only those who might be masquerading under false colors. When Allen hinted that he knew a churchman who might harbor secret rebel sentiments, James had jumped at the introduction. Once again James was impressed. Pigot, the son of a Long Island farmer with a devout wife, had entered the church, but he was a worldly man well versed in New York political currents. Like all that James had met, he was worried about the future. Events in Massachusetts had most frightened. Some concealed their feelings with bluster, but others made no attempt to hide their worry. Pigot was one of these. Unlike many of his congregation, he did not think that the English military would have an easy time subduing the rebellion. Pigot knew that his parents and their rock hard neighbors on Long Island were not soft city people and were fully capable of suffering hardship for principle.

In all of his conversations, James posed as a Virginia newsman collecting information for a series of articles to be published in the *Herald*. Most accepted this story. With only three people did James hint that he might represent more than he seemed. He dropped his veil slightly the first time with York Allen after he concluded he had earned the young man's confidence. On the third day of his visit, late in the afternoon while resting with York Allen in his favorite tavern, James deliberately let slip that he had just visited Cambridge and while there had met with General Washington. Allen's quick mind immediately made the connection between Alexandria, Virginia, where James resided and Washington's home at Mount Vernon. A discreet man, Allen said nothing, and this pleased James. He would have been disappointed if the young man had blurted out his suspicions and begun questioning James about his bonafides. James was looking for New York residents who might continue to live in the city after it was occupied by the English, as it surely would be if James' and Washington's theories about English strategy were valid. A discreet young man working for a newspaper whose owner was flexible enough in principle to adapt to changing political times met most of James' exacting criteria.

The ambivalently loyalist merchant Andrew Partridge and the Anglican pastor Hyde Pigot also interested James. He was not looking for ardent patriots who would flee with the appearance of the first redcoat; he wanted men of influence who might prove useful to the conquering army and thus have the ability to continue to live on in New York with the possibility of access to ranking English officers.

When James departed New York City for Philadelphia the following Saturday, he did so with nascent friendships budding with Partridge and Pigot. He had visited each man several times and had dined with Partridge on his last night in the city. Both men promised to correspond regularly with James and to keep him informed on developments in New York. James, who professed to need their observations for the *Herald* promised to keep their identities confidential. That way they could honestly project their views without fear of retaliation from their friends and neighbors. With York Allen, James reached a closer agreement. He hired Allen to serve as his New York correspondent. They both agreed to keep the salary and the existence of the arrangement secret for their "mutual" benefit.

James suspected the bright young man realized he was agreeing to something more than a business arrangement, and he was right, but neither commented to that effect.

In Philadelphia James intended to follow the same approach since it appeared to work out well in New York, but it did not happened that way. The first thing he contacted his friend Tom Jefferson who had replaced Peyton Randolph on Virginia's delegation to the Second Continental Congress. James, obeying the General's caveat, did not confide to Jefferson the real purpose of his visit to Philadelphia. Tom immediately assumed the role of local host and with the best of intentions occupied James with introductions to the delegates from the other colonies. James knew personally all of the Virginia delegation; he was one of the Burgesses who had voted to select them. Some, proud of what they were doing, and others, anxious to send the best impressions of their personal contributions homeward, worked to fill James' calendar for his visit. He sincerely enjoyed the political talk, particularly the grandiose versions of what would happen after the annoying war in the north was won, and at times found himself imagining what it would be like to be a participant in such a historically important process himself.

James was impressed with John Adams and several members of the various New England delegations. Admitting that a natural bias might be involved, he still found himself less attracted to the representatives of the middle colonies, particularly Pennsylvania. Most appeared more interested in protecting their self interest than contributing to the war effort or planning for the future government of the united colonies; James suspected several of being loyalists masquerading as patriots. He had more respect for some, like Joseph Galloway, the former Speaker of the Pennsylvania Assembly and a representative to the Congress, who made no secret of their conservative views and acted sincerely repelled by the course of events, particularly the excesses committed by the more radical patriots.

Given the political and social shackles his friends imposed on his time, James considered himself lucky to find time to visit two newspaper publishers and to attend two parties hosted by members of Philadelphia society. He was disappointed, however, that the contact with neither the newspapermen nor the social aristocrats produced any leads to potential allies like he had been so fortunate to find in New York. The Philadelphia elite, at least those he met during his short stay, were either sincere loyalists or self seeking opportunists trying to exploit the troubled times for personal profit.

When James finally departed Philadelphia, he did so with a sense of relief. Despite the fact that the Congress contained some of the most impressive and patriotic men he had ever met, James found them so intent on their involvement in the crisis that they lived each day as if it were their last on the face of the earth. James admitted that though tempted at times he successfully avoiding being sucked into the process. As for the cream of Philadelphia society, he did not meet one that he cared whether he ever saw again or not. Some of the young women he met, despite the fact that most were spoiled and vain children who reminded him of some of the daughters of Vivian's wealthy planter friends, entranced him. Peggy Shippen, the young daughter of Edward Shippen, a Philadelphia lawyer and admiralty court judge, was particularly vivacious. James spent a pleasant fifteen minutes talking with the pretty teenager until she bounced off to enjoy herself with young men of her own age. James doubted the senior Shippen's political loyalties, but he admitted that Peggy's effervescence brightened an otherwise dull evening.

Within a week of his return to Alexandria, James found himself fully involved in the ongoing Virginia crisis. Dunmore, angry at the illegal local militia build-up over his objections, had from the safety of his sanctuary on board the British warship in the Bay, dispatched patrols to harass the Virginians. The Committee of Safety, serving as Virginia's governing body, reacted in kind. The result was irritating clashes that shed the blood of both sides. On the night of November fourteenth, about one hundred of Dunmore's men from the King's 14th Regiment with the assistance of about twenty loyalists clashed with militia troops at Great Bridge south of Norfolk. The militia, inexperienced at ambush, was driven back with a loss of seven dead. Eighteen militiamen were captured. High on this minor victory and anxious to punish the rebelling Virginians, Dunmore released a proclamation he had signed a week earlier. He was confident that this paper stroke would shake Virginia society to its foundations. The proclamation declared:

"...I do hereby declare all indented Servants, Negroes, or others (appertaining to Rebels) free, that are able and willing to bear Arms, they joining his Majesty's Troops."

Dunmore had carried through with his often-repeated threat to free the slaves.

The planters of Fairfax County reacted to the Governor's spiteful action in the same way as did their fellow slave owners further south—they suffered immediate fear and panic. Even those like Vivian and James at Eastwind who treated their slaves with compassion and kindness slept uneasily, afraid of being murdered in their beds by their human possessions before they marched off to join what they considered to be Dunmore's unholy war.

James insisted that Vivian join him in Alexandria where she would be safe from retribution, but she refused. She insisted the slaves at Eastwind were her friends who had known her from childhood and would do her no harm. James, who possessed a healthy skepticism about the inherent good of man, black or white, uneasily spent a week at Eastwind with Vivian. He slept at night with a pair of loaded and cocked flintlock pistols on the stand beside his bed. Even the confident Vivian did not protest.

Passions among the planters ran high. They accused Dunmore of the blackest kind of hypocrisy without recognizing that their charges cut two ways. They asked how could Dunmore free slaves in the name of liberty while at the same time attempting to suppress with military force the rebels who were simply fighting for their own freedom. James noted that the planters did not ask how they could own human beings as chattel while fighting a war for their own liberties.

Dunmore organized an Ethiopian Regiment to accept the black volunteers answering his clarion call. Slaves numbering in the hundreds made their way to Norfolk to enlist. Despite the worries of the planters, most of Virginia's some two hundred thousand slaves stayed home. James knew of a few Fairfax plantations that lost workers, but most did not. At first, most had overlooked the fact that Dunmore's call had been aimed at African males. In order to take advantage of the opportunity to earn freedom by taking up the King's arms against their masters, the slaves had to leave their families behind. It did not take long for the threat of death for those left behind to spread.

James reported in the *Herald* the news of Dunmore's epic proclamation and its aftermath as calmly and objectively as he could. He irritated many of Vivian's friends with his dispassion, but the Quakers and small farmers of northern Fairfax applauded his stand. When days then weeks passed and no slave uprising occurred, James felt justified. Vivian reported, however, that many of their neighbors continued to harbor a strong bitterness towards James personally.

Dunmore's Redcoats occupied Norfolk on November 23 and began erecting fortifications. Some escaping slaves and many loyalists rallied there behind him. Skirmishing continued. James obtained most of his information on developments in the south from the Virginia *Gazette*. The reprinted *Gazette* articles when joined with reports from the North that James garnered from his New York correspondents made the *Herald* the most influential weekly newspaper in the northern Virginia, Maryland and Pennsylvania areas. The *Herald's* circulation increased, and James, after hiring four extra workers, expanded by purchasing the building next to his.

On December 1, 1775, James reluctantly left Alexandria to ride with George Mason one more time to Richmond to attend the Fourth Virginia Convention. They no sooner arrived than the delegates voted to adjourn to Williamsburg to meet in the College of William and Mary. James and a crotchety George Mason traveled with their companions to Williamsburg. The meeting at the College brought back old memories to James. As a student, he had watched as the Burgesses met at the College to vent their spleen over Governor Dinwiddie's attempt to impose a tax on land transactions, the famous Pistole Fee crisis. Then, James had been a youthful observer who shared a room with two other students that was located directly over the hall in which the delegates were now assembled.

James was sorry that he had attended this fourth meeting. Most of the session was devoted to resolving a dispute between Patrick Henry and a man named Woodford, who were involved in an argument over militia command. The convention authorized the Committee of Safety to form a Virginia navy, a pet project of the energetic Henry. The convention also restored the judicial system; the year and a half hiatus had produced a mountainous backlog of civil disputes. Loyalists received short shrift; the convention ordered that all males had to enlist in the militia or leave the colony or face arrest. Responding to Washington's requests for more troops, the delegates increased the number of Virginia regiments to be raised from two to nine. They also enhanced the power of the Committee of Safety to govern during periods the Virginia Congress was not in session. For all its status as an illegal and unconstitutional organ, James was struck by the congress' attempts to give an aura of legality to its decisions. On the last day of the session, the delegates, reacting to Dunmore's blockade of the Bay, opened the ports of Virginia to trade by all ships except those of the English Crown. In doing so, they took a large step towards undermining the very basis of the English Empire, its mercantile monopoly.

The congress ended, and James and George Mason wearily trudged home. At least James was tired of politics, but Mason had gotten his second wind. Mason devoted the long ride through a leafless countryside over frozen mud to a discussion of his plans for a new constitution for Virginia. Mason was already working on his draft, which would institutionalize the citizens' rights in an article that Mason labeled a Declaration of Rights. By the time they reached home, James decided he could not possibly attend a congress devoted exclusively to Mason's proposed constitution and began considering excuses he could devise to avoid the daunting prospect. He decided he was even willing to consider another trip to Philadelphia and New York if not Cambridge. He feared another meeting with Washington would cost him his own independence.

In December 1775, the skirmishing in Norfolk continued. Firefights diminished, but both sides continued to get on each other's nerves. British ship captains took exception to ostentatious parade ceremonies by rebels in full few of the ships. The Americans, who had retaken control of Norfolk after Dunmore had once again retreated to his ship, replied the parades would continue. On New Years day, 1776, the American militia conducted an enthusiastic martial demonstration. The British ships showed their exasperation by replying with a long threatened bombardment. By nightfall, Norfolk's waterfront was ablaze. The Americans, who had no regard for the city's decidedly loyalist population, were not the least troubled by the flames. They had in fact recently obtained Committee of Safety permission to burn a distillery belonging to an obstinate loyalist, thus the militia officers and men laughingly let the British do their work for them.

During the night the flames spread. Norfolk burned for three days with neither side troubling to fight the conflagration. Some complained about rebel properties being destroyed indiscriminately along with the loyalist buildings, but no one paid much attention. The militia, most of whom were rough country folk, got into the rum and spent their time cheering the flames as they methodically worked their way through the fated city.

Word of the disaster spread throughout Virginia. In Alexandria, James labored to ensure that Dunmore got full credit for the destruction of a Virginia city. Later, it was estimated that the Americans had been responsible for the destruction of 863 buildings and the English nineteen. Spurred by an imaginative article written by Corney Goodenough who had become a full fledged member of the Sons of Liberty, the ardent patriots of Alexandria gathered at the Court House Square and burned an effigy of Lord Dunmore along with a second named His Bloody Majesty George the Third. James remained a spectator at these frequent events, but he found his attitude one of encouragement rather than concern.

In James' opinion, news from the North was not particularly dramatic when viewed in the perspective of the times. As in Virginia, skirmishing continued. Patriots harassed loyalists, and both sides blustered. The English fleet worried patriot coastal towns with raids from the sea; one such effort resulted in the town of Falmouth suffering the fate of Norfolk. As best as James could tell, no one but townspeople grieved the loss of the two towns; each side tailored reactions to justify their cause.

In January 1776, near Boston, one event occurred that would have dramatic long-term implications, but it passed outside James' awareness. Last May before Washington took command and as rebel troops enthusiastically encircled Boston, it had become obvious that the Americans lacked the wherewithal to really confront the English. Many realized that if they only had cannon they could wreak real harm on the British who were comfortably ensconced in Boston. To their amateur eyes, several hills appeared ideal spots for emplacements, but their citizen army had no artillery. Several eager officers suggested that an easy foray to Fort Ticonderoga on Lake Champlain could rectify this deficiency. The Massachusetts Committee of Safety authorized a Connecticut druggist by the name of Benedict Arnold to undertake the mission. Arnold, who had been apprenticed at the age of fourteen to his mother's cousins who ran an apothecary shop, had served briefly as a private in the French and Indian War. Following this experience, he returned to Norwich, completed his apprenticeship and opened his own shop. He prospered and in December 1774 had been elected a militia captain. Allen, accompanied by some eighty men, fulfilled his proposal on May tenth when he captured Fort Ticonderoga without a shot. They caught the English defenders sleeping in their beds. The rebel army now had over a hundred English cannon, but they were on the wrong side of the mountains from where they were needed.

The cannon remained at Fort Ticonderoga until the young man who had so impressed James during his visit to Cambridge, Colonel Henry Knox, devised a scheme to bring the cannon to Boston. Despite the scoffing and pessimism of the more senior generals around Washington, Knox succeeded. In late January 1776,

Colonel Knox presented the commander-in-chief with a belated but much appreciated Christmas gift, forty-three cannon and fourteen mortars.

Two of the *Herald's* most prominent news stories that winter dealt with espionage and conspiracy. James felt a nebulous link to both and followed them closely. One had developed in Cambridge during James' visit; he later surmised that Washington must have been addressing it at the same time he joined James in lengthy conversation. According to the story as reported in the New York papers, a prominent American doctor by the name of Benjamin Church, a Boston physician, a delegate to the Massachusetts Congress and the respected director of the first American army hospital, had been brought to trial on the third of October charged with having carried on a criminal correspondence with the enemy.

The case had come to the rebel attention by chance. Church, who had been spying for the English for some time—at least since before April 1775 when he reported to General Gage that the rebels were collecting military supplies at Lexington and Concord, leading Gage to dispatch troops on an ill fated mission to seize them—had a mistress. In July 1775 Church had sent the young lady to Newport with a letter containing cipher which she was to deliver to any British official with instructions to pass it on to General Gage. Unfortunately for Church, she failed in this task and left the letter with a patriot instead. After reading the letter, the loyal American became suspicious and sent it to General Washington for investigation. The General had the mistress apprehended. She confessed and the continental army arrested Church and confiscated his papers. The subsequent trial shocked James and others with its conclusion; this prominent American patriot was guilty of having spied on his comrades for money.

The second case developed much closer to home in Virginia and involved the persistent Governor Dunmore. As part of his struggle to teach the rebels a lesson, the Governor formulated a plan to separate the Virginians from their wealth, western land that had long attracted General Washington and other Virginia speculators. Dr. John Connolly, a native of Pennsylvania, which naturally contested Virginia in the west, was an opportunist by birth. Connolly acquired a number of Virginian land grants and changed his loyalties from Pennsylvania to his new potential benefactor. He succeeded in getting himself elected captain of the Virginia Militia Company at Fort Pitt. After the battle of Lexington, Connolly decided to exploit the situation by becoming a loyalist; he traveled to Williamsburg and made his way to Dunmore's abode on a British warship in the Bay. Connolly proposed that he be authorized to raise a loyalist regiment to fight for the King in the west; his plan called for him to set up a headquarters in Detroit and from there to march on Fort Pitt and from thence eastward to Alexandria. James was shocked to learn that Connolly had intended to join forces at Alexandria with other loyalists to be mobilized in Virginia by Dunmore. Dunmore planned that Connolly fortify Alexandria and use it as a base to divide the colonies in half.

After considering the plan, Dunmore sent Connolly north to Boston to discuss it with General Gates himself. The Governor was sure that Gates would be delighted to encourage the loyalists to fight the rebels for him. Connolly with Gage's approval returned to Virginia in November at about the same time that Dunmore issued his proclamation freeing the slaves. After further conferences with Dunmore, Connolly and two companions began to make their way west by the shortest route. They sailed up the Chesapeake Bay carrying their written authorities from Dunmore concealed in the pillion sticks on which a servant carried his belongings. The sticks were nothing more than hollowed out poles covered first with tin and then canvas.

When the small party reached Frederick, Maryland, north of Alexandria, a second servant informed the local Committee of Safety of Connolly's plans. They seized Connolly. A search failed to disclose the hidden authorities but did uncover a piece of paper that confirmed the servant's allegations. The Frederick Committee of Safety reported their find to the Second Continental Congress which responded by ordering that Connolly be sent to Philadelphia. Connolly was found guilty as charged and sentenced to jail.

In Alexandria the Connolly case was a sensation. Virtually every issue of the *Herald* in December and January carried inflammatory revelations, many of which were devised by Corney to excite their readership against Lord Dunmore. James felt guilty distorting the news for strictly monetary gain, but the story increased his already growing circulation. He rationalized Corney's elaboration on political grounds. The patriots were engaged in war and had to do whatever was required to win.

Chapter 13
Eastwind
January 20, 1776

James, holding Vivian's hand for support, not knowing whether the encouragement flowed from himself to his wife or the reverse, stood near Eastwind's large front door. His back braced against the thick wall was chilled despite his heavy wool suit and the heat of the room. He did not know how Vivian in her tasteful gray gown withstood the drafts of frigid winter air that crept in around the doorjamb and reflected off the opaque glass windows. She wore a thick wool scarf draped over her bare shoulders, but still her skin was exposed. Vivian, sensing her husband's scrutiny, turned and smiled encouragement at him.

"It's all right, James. I'm warm enough. After all, I'm not a brittle porcelain doll."

James smiled back. He released her hand and draped his arm over her shoulders in an attempt to share body warmth.

"Besides, I'm too excited to be cold," Vivian continued.

James clutched his wife to him and stared at Eastwind's crowded ballroom. It was filled with long wood benches borrowed from two local churches. The benches, pews really, were occupied by their friends and neighbors. James estimated that every single person he knew, at least those he respected and loved, were present except for his twin brother John, who had been captured in his western mountain home by a winter snowfall—otherwise, he would have been at James' side during this time of personal stress—and George Washington, who was occupied in the North, and of course Martha, George's wife. Martha had joined George in Cambridge to cheer her husband through the tedious days of maintaining his diminished army in its winter encampments.

James' father, Young Tom, bent from age with rigid joints, sensed his son's scrutiny and turned. He, along with the rest of the Satterfields from the Short Hills, sat in the front row of seats on the right hand side. Although their backs were to him, James could see his sister Sally and her husband and their two children; seated next to them was his younger brother Will, easily identified by his broad shoulders and thick arms, and his family. Will's two sons, Jessie and Jackie, aged eight and nine respectively, fidgeted in their seats. James smiled when he saw Jessie, the spirited one, pull Jackie's hair from behind. Jackie turned and glared at the innocent young Randolph boy, the son of Ritchie and Remmie Randolph, Vivian's planter friends.

James, feeling his own burst of paternal contentment, waved at his father. Young Tom raised a gnarled hand to return the greeting before turning to face the front.

"I think your father is getting impatient," Vivian whispered as she snuggled closer to him.

"Do you want to sit down?" James asked, glancing at the two vacant places in the front row reserved for them as the mother and father of the groom.

"Not yet," Vivian replied with a look at the staircase on the left.

"Do you think she's ready yet?" James asked, trying to mask his growing impatience.

"Calm down," Vivian ordered, smiling to soften her words. "This is Lily's day."

"It's too bad her mother can't be here," James said sincerely. Lily's mother had died in October while he was in Cambridge. James had been fond of both John West and his wife and had been genuinely dismayed to learn of Lily's mother's sudden death when he returned from Cambridge. Because John West did not feel up to hosting a large wedding himself, he had gladly accepted Vivian's offer to fill in and plan the wedding. She naturally had jumped at the opportunity to have her only son married at Eastwind.

When the young couple in their eagerness opted for a winter wedding, James had had his reservations. He worried about a sudden winter snowfall preventing the travel of the wedding guests, and lodging was also a problem, but the fickle gods of winter had cooperated, so far. The weather was bitter cold, but a feeble, pale sun had brightened the days, holding the snow clouds west of the mountains. Vivian and James' friends had solved the second concern. George Mason had thrown open Gunston Hall and Lund Washington, who was managing Mount Vernon in George and Martha's absence, graciously welcomed some of the wedding party overflow. George with his fine sense of courtesy had written a warm letter insisting that James and Vivian's guests avail themselves of his home. James' concerns were not completely unfounded. Even those three large mansions were inadequate to house the numerous guests who had appeared. As a consequence, friends to the south opened their homes. Guests were lodged with Martin Cockburn at Springfield and Daniel McCarty at Rover's Delight. Many others traveled from their own homes at nearby plantations or from Alexandria.

While James watched, two of Eastwind's house slaves fed large logs to the huge fireplaces located at each end of the room.

"We must have at least two hundred people crowded in here," James whispered.

"One hundred and seventy-six," Vivian, the efficient organizer, corrected. She had twice told James the exact number of firm acceptances they had received, but the figures had not registered.

James smiled contentedly at his wife until the Anglican pastor from George Washington's church coughed loud enough to be heard over the nervous whispering and shuffling feet of the guests. James looked up and stared at the gaunt man. He could have been Corney Goodenough's older brother. James estimated the preacher was about fifty years of age, but his long hair was still coal black. It hung over his forehead, reminding James of the mane of a horse his brother John once owned.

Vivian slid out from under James' comforting arm and took his hand.

"Come. We're about ready to start. We've got to take our seats."

James, who naturally did not like being told what to do, not even by his wife, pulled back then good-naturedly acquiesced. He accompanied Vivian down the aisle that divided the two families and their friends. James looked to his left and performing still as host nodded to John West's friends and relatives, most of whom lived in Alexandria and were connected one way or another with West's several enterprises. James acknowledged to himself as he walked that his son had chosen wisely. Not only was he acquiring the prettiest girl in Alexandria as his wife, but also he was joining what was probably the wealthiest family in town. Lily had a brother who would inherit the family wealth, but she undoubtedly would bring Jason far more than her father's generous dowry.

James and Vivian had just taken their seats when everyone turned to watch Jason and Skinny Potts, who was serving as best man, walk down the aisle. The two young men moved quickly. Skinny smiled nervously at friends who waved. Skinny lifted his hand in enthusiastic reply, happy to be sharing the attention with his friend. James had time to be proud of his son. Jason had turned out to be a handsome young man. He was now two inches taller than his father who was a healthy six-foot even. Jason's physical labor at the boatyard had toned his muscles. James watched his son's light step and suddenly felt old and soft. Despite himself, he envied his son his youth and fresh bride. James shared the stocky Satterfield build with his twin, John, but for some reason had always felt himself to be the smaller of the two despite their identical size. All Satterfield men were husky, muscular men, generally larger than their friends of like ages. James had often pondered the question. Were the Satterfield males muscular because of the physical exercise and demands of the blacksmith trade most of their ancestors had practiced, or were they blacksmiths because of their bulky physiques. Whatever the explanation, James knew that the genes over which none of them had any control were responsible.

James reached behind Vivian and patted his father on the back. James swallowed hard and fought to deny the tear drops of emotion seeking escape. Vivian, sharing his pride and emotion, took his hand and squeezed. Feeling separated from James, Vivian slid closer to him until their bodies touched from shoulder to thigh. James, feeling masculinely protective of his wife, willed the teardrops back.

Jason and Skinny turned and stood to the right of the Parson. The man, dressed in his black robes of office, tugged at the tight white collar with a bony finger. James noted a smear of winter mud on one side of the collar. Before he could point it out to Vivian—James could not restrain himself from disparaging the office holders of organized religion; after all the Anglican form of state church was one of the institutions that James and George Mason were trying to upset in Virginia with their new constitution that was still in the drafting stages—the organist that Vivian had hired began to play.

James, like everyone else, turned to stare as Lily and John West self-consciously descended the Eastwind staircase. Again, James marveled at how beautiful his son's bride was.

"She's lovely," Vivian whispered before James could speak. "Jason made a good choice." Vivian surprised herself. She had always thought she would never be able to say such a thing about the woman who was taking her son away from her. Vivian knew instinctively that their relationship was changing with each step Lily West took towards the altar. Vivian realized she would never again be Jason's best friend and confidant. He now had someone else to share his secrets and concerns and doubts. Vivian and her son, just like James with Jason, would always be close, but the sense of authority that was always included in any parent's relationship with a child was ending. Love and the memory of shared experiences would always exist, but Vivian knew she had been replaced.

Following the brief ceremony, the guests milled around while Eastwind slaves moved the benches to the side of the ballroom and set up tables at one end. Before long, the guests crowded around the tables and filled their plates from the many steaming platters of venison, lamb, pork and beef. Given the season, vegetables were in short supply but bowls of apple dressing, potatoes prepared in every imaginable form and stacks of bread and rolls made up more than adequately for the absent greens.

James, now relegated to the background, resumed his position near the front door and watched as his son and his new wife circulated through the room, greeting friends and relatives. Most of the guests were hard drinkers, and as James watched, the males made frequent trips to the bar that had been set up in one corner. Rum from the kegs carried on Jason's first Martinique run and Eastwind distilled whiskey using plantation grown peaches as its base appeared to be the drinks of choice. The women with a few exceptions ignored the bar and sipped at the non-alcoholic punch that Vivian had brewed from a variety of home grown ingredients.

After about an hour, James found himself a seat on a wall bench. He smiled to himself when he noticed that it was clearly marked as Colonel Washington's pew from the Puke Church. James wondered how his friend tolerated being lectured every Sunday by the humorless Anglican pastor who had fixed himself among the women no more than ten feet from the punch bowl.

About three o'clock, reacting to some kind of signal from Vivian who had continued to effortlessly manage the affair, Jason and Lily began moving through the crowd, shaking hands and kissing cheeks and effusively thanking all the guests for their consideration in attending the ceremony. After about a half an hour, they reached the front door. As soon as James had seen them preparing to depart, he had arranged for the one seat buggy pulled by a team of matched grays to be brought to the front door. James frequently used the conveyance on his short journeys between Alexandria and Eastwind, but today, he had allocated its use to Jason and his bride. Jason had tried to keep the location where he and Lily would spend the night a secret, but James doubted that few of Jason's friends, including Skinny Potts who was spreading the word, did not know they would be at the couple's new home in Alexandria that James and Vivian had presented to them as a family wedding gift. James assumed his son and Lily would pass the night being harassed from the street by Skinny and his colleagues fortified by frequent visits to the Pig. James, for his son's sake, hoped the night would turn cold and drive the revelers away.

After the happy couple had endured the usual taunting on Eastwind's verandah and front steps, they departed to the loud cheering and polite clapping of the assembled guests. As soon as the buggy disappeared from view—James noted that Jason was driving fast—the guests returned to the ballroom and resumed their celebration. James sought out his wife and silently embraced her. Vivian's face glowed with happiness. While some mothers shed tears over the loss of an only son, Vivian was happy for Jason. She genuinely liked Lily and would have selected none other if the final choice had been hers and not Jason's. Vivian kissed James fully on the lips, then patted him on the cheek.

"We did all right for ourselves, didn't we?" James bragged, referring to Jason who had been a picture book groom.

Before Vivian could answer, the three slaves who provided the music at Eastwind broke into a lively jig.

Vivian, with a single tear running down her cheek, took Jason's hand and led him in a lively, dancing circle of the ballroom. The guests applauded and cheered some raucously. After James and Vivian had completed one turn, the guests crowded to join them. James who had been delighted to relinquish his responsibilities after one turn watched as the women sought out their husbands. James assumed that they hoped to draw their spouses away from the whiskey as much as they wanted to share their company on the dance floor.

James resumed his seat along the wall and watched with unseeing eyes for the next hour as his mind floated through the past filled with memories of Jason as a child. Occasionally, friends would interrupt his reverie or Vivian would appear with a hosting chore to be fulfilled, but always James returned to his spot on George Washington's pew. The room grew hotter and noisier as the guests danced and jostled and drank.

"James, may I join you?" His friend Ritchie Randolph spoke softly as if embarrassed at his temerity in interrupting James' reverie.

"Certainly, Ritchie," James replied, indicating a spot on the pew next to himself. "Sit right here on the end and you will be sharing an experience with our commander-in-chief's posterior."

Ritchie laughed nervously.

"It wasn't that funny, Ritchie," James good-naturedly admonished his friend.

Noticing that Ritchie's hands were clasped together and that his friend had apparently been eschewing the bar, James asked:

"Can I get you some refreshment? Before it's gone?"

"No chance of that despite their best efforts," Ritchie replied indicating the bar. "Vivian knows her friends. She has more rum and whiskey stockpiled than the Pig," Ritchie referred to the Alexandria tavern preferred by the wilder elements.

"Are you sure?" James asked. Ritchie's strained demeanor troubled him.

"I know this is no time to raise such a subject," Ritchie began, "but I don't have much choice."

"Tell me Ritchie," James spoke softly.

"Well... ." Ritchie began then paused.

"Out with it," James ordered. "What can I do to help?"

"I have to sell some property," Ritchie began again.

"No need for that," James interrupted quickly. "If you need a loan... ." James knew that frequently planters, no matter how land rich, ran short of operating cash. Their self-indulgent lifestyles kept them in constant debt. He was surprised at Ritchie, however, because the sober young man had always managed his resources carefully.

"No, thank you James. It's not a loan I need." He paused and studied his friend as if trying to make a decision. Finally, he continued. "May I speak confidentially, James?"

"You know you can, Ritchie."

"I have to sell everything."

"I don't understand," James reacted.

"It's the war. Remmie's parents have decided to pull out."

While Ritchie talked, James listened and thought at the same time. Remmie's parents who had the large plantation to the east of Ritchie's Promised Land had made no secret of their loyalist sympathies. To the best of James' knowledge, and he tried to keep track of such matters, they had not been troubled yet by the Sons of Liberty. Most of their patriotic activity had been confined to town.

"Remmie's father has decided that he cannot support the patriots and for his family's sake must move them to New York. He's convinced the English will soon take over the city and will protect the loyalists. He claims he will return home after the English win and buy up the confiscated rebel land dirt cheap."

"He's entitled to his views," James spoke laconically. The opinions of Remmie's father were not unique. James believed it was possible the elder Randolph might be right about the English taking New York and protecting the loyalists.

"But he persuaded Remmie to take the children and go to New York with him and the rest of the family. Remmie's brother agrees and is pulling out with him."

"Why can't you and Remmie stay here?" James asked. "You have to live your own lives now. You are both adults."

"I know," Ritchie replied, barely able to keep the desperation in his voice under control. "But her father has Remmie scared. He's convinced her the Sons of Liberty will burn our house and kill the children after it becomes known that he has moved to New York. He's made no secret of his views about the war."

"I know," James agreed, "but the talk of killing is nonsense. Can't you convince her otherwise? Do you want me and Vivian to talk with her?"

"It won't do any good," Ritchie shook his head. "I've already tried. They are leaving in ten days, so I have to sell out. Everything."

"You'll lose your shirt," James said soberly. "Your father-in-law is not unique. There are several plantations on the market now, and nobody is buying. Everyone expects prices to drop. Some even say that the land of fleeing loyalists will be confiscated and sold at auction." James knew this to be a fact. At the last Virginia Congress, a confiscation law was almost passed. James expected the next session to provide for confiscation of the property of loyalist sympathizers whether they had fled or not.

"I know. I've arranged to sell my Africans, but I don't know what to do with the plantation or my other land."

James knew that Ritchie had inherited from his father about two thousand acres in Loudoun County.

"Can you help me?" Ritchie pleaded, unable to keep the whine out of his voice.

James shook his head slowly. With his expansion at the boatyard and newspaper and purchase of the small house for Jason and Lily, he too was short of cash. All of his personal reserves were invested. He still had money from the Satterfield Legacy, his one third of Braddock's gold, but his agreement with his brothers required him to invest it in land around Alexandria. Besides, he had no interest in Ritchie's plantation. He was still trying to persuade Vivian to give up Eastwind; he knew this was a losing battle, but he continued to oppose slavery and Ritchie's plantation required African labor to operate it.

"I'm sorry, Ritchie. I can't help. Purchasing the house for Jason has cleaned me out. Besides, you know my views about slavery."

The words struck Ritchie like a slap. He blanched white and leaned back in the pew.

"You were my last hope," Ritchie whispered.

"I'll talk with Will," James was shocked into replying. "He might be able to offer you something for the Loudoun land."

"Would you?" Ritchie pleaded. "With money from the slaves and something from the Loudoun land I might be able to last in New York for a year."

"If you go, you'll lose your plantation," James cautioned. He looked around to make sure they were not being overheard.

"I know," Ritchie nodded.

James looked at his friend thoughtfully. He could not help himself from wondering if he could rely on Ritchie in New York. He had been unsuccessful in his search for loyalists he might be able to encourage to move to New York to work for the patriots. James shook his head no. He had not yet reached the point where he would exploit friends for political purposes, and besides, he was not sure that Ritchie had the courage for the job. He had not been able to stand up to his father-in-law, not even on behalf of Remmie and his children. James patted his forlorn friend on the back and rose.

"Stay here, Ritchie. I'll see what Will has to say."

James was making his way around the crowded dance floor filled with laughing and red-faced guests when a sudden shout from the vicinity of the bar caught his attention.

"You clumsy bastard."

James looked in time to see Elizah Bayley viciously shove one of Vivian's house servants. The African had been serving drinks from one of Vivian's two silver trays she had inherited from her father, Ethelburt Randolph. The trays had belonged to her grandmother. The African landed on his back and the tray and drinks crashed to the floor. James stared at Bayley trying to determine what had aroused the bully. His face was red, and he obviously had been drinking heavily.

"And if anybody wants to make something of it, come ahead," Bayley blustered in a loud voice."

The crowd near the bar, still mostly men, drew back. Nobody wanted to tangle with a drunk Bayley. The large man towered over the others. All knew he liked to brawl when drunk, particularly with those half his size.

James saw Vivian standing near the food tables with Elizabet, Bayley's wife, Vivian's childhood friend. She and Bayley lived on Elizabet's father's plantation, the closest to Eastwind. James saw the concern on Vivian's face and Elizabet turn white with shock. He nodded to Vivian to indicate he would handle Bayley. This was not the first time. James knew he would have to swallow his pride and placate Bayley before he turned on other guests. James rushed to the bar.

"What's the trouble, Elizah?" James asked as if the incident had been an accident.

"Don't come near me, you bastard," the obviously drunk Bayley shouted. "You probably put the nigger up to it."

James looked at the men who had been standing near the irate Bayley. Several shrugged their shoulders, and one raised his hands, palms up in gesture that said who knows. James decided quickly the best thing he could do was approach Bayley who was spinning his head from side to side challenging any who stood near him.

"What can I do, Elizah, to solve the problem?" James asked in a quiet voice intended to soothe the raging man.

To his surprise, his tone had the opposite effect. Bayley turned back towards James and shouted in a demented voice.

"I'll kill you Satterfield," and charged across the remaining few feet in a bull rush at the astonished James.

Bayley staggered as he moved. James stepped quickly to his left and the angry giant stumbled to his hands and knees. He looked about and reacting to the shocked people staring at him pushed himself to his feet. James, embarrassed to be involved in a public dispute, hoped the man would regain his senses.

"Come and have a... ."

Before James could finish his sentence, Bayley was swinging at him. James was going to say, "have another drink," but suddenly he too lost his composure. Even crouched, Bayley towered over James. As Bayley swung his massive right fist in a wide arc, James stepped towards the man and with as much strength as he could muster instinctively punched at Bayley underhanded. James' clenched fist traveled twenty inches but it caught Bayley square in the stomach. To James' surprise, Bayley stopped in mid-swing. He groaned loudly and exhaled all the air in his lungs. Bayley bent forward, his chin almost to James' waist, and clutched his mid section. James, who had never been a fighter, not even as a youth—somehow John had always fought the twins' battles—did not take the time to be surprised at his behavior. He swung again with his right hand, this time angling his punch upward from the floor towards Bayley's inviting chin. James had not even paused long enough to realize he had to stop the bull of a man before he could recover. James' balled fist caught Bayley squarely under the jaw and snapped the man's head back with such force that he toppled and land-ed sprawled on the floor sending his arms and legs askew. Bayley's glassy eyes stared unseeing at the ceiling. James immediately grabbed his right hand with his left. The pain he had felt when his blow landed had shot up his arm all the way to his shoulder.

James immediately realized he might have broken his hand. The pain stilled his temper, and he involuntarily jumped up and down twice shaking his hand and arm trying to stop shooting bolts that ran up and down his arm. He clenched and unclenched his fist and realized with relief that he had not broken any bones. He studied his hand and was surprised to see it already swelling. As the protest-ing nerve endings in his arm subsided, James looked down at Bayley. The man remained motionless. James was still angry enough not to care whether he was dead or not.

"I think you're supposed to kick him now," James heard Vivian speak behind him. James had calmed enough to catch her facetious tone.

James spun around. Vivian stood behind him, grinning widely. Elizabeth Bayley stood wide-eyed and white-faced beside Vivian.

"You surprise me, James," Vivian continued with a smile. "Brawling on your only son's wedding day."

Before James could speak, he noticed Elizabet turn blood-red with embarrassment. As James watched, Elizabet's father took her arm and led her across the crowded dance floor towards the front door.

"Good work, James," Elizabet's father called over his shoulder. "If you will have somebody drag the body out front, I'll arrange to get the wagon, and then we'll cart the creature home." Neither Elizabet nor her father looked back towards the still motionless Bayley.

While James stood speechless, staring first at his wife and then the backs of the departing father and daughter, James tried to collect his thoughts.

"Vivian, I'm..." James tried to speak through his parched mouth. He noted he was not even breathing heavily. "Vivian, I... ." James began again but before he could finish, someone on his left began to clap.

James turned in surprise and saw George Mason, grinning broadly, clapping in approval. As James stared, Mason applauded. Within seconds others in the crowded ballroom joined Mason. Soon, the entire room was clapping and cheering loudly.

"Good work, James," Vivian whispered as she kissed James on the cheek. "But don't make a practice of it."

James raised his hands to embrace her, but winced involuntarily at the pain that shot down his arm from his numbed hand.

"I think you had better go soak that hand in some cold water," Vivian laughed, her eyes sparkling with amusement. "I'll go see to Elizabet."

Before James could speak, Vivian turned and hurried after her departing friend and her father. James turned back to examine the still prone Bayley. Skinny Potts and another of Jason's friends from Alexandria were bending over Bayley. Each was grasping one of Bayley's boots. When he stood up, Skinny turned with Bayley's foot tucked under his arm. Noting that James was staring at him, his right hand held protectively against his chest by the left, Skinny laughed.

"Boy, that was some punch," Skinny shook his head from side to side in feigned amazement. "Don't worry, he's breathing. Just taking a little nap. We'll take him out for some air."

Skinny nodded to his companion, and they began to pull the still unconscious Bayley across the floor towards the door. The applause continued until they reached the front door. James felt the blast of cold air as someone held it open for the two young men to drag the inert Bayley out onto the verandah. When the door closed behind them, the clapping gradually subsided only to be replaced by the hum of many voices discussing with approval Bayley's fate. The three Eastwind house servants began again with their music, and the party continued.

"Come over here and sit down," John West, Jason's father-in-law, took James' left arm.

James realized that he felt weak as his rush of excitement abated. He let himself be led across the room to a bench along the wall. One of the servants appeared with a bucket of freezing water.

"If James didn't need that, Bayley might find it refreshing," West laughed.

West took the bucket and set it beside James on the bench. James gingerly lowered his aching hand into the water. He realized it must have come from the horse trough out back. The cold quickly numbed his hand easing the pain. Someone handed him a glass of whiskey, and those gathered around him drank a toast to his quick victory. James was soon smiling and talking as excitedly as his guests. He kept an eye on the front door, anxious that an enraged Elizah not return. The man was not one to let a grudge smolder. James did not relax until Vivian returned in about half an hour to check on him and to reassure him that Bayley, Elizabet and her father had departed for home. James had to laugh at Vivian's description of a hurting Elizah huddled in the back of the two seated chaise holding his jaw with one hand and his stomach with the other.

The wedding celebration continued for another hour then began to run down as guests departed in the twilight hours for the nearby mansions and Alexandria. James had no doubt that the celebrating would continue as most of the participants, particularly the males, were enjoying their hilarity. The women, worried about the long cold rides in the winter nightfall, were insistent. Soon, only those staying at Eastwind remained. James was relieved he had accepted Vivian's suggestion that only the Satterfield kin from Loudoun be given the hospitality of Eastwind. James had been willing to crowd as many of his friends into the mansion as possible, but Vivian had been adamant. Now that the excitement had abated, James suffered not only from his aching hand but also from a gently throbbing headache. He even welcomed the cup of hot tea that he shared with Vivian, his father and his brother and sister and their families before the hot fire. Even though the Satterfields made a small crowd all by themselves, they were family and provided comfort not emotional drain.

Chapter 14
Eastwind, Alexandria
January, 1776

At midnight following the wedding, a soft snow began to drop. As the hours passed, the flakes grew larger and the winter storm increased in intensity. A strong wind whirled the snow blanket into drifts that began to build against fences and buildings. Inside Eastwind, James slept fitfully. The others, exhausted by the physical and emotional drain of the day, were oblivious to the gathering storm. James, troubled by the ache of his swollen hand, heard the winds increase. Once, he had risen to look out in the darkness and see the swirling snow, but Vivian had ordered him back to bed. Finally, near dawn, the pain in his hand subsided enough to allow James a few hours of rest.

By the time the family had gathered for a buffet style breakfast in the large dining room, snow had smothered the area.

"There's at least eight inches, and it's still falling," Young Tom announced to his assembled clan as James entered the room. The adults were seated around the walnut dining table with the children squatting on the floor before the roaring fireplaces. All had heaping plates of fried potatoes, scrambled eggs and strong country bacon before them.

"Good morning, James," Young Tom welcomed his son. "Afraid you're going to share our company for a few days."

"Eight inches," James quoted his father. James had planned to return to Alexandria this morning, and he knew the family had a full day's ride back to Loudoun.

"And drifting," his brother Will added, chewing on a thick piece of the salty bacon.

The food all looked too greasy to James who after his difficulty with Bayley had let himself be plied with too many glasses of celebratory whiskey.

"Will you have some fried potatoes and bacon?" Vivian smiled helpfully at her husband.

James immediately decided she had noted his queasiness and was continuing to enjoy herself at his cost. He should not have been surprised at Vivian's reaction to the contretemps. Vivian did not react like other women. She obviously was highly bemused by the fact her normally imperturbable husband had been provoked into a brawl.

"Does your hand hurt, dear?" Vivian asked sweetly, feigning concern. "You must be more careful about whom you hit. And where."

All the children caught Vivian's intent and laughed uproariously at James' expression of dismay.

"Thank you for the advice, dear," James replied with as much dignity as he could muster, "and for the offer of assistance. I think I will only have a cup of chocolate and toast this morning."

"I don't blame you, dear," Vivian exaggerated the concern in her voice, making no move to fulfill her offer to assist her husband.

"Don't trouble yourself, dear," James said. I'll serve myself."

After breakfast, the family dispersed throughout the house. The children disappeared upstairs to dress for a sleigh ride already arranged by Vivian. Hardy country children, they were exhilarated by the season's first snowfall. Vivian and Sally and Will's wife adjourned to the kitchen where all three women needlessly supervised the house slaves in their continuing effort to restore the mansion to order after the previous day's chaos. James, Will and Young Tom gathered in the dining room in front of the large fire. Outside, the snow continued to fall.

"We're going to be here for a few days, James," Will observed ruefully. "Look's like we'll get at least a foot."

"And its drifting," James added.

"No loss," Young Tom contributed. "Work around the farm can wait in winter. Sally's relatives and the indentured fellow are taking care of the livestock."

James studied his father as he spoke. Young Tom was clearly aging and not just physically. James noted his father had trouble remembering the names of people, even George White, the indentured helper who had lived with the family for the past two years. Young Tom now looked just like Old Tom, James' grandfather, had looked when the family was young and living on the farm in the foothills. Those had been carefree days, James thought, at least for the kids.

"It's good to have the family back together," James began, pausing when he thought of his twin. "Except for John. I had hoped he would have been able to come."

"He would have if he could," Young Tom admonished.

"Jason's got himself a pretty bride," Will said, changing the subject. Young Tom easily slid into irascibility these days.

"Just like your mother was," Young Tom observed.

James studied his father. Sally had told him that their father was missing their mother now even more than he had in the early days after her death. Sally had asked James if he remembered how Old Tom used to sit by his smithy in his rocking chair and stare for hours at Rebecca's grave. Old Tom had buried her on the spot where the Indians had brutally killed her. Sally had said with tears in her eyes that now Young Tom had taken to sitting in the same chair and staring at the same gravesite where he had buried his wife Agnes near his mother and father. Now, the two women and Old Tom lay interred in the family plot.

"I miss her more than ever," Young Tom said softly.

James had to strain to hear his father's voice.

"Time passes so quickly. I remember when you kids were young, and we were so happy on the farm with Agnes and Old Tom."

James and Will exchanged worried glances as they nodded agreement with their father. He had always been the strong one they could turn to when in trouble. James had often felt that as long as his father lived he would always have someone to support him in times of trouble. Now, Young Tom was growing old. It was like Young Tom was regressing to his childhood, and he and his children were exchanging roles. The thought troubled James. He did not want to assume the responsibility for his father when he became a child in an old man's body.

"The hardest part is living without your mother," Young Tom continued. James noticed a tear trickle down over his father's wrinkled face. James had never before seen his father cry.

"She worked so hard," Young Tom continued. "Life on the frontier in those days was so brutal for women. They raised their families, sewing all their clothes, doing the cooking and laundering and making candles and growing vegetables besides working in the fields like a man. And the savages... ." Young Tom stopped.

James knew that his father had been a young man when his mother had been scalped and mutilated by the Indians. He recognized how deep the hurt must have been. His own mother had died of a weak heart and that had been awful but to die being cut to pieces by screaming savages was beyond comprehension. One of the reasons James had no faith in the concept of a God was his belief that no super being could permit his creations to commit such atrocities as men imposed on each other. James could not accept the rationalizations offered by the preachers, not in any way.

"But life goes on," Young Tom regained control of his emotions. "Jason and Lily will start the next generation of Satterfields. My great grandchildren," Young Tom mused.

"You know," he continued as Will and James listened silently. "We only live for two generations beyond our own."

James did not understand what his father meant. He looked at his brother, but Will only shook his head indicating he did not understand either.

"I, of course, knew my father and mother and my four grandparents well. Just like you. You remember Old Tom and me and Agnes. You don't remember Rebecca, your grandma so clearly, but she died so young. You know everything about me. I told you every story I knew, but dad, Old Tom to you, was just a nice old man who treated you kindly and who sat in his rocking chair and grieved his wife. You don't know what he was like as a young man, just as you were, with parents and old grandparents. We only continue to live in the minds of our descendants for two generations, then all knowledge of our existence, how we really were, whether we were good or bad, brave or weak, that we existed, dies. Our children, that's you, and our grandchildren know us, but not our great grandchildren. If they know anything about their great granddaddy, it's just the recollection of an old man about to die, and the memory itself is faded and blurry. You don't know anything about your great granddaddy, John, Old Tom's father. I do. He was a blacksmith, like old Tom and Will here. I'm sad because Jason's boy, my great grandson, will never know me, and neither will your boys' sons, Will." Young Tom paused to study his youngest son. "Not one of them will ever know I existed. Life is so short," he continued. "We only live two generations. Our sons and our grandsons know us. We live in their memories just as your mother and grandmother still live in my memory and yours, but then, the great grandchildren come and the great grandparents are unknown, just mysterious ancestors who have passed along their genes to be mixed with others and then forgotten. I don't know what its all about, James. You're the family smart one. Tell me. What's the purpose of life?"

James stared at his father and swallowed hard to force the lump of emotion back down his throat. Tears began to stream down his face. He looked at Will who was also crying. A Satterfield trait, he decided.

"I don't know, dad. I don't know what it's all about," James almost stammered. "You're right. We only live for two generations after our own." For the first time in his life, James felt his own mortality.

After James spoke, the three Satterfield men sat in front of the fire, each lost in contemplation of mortality. They thought of unknown Satterfields responsible for their existence. Not one of them considered the house in which they sat. It had been built by the Ethelburt Randolphs, Vivian's now dead father and mother, and not one of the three grieved or celebrated the men and women of that blood stream that would now mix with theirs to produce Jason's offspring. They pondered only the loss of their Satterfield ancestors whose genes they carried. When James and Will finally, quietly, left the room, leaving Young Tom to doze in front of the fire, James knew he would never forget the conversation. He vowed someday to share it with Vivian and Jason. His father had made him realize how finite and precious were each minute allotted to a human that he had to find a way to share more of it with those he loved most.

The snow continued to fall for another twenty-four hours. Twenty-four inches blanketed Eastwind and the neighboring mansions. Travel ceased, and the isolated wedding guests played, at first. Eventually, they got on each other's nerves as human foibles emerged during the long periods of confinement. The snow was a light powdery one that swirled in the wind gusts building drifts as deep as six feet. James, who had considered harnessing a strong team to Eastwind's solitary sleigh and forcing his way to Alexandria, abandoned the idea and spent the week sharing memories and experiences with his family in a depth that had not been plumbed since childhood. Young Tom, as family elder, was the focal point of much of the tale telling, and he enjoyed himself fully. A sparkle appeared in his eye and demeanor that had been absent for years. James took advantage of the enforced idleness to discuss Ritchie Randolph's problems. To James' surprise, Will at first reacted negatively to the idea of purchasing Ritchie's Loudoun lands.

"There's no way I'm going to help one of those English loving bastards escape," Will declared.

James had never known Will to be political. Will had always been a friendly, outgoing boy and man who brought cheer into the lives of everyone he met. He had a circle of friends who gathered at the smithy to share stories while he worked the iron, laughing and cheering each other with good humor. Finally, James prevailed, and Will reluctantly agreed to use Satterfield Legacy money to purchase Ritchie's Loudoun lands, but at a price that embarrassed James. James' only solace was knowing that Ritchie would be delighted to sell the land at any price.

Finally, the weather changed abruptly, as it was prone to do in Fairfax County. The winds abated, and the clouds dissipated. The sun focused its rays on the frozen earth, and in a matter of hours water drops began to fall from Eastwind's roof and poke holes in banked snow. By evening, the fine, powdery snow had settled several inches, compressing itself into a moist, messy mass. Young Tom stepped from the verandah and tested the snow. His foot sank in about ten inches.

"Two days," he declared with his farmer's certitude, "and we can start out."

James looked skeptically at the soggy snow still heaped high in drifts.

"I'm not sure, Dad," James observed. "The snow could be impassable between here and Leesburg."

Young Tom studied his son with an old man's scorn.

"Two days," Young Tom declared with finality.

True to his word, Young Tom rose at dawn two days later and hitched his two muscular farm teams to the wagon. Will, unable to let his father, Sally and her two boys start out alone on what could be a difficult journey, followed suit. Vivian, an early riser, woke James from a deep sleep and told him what was happening. James, unable to let his family depart without him, grumbled as he hastily dressed to join them. He sent instructions to the stables for the field hands to hook up a strong team to the Eastwind sleigh. The least he could do, he thought, was go first with the sleigh and break a path on the familiar road to Alexandria so the others could follow.

By the time James reached the front door, the entire family was gathered on the verandah. The travelers were all bundled in their heavy farm clothes. Vivian had the front door wide open and a string of house servants carried blankets and comforters to be stacked in the wagons. Young Tom climbed with difficulty on to the driver's seat of his wagon. Sally's children, excited about the pending adventure, scrambled into the mound of blankets in the wagon bed. James helped Sally and Will's wife climb into the wagon to join them. They had decided to ride together as far as Leesburg, some forty miles ahead of them. Will and his two boys patiently waited on the bench of the second wagon. The horses in both teams snorted and pranced, pounding the snow under their large feet. The snow had continued to melt overnight, and the earth underneath was coated with a soft veneer of mud. Since each wagon had four large horses pulling it, the snow under their feet began to turn a rich brown.

"Pa," James called. "I have the sleigh hooked up."

"I'd be blind not to see it," Young Tom laughed. "Going for a pleasure ride?" He turned and looked with disdain at the handsome team of matched stallions who had obviously never pulled their weight in a plowed field.

"I thought I'd go first and break a trail for you," James said.

"With that light thing," Young Tom laughed scornfully at the thought of the fragile sleigh designed to ride on top of the snow not smash through it. Young Tom waved to Vivian who he had already kissed good-by, spoke softly to his team, and snapped the reins lightly on their backs. Snorting loudly, the four horses moved out easily pulling their lightly loaded wagon behind them.

"Shit," James swore under his breath. Vivian, who was standing beside him, took his arm to calm her husband who seldom used profanity, and called her farewells to her departing in-laws. As the wagons crunched down the farm lane leading away from Eastwind, Vivian turned to James.

"You had better hurry if you are going to break trail for them," she prompted, not trying to hide the amusement she felt.

James watched his stubborn father's stooped shoulders bounce as the wagon smashed its way effortlessly through the first drift.

"But I haven't even had any breakfast," James protested.

He looked at Vivian who smiled demurely back. He glanced after the departing wagons and was torn by indecision. Finally, he grabbed his wife, kissed her on the lips, hugged her once then ran to the sleigh.

"I'll take Joseph with me," he called, referring to the field slave who stood patiently holding the sleigh's team. "He can bring the sleigh back."

"Don't hurry," Vivian called. "I'm not sure those old farm horses will be able to keep up," Vivian laughed as she watched Young Tom turn his teams onto the Alexandria Road.

James, now seated on the sleigh with the field slave at his side, looked again at the farm wagons as they easily made their way down the road. He looked at the tracks left by the wagons and finally smiled.

"I think I'll let them break the path for a mile or two," he declared ruefully. James waved to Vivian and coached the sleigh's team into motion. The horses, which had been bred for speed and beauty, started slowly, less interested in testing the snow's challenge to their strength than the muscular farm teams.

James and the Satterfields had been gone about three hours and Vivian was in the Eastwind ball room directing the house staff as it stacked the borrowed benches and pews near the front door—the next day was Sunday and they had to be returned to the two churches—when the front door burst open and a tearful Elizabet Bayley burst in.

"Oh, Vivian," she called mournfully.

Vivian embraced her childhood friend and led her to the warmth of the sitting room fireplace. This was their first meeting since the brief skirmish between their husbands on Jason's wedding day. Vivian, who assumed her emotional childhood friend wanted to apologize for her husband's boorish behavior, took Elizabet's coat, handed it to a house servant who had followed the rushing visitor, and turned back to her friend.

"Will you have some chocolate?" Vivian asked.

"No thank you, Viv," Elizabet used Vivian's childhood name. "I... ." she began, then broke into tears.

"There's nothing to worry about," Vivian consoled her friend. "Elizah was just drunk."

"Oh," Elizabet sobbed, "that's not it. He's always drunk."

Elizabet raised her head and looked directly at Vivian for the first time. With shock, Vivian noticed the purplish bruise around Elizabet's right eye and the dark red and black welts on her face.

"My God, Elizabet, what happened?" Vivian raised her voice.

Elizabet lowered her head and continued to cry. Vivian walked quickly to the door of the sitting room, ordered two cups of chocolate from the waiting maid, then shut the door for privacy.

Vivian waited patiently. After several minutes of frantic sobbing, Elizabet slowly regained control of herself.

"This is about last night, not James," Elizabet finally began to explain. "Elizah has been sitting alone drinking ever since the incident," she began. "He didn't eat, just sat in his room drinking. He blames me for what happened. He said if I weren't your friend, he would not have been here. He doesn't like you or James. I think he's jealous."

"Elizabet," Vivian said firmly. "Elizah doesn't like anyone. He's a mean, selfish man."

"Last night I tried to creep into bed, and he was waiting for me. He hit me. He hurt me bad. I tried not to scream, but he hit me so hard that I had to get help. It's not the first time. I'm so embarrassed."

Vivian pulled her chair beside Elizabet's and put her arm around her friend's shoulders.

"I know," Vivian patted Elizabet who began crying again. "You should get free of him," she whispered.

"But I am," Elizabet sobbed harder.

When she finally stopped crying, she resumed her story, gasping as she talked.

"Daddy heard me screaming. He got his gun and came running. He threatened to kill Elizah. He hit him with the barrel, then made Elizah go downstairs. Daddy sent for two of the big field hands. They threw all Elizah's clothes out the window into the snow. They put Elizah in a buggy and made him go away.

Daddy said if he ever came back he would kill him." Elizabet stared at Vivian wide-eyed. "What shall I do?"

"Do? Cheer. You're lucky he's gone. Too bad your father didn't shoot him," Vivian declared, meaning every word she said. Neither Vivian nor any of her friends could understand why Elizabet had married the oaf in the first place.

"But he's my husband. What shall I do?" Elizabet asked mournfully. "What will everyone say?"

"They'll say good riddance," Vivian declared. "And I'll tell you what we shall do. We'll celebrate."

Vivian walked to the door, called to the maid who was preparing chocolate and told her to stop the chocolate and instead bring the sherry. Vivian left the door open and returned to the fireplace where she put another log on the large andirons then waited for the maid to appear. Recognizing an emergency, the girl hurried into the room with the crystal decanter and two glasses rattling precariously. After setting the tray on a table near where Elizabet sat, the girl rushed from the room. Vivian poured two small glasses of the dark red wine, handed one to Elizabet, and then stood facing her. She raised her glass in toast and declared:

"Good riddance to the fat pig. May he freeze in Hell. "

Elizabet's eyes shined as she sipped the wine and stared at Vivian.

Vivian turned and threw her empty glass into the fireplace where it shattered. Both women watched as the glass shards reflected the roaring flames.

"Oh Vivian," Elizabet exclaimed. "Your best crystal." Despite her misery, Elizabet was impressed with her friend's vehemence.

"Drink you wine and throw the glass," Vivian ordered.

Elizabet obediently sipped the sherry, then rose and walked to the fireplace. She looked at Vivian for instructions.

"Throw it. That's your old life. Smash it."

Elizabet turned back to the fireplace and threw the crystal goblet as hard as she could. The glass smashed against the field stone front of the fireplace.

"Oh shit," Elizabeth spoke loudly. "I can't even hit the damned fire."

She turned back towards Vivian who to her surprise broke out laughing. Elizabeth stared at her friend, then began to giggle herself. Finally, she laughed until her face hurt. When they had regained control of their emotions, Vivian spoke first.

"And we will never speak that oaf's name again. "

Chapter 15
Quebec, Lancaster, Boston, New York, Alexandria
Spring 1776

Lieutenant John Andre's passage from England to his assignment with his regiment, the 7th Foot, was a most unusual one. Not only had he stopped in Philadelphia where he had seen the tall Virginia colonel named Washington arrive to attend the illegal congress, he had continued on to Boston and then back to New York. From there, he had journeyed by sloop up the Hudson to Albany. He had walked from that colonial outpost to Lake George. A boat had conveyed him up the lake to the waterway connecting Lake George with Lake Champlain. He paused at Fort Ticonderoga then followed the Richelieu River into Canada. After a visit to the British outpost at St. Johns, a place he later described as one of the most dismal he had ever seen, he had continued northwest to Montreal, and then onward to his assignment in Quebec.

To one and all, Andre had concealed the fact that he had been appointed one of his regiment's intelligence officers and had been dispatched on this unusual route in order to acquire first hand knowledge of the men and terrain he would one day face in arms. Andre's chief regret about the trip developed the day he learned that the Virginia colonel had been appointed commander-in-chief of the rebel army. If only, the ambitious Andre speculated that day, if only he had taken the opportunity to cultivate the man who was to become the enemy's general, he would have been the toast of the 7th Foot.

Andre enjoyed his Quebec assignment. Being eager, he would have preferred the battlefield where he could demonstrate his courage and win honor sufficient to enhance his reputation and rank, but Quebec was pleasant. His first night at his new duty station had begun with a fancy ball; the following winter brought heavy snows, sleigh rides and parties with the fun seeking young daughters of the local French aristocracy. Andre, still new to his profession, was fascinated by everything that he encountered. Andre played until the day that a countryman from St. Johns galloped into the city to report that the rebels led by two unknowns, Ethan Allen and Benedict Arnold, had captured Fort Ticonderoga. The rebels had also raided St. Johns but had been driven off. The news shocked many, but not Lieutenant Andre. Fort Ticonderoga and its casual garrison had not impressed him, and he considered St. Johns a disgrace as a British military outpost.

The British reacted by sending to St. Johns units from the 7th Foot including young John Andre whose task was to gather information about the plans of the enemy. The reinforcements spent the summer improving the outpost's defenses. Andre's sources, traders who crossed between the lines, returned from Fort Ticonderoga with reports that the rebels had selected a General Schuyler to lead an American army against Quebec. Andre, like his comrades at St. Johns, found the rumors laughable. If the rebels came, they gloated, they would fall into an English trap. The 7th Foot wanted nothing more than to meet the rebels on an open battlefield, but nothing happened at St. Johns other than a few skirmishes with rebel scouts. Then, in November, a ragged rebel army appeared and laid siege to St. Johns. After seven weeks of bombardment and skirmishing, food and powder ran low and the English surrendered. Lieutenant Andre found himself a prisoner of one of the most disreputable appearing armies he had ever encountered.

Andre, his fellow officers and the surrendered ranks were marched southward. At Fort Ticonderoga, Andre met and dined with a considerate rebel leader, Major General Philip Schuyler. The march southward continued over trails that Andre had followed on his journey northward. At Lake George the weather turned bitter cold, and Andre gasped with relief when he learned they would overnight at the very same inn that he had stayed previously. The northern winter was no longer a lark. The log cabin was already jammed, and Andre found himself sharing a bed with a rebel officer who said his name was Colonel Henry Knox. Andre, still a lieutenant, had a difficult time believing that the young man who appeared the same age as Andre himself was already a colonel. Knox, despite his rank and ignoring the fact that Andre was a prisoner, treated Andre with courtesy. He did not tell the young captive that his mission was to collect the former English cannon from Fort Ticonderoga and convey it over the mountains to Boston where it would be used to drive General William Howe's redcoats into the sea.

At Albany, the prisoners tarried for over a month while their captors tried to decide what to do with them. The English officers, free on their parole not to attempt to escape, roamed about the village that Andre had previously dismissed as being totally without charm. To his surprise, Major General Schuyler included Andre with several senior officers in an invitation to dinner. Despite his prejudices, Andre had been impressed. Schuyler, their commanding captor, treated the guests with grace and courtesy. Andre almost liked some of the charming rebel officers who attended.

When the time came to continue their journey, the British were surprised. Their destination was changed from Connecticut to a place called Lancaster in Pennsylvania. The Redcoats, officers and men, were split into two groups. Andre's proceeded southward via Philadelphia. There, Andre, still on parole and beginning to enjoy himself, met a young charmer by the name of Peggy Shippen. He was so entranced by her that he painted her picture for her before continuing on his journey to his place of exile. Finally, Andre and his companions reached Lancaster, some seventy miles from Philadelphia. Andre and another lieutenant from the 7th Foot were lodged with a family named Cope. Restricted to a six-mile area circumscribed around Lancaster, Andre and his friend settled into their life as prisoners.

In Cambridge, George Washington spent the winter rebuilding his army. Thousands of his militia departed when their enlistments expired on the last day of the old year, and for several weeks until their replacements arrived, General Washington's siege lines had gaping holes, but General William Howe, intent on passing his winter confinement in as comfortable a fashion as possible, could not be bothered with taking his troops into the icy Massachusetts' fields, gaps or not.

At the end of January 1776, Washington began to receive reports from Boston indicating that the English were outfitting their ships. It appeared that Howe was preparing to depart Boston, and Washington, whose own views had been reinforced by his conversations with James, was convinced that Howe was preparing to evacuate Boston and move on New York as part of a grand strategy to split the colonies and isolate New England. Washington had already asked the Congress how he should react if the British attempted this maneuver, but the only instruction he received was silence. Washington knew what he had to do; he had learned enough from old Governor Dinwiddie to understand that it was advisable to share responsibility for risky actions whenever possible. When John Adams who was in Massachusetts visiting his wife Abigail and his family paid a courtesy call on Washington at Cambridge, the commanding general seized the opportunity. He described the tactical situation for Adams and tabled his concerns.

"What in your opinion should I do?" Washington asked Adams. To Washington's surprise, the pudgy New Englander replied promptly.

"Take control of New York first and build your fortifications."

Washington silently contemplated the advice. Adams, as if reading the general's mind, continued:

"You are commander of all forces with full authority to act as you think best. Do so."

At these words, Washington smiled broadly.

"Thank you, John," Washington spoke seriously. "I will order General Lee to move into the city immediately."

John Adams nodded. Major General Charles Lee was a professional military man and was a good choice to place the necessary fortifications.

"And you?" Adams asked in his forthright manner.

"I'll stay here until General Howe leaves. Then, I will occupy Boston, garrison it, and take my army to New York to join General Lee."

Washington spoke more confidently than he felt. He knew two things that troubled him. Howe with his army under sail could travel faster that Washington and his army could walk. Washington risked giving Howe the opportunity to take New York with a minimal struggle because the small force under Lee would not be able to hold back the numerically superior English. Washington had doubts about the ability of his full army to hold back the English. Secondly, from his visits to the city, Washington knew that New York would be a most difficult place to defend.

At the end of January, Washington received bad news. Montgomery and Arnold's march on Canada had ended in failure. Montgomery had been killed, and Arnold, who along with Ethan Allen had been the conqueror of Fort Ticonderoga, had been seriously wounded. Losses had been heavy; even worse, the English were now free to use Canada as a base to launch a drive down the Hudson to separate the colonies.

Strange reports began to emanate from New York. Lee, apparently suffering from gout, had delayed his takeover of the city. Lee and the Connecticut troops who had been assigned to assist him were stalled in Stamford. Meanwhile, the Committee of Safety in New York had sent Washington an odd letter. It informed him that the city had no powder and no defensive works and recommended that Washington delay his plans to send troops to occupy it. Washington worried because he recognized the voice of loyalists speaking. He had always suspected that a majority of the citizens of the colonies' largest city looked eastward rather than west. Washington decided the letter's author's words concealed an English general's voice and ignored the bogus plea.

In early February, Washington almost appealed to James for assistance. He had staff problems. Edmund Randolph returned to Virginia to settle estate questions occasioned by the death of his Uncle Peyton Randolph who had died in October. Washington's difficulties were enhanced when Joseph Reed visited Philadelphia to meet obligations arising from his ongoing legal practice. Their replacements proved unsatisfactory, distracting Washington at a time when he needed to concentrate on building his army and determining what Howe planned. Fortunately for James, Washington did not give in to impulse and made do while the replacements struggled.

In February, the reports from Boston noted that the English were placing bedding and heavy guns on board their ships. Barrels of water were being onloaded, and bakers were working overtime producing hard biscuits. The loyalists who had flocked to Boston with their families were worried. Rumor had it that Howe was preparing to sail to either New York or Virginia.

Washington had made his plans for New York, but word of Virginia as a possible destination for the British army worried him. There was no way he could march his army to Virginia in time to prepare defenses against the English. Virginia was made for a sea campaign, and the English controlled the ocean. Washington had no navy, no ships for fighting, and none for transport. On board his ships, Howe could sail into the Chesapeake Bay and strike anyplace in five hundred miles along the Virginia waterways from Williamsburg to Alexandria to near Baltimore. Washington belatedly worried that his home colony could be lost before he could react. Recognizing he could do nothing about such a problem but agonize, he set his staff to working on plans for the formation of a rebel navy while he continued with his tactical formulations for Boston.

In March, Washington estimated he had about 14,000 farmers and townsmen, most with some kind of arms including pitchforks and antiquated muskets, facing 8,000 English professional soldiers. Seeking an edge, he ordered Colonel Henry Knox to move his cannon from Fort Ticonderoga into positions on the hills overlooking Boston. If the British were planning on withdrawing, Washington hoped to hurry them on their way. On the night of March 2nd, Knox commenced his cannonade. The English guns returned the fire. They exchanged fire sporadically with minimum results over the following days until on March 8th, under a flag of truce, a delegation of citizens from Boston, accompanied by a solitary British officer, appeared. They carried a letter from the Selectmen of Boston to General Washington. It reported that General Howe and his army had decided to withdraw from Boston and stated that a committee had asked the general about his intentions towards the town. Howe replied he had no plans to destroy the city unless Washington's forces "molested" his while they were withdrawing.

Washington had his doubts about the bonafides of the message. He consulted his advisers and decided to reply succinctly. Since the proposal contained in the message was not authenticated in any way by General Howe, Washington planned to ignore it. Washington did not point out that if the English were planning to sail away, there was not much he could do about it. His cannon could do little damage to the English ships. The English continued to load their ships. On Sunday morning, March 17th, Saint Patrick's Day, the wharves suddenly filled with uniformed men. They boarded long boats and were ferried to the ships waiting at anchor. Excited reports from Washington's hilltop sentries noted that the English were withdrawing from their lines.

On Washington's order, the American guns remained silent. Undisturbed, the English completed their withdrawal in full view of the rebel armies on the hilltops. Washington sat silently and alone in his office with his door shut. He quietly reviewed the situation. He had won a major battle. The English were leaving Boston as he had anticipated, but now he had a major problem. He had to determine where they were going and what he would do about it. He put thoughts of his native Virginia out of his mind and concentrated on New York.

The last English soldier boarded his ship, and the fleet weighed anchor and sailed a few miles only to anchor again. They spent the night in the harbor, and then the next night and the night after. The English had boarded their ships only to stop in the harbor. All knew they could return. They did not. Finally, on March 27th they sailed.

Meanwhile, the rebels streamed into Boston. Washington found some damage had been wreaked by the occupation, but Boston was in a better condition than he expected. Most of the physical harm had been done by the encamped soldiers who had torn down fences and buildings to obtain firewood to keep themselves warm.

On March 18th, 1776, General Washington sent a vanguard from his army to New York. Brigades commanded by Heath, Sullivan, Greene and Spenser began their quick march south. Washington placed Major General Israel Putnam in overall command. General Lee had recently been relieved in New York and dispatched along with his dogs to Williamsburg to take charge of the Southern campaign. Washington, after securing Boston and reassuring himself of Howe's intentions, planned to march his the main body of his army to defend New York City.

The British fleet entered the Atlantic and turned northward, eschewing both New York and Virginia.

American fishing boats tracked the English ships to Halifax where General William Howe disembarked his army. There, he rested and regrouped his forces while awaiting the requested reinforcements led by his brother. Word had arrived of Admiral Richard Lord Howe's coup; the older brother had been appointed Commander of His Majesty's Fleet in North America, Commander-in-Chief of all His Majesty's Forces in North America, thus he became William's commanding officer, and a Member of a two person Peace Commission; after much negotiation, General William Howe was made the second member. The Howe brothers were in charge. Since the family remained firm in its belief that the problem should not be solved on the battlefield, both brothers, despite the fact that they commanded His Majesty's army and navy in North America, continued to believe they would win at the conference table with a minimum of American and English blood shed. After all, despite their differences, the English and Americans were brothers.

The "Eagle," Admiral Lord Howe's flagship, set sail from the Isle of Wright at dawn on the morning of May 11, 1776. On board, among others, were Lord Richard and his secretary Ambrose Serle, a civilian. Lord Howe had selected Serle himself.

Lord Dartmouth who was personally acquainted with Serle had recommended him highly. Serle, in his early thirties and married with a daughter named Betsy, served as Solicitor and Clerk of Reports for the Board of Trade. A rigidly moral and ascetic man, Serle had a novel pet theory. He argued in a thesis that he drafted in 1770 that the establishment of a dominant episcopate was essential to the maintenance of the unity of the empire. In North America, Serle argued, the Anglican Church should be allocated a large glebe in each colony which would be used to support the church in that colony. Glebes were not unknown in the colonies; each parish set aside a tract of land, a glebe, which belonged to the church and was farmed to support the needs of the local preacher. Serle simply proposed the expansion of the glebe in scale. He argued that the power and authority that accrued to the Anglican Church as a result of the massive glebe system would provide the Crown with the leverage it needed to maintain the empire. Simply put, Serle believed that the colonies could be controlled via the church hierarchy, and all the Crown need do was make the church more powerful with land grants.

Richard Lord Howe thought Serle's religious rigmarole naive, but he hired the man for his secretarial skills. Lord Dartmouth assured him that Serle as a drafter and organizer had no peer. Howe liked the fact that the man was a stern Christian, a most moderate user of strong drink, and a devoted family man. Since Serle's family would be left behind in London, Howe reasoned Serle would devote himself to Lord Howe's affairs with the passion of a Christian disciple.

After a month of high seas, icebergs, satisfactory religious services and unappetizing food, the "Eagle" reached Halifax shrouded in a thick fog on the morning of June 21st. The "Eagle's" captain, with the Fleet Admiral's permission, decided to set anchor and wait for the fog to lift rather than risk hitting a rock and losing his valuable cargo. Lord Howe, Commander-in-Chief of His Majesty's Army and Navy in North America, had reached his domain and his word was now law, whether the rebelling colonists recognized that hard fact or not. The "Eagle" anchored near a Halifax schooner commanded by a lieutenant in Lord Howe's navy; the eager officer reported the bad news. General William Howe, the admiral's brother, had grown tired of waiting for the "Eagle" and several days before their arrival had set sail with his restored army for New York. The lieutenant raised Lord Richard's spirits by noting that word had been received from Quebec reporting that General Clinton and his army had arrived safely from London. This meant that two important pieces were soon to be in place to implement the Howe strategy: an army in Canada poised to drive southward, and an army in New York prepared to move northward up the Hudson for the strategic link up that would isolate the hotheads of New England. With that accomplished, Admiral Howe expected that the Peace Commission that he and his brother formed would be able to resolve the problems dividing London and its colonies. The fact that Washington's troops now occupied Boston troubled Lord Richard not at all.

On Sunday, June 23d, 1776, the fog lifted and "Eagle" sailed into Halifax harbor. Serle took advantage of the opportunity to send a letter to his wife and daughter, Betsy. The Admiral paused long enough to accept the required protocol visits from his local staff then ordered that the "Eagle" sail that very evening to join his fleet and troops in the south. Serle was disappointed that he had not had an opportunity to attend divine services or even set foot on land and tour Halifax.

As "Eagle" sailed southward, the wind remained brisk and the temperature rose into the eighties. About noon on Friday, July 5th, the crew hallooed the sighting of the eastern tip of Long Island. A stubborn fog obscured the view and again delayed the "Eagle." When the fog finally lifted, Serle and the Admiral were disappointed to learn the crew had been mistaken; they were off Nantucket, some one hundred leagues from Sandy Hook, the entrance to New York harbor. To add to their disappointment, the wind subsided, and their sixty-four-gun man-of-war wallowed, helplessly becalmed, until Tuesday morning when the wind freshened. On July 11th they sighted Long Island for real. All day they sailed along its shore and at evening time reached the mouth of Sandy Hook. The Admiral accepted his captain's suggestion that they lay to until morning then land in New York on July 12th. Upon arrival Sir Richard was greeted by all of the ships of war in the harbor with what Ambrose Serle considered to be a "glorious" salute.

As soon as they anchored, General William Howe, accompanied by Admiral Shuldham, who Lord Howe was replacing as commander of the North American Fleet, visited the "Eagle." After a warm welcome, the visitors cast a pall on the occasion by announcing that on July 4th the rebels in their illegal congress had issued an insulting Declaration of Independence. The news shocked Lord Richard, as his brother William had known it would. The simple act of declaring their colonies free and independent undercut the Admiral's plans for his Peace Commission. Immediately, the two brothers retreated to the Admiral's cabin to confer.

"If only I had arrived two weeks sooner," Lord Richard lamented.

"With your commission you would have been able to forestall this mad act," William agreed. "We had reports from Philadelphia that they had appointed a committee to draft such a proclamation, but we thought it just talk and would amount to nothing."

"We will have to recoup, somehow, William," Lord Richard tried to reassure himself as much as his brother.

"I fear those who have said that the hot heads had this in mind from the beginning were right," William began.

"Yes, but they are still in the minority," Lord Richard insisted. He had no intention of permitting any one ill-considered act, Declaration of Independence or not, thwart his mission, not even if it contained harsh criticism of the King himself, which it did.

At the Admiral's suggestion, the two brothers returned to the "Eagle's" quarter-deck where they consulted with Admiral Shuldham and the rest of the welcoming party. Lord Richard did not want to convey the impression that the Declaration of Independence had discouraged him.

"From where we stand," Admiral Shuldham began pompously, "you have a clear view of New York City and the rebel fortifications. "

Lord Richard, along with Ambrose Serle and other members of their group, turned to study the shoreline.

"Please use my glass," Shuldham offered Lord Richard his opened telescope. "If you look just to the left of that small knoll where I have it focused, you will be able to see Washington's headquarters."

Lord Richard took the glass and studied the area that had been indicated to him. He could see no building that looked like an army headquarters, but he could make out shabbily dressed soldiers scurrying about the streets. He lowered the glass and silently studied the shore. His thoughts were of Washington and what he had to do to bring the man to the peace table. With the exception of his brother, the others assumed he was considering how he would deploy his forces to drive the rebels from New York City so he could establish his base for the northern campaign to link up with Johnny Burgoyne. Already the English foot soldiers who were tired of the cramped confines of the ships were anxious to learn of Black Dick's plans. The Admiral's affectionately bestowed nickname, "Black Dick," had spread from fleet to army.

Black Dick's decision as he stood at the rail studying his unseen enemy was not about how to deploy his troops. Instead, he opted to make known his role as Peace Commissioner and attempt to neutralize the impact of the untimely Declaration of Independence. The Admiral wheeled on his heel, indicating with an inclusive wave that William, Admiral Shuldham and his secretary, Ambrose Serle, should accompany him to his cabin. There, as Serle took notes, Lord Richard dictated his first message to the colonists.

As Peace Commissioner—he assumed his brother William would do as he directed—he was empowered to protect all Americans loyal to the King, but he had no fiat to negotiate with anybody until they recognized the authority of the King and disbanded their illegal armies and congresses. This caveat put Lord Howe in a difficult position. The rebels had to surrender before he could offer them conditions. He was authorized to work out compromises only after the rebels capitulated. He could not entice them to the peace table with promises. He recognized that the advocates of force had tied his hands, but acceptance of the conditions was the only way he had of achieving his appointment. He had accepted, confident that he was clever enough to circumvent his opponents self defeating machinations.

That afternoon Serle sent Lieutenant Samuel Reeve to Perth Amboy with the announcement of Howe's appointment as Peace Commissioner and carrying letters to all governors south of New York asking their assistance in making peace. The Admiral calculated that by making his first order of business on arrival a declaration of his intention to attain a peaceful solution he might be able to negate some of the bad effects created by the Declaration of Independence. Ambrose Serle, acting on the Admiral's specific instructions, placed the messages in unsealed envelopes, fully expecting that news of their contents would quickly reach both Washington and the Philadelphia Congress. Additionally, Howe on July 14th sent a letter directly to General Washington under a flag of truce. Lord Howe proposed that the two men meet to discuss a peaceful solution to their disagreements. Howe's messenger was escorted to Washington's aide, Colonel Joseph Reed. When told the letter was addressed to "George Washington, Esq.," Reed refused to accept the message. Although he did not know that Howe could not refer to Washington by his title, General, because this would confer recognition on the rebel commander that he was not authorized to issue, Reed recognized a diplomatic slight when he saw one.

When no solution to this contretemps was found, Admiral Howe sent a messenger to ask if "General Washington" would meet with the Adjutant General of the British army. Anxious to complain about reports he had received about American prisoners taken in Canada being maltreated, Washington agreed.

Lieutenant Colonel James Patterson served as Howe's emissary and was received under a flag of truce in New York. Washington tabled his complaint about prisoner treatment, and Patterson replied by noting the Howe brothers strongly disapproved of "every infringement of the rights of humanity." Patterson in turn raised the subject of "reconciliation." Washington countered with praise for the Howes but pointed out he understood they had only the authority to issue pardons. Washington denied knowing anybody who had done anything for which they needed a pardon, and the consultations ended. Howe's message quickly reached the Continental Congress, but it was immediately ignored. The delegates recognized that the Howes had no authority to negotiate and in any case they considered the Declaration of Independence as having foreclosed that option.

In Alexandria James followed events in the north as closely as he could. Along with other patriots, he had cheered when the British fleet sailed from Boston. He and his Virginia neighbors were proud of their friend from Mount Vernon. They bragged that General George had taught the English a rebel lesson and had won a major victory. James knew George had won only by not fighting battles he would probably lose. He recognized the English were not running, only preparing to fight elsewhere, but that knowledge did not diminish the joy that the British withdrawal from Boston occasioned.

James expected a summons from Washington to appear as soon as he heard the General had begun moving his troops from Boston to New York. James' sources were still reporting, and he eagerly used their information to make the *Herald* the most informed newspaper in Virginia, outsurpassing even the respected Williamsburg *Gazette*. Since the *Gazette* was preoccupied with Governor Dunmore's machinations and developments in Williamsburg, James discounted his achievements. As time passed, his concern about the possibility of a summons degenerated into disappointment. James at times was forced to admit to himself the possibility that he was selfishly letting his friend and his country down by insisting on his preference to remain in Alexandria. Important events were marching, and James sat comfortably in Alexandria enjoying his family, making money building ships, and publishing the *Herald*.

In July James' sense of unease increased. His friend Tom Jefferson became an instant celebrity with his drafting of the Declaration of Independence. James acknowledged that Tom, now becoming known as the Revolution's penman, was an excellent writer, and James was proud of the success of another Virginian. At the same time, he was privately jealous. James knew he could write as well as Tom; James after all was a professional newspaperman whose vocation was the printed word, but he recognized that the decision to remain in private life had been his own. James wanted to share his disappointment with someone, but he was too embarrassed at his own vanity and jealousy to even talk with Jason, Vivian or Corney.

James finally rationalized his views by telling himself that when Washington called he would respond. He began praising Washington and Jefferson at every opportunity, so much that even Vivian and Corney protested his preoccupation.

"James, if you want so badly to be a politician in Philadelphia or to join George and run the risk of.getting yourself killed, do so," Vivian had finally decreed. "But for God's sake, please stop talking constantly about it."

James tried to mute his concerns, but as events in New York continued to evolve, James became even more anxious. One passion in Alexandria continued to occupy him. He searched diligently for new business for the boatyard. He wanted to keep Jason so busy that he could not consider joining Washington's army. When Jason's friend Skinny Potts decided to march northward to join the Virginia regiment, James had a difficult time persuading Jason to remain behind. He had argued that Jason's work building fast ships like the "Ghost" was more important than anything Jason could do with a rifle. James also encouraged Vivian to promote the advantages of parenthood in her conversations with Lily. He reasoned a family might tie Jason closer to home and keep him secure from the bloodshed. In July James was exhilarated to learn that this machinations had apparently worked; Lily announced she was pregnant with the first of the next Satterfield generation.

Chapter 16
Alexandria, New York
August, 1776

James sat in misery at his table at the *Herald*. Outside, the mid- August sun showed no mercy. It was high noon, and the streets of Alexandria were deserted. James was thankful that the last edition of the *Herald* had been dispatched, and he was free to sit motionless and suffer. He had never known it to be so hot. The thick, humid air hanging over the riverbank stifled every urge to move. James wiped the sweat from his forehead and pulled at his soaked shirt that clung to his body as if it were glued. James looked about the empty office, spotted his sandwiches waiting on the table at the rear of the room, studied the swarm of flies hovering over them, and then dismissed them. His stomach turned at the thought of the hot, greasy almost rancid from the heat ham and decided it was not worth the effort. He watched an adventurous fly land tentatively on the table in front of him and only half seriously slapped at it with the palm of his hand. The fly, also languorous from the heat, hopped a few inches away and landed on the table again. James ignored it, too sapped by the heat, to try again.

James thought about walking to the Grape and having a glass of warm ale for lunch, then decided against it. He doubted the tavern would be any cooler than his office. He studied the droplets of sweat on the backs of his ink-smeared hands and wondered if the weather in New York City was cooler. He glanced at the calendar. August fifteenth. He wondered what was happening. He knew an attack on Washington and New York City was imminent. York Allen's last dispatch, written ten days earlier, had predicted the Howe brothers had no choice but to attack.

James studied the rough, pencil map that he had drawn for himself. General William Howe at the end of June had arrived from Halifax and landed 10,000 men on Staten Island where the general had established his headquarters. George Washington, who had arrived first on April 13th had situated his headquarters on the southern end of Manhattan between the North and East Rivers. The two armies had glared at each other across the Upper Bay for a month and a half, but now time was crucial. On July 12th, Admiral Richard Lord Howe had arrived with his fleet of some one hundred and fifty ships. English sail now filled the New York harbor, and some 32,000 troops were encamped waiting action. According to York Allen, New Yorkers worried particularly about the some 9,000 Hessian mercenaries at General Howe's disposition. Their reputation for brutality was frightening.

While the English polished their bayonets and paraded in straight, tight lines, Washington struggled with familiar problems. His last letter to George Mason described his difficulties meeting weapon and powder shortages, lamented the slow progress in recruiting to replace departing militiamen, and laid particular stress on his dearth of experienced officers. The defeat of the northern army in Canada worried the General. The English had regained control of their northern bastion and were now in a position to mobilize their forces for a strike southward aimed at linkage with the Howes. Washington admitted that New York City was indefensible and speculated that his citizen army would not be able to prevent the link up of their English opponents.

In disgust, James shoved his map across the table. The fate of the colonies was about to be decided, and he sat sweating in the punishing Virginia heat. James, when he had returned from Cambridge last October, had genuinely feared a call to arms from his friend Washington, but none had come. Instead of feeling relief as he had anticipated, James had grown anxious. Obviously, Washington did not need his assistance, and James had to admit to himself that he was disappointed. As he sat at his table wondering what was happening in New York, pondering what the future held for Washington's army, James made a decision.

Personal honor, whatever the sacrifice, required him to go to New York.

Ignoring the heat, James hurried to his home next door, ordered the house maid to pack two bags for a trip and then went out the back door to the stable. He saddled his favorite horse and departed for Eastwind to inform Vivian of his decision.

When James, covered with dust and sweating, arrived at the plantation, he found Vivian sipping tea on the verandah. Following a long morning in the fields supervising the field hands as they cut the rich brown stalks of summer wheat with long scythes, she had taken a mid-afternoon break.

"Welcome, husband," Vivian called as James tied the sweating horse to the stanchion at the base of the stairs. "Another tall, cool glass of tea for Mr. James," Vivian smiled at the maid who appeared in the doorway.

James stomped up the stairs and joined his wife in the chair swing at the end of the verandah.

"And to what do I owe this pleasant surprise?" Vivian asked as she looked at her husband with an expression that did not conceal her concern.

"Nothing's wrong, don't worry," James reassured her. "Jason is busy at the yard, and I have just finished at the paper."

"That's no excuse for your being out in this heat," Vivian said.

James appreciatively noted that she did not complete the phrase with "at your age."

"I wanted to warn you, " James began.

"That you have to travel," Vivian finished his sentence. They had been married long enough that they could anticipate each other's thoughts. "To New York," Vivian continued.

"How did you know?" James asked. Sometimes he thought Vivian could read his mind. Not like John could, but that was different. They were identical twins and had always sensed when the other was near and could come uncannily close to feeling what the other was thinking.

"George has finally answered your prayers and has summoned you." Vivian spoke flatly, neither expressing approval nor disapproval.

"What do you mean prayers?" James challenged. He was still irritable from the heat. The sun had chased him unmercifully on the long ride from Alexandria. James shrugged his shoulders and tried to stretch the fatigue from his tired muscles.

"Be honest, James," Vivian laughed at her husband's irritation. "You have been as grouchy as a hungry bear lately. Your feelings have been hurt because George has not admitted he needs you."   ·

"That's not… . " James began then caught himself. Vivian was right. He sat heavily beside his wife on the swing.

"You smell," Vivian accused and drew back in mock distaste.

"You would too if you had been out in this heat," James challenged, embarrassed because he was usually fastidious about his personal cleanliness.

"I have been, all morning," Vivian laughed. "Now tell me your secret."

James took Vivian's glass from her hand and drank it dry.

"You're right," James set the glass on the table at the side of the swing. "I've got to go to New York."

"Then George has finally asked you."

"No," James admitted. "Not a word. But it's clear trouble is starting soon, and I should be there."

"You're no soldier, James," Vivian admonished.

"But I am a newsman. I can gather information and present it intelligently."

"And you already have sources in New York." James had confided to Vivian every detail about his visit to New York.

James nodded affirmation.

"If Washington is going to need information about New York City, that means the English are going to drive him out of it."

"Yes," James agreed.

"And you are going to New York after the English occupy it?"

"No, of course not," James replied. "I'll ask what Washington needs to know from the English and then see if one of my friends can find out." Both James and Vivian knew he was not telling the whole story.

"And how will you get the information from them if they do find out unless you go to New York?"

"I don't know," James admitted frankly. He had not given the problem any thought. "I'm sure there will be some way."

"James, they hang spies." Vivian did not try to conceal her concern.

"I'm not going to be a spy. Just a staff officer. I won't be near an Englishman with a rope." James spoke with an assurance he did not feel.

"Or a gun?" Vivian canted her head to one side conveying disbelief.

"Or a gun," James said flatly. "Look, Washington probably doesn't even want my help. If he doesn't, I will be back in ten days. Since he hasn't asked me to come, that's probably what will happen."

"I'm sure, James," Vivian laughed.

The maid reappeared with a pitcher and a glass. She filled the glass and handed it to James, then she refilled Vivian's glass that set on the table.

"You can leave the pitcher, Tabby," Vivian ordered. "Mr. James seems to have worked up a thirst."

The maid giggled, set the pitcher on the table, then returned to the house.

"James, stop worrying. I understand. In fact, if you don't have the war settled by the time the harvest is in, I'll come up myself and help you."

James stared at his wife with concern. He knew Vivian might very well do what she threatened.

"After all Ritchie and Remmie are in New York. I could get them to spy for you."

James looked so stricken at her comment that Vivian laughed. She put her hand on James' arm. He could not understand how her touch could be so cool in this heat.

"Oh, don't worry James. I'm just teasing. I'll let you do the spying."

They continued to sit on the verandah and discuss the trip. James, ever practical, briefed her on family matters in Alexandria. Vivian promised to help Corney with the paper and keep track of Jason at the boatyard. They agreed that everything possible should be done to increase Jason's sense that the family was dependent upon his presence in Alexandria. Neither wanted Jason to decide his place was with his father in the north.

James spent the night at Eastwind. It was one of the most pleasant he had ever enjoyed there, primarily because he had Vivian's full attention. James felt almost like a suitor again. Vivian seemed to hang on every word and had dropped her usual pose of light amusement at James' actions. Although neither said anything, they both worried about what the future might hold.

At supper Vivian surprised James by presenting him with a rich looking black felt tricorn hat. She admitted she had purchased it at one of John West's stores as a Christmas gift for James. She assured James that the clerk had sworn it had arrived prior to the non-import ban. Since it was the last English made hat in the store, she had bought it. James, sitting at the large dining room table, had immediately put it on his head. He was embarrassed he had no gift for Vivian.

"It's too hot for summer," Vivian laughed as James ate while wearing his present.

James, despite the heat, continued to wear his new hat all evening, taking it off only when they went to bed.

"I'll wear it all the time I'm gone," James promised. "To remind me of you."

"To remind you that I'm waiting for you to come back," Vivian corrected. She kissed her husband emotionally with a passion that she had not felt for years.

The next morning James returned to Alexandria. His farewell to Vivian was an emotional one, and James felt a heavy sadness mix with his excitement about travel as he rode the tedious two hours back to town. Vivian had offered to ride in with him, but James declined by noting that he would talk only with Corney and Jason and then depart immediately for New York. Vivian stood on the verandah and watched as James, wearing his new hat, rode down the farm lane to the Alexandria road.

A hot, dirty and weary James halted on the Jersey shore north of Hoboken at nightfall on the evening of August 29th. Not knowing the countryside and not having passed an ordinary he would consider patronizing in the past two hours, James negotiated with a farmer who allowed him to stable his two horses and sleep in the barn for what James considered an exorbitant fee. To James' dismay, the farmer and his family were excited with tales of developments in New York during the past two days.

As best as James could piece together from the fragmented stories, the British on the morning of the twenty-second suddenly moved their transports to Gravesend Bay on Long Island and disembarked their troops. The British for three days extended their front and organized their units for attack. The rebels sent reinforcements across the East River and dug additions to the fortifications already in place in Brooklyn Heights where they planned to make their fall back defense. They stretched their forward lines into the foothills several thousand yards in front of the Heights.

According to the farmer, as related by refugees streaming by his house, long after darkness on the evening of August twenty-sixth, the English, undetected by the lax Americans, began to move their army. At one A.M. a strong British patrol of over two hundred troops encountered rebel pickets. Shots were exchanged, and the pickets fled in panic. Reports of the activity spread across the entire front, and rebel troops alerted. The night passed slowly without major action until about nine A.M. on the morning of August twenty-seventh. Then, as anticipated, English cannon pummeled the American lines. A few minutes after the commencement of the cannonade, rifle shots were heard being exchanged behind the lines of the American left flank commanded by Major General John Sullivan. Soon, it became apparent that sizable units of the British army had marched along Jamaica Road undetected during the long night and had successfully got behind the American lines where they opened their pincer movement. The coordinated morning attack panicked the inexperienced rebels who broke ranks and charged through the enemy lines at their rear as best they could.

Many of those trapped in the Long Island marshes had died while in full flight. Those who escaped reached the Brooklyn Heights defenses by early afternoon. There, General Washington himself did what he could to rally his panicked army. Rumors of imminent slaughter by English bayonet rocked the frightened militiamen. They had known their fortifications were weak, and they had been trapped between the advancing English and the East River. They awaited their fate, some even stoically, but nothing happened. The English army, for some inexplicable reason halted its advance. Night fell, and the rebel army survived. To the Americans' surprise, the next day, August twenty-eighth, passed without the feared English attack. General Howe apparently decided to rest his troops.

A heavy rain pelted the soldiers of both armies during the day, and those who could took refuge in their tents. The rain continued on the twenty-ninth. Unfavorable winds on the river kept the British fleet from the East River and the American army's rear. Washington held a command council, and they unanimously decided to evacuate Long Island and save as much of their army as they could. Twelve thousand men had to be ferried across the river to the New York shore. That night the weather continued to favor the Americans. A heavy fog joined the rain to conceal their movements. In a miracle of maneuver, the rebel army withdrew in an orderly fashion. By dawn on August 30th, Washington's army and its wounded had escaped to the New York shore. Washington had suffered as great a defeat as his mentor General Braddock had twenty some years earlier; unlike Braddock, Washington escaped with his life. James hoped his friend would never again place his troops in a position where they had the enemy in front of them and a wide river to their rear.

"Man, turn around. You're crazy to go to New York now," the farmer exclaimed when he learned of James' destination. "Everybody is going the opposite direction. They expect the Howes to attack the city at any time, and those rebel farmers will run again."

James stared with dismay at the New Jersey farmer. He feared he had delayed too long. He was not sure he would be able to find Washington's headquarters in the chaos surrounding the defeated army in New York. James had not expected the rebels to hold New York, but the Boston victory had raised false hopes. James decided he had no choice but to find Washington. He was not sure that if he were lucky and located his friend that George would have time to tell James how he could help.

The next morning, August thirtieth, at daybreak, James saddled his horse, loaded the bags back on the second animal, the packhorse, and departed the farm. Already the road to the ferry that plied the river between New York and the Jersey shore was crowded with fleeing New Yorkers. Many, who obviously were of an age to have been members of Washington's army, made no effort to conceal their status. Having tasted war and not liking it, they were returning home.

"Turn around, mister," was a shout that James heard frequently. James nodded his appreciation for the advice but continued determinedly northward.

James arrived at the river landing just as the crowded ferry was docking. He watched as the overloaded craft discharged its worried passengers. James was the only person waiting to cross to the New York side.

"Mister," the ferry operator laughed derisively. "You are out of your mind. I can take you to New York, but if you go, I'll never get you back. They expect the lobsterbacks at any time, and I can't carry everybody who wants out. I'm getting triple fees, and more, but I will carry you over for free."

James led his two horses on the deck of the barge like boat and the operator shoved off for his return trip to New York as soon as James was on board.

On the other side, the landing was jammed with people for as far as he could see. Men, women and children, carrying what possessions they could, pushed and shoved and shouted as the ferry approached. They did not wait for the ferry to dock before crowding on board. With great difficulty James led his two horses through the pushing mass. After ten minutes he cleared the crowd and paused to get his bearing. He had no idea where to find Washington and his headquarters. He called questions to passing strangers, but they ignored him in their rush to join the fighting crowd at the waterfront. James mounted his horse and rode slowly towards the center of town. Away from the water, he encountered soldiers hurrying in all directions. None had any idea where the General had located his command Finally, he stopped a young lieutenant who muttered something that sounded like mortar's place. The young man pointed toward the center of town and gave James hurried directions. James later learned that Washington had established his residence in a house owned by a New Yorker named Abraham Mortier. The young officer explained that there they would know where Washington had established his headquarters.

James followed the directions as best as he could but was forced several times to halt others and beg assistance. Finally, James located the Mortier house, a large, two story city mansion. There, James learned from a house servant that the General was at his headquarters two blocks away. James remounted his horse and wearily made his way through the filled streets to the headquarters. He wondered where the rushing people were going. He could hear no gunfire, thus had to assume that the British were not yet crossing the East River. James, from what he heard, doubted that an attack was imminent. The Howes had had their opportunity to destroy a good part of Washington's army on Long Island and had let it escape. It did not seem logical that they would now rush headlong across the river.

James tied both horses at the stanchion in front of the headquarters building, another large city mansion obviously owned by a wealthy New York merchant, probably a loyalist who had had his home confiscated.

At the door, James encountered two dirty and tired looking sentries wearing ragged bluff and blue uniforms. Their crossed white bandoleers were filthy; both sentries looked as if they had been rolling in the dirt.

"Halt, mate. State your business," the taller sentry spoke. The two men crossed their bayonet tipped long rifles to block James' way.

"General Washington, please," James responded politely. He did not know what business he could cite.

"Does he expect you?"

"No, but... ."

"Be on your way mate. The general's busy. Something to do with the lobsters coming for dinner." The tall sentry laughed at his feeble attempt at humor, but the crossed rifles still barred James' way.

"I have important business with the General," James tried again.

"I'm sure you do, mate, but the General's busy. Bugger off."

Before James could think of a reply, a familiar voice spoke behind him.

"James?"

James turned and immediately recognized Eric Grey. He was dressed in an immaculate blue and bluff uniform with the pink sash denoting a member of the commander-in-chief's personal staff. He now wore a lieutenant's insignia.

"Eric," James exclaimed with relief.

The two men embraced briefly.

"Welcome to New York," Grey smiled, humor still evident in his voice. "You picked a bad time to visit, friend."

James noted the young aide who had fetched him from Alexandria to escort him to his first visit to Cambridge last October still retained his boyish charm and enthusiasm.

"I know," James agreed. "I didn't plan it this way."

"None of us did," Grey agreed. "The general's frantically busy, having lost Long Island and all, but he will be glad to see you. He looks tired, but don't be worried. He's been over there for two days. Came back by boat last night, so he's not had much sleep."

"And you?" James asked, noticing for the first time the strain lines and weariness in the young aide's face.

"Me too," Grey smiled proudly. "We're shorthanded around here, but the general sent me home at four to catch a nap and to make myself respectable. He still insists that we look like aides to the commander should."

"Do you know this man?" The tall sentry demanded. The two crossed rifles still blocked James' entrance.

"Yes. Mr. Satterfield is a close friend of the general," Grey replied.

"We have orders to admit nobody unless the staff clears them," the sentry commented gruffly.

James noted the large man appeared prepared to implement those orders.

"Mr. Satterfield should be admitted whenever he wants," Grey spoke authoritatively.

James noted the young officer had seasoned and acquired a military bearing in the months since James' last visit. Then, Grey been green and eager, but now he carried himself with confidence.

"On whose authority?" The sentry demanded.

"Mine," Grey responded and stared at the stubborn guard.

Reluctantly, the two sentries returned their rifles to a version of parade rest, opening the way for James to pass.

"Follow me," Grey stepped around James and led him into a long hallway.

On his left James passed a large room filled with anxious officers milling about.

"Our waiting room," Eric explained, having caught James' curious glance. "All with urgent messages for the general."

James silently followed Eric down the hall not wanting to draw attention to himself. He felt guilty about jumping ahead of the queue.

"Not to worry," Eric assured James. "The general will be delighted you are here."

The young man turned right at the end of the hall and entered another room. Another aide, a captain dressed exactly like Grey, sat behind a desk guarding a closed door. The only other person in the room wore a rumpled bluff and blue uniform topped by a major general's insignia. The weary man stared at James and Grey and nodded.

"General Sullivan, sir," Grey greeted the man who merely nodded in reply.

James assumed General Sullivan was waiting to see Washington. James did not speak because Eric made no effort to introduce him. Sullivan sat glumly in his chair and turned to stare out the window, ignoring both Eric and James.

"Is someone with the general?" Eric asked the captain.

"No, but he asked not to be disturbed for five minutes, then he will begin accepting reports starting with General Sullivan here."

Sullivan did not look up at the mention of his name. The man morosely tried to ignore the other three.

"I've an urgent message that will not wait," Grey moved confidently towards the door.

James concluded from Grey's demeanor that he was one of the few who had the privilege of entering the general's office whenever he chose. Grey with a brief wave of his hand indicated James should wait. The young lieutenant knocked once on the door, then entered, closing it softly behind him.

Chapter 17
New York
August/September, 1776

No more than a few seconds passed after Lieutenant Eric Grey had entered the Commander-in-Chief's office than the softly closed door reopened and Grey beckoned for James to enter. James quickly walked through the doorway, embarrassed at having crowded in ahead of General Sullivan who undoubtedly had pressing battle matters to discuss with Washington while James had no idea how he was going to explain his sudden appearance at this most inauspicious time.

"James, welcome," Washington spoke as he strode across his office towards James. Grey discreetly stepped out of the room and closed the door behind him. The captain and Sullivan looked at Grey expecting an explanation but got none. Grey took a seat behind a desk on the opposite side of the door from the other aide.

James studied his friend and was relieved. Washington's uniform was immaculate. His face had a gray pallor, and James noted worry lines that had not been there before, but otherwise Washington was unchanged.

The two men embraced and Washington took two steps back and studied James thoughtfully. James did not know what to say to explain his presence and let Washington speak first.

"I'm glad you're here. I need you," Washington spoke softly. "Unfortunately, I have no time to talk. I have to finish my report to Congress on our terrible losses on Long Island and announce our successful withdrawal. If it had not been for the fog... ." Washington shook his head.

"James, you are on your own. Assume that we will not be able to hold New York City much longer than a few days. Contact your friends, find as many new sources as you can, then arrange a means to communicate with them from the other side of the English lines, wherever that may be."

James nodded agreement. He asked no questions because he knew Washington had other more pressing problems to handle himself. James vowed to take as much pressure off his friend as he could.

"You have two responsibilities," Washington spoke flatly. "You are responsible for obtaining information on what the Howe brothers plan to do against us. Don't worry about what they have done or are doing; just find out what they plan to do next. Secondly, you are my political liaison to the Congress in Philadelphia. Take over responsibility for the politicians."

"I'll do my best," James replied. "But... ."

"I'm sorry, James," Washington spoke politely, "but I just don't have time now for a friendly discussion. You handle it. Since you're a civilian, you will not attend my staff meetings. Don't come back to this headquarters, and don't discuss your responsibilities with anyone else, military or civilian, except... ."

"But how will I keep you informed?" James had to ask.

"Except Lieutenant Grey. I give him to you. He's yours. Have him serve as liaison between you and me. Tell him what you need, and he'll get it. He's a good boy."

"Does he know about this?" James asked, wondering how Washington could have set everything up, not knowing James was coming.

"No. You brief him. Also find your own quarters and office. Grey will know how to handle the expenses. I have a confidential fund. Now, I must beg your pardon."

The two friends had remained standing during the conversation. Washington patted James once, reassuringly, on the back, then retreated to his desk. James recognized he had been dismissed. Their relationship had changed.

When James reached the door, he paused and looked back.   Washington already had his quill in hand.

"Send Grey in," Washington ordered.

James opened the door and indicated that the commander-in-chief wanted Eric. The young officer jumped up and slipped past James. As the door was closing, James heard Washington speak softly.

"Go with Mr. Satterfield, stay with him, and do whatever he says. Tell no one else."

Recognizing that nothing more was going to be said, Grey caught the door before it closed, opened it and stepped back into the outer office with a quizzical expression on his face.   James glanced at General Sullivan who still stared morosely out the window. James nodded at the captain then strode confidently into the hallway without a word to Eric. The young lieutenant paused, shrugged at the captain, and then hurried after the departing James.

As he walked, James reviewed in his mind what he knew about General John Sullivan. Sullivan was a political general from New Hampshire. He had represented his colony at the first Continental Congress, so James had to assume that he had been a man of stature at home. He had also attended the Second Continental Congress and had been one of the New Englanders selected as a brigadier general to offset the northern disappointment at the selection of a Virginian to be commander-in-chief. Sullivan had served with Washington during the siege of Boston and had been dispatched with reinforcements for the failing northern campaign after Montgomery's death and Arnold's wounding. Sullivan had distinguished himself by getting involved in a political maneuver intended to earn for him command of the northern expedition. He was disappointed when the experienced Horatio Gates who had fought with Braddock and who had cultivated Washington at his home in Mount Vernon was selected over him. Some blamed Sullivan for much of the chaos and disaster that plagued the rebel army in Canada before Gates' arrival. The criticism had been so strong that Congress had considered withdrawing Sullivan's rank, but Washington had compassionately interceded on the fiery Irish politician's behalf. Congress had reacted by promoting Sullivan to Major General in August and sending him to assist Washington in the battle of Long Island.

Outside the headquarters, James paused in front of the stanchion where he had tied his horses and waited for Grey to catch up. James had no idea where he would go next. He needed to find a house or ordinary with stables to board his horses and a bed where he could spend the night. He had no idea how long the army would be in New York. He then had to find York Allen who could assist him in contacting the others. He hoped that Hyde Pigot, the Trinity Church Pastor, and Andrew Partridge, the merchant, had not fled the city.

"General Sullivan's in trouble," Grey confided as he approached James. "He's responsible for the Long Island defeat. The general appointed Sullivan to command the forces on Long Island but replaced him after two days with General Putnam. Neither understands much about military tactics, and Sullivan commanded the left flank. He knew nothing about the terrain or the troops he commanded and did not try to learn. Unfortunately, he ignored reports of a minor road on his extreme left and concentrated his forces in front of him. The Howes discovered the Jamaica Road was unguarded and sent a strong force on a flanking movement around Sullivan. The English swept behind Sullivan and the American lines, and our army panicked. With good grounds, I might add, because they had English bayonets to their front and rear and were being pounded by English artillery. We broke and ran. Washington tried to rally them at Brooklyn Heights but realized they had to get off the island before being exterminated. Thanks to the general and a lot of luck, the fog and rain, we got off last night. Sullivan's waiting now to find out what will happen to him for his mistakes."

James listened carefully to Eric's report, nodded, then asked:

"How long do we have before the English attack here?"

Eric looked around to make sure no one was listening before answering.

"We have no idea. We don't have a single spy in the English camp. The generals all predict that the English will invade soon and that we will not be able to hold New York. The city's not indispensable. Some want to burn it to the ground, but the civilians won't allow that. They are already sending appeals to Congress. I think the general is asking Congress for instructions, but I'm not sure."

James untied his two horses and led them away from the headquarters. Eric walked along beside him.

"The general said I'm supposed to do what you say," Eric began with the confusion evident in his voice. "What are we doing? Where are we going?"

"First, Eric, take me to an ordinary or someplace we can spend the night," James ordered.

"What about my house?"

"No. We must go someplace where you are not known."

"We?"

"Yes.

"I have to give up my house?"

"Don't worry. It will be only for a few days." James had to smile at the relieved expression that appeared on Eric's face. "But don't get your hopes up. The English will take it from you before you get back."

"And then what?"

"We'll see," James replied laconically.

Eric led the way to a dilapidated building not far from the waterfront. A large black crow decorated the fading sign.

"I've never been here," Eric explained. "I'm told it's a pretty rough place, mainly for sailors."

"Good," James approved. "Now, you with your fancy uniform should disappear. I don't want to be seen with you."

The young officer looked at James with dismay on his face.

"But General Washington said... ."

"Go," James ordered. "Buy yourself some farm clothes if you don't have any and get out of that fancy uniform. Stop shaving and be dirty when you appear here tomorrow morning at eight o'clock."

James turned his back on the stricken young man and led his horses to the run-down ordinary. He had no difficulty finding lodging and a stable for his horses. Everybody who could was fleeing the city. James assumed that the majority who remained was preparing to welcome the English, and these were not the kind who frequented the shabby Crow.

James turned his horses over to a poorly dressed stable hand, an old man with brown, rotted teeth, who immediately put the horses to pasture behind the barn.

"Exercise them both and rub them down, good," James ordered, "and there will be two shillings in it for you."

"Right, Guv," the old man bared his brown stumps in a version of a smile.

"And make sure they are here when I get back," James continued. "There will be something more for you." Given the chaotic state of New York in the pre-battle atmosphere, James was not confident that either his bags or his horses would be at the Crow when he returned.

James, who had much to do and little time to do it, hurried off. His travel clothes were dirty, his black tricorn dusty, and he needed a shave and bath after five days on the road and the night in the farmer's barn.

It took James twenty minutes to walk from the Black Crow to the wood building that housed the offices of Hugh Gaine's New York *Gazette*. With luck, James
hoped to find York Allen inside working on a story. James strolled slowly past
the open door and peered inside. Gaine, the fat proprietor, stood near the door
talking with a well-dressed man. James smiled when he saw York Allen sitting at
a table in the back of the room, apparently writing a story. Allen was studying a
piece of paper on the table in front of him and scratching his nose with the feather end of the quill that he held in his ink-stained hand. James kept walking. He
did not want Gaine, York's boss, to see James contact the young man. As James
pondered his dilemma, he spotted two tough looking youths loitering on the
steps of a brownstone building diagonally across the street from the *Gazette's*
office. James made up his mind quickly. He crossed the street and approached
the young toughs who stared at him belligerently. James decided that neither
looked over fourteen, but they already had the veneer of young bandits.

"Want to earn a shilling, easy?" James asked.

The two youths studied James suspiciously for several seconds before the
larger one, almost James" size, answered rudely.

"Doin' what?"

"Taking a message," James tried to match the belligerent tone.

"Where?"

"There," James indicated the newspaper shop with a short turn of his head.

"Why don't ya do it yourself? Your leg broken?" The youth looked at his
companion to see if his humor was being appreciated.

James turned and began to walk away.

"Hey mister," the youth called. "Jist a minute."

He rose from the steps and hurried to where James had stopped.

"Gimmie the message."

James reached into his pocket, took out a pencil stub and a scrap of notepa-
per that he always carried and scribbled a few brief words. He folded the paper
several times and then wrote "York Allen" on the outside. He handed the folded
paper to the boy.

"Who to?" The youth demanded.

James watched him study the words on the folded note. He recognized the
boy could not read.

"That's his name," James pointed at the words. "Do you know Mr. Allen?"

"Nah," the youth replied arrogantly. He tapped the folded note against the
palm of his dirty hand.

"He's sitting at the table in that shop." James pointed at the *Gazette* office.

"Gimmie the shilling first," the boy demanded.

"I'll give it to your friend here to hold, and I'll wait to see that you deliver the
message," James threatened.

The youth glared at James, waited until he handed the coin to the second
youth and turned and strolled across the street. He paused at the door to the
newspaper office to stare at James then entered. As soon as the boy disappeared,

James began to walk quickly down the street. Inside the newspaper office, the youth halted before the two imposing looking men.

"Got a message," the youth said belligerently, holding up the folded note so Gaine could see the written words.

"Allen," the proprietor read and spoke the words aloud. "Back there," he pointed at his young reporter who still sat at the table composing his story. Gaine turned back to the prosperous looking merchant and resumed talking in a low voice. He was accustomed to York receiving messages. Most were tips for stories from York's chain of informers.

The youth swaggered to the table trying to appear tough. He handed the note to the man with the feather in his hand and waited. Allen took the note, studied his name, and then looked at the waiting youth.

"Well?" He asked.

"Don't I git somethin' for bringin' that?" The youth demanded.

"Beat it," York ordered. He was not about to be intimidated by a street punk. He recognized him as one of those who loitered on the steps across the street.

The youth stared defiantly at Allen.

York took a handful of coins from his pockets, selected a copper one and flipped it to the youth.

"Beat it," Allen ordered.

The youth caught the coin and defiantly strutted back to the street. Allen watched until the youth exited the door then studied the note. He tapped it a couple of times on the table, wondering who it was from, then opened it.

"Meet me at noon at the Red Fox. James."

Allen crumpled the note and stuck it in his pocket. He picked up the quill and studied the paper in front of him as if nothing had happened. The Red Fox was a tavern no more than ten minutes walk from the newspaper office. York had introduced James Satterfield to it on his first visit to the city. York had no difficulty figuring out what the Virginian wanted. The English were at the city gates and the amateur spy net had to be activated. York smiled. He had been waiting for his new adventure to begin.

James walked quickly from the newspaper office to the Red Fox. Last October, he and the young newspaperman had selected it as a place they could meet discreetly. He walked about a block past the tavern, paused at a storefront, then turned and reversed his course. People were hurrying about in both directions, but James could not identify anyone who might have been following him. At least nobody suddenly aped James' abrupt movements. He doubted that he was being followed; few in the city knew him personally, and none could have anticipated his spontaneous visit.

Only three of the tables in the large tavern were occupied. James assumed that eleven-thirty was early for New Yorkers to eat, even those who planned on remaining in the city to welcome the English army. He selected a scarred table for two that stood along the back wall, as far from the bar and the other patrons as possible. James sat and waited, still wearing his black tricorn that Vivian had given him as a travel gift. James normally did not favor hats, but he had been wearing the tricorn for almost ten days now, and it was becoming a part of him. James had read in a mystery novel that hats concealed hairlines and made it harder to identify a person. He smiled as the thought repeated itself in his mind; maybe he needed a disguise in his new profession. He decided to follow the same advice he had given Eric. He would grow a beard. While he was wondering how a full beard and mustache would look on his smooth face, York Allen entered the tavern. The young man paused at the door as James had and peered into the gloom. He quickly spotted James seated along the wall and hurried to join him.

James rose, solemnly shook the beaming young man's hand, and guided him into a chair facing James. York's back was to the door.

"Like your hat," Allen smiled.

James grinned with embarrassment. He had not yet acquired a professional demeanor.

"Buy yourself one," James replied. "It's fine English felt."

"That's a strange acquisition for one in your position. I thought you rebels all wore coon hats with tails."

"No so loud," James cautioned. "You don't know who might be listening."

"You're telling me," York agreed. "There's nothing but Tories left in the city. Everyone else has already left. Did you see the man talking with Gaine at the paper?"

"The well dressed man?"

"Yes. He's one of Gaine's Tory friends. Gaine has already changed sides and is trying to line up a contact with the English."

James thought briefly about what Allen had said.

"Good," he finally concluded aloud. "Stick with Gaine and become more Tory than he is. Can you do it?"

"Sure," Allen spoke confidently. "Why?" He already knew why but wanted the somber Virginian to say it.

"Your job will be to find out what the Howe brothers plan to do next."

"That's all?" York laughed nervously.

"That's right. Our most important job. Don't worry about reporting what is happening. Just find out what the general and admiral are planning."

"That should be easy," Allen paused then asked seriously. "And who am I working for?"

"That's obvious. "

"I mean specifically."

"Me.

"A Virginia newspaper owner?"

"Yes. And General Washington's chief of intelligence." James decided on the spur of the moment to give himself a title.

"You're kidding. I'm working directly for General Washington?"

"Don't speak so loud," James cautioned. He noticed that the nervous Allen's voice had grown louder with excitement.

"OK." Allen whispered. "What do I do?"

"You will be our key man. The English will want a newspaper to print their views. Encourage Gaine to sell the services of the *Gazette.*"

"He's already trying to do that. I won't have to encourage him. He knows the rebels were getting ready to burn him out."

"Good. So go along with him. When the time comes, write as many pro-English stories as you can."

"No problem," York agreed.

"And make as many English officer friends as you can. The higher rank the better." James did not admit that he was improvising as he went along.

"And if I learn something? How will I get the information to you. Print it in the paper?"

"Certainly not," James replied, not certain if York was joking or not.

"Send a letter?"

"Maybe." James remained silent thinking about the problem as the barmaid brought them two mugs of dark, foaming ale.

"How?" York persisted after the barmaid had departed. He suddenly recognized that his role might be dangerous. "They hang spies, you know."

"I know," James agreed frankly. "We'll have to work something out. Any suggestions?"

Both silently sipped their ale and pondered the problem.

"We have to decide quickly," York said. "The English could land anytime, and you and Washington will be running with your hind sides afire. Any idea where?"

"No," James admitted frankly.

"Then where do I send your letters?"

"I don't know, but I'll let you know."

"Now," Allen blurted.

"Now," James agreed, trying to make his voice sound calm. He instinctively knew he could not admit to the young man that he was as new to the game as he was. Allen would depend on James to protect him and ensure that their communications were secure.

The two men quietly sipped their ales and thought frantically. The barmaid had refilled their glasses before either spoke

"I think... ." Both men used the same words simultaneously. "Go ahead," James directed, pleased that Allen had also developed an idea.

"I have two uncles who I trust implicitly," Allen began. "My mother's brothers. Both are simple men, one is a fisherman and the other owns a small stable."

Allen paused to see if James had any questions. James did not see how a fisherman or a stable keeper could get information from the English officers but remained quiet.

"Neither cares whether the English or the rebels win. Horses and fish aren't political." Allen paused again to see if James would protest, but he continued to passively listen. James had no solution, so maybe Allen did.

"They will do anything I ask," Allen continued. "Especially if they are paid good."

"That's no problem," James finally commented. "But... ."

"Both can keep their mouths shut," Allen began thinking as he spoke. He had not fully worked an idea out in his mind. "A fisherman and a stableman might make good messengers," Allen suggested.

James suddenly recognized what Allen was proposing. "An excellent idea," he began enthusiastically. "I could arrange to have a courier waiting at Powles Hook to meet your fisherman uncle, and he could bring your reports to me wherever I am. I will have to be near the General." James assumed that Lieutenant Grey could commandeer a soldier from the Powles Hook area who could be ordered home to serve as messenger.

Allen nodded agreement.

"Then, this afternoon I will talk with my uncles."

"And I will arrange the contact at Powles Hook. Maybe in two days we can arrange a practice run for your fisherman uncle and introduce his contact."

"If we have time," Allen agreed.

"And we have other important things to do," James made another spur of the moment decision. "Since you will be controlling our message chain we have to arrange for the others to report to you."

"The others?" York was surprised. He had thought he would collect information and then have his uncles deliver it. He immediately recognized that contact with others would greatly increase the risk to him. He knew he could trust his uncles but was not sure about strangers. "I'm not sure I want to get involved with others I don't know."

James studied the young man and recognized this was a critical moment for him. He sipped his ale and wondered how he could persuade York that the risk was minimal. James immediately decided he could not do that. What he was asking would be risky, and not good security either. If he put all his sources in one basket, the loss of one could lead to the compromise of everyone. York Allen was a key figure. He could collect information on his own and send it along via his uncles, and James did not want to imperil him, but he had no idea how he could get information from his other potential sources through the lines to himself. He could think of no solution and decided he had no choice but to trust the young man's judgment.

"Maybe we can work out some way to collect the information without the others knowing who you are."

Allen nodded agreement but his face reflected his skepticism.

"And of course it would be better if you did not know who the others are," James continued. "That way if one is caught, God forbid, the others will not be threatened. You'll have time to flee."

"And how would you do that? Have them give me messages without knowing who I am?"

"Have them hide messages in secret places. "

"Such as?"

"A hollow tree. Under a rock. A hole in the ground. Pinned under a church pew. I don't know. Think of something."

"That could work," Allen agreed. "I could find the places and tell you, and you can tell the others. How would I know there is a message hidden. I can't go to the secret places every day. I would need a signal."

"What about a simple mark on a wall? A charcoal check or a small pencil mark."

"That would work. Let me look around. I know the city better than you."

"Good," James agreed. "I have to contact the others. We can meet tomorrow, and you can tell me if your uncles agree and where the secret places are. Pick places you visit naturally or pass everyday."

"OK. That will take some thought." Allen paused then spoke again. "I'm not going to do this for nothing. I'll be risking everything including my uncles' lives."

"Understood," James agreed. "It's hard to put a price on something like this." He paused to study the young man. He wanted to be fair but at the same time not waste Washington's money. "How does ten pounds a month sound? For you."

"Great," York broke into a smile. The amount was many times what he earned from Gaine at the *Gazette*.

"And one pound a month, each, for your uncles," James continued, getting a feel for the bargaining.

"In specie," York responded.

"Agreed," James answered.

"Paid where?"

"Wherever you say."

"Give me the money for my uncles, one month each in advance, and save my money for me. I'll collect from you when I need."

"Agreed."

"And you pay me ten percent interest on accrued," York added.

"Agreed, and that's it. Let's get to work." James wanted to get away before Allen thought of more conditions. "I'll meet you here tomorrow at noon."

Chapter 18
New York City
September 1776

James, elated at what he and the young newspaperman had arranged, strode slowly away from the Red Fox and tried to plan what he would do next. As he walked, oblivious to the early September heat and the pedestrians who thronged through the streets they shared with hurrying wagons and coaches, James mentally listed his needs. It occurred to him that York and his other sources should protect themselves as much as possible. James knew nothing about invisible writing but reasoned that if the reports were written in secret ink the authors would be protected if the message hiding places were inadvertently discovered. In addition to recruiting a soldier to serve as a contact in Powles Hook, Lieutenant Grey would have to locate a pharmacist who might know about chemicals. James assured himself that Washington's army would have several doctors and pharmacists who might help. He paused to make notes of things to do before he forgot them. He began to feel the pressure of time and regretted having been so cavalier when he had dismissed Eric for the day. He decided one assistant might not prove to be enough. The thought gave him a better idea of his friend Washington's problems. He could not imagine the enormous difficulties involved in recruiting, training, supplying and fighting an army.

James decided he had to contact his other sources immediately. He decided to start with Hyde Pigot, the pastor at the Trinity Church, and Andrew Partridge, the New York merchant. Both men appeared determined to stay in New York, even if the English should come, and both were prominent enough to have contact with senior officers. James tried to identify other individuals in New York City who would meet the Howes. He immediately concluded he had to enlist the help of influential loyalists. The Americans who had fled or been driven from their homes would undoubtedly contact the English for security and assurances. James unfortunately did not know any New York loyalists, of which there were obviously many. A passing pedestrian jolted James' shoulder, hitting him so hard it knocked his hat from his head. James caught it before it hit the ground, noted it was dusty and began brushing it with his hand. The pedestrian hurried off without uttering a word of apology. James glared after him, wondering what the man would do if he knew who James represented.

James replaced the tricorn on his head and thought of Vivian. He smiled as he remembered his wife's joking threat to come to New York and help him by recruiting Ritchie and Remmie Randolph who had so cheaply sold their land and fled to New York with Remmie's father. James involuntarily slapped his hands together in a burst of enthusiasm, startling a couple who had been pushing towards him. They stepped back to give the possibly demented man room to maneuver past. James added Remmie to his list of must contacts. Remmie's father-in-law would be no help; in fact his views made him a threat, but Remmie might be a means of meeting other loyalists with soft allegiances to the English if he was not strong enough to help himself.

The afternoon and evening passed too quickly for the harried James. He found Hyde Pigot at the Trinity Church. Pigot accepted James' sudden appearance as typical of the times, but he had difficulty truly understanding what James wanted from him. Pigot was willing to secretly help the rebels because he was loathe to leave his church despite his support of the colonial cause. James's request gave him the excuse he needed to stay on in the city, solving a personal dilemma. He had no love of the English; in fact at times he had dreamed of Trinity Church being freed from the Anglican hierarchy based in England. Too often, in his opinion, the Crown demanded from the state church more than it could give. Unfortunately for James, Pigot was an unimaginative man; his literal mind required every detail to be explained in full.

Dusk was setting when James escaped from the churchman's grasp. Then, it took James two hours to find Andrew Partridge. The chubby merchant had already left his counting house, and James had difficulty finding the man's home. Once there, James did not regret the time it took. Partridge responded positively and had no difficulty understanding what James wanted. He said yes to every request and promised to make time available as needed to work out the details. James, exhausted from the day's tension, accepted Partridge's offer to meet again and made his way back to the Black Crow through the empty and darkened streets. Several times James crossed the street to avoid what seemed to him to be menacing shadows. He decided it was naive of him to be afoot in such dangerous times without a weapon of any kind.

The next morning James slept later than he planned. He had spent an uncomfortable night fighting the vermin that infested the dirty straw mattress on which he tried to sleep. Shortly before dawn, he surrendered the straw to its many legged inhabitants and retreated to the hard dirt floor. Finally, he had fallen into a fitful sleep that lasted two hours past dawn.

James was sitting in the dank public room of the Crow eating an unsatisfactory breakfast of hard, stale bread, accompanied by cold, weak tea in a cracked cup, when Lieutenant Eric Grey arrived. At first James did not recognize the scruffy farmer who appeared in the doorway. Only when the man laughed did

James recognize Grey and realize that he had obeyed James' orders to exchange his tidy uniform for country clothing. Grey looked like a rural bumpkin except for one jarring note. On his head he wore a new, black tricorn hat identical to the one that set on the table in front of James.

"Good morning, James," Grey posed in front of the frowning James. "How do I look?"

"The hat," James choked on a hard crust of bread he had been trying to chew when Grey appeared. "What are you doing with the hat?"

"You told me I could buy one like yours," Grey laughed. "Like it?"

"It's too fine for your clothes. Look it still shines," James protested.

"I can take care of that." Grey stooped to grab a handful of sawdust and dirt from the caked floor and rubbed it into his hat. "There, now it looks like yours," Grey smiled, looking at James for approval.

Recognizing that Eric had literally followed his instructions, James decided to ignore the hat and let the irrepressible young man have his joke.

"I've got my new clothes and some money from the confidential fund," Eric spoke proudly. He patted the baggy pocket of his worn trousers. James clearly heard the clink of coins.

"Good. Keep the money until we get outside." James, deciding that the bread was inedible, rose and led the way through the door into the street. He scratched the sides of his thighs as he walked. He was sure his body was covered with little red bites.

As they moved away from the riverfront, James briefed his companion.

"I'm going to introduce you to a young man named York Allen. He's a news collector for the *Gazette*. He's our main source. One of his uncles, a fisherman, will serve as our messenger. We will meet Allen now, then you'll have to find a soldier from Paulus Hook who can serve as the fisherman's contact."

Grey nodded agreement.

"Also, I want you to find a pharmacist in the army who can brief you on invisible chemicals. I want Allen to write his messages with invisible ink. Can you do that?"

"Yes, sir," Grey replied already thinking about who he could ask for suggestions.

"After I introduce you to Allen, I will leave you two to work out the details. I have to contact some other sources."

As they turned the corner, James remembered that Allen was going to find some hiding places for the messages from the other cooperators. James explained the idea to his assistant.   As he talked, James could see the young man getting more excited about their plans.

"Give me the money," James ordered. He spoke more curtly than he intended, but the pressure of time and many things to do before the English attack made him nervous. No sleep and little to eat did not help.

Eric straightened his hat, looked cautiously about to see if any of the passing pedestrians were watching, then handed James the leather pouch filled with coins. James took the pouch and stuffed it into his pocket.

When they entered the gloom of the Red Fox, James was pleased to see that York Allen was the only person in the large room. He sat at the same small table he and James had shared the previous day. To James' dismay, Allen also wore a new, black, tricorn hat identical to the ones worn by James and Eric. James whipped his hat from his head and placed it out of sight on the adjacent chair. Allen studied Eric's hat and laughed.

"You must be one of ours," he smiled.

James, irritated, not sure if the two young men were making fun of him or not, introduced the two gruffly.

"Eric Grey, York Allen."

To Allen, James explained: "Eric's my deputy. He speaks for me. I will let the two of you manage the details. I have other work to do."

Without waiting for a response, James recovered his hat and hurried towards the door. He felt like stamping his feet. At the door to the street, he paused and looked back. Eric and York, each wearing a black hat, sat watching James' departure. Both smiled broadly, obviously proud of themselves. Still stern faced, James glared before turning and rushing back into the street. Outside, as he pushed his way through the throngs, he began to chuckle to himself.

James was not sure of his destination. The day before he had been lucky. He had met with York Allen, Hyde Pigot, the pastor of Trinity Church, and Andrew Partridge, the wealthy merchant. From Pigot, whose congregation was composed largely of wealthy New York loyalists, James had learned the location of several areas favored by refugees from the other colonies. James hoped, with luck, to find his friend Ritchie Randolph and his wife Remmie this morning.

The loyalists, obviously preparing for a long stay, had purchased or leased houses in several locations. They tended to congregate with friends from home where possible. Pigot had directed James to a long residential street on the north side of town where the loyalists had found many mansions vacated by wealthy New York patriots who had moved their families outside the city where they would be safe from the Hessian mercenaries and pillaging English troops. Many had no hesitation renting their homes to loyalists at cheap prices in the hope of obtaining some protection for their homes from the marauders.

Pigot had suggested the names of several ordinaries located in the area. James could hardly go house to house asking for Ritchie, so he planned to inquire at the neighborhood taverns.

After three hours of fruitless searching, James began to grow desperate. He had not expected the search to be easy, but he had not anticipated the hostility. Most of the tavern keepers treated his questions with aggressive rudeness. Some refused to answer altogether, and others curtly dismissed James by denying knowledge of anyone by the name of Randolph. Despite the nearness of the English troops, the loyalists still feared the vindictiveness of the local Sons of

Liberty. Many of them had had their homes and shops looted and burned as penalty for their continued allegiance to the Crown.

By noon James admitted to himself that his quest was futile. He had hoped to keep the identity of his other sources from York Allen; not because he distrusted the journalist, but because James recognized that the young man was vulnerable. The closer he personally became to the English, the more possible it was that he might be discovered. If this happened, James reasoned, he owed it to the other sources to protect them as much as possible. However, if he needed help in finding Ritchie, James had to turn to Allen; his knowledge of New York was almost encyclopedic.

James, still hungry from his unsatisfactory breakfast, decided to eat dinner in a small ordinary that grandiosely identified itself as "The Homestead." James was delighted to discover that his spur of the moment choice had been fortuitous. The ordinary turned out to be more restaurant than tavern. The tables were clean; the sawdust floor recently raked, and the barmaid attractive. James accepted the barmaid's recommendation: joint of lamb and boiled potatoes. James sipped a mug of ale as he waited with anticipation. He placed his hat on the chair beside him and watched as the tavern quickly filled with noontime guests. Several couples were among the diners. James felt the curious glances that were cast his way; obviously, strangers were out of place in the small neighborhood establishment.

James kept his eyes focused on his mug of ale and avoided staring in an attempt to diminish the undercurrent of hostility. Here and there James could detect the soft slur of a southern accent. His hopes began to rise. Maybe, some of the guests were from Virginia and could suggest where he could find Ritchie. James occupied himself with trying to select an approach that would not alarm the recipient. He drew lines through the rings that the ale that had spilled down the sides of his mug left on the scarred tabletop. The barmaid brought a second mug. After about forty minutes, James began to worry about the passage of time. As best he knew, he had only hours to accomplish his mission. As he waited, he began to have doubts. He wondered if he was needlessly putting in jeopardy the people he was contacting. Could he really expect to get their messages through the English lines? Would they be able to find out what the Howes were planning? If not, James was asking them to place at risk their lives and family for nothing. James concluded he was realist enough to recognize that he could not answer his questions.

Finally, the barmaid returned with a third mug of ale and a plate heaped with slices of juicy lamb and small white boiled potatoes. A second plate held a long loaf of hot, fresh baked bread. James smiled with anticipation. The meat had a bright red center, cooked just the way James preferred it. Without thinking, he wiped the knife and fork on his pants leg; most of the ordinaries he visited on the road had questionable ideas of sanitation; he cut himself a large bite of the meat, carefully including a section of the red. He stirred the meat in its own juice and was raising the fork to his mouth with genuine anticipation when a familiar figure appeared in the doorway. James' hand froze in mid air. Ritchie Randolph entered the small room, spoke familiarly with several of the guests, and took a table by himself across the room from James.

James placed the meat in his mouth and was chewing vigorously when Ritchie's eyes locked on James' face. Ritchie reacted as if he had been slapped. He stared at James, then quickly looked around to see if any of the other guests had noticed the exchange of looks. Satisfied that none had, Ritchie glanced again at James, shook his head from side to side, negatively, then looked away. James took another bite. He did not have to be a genius to recognize that Ritchie did not want the others to realize that he knew the stranger. James continued to eat trying to ignore Ritchie's presence. It was hard because he had been occupied with his quest for Ritchie since he remembered Vivian's half-serious suggestion that he might be useful as a spy. Now, James sat across the room from his friend and did not know how to approach him. Ritchie ordered a mug of ale and contented himself with a plate of bread and a large piece of country cheese.

James' mind raced trying to develop a way of approaching Ritchie. When he became aware that his plate was empty—he had eaten every morsel—he decided to leave and attempt to approach Ritchie outside. Later, James, to his dismay, could not remember having tasted a single bite of the succulent meat. James paid his fare, leaving a large tip for the barmaid, and left.

The New York September sun still had warmth, but it was nothing like the Potomac heat. James placed his tricorn on his head and walked north. A slight breeze coming off the river rustled the still green leaves. James noticed that some were turning brown despite the recent rains. James walked slowly looking right and left, anxiously searching for a discreet spot to wait for Ritchie. Most of the houses were large mansions that did not invite strangers to linger nearby. James risked a backward glance and saw that Ritchie was now walking about a hundred feet behind him.

A surge of elation made James' nerves tingle. He picked up his pace and walked briskly northward. He did not know where he was going, but as long as Ritchie followed along behind he did not care. He was now confident he would find a place where they could talk. After two blocks, James turned right and headed towards the river. The mansions appeared to line only the street northward. On his left and right, now, the neatly tailored lawns gave way to empty lots and then to open fields. The small lane ended in a path that led into a clump of woods. A backward glance assured that Ritchie continued to follow. Finally, James reached what James assumed was the bank of the East River. To his right, to the south, James could see in the distance rebel soldiers digging a fortification aimed at Long Island. James assumed that before long English soldiers would cross the river and assault these very banks. James stared at Long Island. He could see trails of smoke, from campfires he assumed, rising into the air.

James turned and waited for Ritchie to appear.

As James watched, Ritchie emerged from the tree line. He paused, looked left and right and then behind him, before turning and rushing to greet James. The two friends embraced.

"James," Ritchie gushed nervously. "I almost had heart failure when I saw you sitting there so calmly eating. How did you find me?"

James did not answer Ritchie directly.

"I'm sorry, Ritchie. I didn't mean to frighten you. Did I do something wrong?"

"No," Ritchie began. "Well, yes. Those are all loyal King's men, and they don't take kindly to strangers. All are bitter. With the English so close, they're suspicious of strangers."

"They shouldn't be afraid now. They're winning."

"No, they're afraid the rebels might take their failures out on them. Just when they're about to be safe. All have lost so much."

"It's good seeing you again, Ritchie. How's Remmie?"

"Good, James, but what are you doing here?"

"I'm with George."

"Washington?"

James nodded, closely studying Ritchie face for clues to his reaction. Ritchie, who never hid his emotions, blanched white.

"I was afraid of that," he gasped. "Are you going to do something to us?" He looked at James anxiously.

"No Ritchie. Why would you think that?"

"I don't know James," Ritchie said. "Life is so difficult. I don't know what is going to happen to us all. They say the English will protect us and help, us but I wonder."

James did not know what to say to his friend to reassure him. An unkindly thought crossed his mind: Ritchie liked to suffer.

"What will Washington do when the English attack?" Ritchie asked, his worry etched on his pale face.

James noticed that Ritchie's hands were shaking.

"Ritchie. You'll be safe. New York is indefensible. The English will come, and Washington will withdraw."

"They say he will burn the city. Will he? Where should I take Remmie?"

"Washington will not burn the city." James spoke with more assurance than he felt. He had no idea what Washington would do to New York. Burning did not seem a bad idea to him. In war it made sense to deny comfort to your enemy. In Massachusetts Washington and his men had camped in the snow while Howe's soldiers lived comfortably in the warm Boston houses.

"I'm sorry I'm putting my problems on you," Ritchie tried to pull himself together. "It's just that life here is so difficult. I'm running out of money and don't know how we will live."

"What about your father-in-law? He's responsible for your being here."

"No. It's my fault. I came with Remmie. He will feed us, but he won't let it be easy."

James decided to take a chance. He knew Ritchie was weak, but he was a friend.

"Ritchie," James began. "How would you like to earn some money?"

"How?" The thought seemed to give Ritchie some courage.

"I need to know some things," James began.

"What?"

"I need information about the loyalists." As he spoke, James knew he was not being truthful. He needed information on English plans, but he recognized to say so would simply frighten Ritchie.

"What kind of information?"

"Who is close to the English? What the English say to them."

"But the English aren't here now," Ritchie began then paused, recognizing what James was asking of him.

James saw Ritchie's realization. Ritchie might be weak but he had a sharp mind.

James decided to be frank. He told Ritchie that he needed information on English plans and anticipated that prominent loyalists would become close to the Howes, particularly if the occupation of New York extended into the winter. Ritchie acknowledged that his sojourn in New York had strengthened his doubts about his father-in-law's decision and admitted that he should have stayed in Fairfax. James offered his friend an opportunity to earn his way back into the good graces of neighbors, possibly even of saving his mansion in Fairfax. After considerable discussion, including a candid appraisal of how they would communicate anything Ritchie might learn, the two shook hands to seal their agreement. James, without thinking, took the leather pouch from his pocket and handed it to Ritchie. James noticed that it was heavy. James had no idea how much money it contained; he had not opened it since Eric had given it to him.

Ritchie smiled broadly and tossed the pouch in his palm.

"Specie," Ritchie said. "Coins are rare. My loyalist friends would fight for these."

James nodded agreement and wondered what he had given Ritchie.

The two friends parted after agreeing to meet the next morning at the Red Fox. James decided he would have to learn the name of another ordinary if he were to stay in the city much longer.

Chapter 19
New York
August/September, 1776

At noon on August 29th, Ambrose Serle, Lord Howe's secretary, stood on the quarter-deck of the command ship "Eagle" and watched as the sloop carrying the Admiral's dinner "guests" made its way through the rain gusts. In the near distance, Serle could see yesterday's battleground, Long Island. Serle studied the beaches where General Howe's army had landed. A line of boats scurried between shore and the fleet carrying men and supplies for the troops who had already occupied all but a small fortification on the island's eastern tip. Serle had been present when the general had personally delivered his first action report to his brother, the admiral. General William Howe had been all smiles when he described the overwhelming victory. He had been particularly proud of General Clinton's flanking move through Jamaica Pass. General Howe did not admit to his brother that he had originally opposed Clinton's plan. A member of the general's staff had confided the details to Serle. Clinton, who had become intimately familiar with the Long Island terrain as a young man living with his father who had been Governor of New York, had personally scouted the terrain and appraised Sullivan's defensive deployments. Clinton had been delighted to discover that his adversary had overlooked the Jamaica Road, a path really, on the island's northern shore.

Clinton had suggested a bold flanking maneuver that General Howe had rejected out of hand. After rethinking the proposal overnight, Howe had reversed himself. Howe also had approved two diversions. He sent a British feint against the American right flank, the Hessians into the center and two-thirds of his army with Clinton around Sullivan's left. To everyone's surprise, Clinton's force was in the American rear before they were discovered. The result was American panic and absolute English victory. Clinton's marauding men captured two American generals, Sullivan hiding in a cornfield near his headquarters, and the impostor who styled himself General Lord Sterling. The latter had been Sullivan's senior commander on the left flank. As soon as he heard of the captures of the two

American generals, Admiral Lord Howe had insisted they be transported to the "Eagle" to meet with himself and General Howe.

To the dismay of Clinton and the other victorious English generals, the Howes ordered them to halt their troops who were anxious to complete the rout by driving the Americans into the river. General Howe declared it would be less costly to humble the Americans with siege tactics rather than sacrifice English lives as would happen with a final frontal assault. Serle knew this to be something less than candor. He had personally listened to the Howes discuss their options the previous day. The Admiral was enthusiastic because he believed the overwhelming victory presented he and his brother an opportunity to end the war. The Admiral had suggested that they surprise the Americans by being magnanimous in victory. His proposal was simple. The Howes should revert to their roles as joint Peace Commissioners and offer compromise in place of the demands of the victor. The capture of the American generals provided the means. While Serle awaited Sullivan and Lord Sterling's arrival, the Howes discussed their plan.

"Don't worry, William, you have the rebels in a trap. If the Americans don't accept our peace overtures, you can destroy Washington and his army at your convenience."

General Howe studied his brother before responding. He agreed with the proposal to exploit the opportunity to capture peace, but he had his doubts. As always, however, he deferred to his older brother.

"Just so your fleet prevents the Americans from escaping across the river to New York," the general hedged.

Lord Richard laughed. "Always the pessimist, William. Don't worry. We have the Americans in a box. Pray tell why did Washington place himself in such a dreadful position. He has your army in front of him and the river at his back preventing escape. I thought his troops liked to fire from behind rocks and trees and then run. "

"Remember, Richard, Washington is not a professional. His only military experience was during the war with the French in the west, and there he learned how to lose."

"Just so," the Admiral nodded, "and now, we give him a chance to eke glory from defeat."

A particularly heavy rain squall enveloped the "Eagle" just as the sloop approached. Serle, standing under the quarter-deck's overhang just outside the door leading to the admiral's cabin, watched with dry amusement as the soaked and dirty Americans approached. They appeared as what they were, defeated men, anything but rebellious.

"Welcome aboard the "Eagle," Serle spoke haughtily. He assumed the fact that a civilian greeted them not a military officer was not lost on them. "I am Ambrose Serle, the admiral's secretary."

Sullivan, who had stiffened his back with pride expecting a salute, glared at Serle then relaxed.

"Mr. Serle," Sullivan spoke curtly.

The second man, the bogus Lord Sterling, remained silent. The man's real name was William Alexander. During a visit to England some seventeen years previously, Alexander, while investigating his family lineage, had learned that one of his ancestors had once carried the title Lord Sterling. He had immediately laid claim to the title and despite the fact that the House of Lords had ruled against him continued with his false pretensions in the colonies.

Serle turned and led the way to the admiral's spacious sitting room.

The assembled English officers, taking their lead from the Howe brothers, treated the Americans with respect. Serle noted with amusement that despite their attempts to deal with their captors as equals, the American generals worked themselves into a position near the admiral's fireplace where they dried their wet clothing. The Americans acted with dignity, ineffectively concealing an occasional involuntary shudder.

Lord Richard posed as a genial host entertaining friends; Serle marveled at the facility with which the admiral concealed his disdain for the humbled rebel officers. He put them at ease with frequent references to his brother who had died while serving the colonies. Though neither he nor his "guests" had ever seen it, Lord Richard described in detail the commemorative statue the people had erected to his brother's memory. The admiral insisted that Sullivan who had a reputation as a hard drinker keep his glass filled with the admiral's wine. Serle privately approved that the Admiral had personally ordered that wine from the kegs that met the common sailor's daily ration be placed in bottles that had once contained the admiral's finer vintages.

After the meal, the stewards served the brandy and cigars. For some reason, Howe shared his private stock of cigars made from the delicately aged Virginia leaf. Serle assumed the admiral drew some ironic pleasure from the fact that Washington's generals were thus induced to break their own trade embargoes.

Sullivan appeared to respond to the admiral's hearty geniality and by the end of the meal was sharing stories with abandon. After lighting his guests' cigars, the admiral settled down to business. He began by noting that Sullivan's former colleagues in the Congress misunderstood his intentions. He acknowledged that he wore three hats, two as a military commander, but the third as Peace Commissioner. He stressed that his mission was to restore peace. He denied that he was authorized only to accept surrenders and to issue pardons as General Washington and others believed. The admiral, paused for effect, then declared that he had been assured that Parliament would approve any conditions he proposed. In this regard the admiral confided that no one in his family believed that Parliament had the right to tax the colonists without fair representation and described the war as senseless. He concluded by asking that Sullivan under parole travel to Congress as his emissary and ask that several of its members be dispatched to meet with Howe in an unofficial peace conference.

To Serle's surprise, Sullivan agreed without qualification. Lord Richard quickly sealed the agreement by directing that his brother immediately arrange the return of Sullivan to his army under a flag of truce. Serle assumed word of the commander-in-chief's action would soon spread to the English generals and troops and provide the justification for the unwelcome delay in continuing the attack against the isolated and vulnerable rebel troops on Long Island.

After Sullivan and Sterling's departure, Lord Howe summoned Serle to his cabin and dictated a long report on the Long Island victory for London. Serle noted he omitted any reference to his discussion with the captured Americans.

The next day before the report had been dispatched on a returning ship, the Howes received some unwelcome news. During the night in the concealment of a heavy rain and thick fog, Washington had somehow evacuated his army from its Long Island trap. Dismayed but still optimistic about his peace overture using General Sullivan, Lord Richard rewrote his report deliberately understating the importance of the rebel escape—a success in defeat—and stressing high rebel and minimal English losses.

The next day, General Sullivan crossed the river in a boat under the white flag of truce. Upon arrival at New York City, he was escorted immediately to General Washington's headquarters to make his report. Excited about the prospects for his peace mission, Sullivan had been dismayed to cool his heels while Washington conferred behind closed doors with his friend from Virginia. He was surprised when Washington reacted with disinterest to Howe's proposal. While Sullivan watched, Washington laboriously scratched a short note to his friend John Adams in Philadelphia. Washington, without informing Sullivan of its contents, folded the paper while Sullivan watched, placed it in an envelope then dropped a blob of hot wax on the flap. He pressed a large seal bearing the initials "GW" into the wax and handed the envelope to Sullivan.

"When you arrive in Philadelphia to report to the Congress on your mission for Admiral Howe, please give this private message to Mr. John Adams."

Sullivan took the message and waited for Washington to praise him for his skill in dealing with the Howes. Washington turned back to his desk, silently dismissing the chastised Sullivan. Sullivan in desperation waited.

Washington after a few seconds looked up and acted surprised that Sullivan was still waiting.

"Have a pleasant trip, general," Washington spoke coldly and returned his gaze to the papers in front of him.

Sullivan, feeling his Irish temper rise started to protest, then thought better of it.

"Thank you, sir," he said angrily then turned and stomped from the room.

Washington smiled at Sullivan's departing form and returned to his papers.

As he hurried about the city meeting his informants and making plans, James quickly mastered his environment. He had always known that the city was located on an island situated between the Hudson and Harlem Rivers. Some called the Hudson the North River and the Harlem the East River. The island was thirteen miles long and at places two miles wide. New York City nestled in a three-mile long pocket at the island's southern tip. On the island's northeast corner King's Bridge connected the island with the mainland. On the cliff overlooking the bridge, the rebels had constructed Fort Washington. Although James did not know it, Washington had already decided to surrender the city when the English finally attacked and was transferring his army progressively northward towards Fort Washington. While James made his arrangements, Washington's army moved supplies out of the city. To Washington's concept of a mobile army, the supplies were far more important than the city or the land being surrendered. Unknown to either Washington or James, the Howe brothers, waiting for the congress' answer to the peace offer carried by General Sullivan, graciously gave Washington the time needed to move his supplies and James the opportunity to organize his informant net and test his communications.

General Sullivan rode hard and reached Philadelphia in three days. On September 2nd he reported to individual delegates about his conversation with the Howe brothers. The next day Congress formally asked Sullivan to submit a written report. He did so stressing that Lord Howe was empowered to negotiate peace and wished to meet with a delegation from the Congress.

To Sullivan's surprise, his report created a furor. The New England members protested that this was just another English ploy designed to mislead the colonists. They insisted it be ignored. After several days of debate, the Congress appointed a three-man delegation that included the venerated elder Benjamin Franklin, a hard line patriot, the firebrand Sam Adams, and the moderate Edward Rutledge. On September 11th the delegation reached Perth Amboy and took the ferry to Staten Island. Lord Howe, accompanied by Ambrose Serle and other members of his staff, met them at the beach and escorted them to a nearby house. After a meal of ham, mutton and tongue, which they washed down with liberal servings of a claret that Franklin later described as passable, the Americans declared their willingness to hear what Howe had to say. To their dismay, the Admiral began by noting he had to meet with them as private citizens as he had no authority to receive them as representatives of the Congress. Franklin replied wryly that the admiral could consider them to be anything he wished as long as it was not as British subjects. Howe stressed that if the colonies would retract their declaration of independence and return to their former status he could declare peace, grant pardons and recommend any changes in the imperial system the colonists desired. The Americans replied that they had no intention of making peace until the Crown recognized their independence. On this barrier, the conference broke. The Americans returned to Philadelphia, and Lord Howe ordered his brother to implement his plans for continuing the attack.

On the night of September 14th, James, tired and dirty, returned at dusk to the Black Crow. After a busy two weeks, he was finally satisfied that his net of informants was as ready as he could make them. The principles, Pigot, Partridge, Remmie and York Allen had been briefed and trained. Each had placed one message written in invisible ink in his assigned hiding place. Allen had retrieved the messages with a minimum of difficulty and passed them to his uncles the messengers. The fisherman had delivered three to Perth Amboy and the stable man had rode north to Fort Washington with the fourth. In addition Allen had enlisted the services of two watchers, his elderly mother and father, whose task would be to observe, and the owner of the Red Fox tavern whose recruitment was simply a matter of protection; James and his contacts had met so frequently at the Red Fox that the proprietor and his barmaid daughter had become curious. When York explained they were making plans to harass the English after the expected capture of the city, the self professed patriot agreed to help and purchased his own black tricorn hat.

James went directly to his room, determined to finally get a full night of sleep. He had replaced the vermin infested mattress with a linsey woolsy cover that he stuffed with clean straw. The city that night was rife with rumors, the most troublesome of which was a report that five English ships-of-the-line had been seen sailing northward in the East River. Since Washington had moved his headquarters seven days earlier to the north end of the island, tacitly announcing his intention to abandon the city, the remaining population had tensely waited for the English attack. Washington had again split his army; eight thousand were deployed in the heights between Harlem and Kings Bridge; five thousand were spread along the island's thirteen mile length, maintaining control of the city while carts and wagons noisily hauled supplies northward and guarding points along the island's middle which might be inviting to Howe's troops. Washington and his generals, like everyone else, expected the English to strike north of the city interposing their army between Washington and New York. The loyalists waited for their liberators, and the rebels, common citizens and members of the patriot army alike, worried about being caught behind the English lines. James included himself amongst the latter.

Despite his gnawing concern, the exhausted James slept soundly. He had done as much as he could in the city itself and planned to ride northward the next day to report his progress to Washington. James recognized that his team had little chance of success and that Washington had much larger concerns to occupy his time, but James was satisfied that he had tried.

The first cock had crowed to announce the appearance of the sun on the eastern horizon and the Black Crow was still cloaked in the gray of the departing night, when James was roughly shaken from his sleep.

"James, James, wake up, the English are landing."

It took James several seconds to focus on his assistant's words. James stared with confusion at the shabby form. Lieutenant Grey's black beard was now a disheveled inch long. It was a countryman's unkempt mass of hair lacking the style and shape of a well-groomed officer's pride.

"James, the English are attacking at Kip's Bay and the last of our army is fleeing northward."

James sat up, scratched his beard while his numbed mind registered Eric's words, and asked:

"Are you sure?"

"It may be a feint but the English are moving flat boats into position along side their men-of-war. We can't take a chance of being cut off and confined to the city."

James, recognizing that Kip's Bay was about a third of the way up the island's length thus placing the British army between him and Washington's headquarters, leaped to his feet fully clothed. He slid his feet into his boots. Without a word, he grabbed his only possession, his saddlebags and followed Eric to the empty stables behind the Crow. The neighborhood was still quiet. James and Eric saddled the two horses and galloped out of the barn. Eric led the way to the westernmost of the three roads that led from New York City northward. James knew that at Harlem, roughly two thirds of the way up the island's length, the roads met to become one. James approved Eric's choice. If the English were landing at Kip's Bay, they were on the eastern coast under the protective guns of their fleet. They would have to fight their way the some two miles across the island's breadth in order to isolate the city from Washington's army.

Despite the fact that the army had been moving supplies northward for two weeks as part of Washington's strategic retrenchment, the road was filled with army wagons struggling to take one last load to Washington's troops. The army carts were moving slowly, surrounded by masses of ordinary citizens who had delayed their flight too long. At the edge of the city, Eric paused and studied the jammed roadway. He turned to James and shouted:

"We'll never get through this way. Let's swing through the fields along the river."

James turned his horse and forced his way through the stream of refugees ignoring the shouted complaints. Once free of the people, James spurred his mount and turned northward cutting through the open pastures. After about a half-hour's ride, they encountered a disorganized mass of rebel militia. They seemed to be going in two directions at once. Several officers were shouting at one group driving them eastward towards what James assumed was the point of the English landing. The citizen soldiers in the immediate vicinity of the officers appeared to be responding reluctantly. As James and Eric watched, the militiamen in the ranks furthest from the officers peeled off individually and fled for cover in the tree line that stretched northward along the Hudson.

"What's happening?" Eric shouted at one husky soldier who like them stood watching the panicked militiamen mill about. The man glanced at Eric and James with amusement. James sensed that the man was considering raising his rifle and taking their mounts. He leaned forward and put his hand on the saber he had purchased in the city and now carried in a scabbard on the right side of his saddle. Eric noted James' motion and reacted by placing his hand on the flintlock pistol he carried on his saddle.

"Easy gents," the soldier cautioned, spitting a stream of tobacco juice in their direction. "I was jist admirin' those fine mounts."

"We're scouts collecting information for the general," Eric improvised.

"Sure, and I'm Genril Sullivan myself," the militiaman laughed.

"What's happening?" James asked.

"Black Dick," the militiaman derisively referred to Admiral Lord Howe by his nickname, "finally decided to fight."

"Where?" James asked.

"Don't follow those brave men cause the fightin' is in the opposite direction," the militiaman said. "They're lookin' for the genril so they can report jist like you. Leastwise, most are tryin' to head north."

James and Eric exchanged looks and simultaneously spurred their horses northward.

Later, they learned that they were among the last to escape before the British drove across the island and blocked further flight. One story that James did not know if it were apocryphal or not alleged that the General Clinton's army narrowly missed a major victory. The panicked militiamen that James and Eric encountered were remnants of units of General Putnam's army. According to the story, the invading English generals, accompanied by Governor Tryon, paused at the home of Robert Murray for a rest. Mrs. Murray treated them with cake and wine and good cheer while the general's angry troops waited. The company had been so pleasant and the morning so enjoyable that the generals tarried arrogantly for over two hours. This delay enabled General Putnam's troops to hurry up the west coast road and escape what would have been inevitable capture or death.

The English cordon isolated New York, and the successful troops marched into the city to the cheers of their loyalist sympathizers. Many raced through the city painting the letter "P" on the homes of Patriots marking the buildings clearly for looting by the Hessians and English troops and later for occupancy.

While the New Yorkers cheered, Washington assessed his losses. He had not succeeded in moving all of the needed supplies northward, but their loss was not what troubled him the most. On Long Island and again in the battle of New York Washington had been unable to control his army. Neither the commander himself, his generals nor his field commanders had been able to impose discipline on the frightened militiamen. As soon as a battle began, the citizen soldiers fired one shot from their flintlocks then retreated as individuals. Not one unit maintained solidarity, and this lack of control worried Washington. He knew he could not fight a war with every man acting as his own general.

Washington at Kings Bridge attempted to regroup his army and deploy his defenses for a stand. In New York, the English celebrated. As days passed and the English did not follow up on their total success by moving to eliminate Washington's confused force, Washington puzzled over the delay. Washington ordered that trusted men be sent through the lines to learn what the English were doing.

On the night of September 20th, in New York City a house in the wharf area broke into flames. A river breeze fanned the flames out of control, and they spread rapidly. Many reported seeing dark figures scurrying from building to building as the uncontrolled fire spread. The recently conquered city was still in a state of bureaucratic anarchy. Civilians, no longer in control, waited for the English army to give the orders to respond. Word of the conflagration spread slowly. The church steeples were silent; the fleeing rebels had carted away all the church bells for use in fabricating cannon. The fire companies that eventually responded proved ineffectual. The flames spread during the night and threatened to consume the entire city. During the early morning hours, fate intervened. The wind shifted, enabling the firefighters to confine the blaze between Broadway and the North River. By noon the authorities had regained control, but the city had lost over six hundred buildings, most residences and offices but including Hyde Pigot's Trinity Church.   General Howe's headquarters announced to the shocked city that his army had captured several rebels in the act of setting the fires. Many had matches and other combustibles concealed on their persons. Later, rumors spread of soldiers having killed arsonists at work and having seized individuals busily engaged in obstructing the firefighters by cutting the rope handles on fire buckets and abusing the loyal citizens working to save their homes.

Reports reaching Washington's army in the north of the island indicated that about one quarter of the city had been destroyed. Washington, who had been ordered by Congress to evacuate the city intact, was alleged to have observed that fate, or "some good honest fellow," had intervened to do what they had not been able to do themselves.

Sitting in his headquarters at Kings Bridge, Washington assessed the situation. He had surrendered the united colonies' largest city to the English without a fight. His army had turned its back on the enemy and ran. Officers as well as men had panicked, some trampling each other as they dashed to and fro while fleeing for their lives. The total breakdown of discipline depressed Washington. In his reports to Congress he lamented the poor quality of his officer corps and the undependability of the militia. He argued that only the recruitment of long term soldiers and able officers could save the day. According to the best information he was able to acquire from refugees fleeing the city, the English had lost three men in their attack. Washington wryly noted his own troops had done more damage to themselves in their trampling panic to escape. Washington had New York's church bells but had left behind sixty irreplaceable cannon.

One of those dispatched to acquire information on New York City after the takeover was a young lieutenant from New Hampshire. The Yale educated school teacher had completed a sketch of English fortifications on Long Island and New York and a report on troop dispositions when he stopped in a tavern for a much needed draft of ale. There, he was recognized by a Tory cousin, Samuel Hale, also from New Hampshire and denounced as a rebel spy. A cursory search disclosed the reports. The next morning, September twenty-second, General Howe himself interrogated the young schoolteacher. The rebel officer identified himself as Lieutenant Nathaniel Hale and frankly admitted he had infiltrated British lines to collect information. General Howe ordered death by hanging for the American spy. At about eleven o'clock, after denying Hale's request for a clergyman and a Bible, Howe's Provost Marshall unceremoniously hung Hale. An English officer whose tent stood nearby was one of the few witnesses. He later reported that Hale just before the gallows' trap fell had called out in a loud and firm voice:

"I only regret that I have but one life to lose for my country."

Chapter 20
Autumn, 1776
New York

James and his assistant, Lieutenant Eric Grey, spent the week following their flight northward resting, making plans and readjusting their communications link with their net in New York City. Eric visited General Washington's headquarters and reported that James had established himself in a farmhouse north of King's Bridge. Since Washington had been involved in endless meetings with his generals in military council making plans for the anticipated English attack on Harlem Heights, James had not intruded. His informant net remained silent, and James worried that his intense efforts would amount to nothing.

Finally, on the morning of September 25th, General Washington summoned James and Eric to his headquarters. Both men wore their dirty working clothes. Eric, who had reported receiving curious glances from the sentries and his former colleagues on Washington's staff, had asked James if they should shave their scraggly beards and don clean clothing. Eric during the course of their hasty flight from New York had been forced to abandon his collection of fine uniforms. Now, like James, he owned only the rags he wore on his back. James, secretly pleased with his disarming disguise, decided they should go as they were, dirt, odor and disreputability to the contrary.

This time the surly sentries refused admission to both James and Eric. On James' previous visit, Eric, dressed as an immaculate member of Washington's staff, had ordered James' admission with confident authority. This time only the intercession of a natty captain wearing the pink sash of a staff officer obtained their admittance. The captain, who had previously been a superior of Eric's, frowned his disapproval of the young man's appearance. He assumed that Eric had been one of the many officers who had deserted during the Long Island and City campaigns and had now reappeared to beg forgiveness and reinstatement from the commander-in-chief.

Washington was standing at the door to his office conferring with one of his secretaries when James and Eric appeared. To James' delight, Washington had glanced at them without recognition, sniffed the air in disapproval and then turned his back in dismissal, obviously irritated that the disreputable twosome had somehow talked their way past the sentries.

"General Washington. It's Lieutenant Grey," the captain announced with evident concern that he had erred in approving the admission.

Washington spun on his heel and studied the two more closely. To James' relief, Washington laughed loudly.

"Better than I had hoped," he announced, confusing the captain. "Come into my office. We have business." The taller Washington put his arm on James' shoulder and pulled him into the office. Eric followed and closed the door behind him as the captain watched with amazement.

Washington escorted James and Eric to seats near the fireplace. A light September chill had descended during the night, and Washington's staff, concerned for his health, had lighted the first fire of the season. Washington poured each of his visitors a cup of tea from the chipped porcelain pot that set on the table in front of his chair.

"Sir, if I may... ." Eric gestured towards the teapot, offering to assist. The former aide was uncomfortable being treated like a guest.

"Sit still," Washington ordered. Eric handed one of the cups to James and took one for himself.

Washington leaned back in his chair and consulted his watch. James studied his friend's face. It was even paler and more drawn than it had been three weeks earlier. The worry lines appeared deeper.

"We have thirty minutes before our guests arrive, and I have some matters we must discuss," Washington announced. "Don't worry about my appearance," Washington dismissed his friend's scrutiny. "Vivian wouldn't recognize you as far as that goes."

James nervously ran his hands along his baggy pants and was dismayed to note the small cloud of dust that resulted.

"Tell me what the Howes are planning," Washington smiled, but the edge of the commander-in-chief was discernible in his voice.

"We can't do that yet, George," James replied. He had not intended to use his friend's first name in front of Eric, but it had slipped out. "But we have hopes."

James briefly identified the members of his informant net and described their plans for acquiring information.

"We have yet to receive our first report, but I am confident one will be forthcoming. York Allen is a reliable man."

Eric nodded his agreement but was intimidated into letting James speak for them.

"I hope so, James. The Howes... ." Washington paused and looked at Eric before deciding he could speak frankly. "The Howes have me confused. I expected them to march north and take advantage of our confusion before we could consolidate after the spectacle following their landing, but they haven't. Again, they're giving us time to recover. Why?"

"I'm not sure, George," James replied. "Maybe, they are taking their Peace Commissioner duties seriously."

"They're making a mistake if they are. Certainly they recognize the situation has progressed far beyond simple compromise." Washington shook his head negatively. "They must have something else in mind."

"They haven't been anxious to shed blood," James continued, giving voice to a thought he had pondered for several days. "William Howe resorted to siege tactics on Long Island when one charge would have seriously hurt our army."

"That's right," Washington agreed. "And... ."

"And he may be doing it again," James continued. "I'm not a military man, George, but he may not have to attack Harlem Heights to force you off the island."

"If that is what he wants," George half agreed. "If it were me, I would want to destroy the rebel army not acquire land."

"But that would require shedding English blood," James continued. "If he puts a blocking force in front of the heights then uses his brother's ships to land forces behind you, he can trap you on the island and starve you into surrendering the heights."

"Washington nodded agreement. "You may be right. If he doesn't attack within the next few days, I'm going to have a difficult decision. If I stay here, I risk losing my army. If I retreat again, we may be able to survive to fight another day. I wish I knew how Johnny Burgoyne is doing in his drive down from the north. I haven't had any reports for weeks. I can't let Howe come up the Hudson and link up with the army from Canada."

James remained silent. There was nothing he could say that would help his friend. James' problems with his little group in New York City were minuscule by comparison. Washington glanced at his watch.

"My visitors will be here shortly. I need your help with them James."

"Anything," James replied. He noted that Eric had followed the conversation with a wide-eyed gaze that he shifted from Washington to James as they spoke. James assumed Eric had never seen the commander-in-chief behave like a normal man with doubts and concerns.

"I think you may know all three," Washington continued. "Another committee from Congress. Elbridge Gerry, Robert Sherman and Francis Lewis. Good men. I sent a confidential message last week to John Adams asking him to send a trustworthy delegation with whom I could discuss matters I could not entrust to paper."

James nodded understanding. "I know all three, Sherman and Gerry better than Lewis."

"Good," Washington said. "I want you to take charge of their visit. Your first duty. Then, all congressional matters will be in your hands."

James recalled that on his arrival Washington had told him he would serve as the army's liaison with the Congress.

"Eric," Washington addressed the young aide. "I want you to continue to work with James on your information collecting. Please select some men to help you, but not from my staff. I'm shorthanded as it is. I'll let you and James work out how much you get involved with the politicians. I leave that to James, but for now, you need not waste time listening to us talk."

"Yes sir," Eric replied rising. He had trouble hiding his disappointment at being dismissed.

"Have the new men report to us at the farm by three o'clock," James tried to mask the disappointment by assigning responsibilities. "We will need two men to control the messengers and at least five more to work on acquiring new sources in New York. We can worry about Philadelphia later."

Eric looked at James in puzzlement. He had thought their work was finished with the recruitment and training of the New York team.

"Yes sir," he saluted and spun towards the door.

"That military demeanor looks odd on someone dressed in rags," Washington observed.

James noted that Eric smiled to himself as he walked away. Before reaching the door, he proudly placed his dusty tricorn on his head.

"Is that some kind of uniform?" Washington asked. "I notice you have an identical hat."

James smiled his answer.

"And Eric," Washington called. "Please have my guests shown in."

Eric held the door for the three congressional delegates as they entered the room. James noticed with amusement the puzzled looks that all three cast at the disheveled Eric as they passed.

After appropriate greetings, James and the three delegates arranged themselves in chairs in a semi-circle facing Washington who had formally seated himself behind his desk.

"General," Gerry began with a smile. "Having seen the condition of your aides I am already convinced that your army is in dire need of clothing and supplies."

During the discussion that followed, Washington shocked his guests with his frank comments on the sad condition of his army. He noted the officer corps was unworthy of the country. He told story after story about junior and senior officers who had fled the enemy before their troops turned. He described the majority of officers as incompetents who could not instill discipline in the common soldier because they had none themselves. Washington opined that most of the men were better than their officers, but they looked homeward more often than in the direction of the enemy. In addition to material support, the army, if it were to have a chance against the determined enemy, had to have long term soldiers not militiamen planning next season's crops.

After the long discussion, James escorted the three guests on a tour of the encampments. They were shocked when they met one captain, who proudly proclaimed that he was a barber in private life, shaving a private from his command.

One of the regimental commanders told of his difficulty with an officer who had fled after ransacking the personal possessions of privates who were posted on guard at the captain's orders. By the end of the day, the delegates were convinced. They promised to return to Philadelphia, report to their colleagues, and draft legislation designed to rectify the problems cited by the general.

James missed his three o'clock meeting at the farm with the new officers recruited by Lieutenant Grey, but he returned satisfied that he could handle the liaison with Congress. He knew that all members were not as objective and reasonable as these three, but he was now confident he could cope with the new duties and was pleased with the knowledge that by doing so he could lift considerable weight from Washington's shoulders.

Ambrose Serle, the Admiral's secretary, visited New York City on September 16th, the day following the rebel flight from the city. The many fine buildings and government houses that he found there pleasantly surprised him. He witnessed a party of English marines as they raised the English flag over the fort and surprised himself by cheering as loudly as any person in the large crowd that had gathered for the ceremony. Many local citizens participated and demonstrated their relief at being freed from the tyranny of the rebels by carrying British officers on their shoulders through the streets. As Serle walked, he was amazed by the rebel fortifications. Washington's army had dug redoubts on virtually every street corner. Serle smiled with amusement at the thought of how much chagrin the rebels who had dug the fortifications must have felt when they joined their fleeing comrades without having fired a single shot from the ditches where they had labored many hours.

When he reached Gaine's print shop, Serle decided to enter and purchase local newspapers to gain insight into local opinion. Serle had already heard of Gaine from Governor Tryon who commended the man as a staunch subject of the King who had suffered at the hands of the Sons of Liberty. Tryon recommended that Serle himself take charge of political matters at Gaine's shop, arguing that Admiral Lord Howe should control the content of the New York press. Serle wanted to obtain an impression of Gaine and his New York *Gazette* for himself.

The shop was empty except for a young man sitting at a table at the back of the room, partially obscured by a printing press. Serle walked up to the counter that separated the work area of the print shop from the public and waited for the young man to acknowledge his presence. The young man dipped his quill in the inkpot in front of him and continued writing, deliberately ignoring Serle's presence. Serle had seen the untidy youth who curiously wore a black tricorn hat while he worked glance in his direction when he entered, but he neither spoke nor acknowledged in any way Serle's appearance.

Unaccustomed to such rude behavior, Serle was unable to conceal his anger when he spoke:

"Young man." He repeated himself when the writer did not respond. "Young man. May I please have your attention."

"We're closed," the youth responded sourly without looking up from his paper. He again dipped his pen in the inkpot and continued writing.

"Young man. See here," Serle spoke indignantly. "I want some newspapers."

"We're closed. There's a war on you know."

"Do you know who I am?"

"No, and I don't care. Leave," the youth arrogantly challenged Serle with eyes that sparkled with humor at Serle's indignation.

"I am Lord Howe's secretary, and I demand copies of newspapers."

"I don't care if you are Black Dick himself," the youth replied, staring belligerently at Serle.

"Where is the proprietor?"

"Probably at the Red Fox drowning his sorrows," the youth replied.

"Governor Tryon has recommended Mr. Gaine to me," Serle tried another tack.

"Good for you," the youth laughed. He put his quill on the table in front of him, leaned back in his chair with his hands folded behind his head and stared at Serle.

"You don't look like a redback," the youth challenged. "Where is your uniform?"

"I'm not a soldier. I'm a civilian aide to the Admiral. Serle was surprised at himself for explaining anything to the arrogant young man.

"Well la-de-da," the youth replied. "So am I not a solder. I guess that makes us equals."

Serle was surprised at the young man's attitude. He had already met several prominent Loyalist leaders who at Governor Tryon's recommendation had called on the admiral. All had been servile and had worked to ingratiate themselves with their saviors. Serle assumed that the youth represented the colonial lower class and resented his obvious betters.

"I want some newspapers," Serle repeated his demand, having decided to teach the rude young man his proper place.

"We have no papers. The *Gazette* hasn't been printed for two weeks. Gaine's afraid of being burned out."

"Not now, I assume," Serle smiled sarcastically.

"No, but he's waiting for your kind to come up with some money. He has none."

"And what are you doing? I would have assumed the academies would be closed." Serle tried to imply that the youth would be doing nothing more than schoolwork.

The youth laughed, genuinely amused.

"What's your name?"

"York Allen."

"Then you are not a relative to Gaine. What do you do here? An apprentice?"

"Something like that," Allen replied.

"What are those over there?" Serle pointed at a stack of newspapers piled at one end of the counter.

"Newspapers."

"I want some of them."

"They're old ones. Help yourself. You can read what the New Yorkers think of you."

"What is the price?"

"How should I know?"

"What should I pay."

"Steal them," Allen suggested. "That's what your Hessians are doing to everything else."

Serle was dismayed at the comment. He knew that the Hessians and some of the English soldiers were looting at will with little regard for the distinction between loyalist and patriot.

"Watch your tongue or you could be in trouble," Serle threatened.

At that moment, Gaine, the proprietor, entered the shop, introduced himself and listened gape-mouthed as Serle again explained who he was and what he wanted.

"The Governor tells me we may be able to do some business," Gaine began.

York Allen watched with an amused expression as Gaine fawningly tried to ingratiate himself with Serle. The proprietor collected several copies of the newspapers from the end of the counter and handed them to Serle.

"Please take these, sir. They are a week old but the latest we have in the city. You will find I have copies of all six newspapers that were printing at the time."

"But not the infamous *Gazette*," York Allen laughed derisively.

Gaine glared at Allen but said nothing. He turned his back to Allen and spoke quietly to Serle.

"Please sir. If you will join me for a pint, I have some things to say that may interest you."

"I don't imbibe alcohol," Serle sniffed, "but I will join you for a cup of tea."

Gaine frowned at the thought, and Allen laughed again.

"Better hang on to your poke," Allen called to the departing Serle. "Old Gaine will have it in his pocket before you can blink."

Serle glared angrily back at Allen and appeared about to respond when Gaine took his arm and led him through the door.

"Ignore the fool," Gaine counseled. "He's the best news collector in New York, but also the rudest."

Four days later on Saturday night, Serle was sound asleep in his cabin on the "Eagle" when about one o'clock he was awakened by excited voices on the deck outside. When Serle, irritated to be abruptly awakened, stepped outside in his nightcap and gown to chastise the rude sailors before they disturbed Lord Howe, he was shocked by the red haze that filled the sky over the city. New York was in flames. He choked on the acrid smoke despite the sea breeze and their distance from the shore.

The next morning the Admiral dispatched Serle to obtain a first hand report. He was dismayed to learn that over one fifth of the city, including many fine homes, had been destroyed. The ashes still smoldered and grime smeared soldiers and sailors worked with frantic townsmen to extinguish the remaining isolated fires. Serle was unable to sort the many rumors for truth and falsehood, but he accepted the premise of most that agents of Washington's army had started the fire. Serle heard many first hand reports about the seizure of culprits including one who had been angrily cast back into the flames as penalty. The description of the terrible human deaths did not trouble him as much as the loss of Trinity Church. Serle had considered it the finest edifice in town, an important element of the "fabric" the church used to control the town's establishment. Serle was relieved when he walked along North River to discover that St. Paul's still stood. He arrived at St. Paul's at eleven o'clock fully expecting to find services in progress. He had planned to attend and give his own prayers thanking the Lord for saving that part of the town that survived.

Serle was surprised to discover the church empty and Pastor Inglis, who had visited the Admiral on the "Eagle," standing outside talking with a slender man dressed in black, also wearing a clerical collar.

"Oh Mr. Serle. What a tragic morning," Pastor Inglis wrung his hands and frowned as he greeted Ambrose.

"May I offer my condolences at the terrible losses," Serle spoke solemnly.

"Will we never cease to suffer at the hands of the rebels?" Inglis spoke perfunctorily.

"Not much longer, if Lord Howe has his way," Serle replied. Serle studied the second man whose head was bowed in apparent anguish.

"We don't know for sure who started the fire," the man said.

"Mr. Serle. May I introduce Pastor Pigot. He has just lost his church. Pastor, this is Mr. Serle, Admiral Lord Howe's secretary."

"Pastor," Serle said gravely. "Again, may I offer my condolences at your loss." The man glanced briefly at Serle, nodded, then looked back at the ground. Strangely, Serle thought he detected a flash of interest in the man's eyes that contrasted with his sad demeanor.

"We've lost Trinty, but also many people. We will be days until we know how many," Pastor Pigot spoke softly.

"Trinty was our finest church," Pastor Inglis said nervously. "We at St. Paul's will do our best to help until Trinty is rebuilt."

"If she is," Pigot said. He assumed that Inglis was already counting the collections he could take in from Trinty parishioners in the interim.

"We have postponed services, because of the tragedy, until three this afternoon," Pigot said. "If you would join us, Mr. Serle, and his Lordship also, we would be most grateful."

"Certainly, I will attend," Serle replied. "But his Lordship... ." Serle paused to imply the Admiral was deeply engaged in military plans. In fact, Serle knew that the Howe brothers planned to dine on the "Eagle" to celebrate their New York victory and to discuss the general's strategy for pursuing Washington's army.

"We understand," Inglis observed officiously. "But if yourself..."

"I will be here," Serle promised. He anticipated the Howes would make and change their plans several times before launching the next attack and after all this was the Sabbath and the fire had been a human tragedy. It suddenly occurred to Serle that the loss of Trinity Church might afford opportunity. With his help, the church could be rebuilt on a more ambitious scale. If he could persuade Lord Howe to assist, he might even be able to acquire enough land for the church to enable it to take the first steps in developing a state glebe. Serle resolved to brief the Admiral on his original proposal that the Board of Trade had ignored for using large glebes to build powerful churches that could be used to manipulate and control the colonists. If successful, Serle's plan could revolutionize the empire and harness it for England's benefit for centuries to come.

"We must talk about your plans for rebuilding Trinity," Serle turned towards the distraught Pigot. "It's never too soon to begin the Lord's work anew."

Pigot stared in confusion at Serle before responding.

"With the Crown's assistance... ." Pigot began.

"I'm afraid I cannot speak for His Majesty," Serle interrupted. "But in a small way I may be able to persuade Lord Richard and other influential men to help."

Pigot nodded approval and thought to himself that the Lord indeed worked in mysterious ways. He had lost his church and possibly much of his congregation; now, one of the very men he had wanted to meet on Washington's behalf was offering to help him rebuild his church.

Chapter 21
Autumn, 1776
New York City, King's Bridge, Frog's Neck

During the first week of October, Ambrose Serle visited Hugh Gaine at the *Gazette* three times. York Allen patiently watched as the two men circled. When it became apparent that Serle might become a fixture at the newspaper, York moderated his antagonism. His agreement with James required him to develop contacts within the English military hierarchy, and Allen belatedly decided that despite his civilian status Serle's position as the admiral's secretary qualified him to meet James' requirements.

On Monday the seventh of October, Serle and Gaine reached their agreement. As York Allen watched, Gaine soberly escorted Serle to the shop door and formally shook his hand. Gaine paused in the doorway and observed as Serle carefully stepped around the accumulated garbage in the street as he made his way to the riverfront. As soon as Serle was safely beyond hearing distance, Gaine rushed towards the table where York sat reading Rivington's *Gazette*. Gaine's newspaper, the New York *Gazette* had not been printed for over a month. York had continued to visit the newspaper offices in order to maintain squatter's rights to his job. Gaine had not paid Allen for over two months, and the young man made a demonstration of his poverty by dining frugally on a half loaf of dry bread. York was astute enough to recognize that if he acted otherwise and conspicuously spent his generous wages from James he would arouse Gaine's suspicions.

James had just bitten off a chunk of hard bread and was manfully trying to chew it when Gaine vacated his position at the door. With a shout, the fat proprietor grabbed York's arm and pulled him to his feet. Gaine clutched the dismayed young man in his arms and spun wildly in what Allen assumed was a victory dance.

"I've done it," Gaine proclaimed in York's ear. "We're back in business."

York pulled free of the excited fat man and watched as he continued to dance. To avoid another turn as Gaine's dancing partner, Allen sought refuge behind his table. Finally, an exhausted Gaine collapsed with a whoosh into his own chair.

"We must have the first issue ready for printing on Friday."

"On Friday?" York sat straight in his chair at the thought of collecting enough information to fill the *Gazette's* four pages. "That doesn't give me enough time," York protested. He assumed he would be responsible for writing all the stories. Since the English now controlled New York, they could no longer pirate articles and letters from other colonial papers; their content would be unacceptable. He could tell from reading Rivington's *Gazette* that New York's other newspaper was having trouble generating stories that would not antagonize the English military.

"Don't worry about that," Gaine laughed. "We have our own source."

"Serle?" Allen studied the proprietor as he wiped the sweat from his flushed face.

"Serle," Gaine confirmed. "He's our new political editor."

"And what do I do?" York demanded.

"Whatever you're told," Gaine responded. "The English now own us," he said cryptically.

"You sold them the *Gazette?*"

Gaine paused before answering, obviously pondering how truthful he should be.

"I didn't really sell the *Gazette* to them. Just rented it to them," Gaine laughed at his own cleverness.

"They want a tame paper to print their lies," York spoke accusingly.

"That's right. Any objections?" Gaine adopted Allen's belligerent tone. "Because if you have... ." He put as much threat into his tone as he could muster.

"No objections," York interrupted. He threw the hard crust of bread against the sidewall in a forceful display of his disgust at the owner's cupidity. The crust bounced back and landed on the edge of Gaine's table. "Not if it means you can start paying me so I can eat."

"That's possible," Gaine said.

"Beginning now?"

"Just a small amount on account." Gaine reached into his pocket and extracted a leather pouch tied at the top with rawhide strings. He proudly tossed the pouch in the air, and Allen heard the coins jingle. "Good English specie," Gaine smiled. He untied the rawhide strings and took out four shillings. One by one he threw them to York who adroitly snatched them out of the air.

After throwing the fourth coin, Gaine retied the strings and put the pouch back in his pocket.

"That's all?" Allen protested.

"For now," Gaine laughed. "I need the rest for paper, ink and the boys." Gaine referred to the two men who set the type and ran the press.

"Serle will write the stories?" Allen asked suspiciously.

"All the important stories about the English," Gaine replied. Noting his young protégé's frown, he continued. "You can write profiles of the prominent local leaders and describe how happy they are."

"The loyalists," Allen sniffed.

"Our prominent local leaders," Gaine corrected. "And forget about the rebels. The *Gazette* is now the official English mouthpiece."

"I'm not sure I like that," Allen replied. He knew Gaine expected him to be independent. "What about my journalistic integrity?"

Gaine looked at Allen and responded with a loud laugh "Who are you trying to kid, kid?"

"Why Friday?" York changed the subject. "If we hold off for a week, we can do a better job on the first issue under our new status."

"Money," Gaine replied. "The loyalists... ." He paused and corrected himself. "The prominent local residents will buy every paper we print. Serle will make sure that they all know how much the English respect our journal. Everyone seeking their favor will buy a copy to impress them."

"So," York said accusingly. "You make money from the paper, and Serle pays you to print whatever he wants."

"That's right. So what? You don't like it?"

"It's OK with me, but shouldn't I share a little of the profit?"

"For doing less? Don't press your luck."

"For selling my good name."

"You don't have one."

Deciding that he would not win that argument, Allen changed the subject. "Why is Serle so anxious about Friday?"

Gaine bit his underlip, which York recognized as Gaine's signal that he was thinking seriously. After a brief pause, Gaine looked cautiously in each direction as if assuring they were not being overheard. Allen was tempted to wisecrack but discreetly kept silent.

"Something's happening Friday," Gaine spoke softly.

"Where? Shall I cover it?" Allen immediately assumed the something referred to the delayed English attack on Washington's army but volunteered his services in order to elicit more information from Gaine.

"Don't worry about it. Serle will write all the stories for our front page. You just get some local filler for inside. Write a couple letters praising the Howes or something."

York decided he would get nothing more from Gaine. He doubted that Serle would have confided much more to the loquacious fat man. York rose out of his chair and walked around his table in the direction of the door.

"I better start working my contacts," Allen said.

"Don't bother," Gaine said. "Our news now comes from Serle."

York continued towards the door, ignoring Gaine's comment.

"It's Frog's Neck," Gaine called in a lowered voice.

York stopped as soon as Gaine spoke. He smiled to himself. He knew that Gaine's need to share his self-importance would force him to reveal everything he knew. York, like most thinking residents, had speculated on the Howe brothers' next military action. York had theorized that the cautious general and admiral would not attack Washington's defenses at Kings Bridge head on. They had already demonstrated a preference for siege tactics and flanking movements in the battles for Long Island and the city itself. The speculation centered on the mystery of where the admiral's ships would land the general's troops to begin their flanking movement. Frog's Neck was a small peninsula of land that jutted from the mainland into Long Island Sound some eight miles south east of Kings Bridge.

"Frog's Neck?" York repeated trying to sound impressed. "That's where the English will land?"

Gaine nodded yes.

"On Friday?"

Gaine smiled knowingly.

"Serle told you that?"

Gaine smiled again.

Dumb bastard, York thought to himself. Serle would learn that if he wanted to keep a secret Gaine should be the last person to be informed.

"I'm impressed," York flattered his employer. "Can I go along on one of Howe's ships? You know as the *Gazette's* eye witness."

"I told you. Don't be stupid. Serle will write what he wants to appear in the paper. You just do what I told you."

"Just trying to do my job," Allen tried to appear disappointed. He calculated he had learned all Serle been willing to share with Gaine and recognized he had his first report for Washington. Anxious to get to over his uncle's stables so that he could prepare his message for his fisherman uncle to carry to his contact, Allen turned towards the door.

"Guess I'll go over to the Fox and get me something to eat." York jingled the four shillings in his pocket.

"Save some for tomorrow," Gaine called to his reporter's back. "You'll need it."

On Wednesday, two days later, James was sitting on the front porch of the farmhouse he had made his office and was studying the fall foliage when he noticed a rider approaching at a rapid pace. James had been comparing the brilliant New England colors and had decided two things. Autumn came four weeks earlier in New York than it did in Virginia, and, he reluctantly admitted, the colors were far more vivid. He assumed the colder nights were responsible.

As the rider drew closer, James recognized the familiar form of Eric Grey, his assistant. The black tricorn was a dead giveaway. James had begun to worry about the fact that most of his staff and informants had taken to wearing black hats similar to the one James wore constantly. He belatedly realized that the English would be able to identify his men if one of them were captured and divulged the secret of the hats. Since Vivian had given James his own hat, and he considered it a good luck piece, he was not about to give it up, and if he would not, James did not see how he could order his subordinates to do something he refused to do, particularly since they had purchased their own tricorns without first asking for permission. Secretly, despite the nagging worry, James was proud of the fact that his men had decided to emulate him.

Lieutenant Grey did not slow his mount until he skidded to a halt in front of the porch where James sat.

"It's here, James. I have it," Eric called excitedly.

He jumped from his horse, draped the reins over the railing and ran to the porch waving a sealed brown envelope. Eric handed the envelope to James, then stood holding his black tricorn in one hand while he wiped the sweat from his brow with the back of his forearm with the other. James studied the water stained envelope and asked:

"And what's this?" James asked with the laconic tone he frequently used when talking with Eric. James naturally liked the young man and found himself continually wanting to tease him. It had occurred to him recently that he treated Eric with the same light, sardonic style that Vivian used with him.

"That, sir," Eric drew himself erect and spoke formally, "is your first secret report."

"From New York?" James was unable to conceal his surprise.

"Exactly, sir. The fisherman courier delivered it yesterday and our contact rode all night to bring it here. He had some trouble locating us. Washington's aides did not know where we had located."

James recognized immediately he had erred. He had left instructions for the couriers to find out where he had landed by checking with Washington's army headquarters. James planned to move frequently but had reasoned the army would always be able to locate its commander. Therefore, James simply had to keep Washington's aides informed of his whereabouts and had failed to do so. James paused to wonder if he had been negligent because he had doubted that his New York informants would produce anything of value anyway.

"It's sealed with wax as you ordered." James turned the envelope over and noticed the blob of unstamped yellow wax that he had suggested that York Allen use.

"Please, sir, let's open it and see what it says. It could be important."

"I doubt it. Allen probably wants some more money," James laughed. "Come," James ordered, spinning on his heel. "Inside. We must handle message number one officially."

As he walked, James broke the wax seal and took out the single sheet of paper that it contained. He paused in confusion and studied the paper. It was blank on both sides.

"It's the invisible ink, sir," Eric said excitedly.

"I know that," James replied irritably. The thought had occurred to him at the moment Eric spoke. "Develop it," James ordered, handing the paper to his assistant.

James had proved inept in applying the heat necessary to develop the chemical. He had tried holding the paper over a candle and had succeeded only in burning the message. He had applied an iron heated at the hearth and either got it too hot and scorched the paper or had not heated it enough to make the message appear on the blank sheet. Eric, on the other hand, had developed a knack for getting the iron just right. The messages appeared mysteriously in dark brown on the slightly scorched paper.

Eric retrieved the iron and carefully heated it while James waited impatiently.

"Hurry up," he demanded, anxious to learn what York had reported. He tried not to allow himself to hope that somehow the young man had learned of the Howe brothers' plans.

Finally, Eric licked his forefinger and applied it to the iron, reminding James of a similar gesture used by his mother at the family home in the Short Hills.

"That should do it," Eric declared, approving of his own efficiency.

Eric carefully carried the iron to the table where James had spread out the message paper on a rough piece of wool blanket. Eric ran the hot iron in one smooth stroke across the paper and studied his effort. As if by magic, a single brief line written diagonally across the page appeared.

"Frog's Neck. Friday October 12."

"That's all," James exclaimed. "What's it mean?"

"That's all," Eric repeated.

"Do it again," James instructed, nodding his head at the iron Eric still held in his hand.

"No," Eric refused. "It would only burn the paper. That's all he wrote."

"What's it mean?" James repeated himself. He thought quickly. It could only be the time and place of the English attack, and it could be simply Allen asking James to meet him to discuss a minor problem. James immediately wished he had been more precise in telling York what to report. James had concentrated on the mechanics of collecting the reports and getting them to himself. He had failed to brief Allen to report the identity of the source and advise how the informant had obtained it. James belatedly realized Allen should also have noted when he sent it so James could determine if there was a problem with their courier system. James also acknowledged it was unwise to send blank pages. He assumed the English might suspect the use of invisible chemicals if someone went to the trouble to send envelopes containing blank paper through their lines. York should write an innocuous letter on the opposite side from the report.

"It must be the time and date for the English attack," Eric suggested. His voice trembled with excitement. "Do you think, James?"

"Where's Frog's Neck?" James demanded. He had no knowledge of local geography and no maps.

"I think it's east of King's Bridge," Eric suggested.

"Let's find out," James ordered.

James carefully folded his message and placed it in his jacket pocket. He hurried through the back of the house to the barn where he had stabled his horse. He saddled quickly then joined Eric who had ridden around the house to wait for James at the barn door.

The two men rode hard for Kings Bridge where Washington had temporarily established his headquarters. After conferring with two of Washington's aides, James and Eric learned that Frog's Neck was about eight miles southeast of Kings Bridge on Long Island Sound. It was one of the places that the generals had identified as possible English landing points for their flanking move on the rebel fortifications in the north of Manhattan island.

That information hardened James' decision. The English planned to land at Frog's Neck on Friday. With a shock, he realized the information would give the rebels two days to prepare for the attack. James and Eric immediately interrupted Washington who was in conference with his generals. James asked his friend if they could meet privately for a few minutes. Washington excused himself from the military council and led James and Eric across the hall to a sitting room. James showed Washington the secret message from York Allen. Washington immediately grasped its significance.

"Is he reliable?" Washington asked, referring to the writer of the message.

James swallowed hard before answering. "Yes, sir," he replied formally.

"Then we will go to Frog's Neck and await General Howe, " Washington smiled thinly. He patted James on the back. "Thank you James. And you too Eric." Washington wheeled and left the room.

James was not disappointed. He knew from experience that Washington seldom lavished praise on friends or subordinates. He had accepted James' information and was acting on it. James looked at Eric and shook his head. He did not have to say that he prayed that York Allen was correct. James decided that as soon as the battle was over, he would somehow arrange to meet with Allen, even if he had to sneak into New York City himself. He assumed the fisherman uncle could smuggle passengers as well as messages.

Washington, acting on James' intelligence, took a chance. He stripped his fortifications at King's Bridge and moved his army southeast to Frog's Neck. Wednesday afternoon, Washington himself surveyed the potential battlefield. He discovered that Frog's Neck was more of an island than a peninsula and that a deep marsh connected the solid land with the mainland. Washington had his commanders dig their fortifications facing the marshes and prepare to isolate the English army on their ill chosen landing point. If they tried to flank Washington's fortifications at Kings Bridge by crossing from Frog's Neck, they would pay a heavy price.

At three o'clock in the morning, General Howe loaded five thousand complaining redcoated soldiers on the ships of Lord Richard Howe's fleet. At daybreak, the ships-of-the-line set sails northward up the East River. At Hell's Gate where the East River turned due east and met the Long Island Sound, the ships encountered a thick ocean fog. Fearing that any attempt to anchor would result in numerous collisions caused by the following ships, the British reluctantly pushed into the fog. Somehow, they found Frog's Neck.

The anxious redcoats encountered no difficulty in landing. As the fog gradually dissipated, they formed their units and prepared to march inland. The worried officers were delighted when they completed their landing without harassment from the rebels. The pleasure turned to dismay when advance elements of the army discovered the marsh and the rebel fortifications that had replaced the causeway connecting the island to the mainland. General Howe halted his advance and reconsidered his strategy. The cautious general lost no time concluding that it would be too costly to force his way across the marsh. Besides, surprise, an essential element to his flanking maneuver, was lost. Howe decided he had no choice but to reboard his army and select another more advantageous landing point. By the time Howe and his generals selected Pell's Point, some twenty miles further along the coast, a driving rain began to pelt Frog's Neck rendering reboarding the troops impossible. Howe sent orders calling for additional provisions and reinforcements back to New York City.

The delay cost the English a full week.

On October 18th General Howe's troops successfully landed on Pell's Point. They moved through light resistance inland to the main coastal highway north. The army was at a point near New Rochelle when Howe learned that a Hessian division of 8,000 mercenaries had landed at New York. He halted his advance and waited for the reinforcements to join him. Meanwhile, Washington, having appraised the size of Howe's growing army, had wheeled about and moved his militiamen northward to White Plains. Howe sent several battalions to block the remaining American force at Kings Bridge and followed Washington northward. On the twenty-fifth, Howe reached a point four miles from White Plains and halted. His plan to flank the Americans and pin them on Manhattan had failed, and Howe pondered whether to attack or wait for Washington to retreat.

On November 10th, Washington withdrew westward across the Hudson River. Howe turned back and implemented his plan to clear Manhattan Island. He attacked Kings Bridge and Fort Washington on November 16th. At three in the afternoon, three thousand Americans surrendered, giving Howe the whole of Manhattan and victory. Encouraged by success, Howe turned to follow Washington into New Jersey. On November 20th, General Cornwallis crossed the Hudson and captured Fort Lee. Washington and his army retreated southward. Cornwallis followed.

James and Eric watched with dismay as Washington marched his army in retreat. Their elation over their advance word of the British landing at Frog's Neck turned to despair as events developed faster than their ability to assist. As Washington moved further southward, James decided he had to have one last meeting with York Allen. Nobody knew where the lines would be drawn when the two armies moved into winter quarters, and James opted to take advantage of the confusion to slip through the lines for one last talk with his informants. Eric argued against the plan. When James turned stubborn, Eric swallowed his pride and rode with him to the Jersey shore for a rendezvous with the fisherman courier.

Chapter 22
New York City
December 1776

On Saturday, November 30th, Lord Howe issued a proclamation aimed at undermining morale in Washington's retreating army. Lord Howe called on all armed bodies of men to disperse and all congresses to cease their treasonous activities. In return, Lord Howe promised that all who reported to designated Crown officials and took an oath of allegiance to the Crown would be given a full pardon.

On Sunday, November 31st, Ritchie Randolph entertained Ambrose Serle in his home. Governor Tryon, who had been asked by the admiral's secretary to introduce him to young loyalist refugees, arranged the occasion. At the admiral's urging, Serle had embarked on a project to meet representative loyalists from throughout the colonies in order to obtain a better understanding of various local viewpoints. Governor Tryon asked Ritchie's father-in-law for a list of suitable loyalists from Virginia, and he put Ritchie's name at the top of the list. The insecure Ritchie, who was not certain of his own views despite his commitment to James to assist him, proved a poor choice. He tended to tell Serle what he thought Serle wanted to hear, and because he was so obvious he displeased Serle. Since the latter was not a man to dissimulate, he let his irritation show, making Ritchie all the more nervous. In his anxiety to please the man who was in a position to influence his own destiny, Ritchie Randolph let slip the fact he had once been approached by a rebel friend of General Washington who had asked him to provide information on loyalists in New York. Ritchie implied that the request was confined to the time frame during which Washington's armies had occupied the city, and as a consequence, Serle ignored the revelation. It did not surprise him that the rebels were interested in the loyalist refugee community.

On Monday night, December 2nd, at a point two miles north of Powles Hook, James, accompanied by Eric Grey, met York Allen's uncle, the fisherman courier. The full moon was partially obscured by low sailing clouds borne from the east on the brisk breezes. Despite his heavy woolen coat, James shivered from the sharp winter cold while the icy waters of the Hudson splashed gloomily against the hull of the small fishing sloop.

"James, won't you reconsider?" The worried Eric asked one last time after his commander had stiffly boarded the sloop. Eric, who was shivering from excitement as much as from the biting cold, stood on the shore watching as James took his seat near the bow.

"It must be done," James replied firmly. Now that he was actually preparing to slip through the British lines into occupied New York, James felt his confidence eroding. The idea had sounded better when he was surrounded by Washington's troops.

"Let me go," Eric persisted.

"It's my duty," James replied, "but thank you for the thought. I will see you in two nights. If not... ." James did not finish the sentence because he did not know what to say.

"If not, the British will have you," Eric completed the thought. "Then, what should I do?"

"Carry on," James ordered.

York Allen's uncle looked questioningly at James. He stood in the stern of the boat having difficulty holding it against the tide and the pushing waves. James nodded, and the fisherman shoved away from the rock, sat himself in the stern where he grasped the rudder and tightened the sail hawser. He turned southward to catch the wind and begin his turn back onto the tack eastward.

Eric gloomily watched as the silent skiff disappeared in the darkness. He shivered nervously and tried to dispel the premonition of disaster. This was James' first trip behind enemy lines, and Eric was seriously worried. In a few short months he had developed an affection for the soft spoken Virginian that was as strong as that he felt for his own father. A single phrase kept repeating itself in his mind.

"They hang spies," he thought. He wondered if he would ever see James again.

James crouched low in the bow seat and watched the shoreline quickly recede. He waved one last time to Eric, who did not see him, then stuffed his hands into his pockets. The strong current sent a cold spray showering over him, and James huddled still lower, tightening himself into a ball for warmth.

Although the wind was fresh, and the fisherman skilled, the crossing consumed a tedious forty-five minutes. The fisherman, a weather-beaten man who had not said a word, not even in greeting, pointed straight ahead. James could hear the current lapping on the New York shoreline, but he could see nothing but blackness ahead. Suddenly, the small cloud overhead passed, and the moon illuminated the shore only fifty yards away. Unerringly, the fisherman guided the sloop into a small cove formed by the junction of a diminutive creek and the surging river. The fisherman entered the cove, released his sail and guided the sloop to the shore. The bow crunched into a sandy beach that was no more than ten feet in length. Thick trees and overhanging bushes concealed it. James leaped out and waded into the freezing water to help the fisherman beach his boat. Then, James watched impatiently from the wood line as the taciturn man furled his sail and lowered the mainmast. In a few short minutes, the fisherman joined the shivering James, pointed inland, waved his hand to indicate James should follow, then led the way confidently down a path. James, carefully searching the shadows, was not sure to be thankful for the full moon or not.

Within an hour, to James' surprise and relief, he was sitting in a room in the front of the second floor of the Red Fox. A fire blazed in the hearth, and James crowded his backside as close as he dared. His wet trousers steamed as they dried. A beaming York Allen regaled him with stories of the admiral's secretary, a sober, long nosed aristocrat who according to Allen would have made an excellent preacher.

"Did you get my message on Frog's Neck?" Allen asked enthusiastically. "I got the information direct from the admiral himself."

"From the admiral?" James asked, impressed by his young colleague's enthusiasm.

"Well, not the admiral, but from Serle who got it from the admiral."

"I wish you had told me that," James said.

"What? Didn't you tell Washington?" Allen asked, suddenly sober.

"I did," James replied, "and he moved his troops to Frog's Neck and blocked Howe's flanking move."

Allen smiled broadly and almost glowed with pride. James could not bring himself to observe that the English had simply waited a week, moved further east along the Sound and had completed their maneuver driving Washington north, then west and finally south into New Jersey. As best as James knew, Washington was still retreating.

"I handed your message to Washington himself."

"He actually read my invisible writing?"

"He did and complimented it as the best intelligence he had ever received." James rationalized his exaggeration with the thought that the eager Allen had earned it.

"I don't know how much time we have," James began.

"You go back in two days," Allen interrupted. "We have lots of time." He was enjoying the praise.

"But I have others to see, and we don't know when we will be interrupted," James continued.

"We're perfectly safe here. The proprietor is my man," Allen bragged.

James took a heavy leather pouch from his pocket and jingled the coins.

"Well, maybe we better get our business done first," Allen agreed soberly, studying the bag.

James carefully counted out the coins. Allen's exuberance increased when he saw the five-pound gold coins nestled among the shillings and coppers.

"I've brought one hundred pounds. I'll send more when you need it."

"Well now that you mention it... ." York began.

"In due time," James interrupted. "Now, I have several requests."

James devoted the next two hours to briefing Allen on the need to provide more details in his reports, particularly information about the sourcing, estimates of reliability, and the like. James suggested that Allen begin numbering his messages, that way James would know immediately if one had been lost and posed a risk to his young confederate. Allen enthusiastically accepted the suggestions and promised to send more frequent reports, longer ones, and to write a fictitious letter on the opposite side of the paper as a pretense to cover the correspondence. He admitted that he had wondered about the efficacy of sending blank sheets of paper in an unaddressed envelope.

After about four hours of intense conversation, James suddenly felt weary. He arranged to meet Allen again the next night in the same room.

"Are you sure it's safe for me to stay here?" James asked.

Allen assured him that the innkeeper was totally reliable. In response to James' questions, Allen assured him he should have no difficulty traveling about the streets.

"New York is a large city, and the redcoats think they own it. There are no controls. The streets are filled with uniforms, but they won't bother you. They think all the rebels have fled, and the rest of us are good loyalists." Allen laughed with pleasure at his own duplicity. "Boy," Allen's young face brightened at the thought. "Wouldn't that Serle be surprised to learn that Washington himself read his words."

Finally, just as the first cock crowed, Allen bid farewell and made his way down the stairs, through the deserted public room and out the door. James, who stood inside his room watching through the cracked door to make sure Allen's departure was not observed, winced when he heard the loud creak of the front door when the young man opened it. Allen carelessly closed the door with a slam and James held his breath as he waited to see if any one responded. When the ordinary remained quiet, James eased his own door shut. He noted it had no lock. As a precaution, James wedged a chair against the wood handle. James put two additional logs on the fire, took off his boots and placed them in front of the fire to dry, then lay down still fully dressed. Within minutes, he was asleep.

The exhausted James slept until the loud voices of the noontime crowd in the Red Fox's popular public room woke him. Only a few ineffectual coals glowed in the fireplace when James stirred the ashes, and the room was freezing cold. James broke the thin layer of ice on the pitcher and poured the chilled water into the cracked porcelain bowl. After he relieved himself in the bedpan and shoved it back under the bed, he washed his hands and face, thankful for his full beard that made it unnecessary to shave. James had grown accustomed to the comfort of his worn countryman's clothes. Being dirty was no longer a major problem.

James opened his door slightly and peeked out. The hallway and stairs were deserted. James preferred that no one other than the ordinary proprietor and York Allen be able to associate him with his place of refuge. He did not have to remind himself that he was in a hostile environment, and he did not want to think of what would happen if he were ever captured by the English without the protective sheath of a soldier's uniform, not even that of the enemy.

The public room was crowded and filled with chattering voices and the clink of mugs on wood tables when James descended the stairs trying to act as normally as possible. The pub keeper who James knew by sight stood behind the bar. He glanced at James as he approached the base of the steps, and when his eyes locked with James', he nodded. James tilted his head in acknowledgment, then continued out the door. As best as he could tell, none of the patrons had noticed his departure; at least if one had, he had not indicated any undue interest.

James did not proceed directly from the Red Fox to his first contact. He strolled through the city, looking for changes. He was shocked to discover the devastation of the fire. His old abode, the Black Crow, had disappeared, and in its place jutted a few charred timbers surrounded by a soggy mass of black ashes coated with a scum of dirty ice. None of the buildings in the burned out area was being rebuilt, an observation that led James to wonder what had happened to the residents. When he turned to make his way to Trinity Church where he planned to pay a surprise visit to Pastor Pigot, James stopped in shock. It suddenly occurred to him that Trinity Church had been one of the buildings consumed by the eager flames. Not knowing what else to do, James made his way through the narrow lanes littered with charred debris to the spot where Trinity once stood.

The area was deserted and a high pile of rubble leaned against the charred walls of what had once been a proud edifice. James stood and stared. Here and there, fragments of the stained, leaded glass windows sparkled in the afternoon sun.

"Sad, isn't it," a crackling voice behind him observed. It was a statement, not a question.

James turned with a start. He stared at the little, old poorly dressed lady behind him. She was bundled in a heavy, black coat and had a black scarf looped over her head and under her chin covering almost her entire face. Only her eyes and a long, red nose were apparent.

"Was it your church?" James asked, trying to sound sad, concealing his hope.

"Yes. Did you attend? I don't recognize you," the woman challenged.

"No," James replied honestly before beginning the story he had immediately formulated. "Pastor Pigot was, is my cousin. My second cousin on my mother's side," James began hesitantly.

"Yes. Poor Pastor Pigot," the old woman declared, apparently accepting James' explanation.

"Does he have another church? Do you know where I can find him?" James asked, letting a little of his concern edge into his voice.

The woman who had been staring at the church turned back towards James and began studying him.

"I come by here every day," the woman explained, ignoring James' question.

"It must be sad," James said, recalling the old lady's first remark.

"It is sad. I first came to this church with my mother and father many years ago. Every Sunday."

"Before Pastor Pigot?"

"Before several Pastor Pigots," the old lady cackled mirthlessly.

"But you know where I can find my cousin?" James tried again.

"Pastor Pigot?"

"Yes, Pastor Pigot," James tried to be patient.

The old woman thought before replying.

"Are you sure he's your cousin?"

"Yes, ma'am," James replied dutifully.

"Pastor Pigot?" The woman appeared pleased at James' attempt at courtesy.

"Yes, ma'am. Pastor Pigot," James tried to control his irritation.

"Pastor Pigot? Why he's building a new church. Don't know why. Nobody will go. Certainly not me." The woman frowned and studied James with her hard glare. "You aren't one of those Tories are you?"

"No, ma'am. I'm from Long Island."

The woman accepted James' answer, ignoring the nonsequitor.

"He's using English money to build his new church. I'll never attend," the old lady declared firmly.

"Sorry to hear that," James commiserated. "Can you tell me where I can find Pastor Pigot? Him being my cousin and all."

"Why at where he's building his new church."

"And where is that?"

"Over on Broad Street, near that promenade, that's where."

James thanked the old lady for her kindness and departed in the direction she had pointed. He wondered what she would have thought if he had told her his real identity.

James paused to ask directions several times and finally found Broad Street, a lane off Broadway. The streets in this part of town were filled with citizens and soldiers, mostly soldiers, who walked arrogantly along the paths forcing the civilians out of their way. James had tensed when he first encountered the redcoats, but quickly followed the pattern used by the other civilians. Whenever the noisy soldiers approached, James stepped back, smiled and obsequiously yielded the right of passage.

As soon as he turned into Broad Street, James saw the construction site. About thirty men were bustling about raising the first walls. Pastor Pigot had indeed acquired money somewhere because so many workmen were a rare sight. Usually, one or two men constructed buildings. So many were an extravagance. It looked like the new church would be much larger than the old Trinity. The rising walls were situated in the center of a lot that occupied the entire block. James asked a workman where he could find Pastor Pigot and was directed to the rear of the building. James found Pigot standing at the back of the lot studying the site.

"James!" Pigot exclaimed. "What a surprise. I have so much to report."

Pigot took James by the arm and led him away from the workers. As they walked, Pigot excitedly described his fortuitous contact with Ambrose Serle who was mobilizing support to assist Pigot in rebuilding Trinity. Pigot apologized for not having sent James any reports, explaining that he had yet to unearth any military information. Pigot and Serle were spending considerable time together—Serle was a sincere Christian—and Pigot was confident that in time he would begin confiding about his work with Lord Howe. James walked the back streets with Pigot for about two hours. When they finally parted, James was confident that he would soon be receiving significant information from the earnest pastor. With both York Allen and Pigot reporting on Serle, James anticipated he would soon be learning everything that Serle knew. The thought excited him.

By four o'clock when James bid farewell to Pigot, James had begun feeling uncomfortable. He did not want to become a familiar figure on the streets that were crowded with English soldiers. James feared that one untoward encounter or confrontation could invite disaster.

The public room of the Red Fox was deserted when James entered the front door, and he hurried up the stairway to his room. He decided to remain there and rest while waiting for his evening meeting with York Allen. James reasoned he could meet with Andrew Partridge, the dry goods merchant, on Tuesday morning, Ritchie Randolph in the afternoon, and still have time for his rendezvous with the fisherman courier who would ferry him back to safety on the New Jersey side of the river.

The meetings with York Allen and Andrew Partridge went as well as James could have hoped. York Allen remained his cheerful, positive self, and Partridge, like Pigot, brimmed with enthusiasm about his prospects. General William Howe had fortuitously located his headquarters in a building across the street from Partridge's emporium, and already several members of Howe's staff had become customers. Partridge promised to seize every opportunity to ingratiate himself with Howe's officers and to promptly report any information he acquired. As he had with Allen and Pigot, James briefed the merchant on James' new procedures for preparing his messages.

Only one unpreventable incident caused James' worry. In order to diminish the time he spent on the streets and to lower his profile as much as possible, James returned to the Red Fox to hide out in his room until about three o'clock when he planned to visit the Randolph home hoping to find either Ritchie or his wife Remmie present. James descended the stairs of the Red Fox on his way to the Randolph home when just as he approached the door of the ordinary it suddenly opened and James found himself face to face with a giant of a man. James involuntarily stepped back to make way for the newcomer who rudely brushed James aside. One glance at the man's face almost paralyzed James with shock. It was Elizah Bayley, the husband of Vivian's best friend. James' right hand still pained in damp weather as a consequence of the bruising suffered when James had hit Bayley at Jason's wedding. James lowered his head and hoped that his shabby country clothes and beard were sufficient to conceal his identity.

Bayley pushed past, and James meekly rushed to the door. James was reaching for the door handle when a loud voice behind him shouted:

"Hey you. Wait a minute. Don't I know you?"

James, without pausing or looking back, opened the door and hurried into the street. He heard footsteps behind him.

"Hey, Satterfield. I recognize you, you bastard, what are you doing here?"

James walked quickly away from the Red Fox. He looked back, saw that Bayley was standing uncertainly in the doorway, watching as James hurried away. James realized that Bayley was not sure of his identification and was not pursuing him. James silently cursed his luck. Bayley, who he was sure was determined to wreak revenge on James as a consequence of his humiliation at Jason's wedding and subsequent expulsion by his father-in-law, was one of the last persons James expected or wanted to encounter in New York. Bayley's presence indicated that he had made his peace with the loyalists.

As soon as he turned the corner, James began to run. He continued for about ten minutes and did not pause until other pedestrians began to stare at the unusual sight of a grown man running through the streets without pursuit. James slowed to a walk but was still unsettled by the incident. He wasted an hour making sure that Bayley had not set off an alarm. Bayley knew that James was a close friend of Washington and George Mason and that his visit to New York City could not be a friendly one.

James had no difficulty locating the Randolph house and flattered himself with the thought that he was becoming an expert on the back streets of the city. James approached the Randolph house with trepidation, wondering if his luck had soured. He knocked several times on the oak doorway and waited for a house servant to open it. He assumed the Randolphs still lived in the planter style of Virginia. To his surprise, Remmie herself opened the door, and she immediately recognized James despite his disreputable appearance.

"James," she shouted excitedly. She threw her arms around James and hugged him tightly.

James responded. He sincerely liked Remmie. After several seconds, she stepped back.

"Where is Vivian? Is she with you?"

"No," James laughed. "She sends her best but could not make this trip." Noting the dismay on Remmie's face, James continued. "I'm afraid I'm here on business."

"Oh, yes, I know. At least Ritchie told me about his last conversation with you. You want him to be friends with the English."

James looked around in alarm, concerned that Remmie's blurted words might have been overheard.

"Don't worry, James. You're safe. I'm home alone. No one can hear." Remmie reacted to James' stricken look.

"No servants?"

"We don't have such luxuries. We couldn't afford to feed them and had to free Momie and Abe."

James recognized that she referred to two of the Randolph house slaves who had been in the family for years.

"Are they in New York?" James asked, not knowing what else to say.

"No. They left New York before the English came. I don't know where they are now. Poor things."

"Is Ritchie here?" James changed the subject, suddenly conscious that they still stood in public view.

"No. He's in town with his English friends."

Remmie seized James' hand and pulled.

"Come in before you freeze to death out there."

James followed Remmie into the house. She led him down a long hallway past a sitting room. James noted that it was empty of furniture.

"We've found hard times," Remmie shook her heard. Her eyes suddenly filled with tears. She had caught James' glance at the living room. "We've had to sell all of our furniture to eat."

Remmie led James into a room at the end of the hall. It was furnished sparsely with a scarred table and three handmade chairs placed close to the fireplace. A small blaze gnawed at two short logs. The room was cold; shards of ice had collected on the room's one tiny window. Remmie sat in a rocking chair near the fireplace, gestured for James to take the one opposite her, and pulled her heavy shawl tighter around her shoulders.

"It's so cold here, James," Remmie complained with a shudder.

James tried to think of something to say to console his friend. Failing, he repeated his question.

"Ritchie isn't home? Will he be coming back soon?"

"He's having dinner with some of General Howe's staff. If he's not with them, he's with Ambrose Serle, the admiral's secretary. Always stag. No women allowed." Remmie shrugged her shoulders in disapproval. "At least he's getting a free meal."

Ambrose Serle again, James thought. The man certainly got around. He meets with York Allen, then Pigot, and now Ritchie also. As he thought, James became concerned about the implications of Remmie's comment. He was still not sure of the wisdom of his having selected Ritchie to help them. James in retrospect was concerned that Ritchie was too weak to face the challenges of being an informant, particularly given the family's circumstances and Serle's obvious competence.

"Will you stay with us?" Remmie asked.

James paused before answering, wondering how much he could tell his friends.

"No, thank you Remmie, but... ."

"Is it because we are so poor?" Remmie smiled thinly.

James studied Remmie's drawn face. He remembered she had been so beautiful and vivacious, and now, her slender face was worn and carried deep worry lines, all because of the folly of her father's politics. James leaned over and took both of Remmie's hands in his.

"No Remmie. I must leave tonight. It's not safe for me here, nor for any one I visit."

Remmie nodded understanding.

"I wish we were all back in Fairfax," she said, struggling to hold back the tears.

"I know," James said, recognizing that words were small consolation. "When will Ritchie return?"

"I don't know. Sometimes he stays late drinking with his English friends."

James still did not know how to interpret Ritchie's actions. He could be following James' instructions to make friends with the English, or he might have his own agenda for salvation. James recognized that Ritchie, weak as he was, had to be desperate. He decided he had to see Ritchie on this trip and find out; otherwise, he would not know how to treat any information Ritchie passed along, and besides, Ritchie might endanger the rest of the network.

"I must leave now, Remmie, but I want Ritchie to come and see me. Maybe, I can help... ." James was reluctant to tell Remmie where he was staying, and at the same time he did not want to roam the streets for hours. The accidental confrontation with Bayley had unsettled him.

"Did you know that Elizah Bayley is in New York?" James asked.

"Yes. Ritchie has seen him a couple of times. Bayley's still bitter. I don't recommend that you meet him. He's angry at you and blames you for his troubles."

"I can't do anything about that," James said. "Has Bayley made friends with the English? He used to criticize both the Crown and the rebels."

"I don't know. I haven't talked with him. Ritchie says he's still bitter, hates both sides, but he lives in New York, so he may have worked out an accommodation."

"Like the other loyalists," James blurted, immediately regretting his words.

"Yes, James, like us," Remmie said bitterly. "I hate politics and war."

"I'm sorry, Remmie, I didn't mean that. I hope you and Ritchie are still our friends, despite everything."

Yes... ." Remmie tried to continue but stopped.

James abruptly decided. Remmie and Ritchie were his friends. If he couldn't trust them, he could not trust anybody.

"I will be at the Red Fox until nightfall. Tell Ritchie to come to the first room on the right at the top of the stairs. Tell him I need to talk with him."

As soon as the words were out of his mouth James knew he had made a mistake. He had surrendered control of his environment.

"I'll wait for him," James continued, now nervous himself.

Remmie with tears still running down her cheeks walked to the door with James.

"I promise. I'll tell him," were her last words to James as he hurried back to the streets.

Chapter 23
New York City
December, 1776

James waited in his room at the Red Fox until an hour after darkness, but Ritchie Randolph did not appear. Finally, James decided he could wait no longer. He was anxious to escape from the city, and the fisherman courier was waiting at his sloop. James looked once about the room. He had brought nothing with him and was leaving nothing. He blew out the single candle that flickered on the table and approached the door. He opened it slowly, wincing at the loud squeak. He glanced up and down the hallway. It was dark and deserted. James took a deep breath and moved towards the staircase. He could hear the noisy clatter of the public room. James had no way of knowing if Elizah Bayley was on the premises or not. The public room had been deserted when he had returned from the Randolph house, but now it was filled. Since he had no choice, James descended the stairs slowly. He tried to look relaxed and natural, hoping that any who saw him would dismiss him as another boarder unwisely going out to brave the December winds.

James glanced at the public room and did not see Bayley. He exhaled a relaxing breath and crossed quickly to the outer door. He opened it and stepped into the cold. A sharp wind filled with blowing snow slapped him in the face and strong hands gripped each of his arms.

"Got 'im," a deep masculine voice grunted.

Two burly men pulled James to the street. He heard the clatter of a saber behind him. There were at least two more men behind him. A black coach pulled by two large teams rattled to a stop in front of him. The coach driver, like the men around him, wore a red uniform.

The English had captured him.

The coach door was thrown open. James glimpsed an English officer sitting near the door.

"Inside, Satterfield."

Shocked to hear his name spoken, James paused, wondering how they had learned his identity. Suddenly, something struck the back of his head. James slumped to the ground. The last thing he saw was his hat falling beside him. Eric was right, it's too dangerous, James thought, then lapsed into unconsciousness. The soldiers threw his crumpled form roughly to the floor of the coach then climbed over him to join the officer.

Snow was falling on western Pennsylvania when the rider appeared to announce that Major John Andre and several of his officer companions had been included in a prisoner exchange. Despite his anxiety to escape from his enforced isolation, Andre and his companions were forced to delay their departure. The snow accumulated twenty-four inches, an unusual occurrence for that early in the winter season. Andre wondered if fate were punishing him for an unusual transgression. After a week of impatient waiting, Andre and two of his friends could delay no longer. Traveling on foot, carrying their meager possessions, they trudged across Pennsylvania to the east, turned northward into New Jersey and slowly made their way towards New York.

Unlike his companions who were interested only in reaching the safety and warmth of New York behind the protecting arms of Howe's army, Andre carefully studied the roads, villages and countryside that they passed. Evenings, while they sought refuge from the freezing cold in the drafty barns of compassionate farmers, a shivering Andre, ever the ambitious intelligence officer, drew sketches and made notes while his companions burrowed in the hay seeking warmth.

Upon arrival in New York, Andre was dismayed to learn that his regiment, the 7th Foot, was being shipped home. The ambitious young man who had spent most of his time in the colonies as a paroled prisoner had not earned the honor and advancement he so eagerly sought. No longer anxious to find his place with the troops but still desirous of honor, Andre decided his future rested on his finding a billet as an aide-de-camp to a senior officer, General William Howe, himself, if at all possible. Using the salary that had accumulated during his year of prisonership, he bought a captaincy in the 26th Regiment that was now assigned to garrison duty in New York City. Andre promptly submitted his maps and sketches to his superiors. To Andre's delight, General Howe summoned Andre to describe personally his recent journey through Washington's New Jersey lines. Andre seized the opportunity and let slip the information that he spoke fluent French and German and was willing to serve as an interpreter for the army's difficult Hessian mercenaries. Impressed with the ambitious young officer, Howe assigned him as aide-de-camp to General Charles Grey.

Andre attained his goal as aide to a senior officer, but not exactly as he had planned. General Grey, accompanied by his aide, abandoned the comfort of New York City for the fighting front in New Jersey.

Ironically, James who would have liked nothing better than to cross through the lines to join his friend Washington, languished in New York while Andre who preferred to remain in New York galloped to the front.

On Tuesday night, December 3rd, Lieutenant Eric Grey maintained a lonesome vigil by a flickering fire on the frozen riverbank waiting for James to return. Eric sat on his blanket with his back to a tree and his feet to the fire staring at the empty river. The night passed slowly, and Eric worried. He had had a presentiment that something bad was about to happen and had warned James, but James had stubbornly followed through on his plans.

Dawn broke, but Eric did not abandon his vigil. He decided he would wait for his friend until he returned. He tried to cheer himself by speculating that things had gone so well for James that he had decided to stay an extra night. James had warned that this was possible and that Eric should not worry if he did not return as scheduled. He had made Eric promise to wait at least two days before spreading the report that James was missing.

"One must remain flexible in this business," James had insisted.

Eric abandoned his vigil only once, and then he did not stay away long enough for his fire to die. He rode to a nearby farmhouse to purchase some food; he was gone only an hour, but nothing had changed.

Wrapped in his blanket, Eric dozed. To his chagrin, he was asleep at midnight of the second day when the fisherman courier beached his boat and approached the dying fire.

The fisherman, stiff from the cold, threw two logs on the fire then shook the sleeping Eric.

"James," Eric spoke with a start when consciousness returned. He studied the back of the silent fisherman who had turned to face the fire.

"James," Eric repeated.

His bloodshot eyes studied the unfamiliar back. The recognition that the form before him was not that of his friend startled Eric to full alertness. He leaped to his feet and found himself facing the fisherman.

"James is here?" Eric asked hopefully, fighting the knowledge that something dreadful had happened.

The fisherman shook his head negatively.

With difficulty Eric extracted a story from the taciturn man. His nephew York Allen had learned late that afternoon from the proprietor of the Red Fox that English soldiers had seized James as he was preparing to return. It had taken Allen several hours to learn that James had been taken to General Howe's New York headquarters, held there incommunicado before being escorted under heavy guard to the harbor front. All York could learn at that point was that James was being held on one of the many English men-of-war anchored off shore. York's main concern was that they had not immediately hung James as a spy like they did Nathan Hale. Fearing that James would be forced to identify his contacts, York requested immediate instructions.

The news staggered Eric. He stared speechless at the fisherman. Then, he sat down on his blanket, wrapped himself tightly and stared at the fire. He could not believe the fisherman's story. James would not have allowed himself to be trapped unless he had been betrayed. Eric looked suspiciously at the fisherman and wondered if he could believe the man. York Allen, the man's nephew, was the most likely traitor. Eric did not like the brash, young newsman and thus did not trust him. However, he reasoned, Allen would not have sent his uncle with the report if he had been the betrayer. He would have left Eric and Washington in doubt about James' fate. Eric pondered what should he do. If Allen had not betrayed James, Allen and his uncles would soon be in jeopardy. Eric and James had discussed the possibility of capture several times, and both had agreed that any man would divulge all his secrets if tortured. The problem was that Eric did not know if General Howe would use torture or merely hang James promptly. He decided that he needed information and that he had only one way of obtaining it.

He sent the fisherman courier back to New York with instructions to Allen to stay where he was and to learn as much as he could. James directed the man to assure his nephew that James would not divulge his name under any circumstances. Eric directed the fisherman to return in two days with any information his nephew could acquire, and Eric would give him further instructions.

After the fisherman silently disappeared in the blackness that hung over the river, Eric sat before his fire and thought. He had to inform Washington of his friend's arrest, and he had to make plans for James' rescue. He could inform Washington, but rescuing James was impossible. The thought of the difficulty inherent in the task made Eric desperate; he sat in front of the fire and lamented his loss, and in doing so began to sob. The situation was hopeless.

On Tuesday night, December 3rd, John Satterfield, James' identical twin, sat in his snug cabin in the mountains high above the Gauley River and watched his family settle down for another long winter evening. A fire blazed in the huge stone fireplace that John had built with his own hands over twenty years before. The cabin was small for his family, but it was well built. John had used only large, oak logs. Then, he had been interested in protection more than comfort; because of his concern, the cabin despite the help of his two nearest neighbors had taken two months to build. The two mountain men had difficulty understanding John's insistence on the oversized oak logs that he notched for walls, and they watched with total incomprehension as John tediously lined the interior of the cabin with a second wall of medium sized logs. Between the two exterior walls, James heaped large rocks packed hard in dirt scraped from the cleared area around the structure.

John Satterfield, a mountain man who kept his thoughts to himself, did not explain. He never did, but his neighbors had learned to respect the man. He was one of the most famous Indian fighters on the frontier. He had fought with Washington against the French and had personally killed more than his share of the savages. When John had settled high in the Alleghenies above the Gauley, he had been the first white man in the area. There had not been many Indians around when John arrived—that was one of the reasons he had selected his homesite—for he hated Indians. The few marauding Algonquin renegades who had called the Gauley home made the mistake of trying to persuade the intruding white man to settle elsewhere. Then, suddenly, there were fewer Indians to trouble the lone settler. John killed them, every last one of them, including their squaws and children.

John, using money that others assumed came from his family back in the Short Hills of Virginia, had purchased over five thousand acres of mountain land. His neighbors assumed he wanted privacy. Over the years, settlers, mostly Scotch and Irish fleeing the crush of society, pushed into the mountains. A few settled along the Gauley, but only those who had John Satterfield's permission did so. In his mountain domain, John Satterfield was king. Those he assumed would make good neighbors and provide companionship to his wife and children, John allowed to remain. The others, with minimal encouragement from the mountain legend, moved on to other mountains.

That very morning John had returned from a weeklong foray with the local militia that he commanded. It was not really a militia company, just a loose grouping of every single white settler in a fifty-mile area. When John called, the men came. They did not parade or threaten Tories, for there were none in the mountains; they simply killed any savages that were unwise enough to venture into John Satterfield's kingdom.

The previous week, a band of Cherokee had been sighted to the south. John had ambushed them thirty miles from the Gauley, and they no longer wore warpaint, or anything else, including hair.

John loved his family and enjoyed watching it settle into the evening. His wife Nancy, the mother of Becky and Little Romp, short for Romper, was ten years younger than John. He had married her following the death of his first wife, Maggie. John had found Nancy huddled in the smoking remains of a cabin in the north near the Monongahela with her dead husband's head in her lap, a victim of an Indian raid from the north. Nancy thought the savages had been Algonquins, but she was not sure. She had hid in a refuge her husband had dug in the cabin floor and had not dared to come out for two days after the last Indian shout.

Nancy, a tough frontier woman, had survived. Now, she seldom mentioned her tragic experience, but it was obvious it still troubled her. She refused to let John dig a safe hideaway in the floor of their Gauley cabin. She vowed she would perish this time fighting at John's side rather than whimpering underground while her husband died.

John leaned on the family table, one of the cabin's few pieces of furniture, and watched his family. His son Eli, short for Elias, John's first wife Maggie's only child, sat in a corner reading a book. Eli, nineteen, the same age as James' Jason, seemed to John to be a mixture of the twins. Eli was a mountain man like his father, but he tempered his father's hardness with James' love of books. Becky, aged ten years, played on the large bearskin in front of the hearth with five year old Romp. Becky was trying to teach Romp a card game of her own creation that John did not understand. Nancy, whose hands were never still, rocked in a chair and knitted a wool sweater intended for Eli. Nancy made all of their clothes, including the deerskin pants and hunting shirts that John, Eli and Romp wore in winter.

As he watched his family, John was reminded of his own childhood in the Short Hills. He recalled the many nights that he and his brothers and sister had sat around the fireplace with their father, mother and Old Tom. Then, their grandfather had entertained them with long stories of the family. John had long exhausted the family stories for his own children. They had learned not to press for stories of John's life on the frontier west of the Blue Ridge. They had heard tales of his bravery and savagery from others, but never from their father's lips. Not even Eli who knew his father best could believe the legends that other families told about John. With the family, John was kind and considerate. Eli had never known his father to strike one of his children. Their mother handled the discipline. Eli sensed, however, a hard inner core in their father that his enemies had to fear.

John's memories reminded him that he was overdue in visiting the Short Hills. He wanted to see his father, Young Tom, one last time before he died. The letter James had sent with a new settler over a year before had reported that Young Tom was aging fast. John loved his entire family, but he missed his twin James most. As John watched the fire and reminisced, he was taken by a sense of unease. He suddenly set straight on the bench and pounded his large fist against the table, frightening his family with the move.

"What is it John?" Nancy asked.

John did not reply. Eli studied his father and waited. He had seen the look before. John's brilliant green eyes turned hard with little light specks that seemed to flash.

"John?" Nancy repeated.

The room was silent with the two smaller children on the bearskin anxiously watching their father.

Finally, John moved and broke the tension by shrugging his shoulders, blinking his eyes and relaxing. The specks seemed to disappear.

"It's James," John declared. "Something has happened to James."

Neither Nancy nor Eli questioned John. They had long ago accepted the curious relationship between the twin brothers. John had told them of the many occasions when one brother knew, just knew, what the other was thinking.

"James is in trouble. He needs me," John spoke flatly.

"Then go," Nancy said. "We're ready for the winter. Eli can handle the hunting and the traps."

"Should I come too?" Eli asked.

John looked at his son. Eli was already two inches taller than his father, but lacked John's muscular bulk. That would come with age. Eli had acquired John's mountain skills and had already demonstrated his reliability in a crisis. Although the family did not discuss it, Eli had helped to devastate several war parties who had unwisely ventured into their mountains.

"Thank you, son, but you should stay here with your mother. I don't know how long I will be gone."

The decision was made. Five minutes earlier, John was sitting comfortably sharing a cozy family evening; suddenly, he found himself making plans for the long trip eastward. He would trek southeast to the New River and the settlement at Lewisburg where he would purchase horses then ride fast east to Williamsburg then north to Fairfax. He would be in Alexandria in ten days.

On the morning of Thursday, December 7th, James woke with a throbbing headache in the room that they had confined him in two days previously. His back ached from swinging during the sleepless night in the short hammock that served as his cot. The room was too small for the hammock to be extended, and James was forced to lie in a doubled up position. He had one dirty blanket that offered inadequate protection from the cold sea wind that blew through the open porthole. The room's size forced James to lie with the frigid, damp air striking his back. He did not know how long they would keep him in the cell, but he had learned that he was on the "Eagle", Lord Howe's flagship, and confined in the ship's brig. When he complained about the cold, the ugly seaman who visited him twice each day to give him a cold bowl of tasteless gruel only laughed.

"Don't worry, mate. Ye'll be warm enough soon. They say that after Black Dick talks wid ye, ye'll be swinging high."

"But until then, give me another blanket," James shivered.

The sailor ignored James' plea by kicking the small bowl of gruel with the toe of his boot. It slid in James' direction, then toppled over, spilling the greasy mess onto the dirty floor.

The sailor laughed at his own cleverness, slammed the door shut, and strutted down the dark passageway.

"They hang spies, you know," he shouted as he departed.

James stared at the unappetizing slime on the floor and turned in the hammock trying to draw the thin blanket tighter.

Several decks over James' head, Ambrose Serle stood in Admiral Richard Howe's warm cabin and listened while the commander-in-chief discussed the spy's fate with his brother, General William Howe. Serle did not understand why the two brothers were taking so much time discussing the miserable creature locked below. Serle personally knew the man deserved to die. He had been instrumental in the spy's capture. One of his loyalist contacts had reported to Serle that a rebel spy that he knew personally was a close friend of George Washington was hiding at the Red Fox. The man had agreed to bear witness against the spy who he identified as James Satterfield, a newspaper publisher from Virginia. Serle had watched as the guard officers seized Satterfield at the Red Fox, then had accompanied the group to military headquarters where he listened as the captain reported to General Howe of their find. Howe, who frankly admitted he had an engagement that evening with Mrs. Loring, the wife of the permissive Chief of Prisoners, did not have time to discuss the matter.

"Lock him up and we'll hang him in the morning," General Howe dismissed Serle and the captain.

Serle had watched while the guards stripped the prisoner and searched him for compromising materials. The other spy, Hale, had carried sketches and descriptions of British forces, but unfortunately Satterfield had no such thing on his person. A search of the Red Fox failed to develop any evidence. Never the less, Serle was convinced of his guilt. His loyalist contact remained firm in his accusations. Serle had listened while the officers questioned Satterfield. He denied that he was a spy, but he had no believable story to explain his presence in New York. He tried to claim he was merely visiting old Virginia friends, but he declined to name them for fear of the British punishing innocent people.

Serle had returned that night to the "Eagle." To his later regret, he had met Lord Howe on the quarter-deck and had recounted the story of the spy's capture. Unfortunately, the Lord had made an issue of the lack of incriminating evidence and ordered that the suspect be brought to the "Eagle" so that he could personally interrogate him. Serle's chance meeting with the Admiral had resulted in the delay in the hanging. Serle suspected that Lord Howe was concerned that a summary hanging of another spy would discourage any would be defectors from responding to the Admiral's proclamation offering amnesty to any deserters.

"Has he asked for amnesty?" The admiral had asked.

Serle, who doubted that the spy had even heard of the amnesty offer, had assured the admiral that the spy had not.

Now, the two Howes frankly discussed the problem.

"I don't think he is worth discussing," the general assured his brother. "Just let me hang him as a lesson to others."

"Now don't be in such a hurry, William," Lord Richard said.

Serle feared that the Admiral who did not like to be pressed by others, not even his brother, was getting his back up.

"The man's a spy. That's clear," the general said.

"And the evidence?"

"We have a witness."

"What did he see?"

The question caught the general off guard. Serle was tempted to speak but knew better. The admiral was not in a mood to be challenged. He had already heard that criticism of his latest amnesty offer was circulating among the officers, and he was sensitive to the fact that not one deserter had yet crossed through the lines.

"Well, he didn't actually see anything. How do you see a man spying?"

The admiral looked with disdain at his younger brother.

"Now, William," he admonished, ignoring the question. "We can't hang the colonials just because they might be rebels. We are here to settle the problem, not decimate the population. They're Englishmen after all."

"I agree," the general capitulated. He knew his brother well enough to recognize he was in one of his stubborn moods. "What should we do?"

"Let him sit below until I get a chance to talk with him and decide."

The decision made, General Howe departed and Admiral Howe began dictating reports for London ignoring the subject of the spy.

After capturing Fort Washington and relieving General Greene of three thousand soldiers, General Cornwallis crossed the Hudson and pursued Washington's army south. Cornwallis had Washington's decimated army in his grasp and was about to seize it when General Howe ordered him to pause to give the army commander time to join the victors. The scurrying Washington took advantage of the opportunity to retreat to Trenton, arriving on December 3rd. Washington sent patrols thirty miles in each direction along the Delaware and confiscated every available boat. Before General Howe reached Trenton, Washington and his army had again rowed across a river seeking refuge, this time in Pennsylvania. Worried that Howe would now wheel on Philadelphia, Washington sent warnings to Congress. On December 12th, the complaining delegates moved to Baltimore, and General Howe returned to New York to report to his brother.

On Sunday, December 15th, Eric Grey again leaned against the tree in the dark and watched his shimmering fire as he waited for the fisherman courier to appear with a message. Eric morosely shivered in the blanket he had draped over his shoulders and worried. He had alerted Washington to James' capture and dispatched one of his soldiers to Alexandria with regretful letters from himself and Washington for James' wife. He had had one message from York Allen that contained no news other than the fact that James was being held on the "Eagle." Serle refused to discuss the subject. Allen had requested that Eric meet him personally on December 15th, hence Eric again faced the cold night. He had grown to hate the numbing chill of the penetrating sea dampness. No matter how large he built the fire, the wind dissipated the heat.

Braced for a long wait, Eric was surprised when the sloop suddenly appeared out of the mist about an hour before midnight. Eric watched as the boat approached. He could see two figures. At first he thought the man in the bow might be James, but he soon discerned the more diminutive body of York Allen.

Eric walked to the shoreline, dispiritedly greeted the fisherman and Allen, helped them beach the sloop, then led them back to the fire, which provided light but not warmth. After half-hearted pleasantries which neither man felt, Allen reported on recent information about James. He was still on the "Eagle." Serle had denied peremptorily York Allen's request that he be allowed to interview the spy for a first hand report for the *Dispatch's* readers.

"No one cares about the fate of a spy," Serle had sniffed and changed the subject.

York Allen produced one piece of information that Eric realized would be of interest to Washington. If it had not been for James' capture, the report would have excited Eric, but given the circumstances he only nodded matter-of-factly when Allen reported.

"General Howe has decided to go into winter quarters," Allen said.

"Where?"

"Manhattan."

"New York City?" Eric asked, not trying to hide his disbelief.

"Yes."

"Not Philadelphia?"

"New York City."

"How do you know this?"

"Serle introduced me to one of General Howe's aides at headquarters. I've been developing him," Allen bragged.

"And he told you the general's plans?" Eric studied the young man scornfully.

"No way," Allen replied. "He asked me to help him find the general a more posh mansion for the winter. While I went through the pretense of helping him look, he let slip that the army was returning from New Jersey."

"Are you sure?"

"General Howe and Elizabeth Loring spent last night in the house I found for them. I'm told they enjoyed it very much," Allen laughed.

The young man was so proud of his information that Eric had to smile.

"I'm sure that General Washington will find this information most useful," Eric said honestly.

"Enough to pass along some more expense money?"

Eric had anticipated the request and had brought along a leather pouch filled with coins from General Washington's confidential fund. He had intended to give the money to Allen along with the demand for more information on James, but recognized the request was futile. Instead, he simply handed the pouch to Allen who quickly pocketed it with a knowing glance at his uncle. Eric told Allen he would have a messenger waiting at the spot every third night for the immediate future. Information on James had priority. Eric accompanied the fisherman and his nephew back to their boat, shoved the bow into the river after they had boarded, and cursed when the current lapped over the top of his boots. He watched while the sloop disappeared into the night then returned to extinguish the fire. He had to ride south and report the information on Howe's army to Washington.

It took three days for Eric to locate Washington's temporary headquarters in Pennsylvania. The General was delighted. Eric's report coincided with information Washington had received from a Griggstown, New Jersey butcher who had learned that rumor had it that Howe's army was going into winter quarters. The butcher, a man named John Honeyman, had also learned that Howe's Hessian mercenaries were being quartered in Trenton to keep them away from the temptations of the larger city.

Acting on this information, Washington boldly launched his Christmas Eve attack on the Hessians in Trenton. The Delaware crossing required nine hours, and Washington's men reached Trenton on the day after Christmas where they caught the Hessians in the midst of their holiday revelries. The victory was complete. The rebels captured over one thousand Hessian prisoners, a number of cannon and wagonloads of badly needed supplies.

An angry General Howe summoned Cornwallis from the ship on which he was about to embark for a visit home and dispatched him to the battlefront. Before he arrived, Washington confounded the English by attacking at Princeton rather than retreating, as was his wont. Surprise produced another unexpected victory. Washington went into winter encampment at Morristown, and Howe, ignoring the two defeats, settled down in New York.

Chapter 24
New York
December 1776

On his twenty-first day in the cell on the "Eagle," James woke with the same thought that had crossed his mind each of the preceding dawns:

"When will I get out of this Hell on earth?"

James' life had improved by inches. He was no longer threatened with an immediate trip to the gallows, though he knew that fate was only a few words away. Consequently, he lived from hour to hour waiting for Lord Howe to question him, for the Admiral had stayed James' execution pending a personal meeting with the accused spy. James was thankful that Black Dick did not appear to be in as much a hurry as his subordinates to witness James' last day on earth.

James' tormentors had marginally relieved his misery; one had given him a second blanket, which James wedged in the open porthole to control the harsh ocean wind; somebody had decided that he had better keep James alive long enough to meet the Admiral, obviously fearing Black Dick's wrath more than losing James, and had now included a crust of bread with the daily gruel. James, once he had gained control of his fear, adjusted to life in his confined world.

This day, as on every other, he awoke to the clatter of the ship's crew. He pulled back the blanket curtain and peered through the porthole at the gray dawn in a sky devoid of warming rays from the cloud-screened sun. He inhaled deeply the heavy sea air, barked a phlegmy cough, and tried to convince his body that the Spartan regimen was good for it. He replaced the blanket curtain and began exercising. Four times a day he bent and twisted his body, trying to stretch the fatigue of confinement, but never succeeding. In three weeks James had lost at least twenty pounds, maybe more; the exercise and meager diet had trimmed James' body of the fat that had accumulated over the years. James approved of the results but worried that soon his body would begin consuming its muscle and sinew. The fat was almost gone.

When he finished his exercises, James sat erectly on his hammock and waited patiently for his gruel and crust. The anticipation was important to him because the actual consumption of the tasteless, gray porridge was difficult. James mentally counted the minutes as he waited. He had developed a knack for estimating the passage of a minute. At first he had counted seconds, but now he could sense the moment of each minute's passage. He preferred marking time to torturing himself with memories of his family.

Finally, his cell door opened, and one of his jailers entered. It was the large, fat one with the missing front teeth. James hid his disappointment because he would have preferred the skinny sailor who always paused to talk. James looked forward to the visits, even though the man only described the weather, because they reminded James that life continued outside his closet.

"Merry Christmas," the large man laughed and spit on the floor.

James studied the large glob that rested inches from his bare feet.

"In here," the cruel man snarled.

To James' surprise, a second man, another sailor, crowded into James' cell carrying a bucket. He set it on the floor near the door and backed out as if he feared James carried the pox.

"Wash yourself," the jailer ordered. "Black Dick will see you in two hours."

James began counting, no longer content to trust his intuition to mark the passage of time. The jailer turned to the door, held his hand out into the hall, and turned with James' gruel and crust.

"Eat this," the man glared. "When you finish. Scrub yourself, then your filthy deck. I will inspect when I return."

The evil man laughed as if he had said something funny and departed, slamming the cell door behind him.

Two hours later, James, looking as presentable as a half of bucket of cold sea water could make him, was escorted by two immaculately clad sailors, carrying polished rifles, to the Admiral's cabin. They stood at attention, flanking James while the sentry outside the admiral's cabin knocked and announced their presence. James, his eyes smarting from the daylight after three weeks of prison gloom, blinked as he stared at the "Eagle's" sanded decks. In the distance, he saw what he presumed to be the Manhattan shoreline. He had already forgotten what solid soil under his feet felt like. He wondered if he was developing sea legs that involuntarily rocked to adjust to the slow roll of the deck in the gentle waves.

The sentry opened the door, turned, stood at attention and shouted "Enter" out of the side of his mouth.

James, accompanied by his two guards, did as he was told. He was immediately impressed by the size of the admiral's office compared with his cell. It was all highly polished wood and glittering brass. A large man with white hair and a walrus mustache sat behind a polished desk. It was completely bare. To the man's right stood a large globe. The Admiral was dressed in a freshly pressed blue uniform trimmed in white and decorated with shiny brass buttons. To the admiral's left stood a tall, slender man with long black hair that hung over his high forehead almost touching the tip of a prominent, bony nose. He wore a sober black suit. James stared at the civilian in amazement.

He immediately assumed the man was Ambrose Serle, the admiral's secretary, James' unwitting source of information. James had long aspired to covertly view the man, but not under circumstances such as these. The admiral pretended to be reading from a document that he held in his soft, chubby fingers. James, like the civilian, Serle, and the sentries, silently watched as Black Dick read. James began counting time. After two and a half minutes, the admiral looked up. He smiled benignly at James, as if he were welcoming a chance visitor, and spoke to the sentries.

"You may wait outside."

The guards in unison took one step back from James, clicked their heels together in what James assumed was a positive response to the order, pivoted and marched out of the cabin. The door shut softly behind them.

"Please seat yourself, Mr. Satterfield." The Admiral indicated a chair on the right of his desk.

James did as he was told and sat in the chair. He was conscious of the tattered condition of his clothing and his bare feet. He looked at Serle, expecting the tall, thin man to also take a chair. He remained standing, staring at James through watery blue eyes. James noted the man had a small chin, almost no chin, and stared. The man appeared to read James' thought and glared disapprovingly back.

"Mr. Satterfield," the admiral coughed to regain James' attention. "What are we to do with you?"

James, who did not know what to respond to such an absurd question, said nothing.

"We hang spies, you know," the Admiral continued, laughing at his feeble attempt at humor. "Do you know of any reason why we should not?"

"If you refer to me, I can't think of a reason why you should," James' voice cracked from disuse. "I'm not a spy."

"Please get Mr. Satterfield a drink of water, unless he prefers brandy. I do believe his throat is dry," the admiral ordered his secretary.

Serle glared at James as if he were responsible for such a demeaning order. It was beneath his dignity to serve prisoners.

"Yes, sir," Serle turned. He walked to a sidebar, splashed a glass half full from a decanter filled with a clear liquid which James assumed was water and returned to hand it to James.

James slowly raised the glass to his lips. It was the first taste of non-brackish water that James had had since his arrest. It was the finest water James had ever tasted. He noted but did not regret that Serle had not offered him a choice as the admiral suggested.

"And now that you are refreshed," the admiral continued, "please tell me what we should do with you." The admiral had detected James' delight at the small gesture of water. "But first," the admiral held up his hand as if to forestall James from answering the first question, "tell me about your spying."

"I am not a spy," James insisted. I... ."

"Are you not from Virginia?" Serle interrupted.

"Yes, but... ."

"Alexandria?" Serle's words were an accusation.

"Yes, but... ."

"A neighbor of George Washington?"

"Yes," James, resigned to the questions, did not attempt to explain this time.

"A friend of Washington?"

"Proudly," James declared.

"And Washington's spy? "

"No," James protested. "I... ."

"Enough of that," the admiral interrupted as if James had rambled on too long. "Do you want amnesty?"

"What amnesty?"

"The admiral's too kind offer... . " Serle paused and glanced at Lord Richard to see if he had caught Serle's disapproval.

"Renounce your rebellion, acknowledge the authority of His Majesty, and I have it in my power to pardon you," the Admiral interrupted his secretary. He glared at Serle, cautioning him to remain silent then waited for James' response.

"I have done nothing to require a pardon," James challenged. "I... ."

"Then return Mr. Satterfield to General Howe with instructions to hang him tomorrow morning at dawn," the admiral spoke without emotion.

"Yes, sir," Serle smiled at his superior.

Ignoring James' shocked reaction, Serle walked to the door.

"Return the prisoner to his cell and prepare him for transfer," Serle ordered the guards.

"Sir," the two immaculate soldiers slapped the butts of their rifles on the floor, clicked their heels together and marched into the room.

Stopping, one on each side of James' chair, each grasped an arm, lifted James erect then marched him out the cabin door. James had to hurry to keep from being dragged. He heard the door slam behind him, and he was rushed back to his cell in the hull of the ship.

"Your social visit finished?" The cruel jailer asked.

He waited at the door of James' cell as the guards pushed James inward. James tripped to the floor.

"Tomorrow morning in the square," one of the guards smiled to the jailer.

"Justice is served, me mate," the jailer laughed and slammed the door shut. "Pack your gear. They'll be comin' for you soon milord."

James stared disbelievingly at the door.

"The buzzards, I mean," the jailer cackled as he walked away.

At the very same time that James was meeting with Lord Howe, John, Eric, three husky volunteers from James' staff and York Allen were crowded into the small river shack that served as the fisherman uncle's home. A surprisingly quiet York Allen had just arrived, and all were waiting for James' twin brother who was the group's obvious leader to speak.

Eric, who had been transported along with John and the three volunteers from the New Jersey shore by the fisherman uncle the night before, could not believe he was sitting in this shack behind English lines getting ready to plan an impossible rescue. John, who sat silently with his elbows resting on the fisherman's table while he collected his thoughts, still was a source of amazement. John, having changed his deerskin trousers and hunting shirt for a set of James' old clothing, was the very image of his brother. If it were not for the hard green eyes that bored deeply into any animate or inanimate object they beheld, Eric would have sworn that James had somehow miraculously returned. John, who had appeared the morning before at the farmhouse where Eric maintained his vigil, had been escorted by the three volunteers from Washington's army. John had been a surprise, but the presence of Vivian, James' wife, had been a shock. When asked for news of James, Eric had honestly replied he had none, that to the best of his knowledge James remained a captive on the admiral's flagship, but volunteered that the courier would arrive that night, possibly with new information.

Eric had intended to reassure the tearless Mrs. Satterfield. Instead, she had fixed a flinty gaze on John. He had nodded in response and had informed Eric that they would return to New York that night with the fisherman. Eric had protested that it would do no good to risk more lives until they had word that James was back on shore where a possible rescue could be considered, but John had merely silenced him with one glance of those hard green eyes. The three volunteers nodded their approval, and Eric had no option but to agree. When Vivian had expressed her intention to also join in, John had vetoed the idea with six words.

"No Vivian. We need you here."

Eric had been surprised that the words had been sufficient. He knew he would have been overwhelmed in argument if he had spoken, but Mrs. Satterfield had simply paused silently and stared at her brother-in-law for what seemed like minutes before acknowledging the decision.

"Very well, John," she had replied. She had not needed to use the unspoken response that every man in the room felt. "If you don't succeed, I will come."

Eric shivered as he thought of the moment. Mrs. Satterfield, as nice as she was, as beautiful as she was, was every bit as uncompromising as John. Each simply assumed that others would accept their decisions. Eric hoped that if he ever got into difficulty he would have such friends prepared to assist him.

"And he is still on the "Eagle?" John's question was aimed at York Allen.

"Yes, but I know from Serle that the admiral planned to meet with him this morning."

"For a decision?"

"Serle seemed to think so."

"When will you learn the result?"

"Serle will come to the *Dispatch* this afternoon. If a decision is made, he will write a story for a special edition."

"If they decide to hang him," John's word were a statement not a question.

"Yes." York was intimidated by the twin brother in a way he had not been with James. Otherwise, he would have replied: "Yes, a pardon is not important news. Only hanging is."

"They will hang him," John declared. "Tomorrow morning. We will have to act as soon as he is on shore."

"They'll move him to the military headquarters tonight," Allen suggested.

"Probably at dusk," John continued.

Eric could see that the decision had been made. They would attempt to rescue James. The very idea frightened Eric, but he was determined to assist. Somehow, he felt, if anyone could do it, the man with the hard flashing green eyes could. Eric had already stopped considering him as James with different colored eyes. John, who lacked all of the self-denigrating softness that made James so attractive to friends, was something completely different. Eric knew that John carried the group's only weapon, a long bladed, vicious looking knife with the initials "JS"" on the handle. John had insisted they leave their long rifles on the New Jersey shore with Vivian. He had self-confidently assured them that they would acquire whatever they needed from the English, and not one of them, not even Eric, had doubted his words.

"You, York," John spoke directly to York Allen. "Check with your friend at the military headquarters and then go to the *Dispatch*. As soon as you learn anything about James, report back here."

Dismissing the submissive Allen, John turned to the largest volunteer. "You and I will collect English uniforms and weapons."

John looked at the two remaining volunteers and Eric. "You three wait here.
"

The two volunteers nodded agreement. Eric considered protesting, demanding to know what John planned, then thought better of it. He too nodded and silently watched as Allen, John, and the largest volunteer filed from the shack.

By late afternoon, John and the large volunteer returned carrying four English long rifles of the kind used by sentries and four English uniforms, three for common soldiers and one for officers. Eric, who was about to explode from tension and boredom, examined the uniforms, discreetly looking for bloodstains or evidence of violence; he found none, but did not ask how the uniforms and weapons had been acquired. John noticed Eric studying the officer's uniform and spoke:

"Try the uniforms on," John ordered. "We tried to obtain approximate sizes."

Eric held the officer's uniform against his chest then turned sideways to remove his boots.

"Not that one, Eric," John smiled. "It belongs to Sean." John pointed at one of the volunteers who was about Eric's size.

Noting the look of dismay on Eric's face, John explained:

"Sean will wear the officer's uniform and be our spokesman."

His response at first puzzled Eric, then realization hit him. Sean, a recent immigrant from Scotland, spoke with a soft Scottish burr. Eric nodded his understanding and selected one of the English private uniforms. When the three volunteers and Eric were dressed in the uniforms, John had them stand in a rough formation. Sean, the officer, was placed in front with the four common soldiers placed in a short column of twos behind him.

"Not bad," John nodded after inspecting the squad.

The uniforms were not exact fits, but for their purposes they were adequate. The large volunteer was unable to button his uniform, and the shirt gaped at the neck. John placed him in the back row. Then, to Eric's surprise, John had Eric and his companion in the front row step one pace apart. John stepped between them, joining the formation. While Eric and his companions watched, John ran both hands roughly through his hair making it as disheveled as possible. Satisfied, John slumped his shoulders and let his head hang slack-jawed to one side. He looked exactly like his brother James. Eric stared sidewise studying the formation, then he suddenly grasped John's plan. He began to laugh.

"It might work.".

The others looked at Eric in puzzlement.

"We are going to pose as the ship's party delivering James to military headquarters," Eric speculated. John did not respond, and Eric continued. "We will arrive first, gain admittance to the headquarters and take it over. The guards will think we are delivering James and will be relaxed. We lock them up or kill them, then wait for the real party to arrive. We overpower them, free James, head for the boat and escape to New Jersey."

John nodded.

"It will work," the large volunteer declared, and the others began talking excitedly.

"Do you think you can pose as our officer?" John asked Sean.

"Aye, man, and let's stop talking in the ranks," Sean responded.

For the next fifteen minutes the unit practiced marching in formation. Since all but John were soldiers, they had no difficulty. John was posing as James, a civilian who had been confined for almost four weeks, thus he was not expected to be martial.

While they were practicing, an excited York Allen arrived. As soon as he burst through the door, he halted and stared.

"Christ," he exclaimed. "You gave me a start. I thought the lobsterbacks were here."

He held one hand to his chest in mock exaggeration. The unit stood before him in formation. Allen immediately grasped the plan. "You look perfect," he approved. "And you are going to have to. Serle is at the *Dispatch* now writing his report. He says they will bring James in at dusk, confine him overnight at military headquarters, then hang him in the morning. Serle ordered me to stay away from headquarters tonight but gave me permission to watch and report the hanging in the morning."

"It will be dusk in about half an hour," Eric observed superfluously.

"Right then, men," Sean spoke with his Scottish burr. "Let's be on our way."

"Sean," John ordered, "march your men to the waterfront, turn about and proceed to military headquarters. I'll wait for you one block from the building and join you. We'll march quickly to the headquarters. You intimidate the sentries if needed and gain us entry. Once inside, we'll have to play it by ear. We'll overpower the guards, call the sentries for assistance, dispose of them, and then two of you will replace the sentries outside. When James' party arrives, let them into the building, and we'll free them."

It sounded easy, but Eric had his doubts.

"And me?" York Allen asked.

"You alert your uncle to standby the boat and then return to the *Dispatch*. Keep an eye on Serle. We don't want him to come to the headquarters to watch the proceedings."

"But... ." Allen began to protest being left out of the action.

John glanced briefly at him. Allen caught the glare of the hard, green eyes and did not continue.

"Right," Allen agreed. He opened the door a crack. "All clear," he announced turning his head to look at the group one last time. "Good luck, boys," he said softly then slipped out of the door.

Chapter 25
New York
December, 1776

John stood in the doorway of the dark storefront and patiently waited. The wind howled through the deserted street blasting dead leaves and pieces of refuse against any obstacle with the temerity to stand in its path. John soberly studied the planks of the wood walkway that paralleled the frozen mud of the wide street. The odd wood path, the first in the city, was designed to protect New York's nobs from the mud and manure filled street. John, who had spent all of his adult life in the mountains, passively accepted the city man's foibles. He wondered what his wife Nancy would think of women who required a wood walkway to keep their dainty feet dry.

While he waited, John's finely tuned senses scanned the environment. He could smell a wood fire with a hint of frying meat wafting on the air. The smoke was thin, obviously originating in the distance, not a threat. Except for the howl of the wind, the street was soundless, for a gloomy dusk had descended cloaking the city in a gray haze. John could see the inky blackness of night dropping from the moonless sky where heavy, dark clouds obliterated the stars. John, totally immobile, blended against the side of the doorway where he patiently waited as he had in countless ambushes, silently frozen in time contemplating his prey. He cautioned himself against overconfidence. John had been with Washington and Braddock when the redcoats had panicked and fled for their lives, running out of control before the outnumbered French and their shrieking savages. Recalling the battle, John shook his head in disgust. Any frontiersman knew that Indian battles always involved one of two options. Either the Indians frightened their opponent to flight and they pursued, or the Indians turned and fled. Indians were too wise to stand and die, preferring to live to fight another day. John, who did not respect the English, struggled to persuade himself that they posed a creditable threat to his plan.

Suddenly, John heard the tramp of boots as a marching patrol abruptly mounted the wood walkway about two hundred yards to John's left. He did not

move, waiting for the military cadence of the stamping feet to bring the group
into his field of vision. As expected, it was his small patrol. Sean, puffed with
apparent self-importance, marched in the right front of his file. Eric and his three
companions stamped in step, stern faced, white hands clutching the long rifles
they carried angled over their shoulders.

When they were about ten paces away from John's hiding place, he stepped
in front of them facing the direction they were marching. A startled Sean paused
imperceptibly but did not lose his stride. Without a word, he passed John. Eric
and his companion parted, and John fell into step between them. The other two
volunteers continued behind. John's deliberate civilian shuffling broke the rigid
cadence.

"Move along, prisoner," Sean shouted for the benefit of the empty street.

The prisoner and his escort continued along the wood walkway until it ended
in a small square. To their left stood the military headquarters. The escorts
wheeled left and crossed the frozen mud of the street carrying the reluctant prisoner with them. The two sentries guarding the building entrance snapped to
attention.

"Prisoner Detail, Halt," Sean shouted with authority.

Eric and his three companions stamped to a stop. John stumbled one step
further. Eric reached out, roughly grabbed him by the shoulder and savagely
pulled the pliant John backwards.

"Prisoner detail from the "Eagle" on the admiral's orders," Sean barked.

"Yes, sir," the sentry on the right, obviously intimidated, snapped back.

He turned, opened the door and shouted into the long, dark, empty hallway:
"Prisoner detail reporting, sir."

Without waiting for a response, Sean strode arrogantly into the hallway. Eric
and his guard companions followed, pushing the compliant, intimidated John in
front of them.

The sentry slammed the door shut behind them. Sean paused uncertainly,
trying to decide where to go. At the end of the hall, a door on the right opened,
and a portly, red-faced English sergeant stepped into the hall. Candlelight from
the room behind him reflected on his thinning but pure white hair. The sergeant
stroked his mustache with the thumb and forefinger of his right hand while a
large ring of keys jingled in his left.

"Ah, our guest has arrived," the sergeant smiled.

"Please bring him this way, sir." The sergeant had spotted the epaulets on
Sean's shoulders.

The sergeant stepped back into the lighted room. Sean followed. Eric shoved
John in the back forcing him to stumble to his knees in the center of the small
room. Its three occupants stared at the fallen prisoner while Eric and his companions studied the room. It was obviously the guardroom. A large fire blazed
in the hearth, and the table in the room's center was littered with empty wine bottles and the unfinished remains of supper. The portly sergeant stood near an

open door at the right of the fireplace. Two other soldiers, obviously fellow guards, sat at the table staring at the prisoner and his escort.

The sergeant turned and descended the staircase, which was lighted by one flickering candle mounted high on the sidewall. John struggled to his feet and weakly followed. Sean paused at the head of the stairwell and turned to his guard patrol.

"You men wait here. I'll be right back after I make sure the prisoner is in his cell."

"He doesn't look like much of a spy," one of the two sitting men sneered.

Eric and the large volunteer ignored the comment and moved past the seated guards to stand behind them near the fireplace. Eric leaned his rifle against the stone hearth and made a show of warming his hands.

"Colder than a witch's behind," Eric said.

Eric turned and faced the backs of the seated guards.

His three companions watched Eric for a signal. Unseen by the guards, he retrieved his rifle and raised it with the stock pointed towards the back of the head of the man seated in front of him. The large volunteer mirrored Eric's movement. The two men swung their weapons striking the heads of the seated men almost simultaneously. Eric thought he heard bone cracking as his victim's head snapped. Both men slumped forward on to the table, scattering bottles and tin plates with a clatter. Eric turned towards the stairwell, concerned about having alerted the guard sergeant in the cell room below.

"Not to worry," Sean said as he appeared at the same instant in the doorway. He smiled broadly. "The sergeant decided to take a nap in the cell below."

A silent John pushed past Sean, took in the guardroom with a glance, and hurried to the hall doorway.

"You two," John pointed at the volunteers. "Take these men below and put them in the cell with the sergeant. Tie their arms and legs and gag them, whether dead or alive." John turned to Eric, Sean and the large volunteer. "Come with me," he ordered.

John pointed at the front door. "Now, those two," he indicated the two sentries who stood outside. "Summon them in, Sean."

Eric and John took positions in the two opposing doorways mid-way along the corridor.

Sean nodded and walked briskly to the front door stamping his heels as he walked. He opened the door.

"Come," he ordered. "We need your help in subduing the prisoner."

Sean saw the two sentries exchange quick looks. They were obviously puzzled that all those guards needed help in handling one prisoner.

Sean stood back and allowed the two sentries to rush past.

"In the cell," Sean called. "I'll watch the front door."

The two soldiers raced down the dim hallway. As Eric watched, John stuck out his foot and tripped one of the running soldiers. The other stopped when his companion stumbled. John stepped out of the dark of his hiding place. Before the surprised sentry could react, John thrust his long knife under the sentry's breast-bone. Eric, who had never seen a man killed with such cold efficiency, was para-lyzed. He watched as John withdrew his knife and spun to a position directly over the second sentry who was on his hands and knees trying to rise. John, reached around the man's head with his left hand, caught the man's nose, mouth and chin in his large hand and pulled back. Before Eric could blink, John sliced his long knife horizontally across the sentry's neck. John turned the bleeding man on his back and pulled the man with the chest wound parallel to the first. Eric stared at one and then the other, watching the air bubbles froth in the dark arte-rial blood. John grabbed the two lifeless forms by the back of their collars and dragged them down the hallway.

"Find rugs quickly to cover the blood," John calmly ordered Eric. "Sean, watch the door until I get our sentries out there to replace these two."

Within three minutes, two of the volunteers were guarding the front door. John, Eric, Sean and the third volunteer gathered in the guardroom. John nodded approval as Eric and Sean rearranged the scattered dishes and food on the table.

"You sit here, Eric," John indicated a seat behind the table. "Sean, you meet the arriving party at the front door and escort them to the guardroom. I'll take the two rear guards as they enter the guardroom. The rest of you do what you can, but watch out for James. He'll be in the middle. We don't know what kind of condition he is in."

John pivoted and took his position in the doorway of the room mid-way down the corridor. Sean exchanged a worried look with Eric then hurried to the front door.

Within five minutes, although it seemed much longer to Eric who sat and sweated in the hot guardroom, one of the sentries tapped on the front door.

"I assume that means they're coming," Sean called softly.

Sean listened as words were exchanged outside the thick oak door. Suddenly, the door was thrust open and one of the sentries stuck his head into the hallway.

"Prisoner detail has arrived," he shouted, mimicking the words the original sentry had used ten minutes earlier.

A burly sergeant, much bigger than the largest volunteer, pushed past the sentry and stomped into the hallway.

"I don't know you," he complained to the sentry. He marched towards Sean who had retreated to a position outside the guardroom.

He halted opposite the darkened doorway where James waited, stamped his feet, clicked his heels, and saluted Sean.

"The prisoner detail reporting as ordered, sir!"

John reached out, grabbed the saluting sergeant by his raised arm and jerked him into the dark room. The large man stumbled sideways. John drove his knife under the unbalanced man's breastbone, hitting the identical spot below the heart that had felled the first sentry, then stepped back and let the sergeant's body crash to the floor. John was not dismayed by the change in plans. He had fought enough hand to hand combat with undisciplined savages to know that he had to take what was offered.

In the hallway, Sean and the two volunteer sentries were as surprised at the sergeant's sudden disappearance as were the guard escort and their dejected prisoner, James. The bogus sentries had been dismayed to see that the escorts outnumbered them. The large sergeant and six men bearing shiny English long rifles had escorted James.

John prolonged the paralyzing surprise by leaping from his hiding place and landing on the balls of his feet facing James and his six guards now crowded in the short expanse of narrow hallway between John and the two sentries. Without a word, John threw his knife underhanded, striking the guard on James left squarely in the throat. The man dropped where he stood, unable to scream protest at the sudden pain. James, startled, jumped backwards, tripping into the guard immediately behind him and knocking the man into the guard behind him. The two bogus sentries, still near the front door, lowered their bayonets and thrust them into the backs of the two members of the guard detail nearest them. The three remaining guards dropped their rifles and raised their hands in surrender. Before they got them high enough to signal their intent, the two bogus sentries had withdraw their bayonets and thrust them into the next two guards. Within seconds, five soldiers and the husky sergeant died. The remaining guard stood behind James with his hands in the air. John calmly retrieved a dropped rifle and smashed the stock into the guard's face. He dropped on top of two of his slain companions.

For a shocked few seconds, Sean and the two sentries stared at the tangled, bloody mass before them. James, speechless, slouched weakly against the wall. John dropped the rifle he had used to smash the last guard, bent and retrieved his knife from the throat of the first guard private to die, and calmly wiped the blade on the man's dirty shirtfront. John put the knife in its sheath at his back and spoke quietly to his two bogus sentries.

"Take two of the rifles with clean bayonets and resume your posts outside the door. Let nobody enter."

John turned to Sean who had been joined by Eric.

"Get these bodies to the basement. Tie up any who are still alive," John indicated the man with the smashed face, and gag them if you can."

John turned and for the first time studied his brother. James, still in shock, continued to slouch against the wall. He stared in disbelief at his twin.

"John," James whispered. He shook his head trying to clear the confusion and looked at himself in the mirror that was his brother's face. The diamond flecks flashed in the bright green eyes as they always had when John was excited.

John put his arm about his brother who was thin and weak, guided him into the guardroom, and helped him into a chair near the fire.

"John," James tried again with the raspy voice that was dulled by disuse.

"Later, James," John said softly and turned to assist Eric and Sean drag the last three bodies to the basement cell.

Within minutes all of the rescue party had gathered in the guardroom except for the two sentries outside.

"Sean and one of the volunteers began to chatter excitedly about what had happened. Eric leaned over James studying his friend for external signs of damage.

"Do not linger," John ordered. "Get a weapon and form up outside. Quick march to the boat. All except you, Eric. Take off your uniform."

The men did as they were told without question. Not one was prepared to cross the man who had so quickly killed five men, maybe six, in a matter of seconds. Eric, like the others, had carried his countryman clothes in the small knapsack that the English soldiers wore on their backs. Eric's fingers trembled as he hurried. As soon as he was dressed, he joined John in assisting James to his feet. Eric draped James' right arm over his shoulder, and John did the same with the left. John grabbed a half-empty bottle of wine from the table and led the procession down the dim, empty hallway. If stopped, the three civilians would pretend to be farmers returning from a night at the ordinary.

Fortunately, the cold December wind had emptied the streets of all but an occasional English patrol, and even they were not interested in pausing to question nighttime pedestrians. The bogus English patrol and the three countrymen made their way to the boat without challenge. The fisherman uncle had his sloop in the water waiting when the Satterfields and their volunteers arrived. Within minutes, the heavily loaded boat cleared the creek inlet and was sailing with an easterly wind behind them directly for the Jersey shore. Eric was relieved that the fisherman did not have to tack. The river water lapped a short six inches below the sloop's gunwales.

Chapter 26
New York, New Jersey, Philadelphia
Spring, Summer 1777

On Sunday, April 21st, 1777, at two o'clock in the afternoon, James sat on the swing of the porch of his Alexandria town house. James knew exactly what time it was. Since his "December Experience," the euphemism he had assigned to his personal purgatory on the "Eagle," James had remained unusually conscious of the passage of time. He still silently measured the minutes, not by counting, but instinctively, using the skills he had honed in his cell. James sat quietly with Vivian at his side. She had become accustomed since his rescue to James' long lapses into unshared introspection.

Physically, he was in better condition than he had been before his capture and deprivation. The weight loss, unwelcome and unpleasant as it had been, had been good for him. His appetite still had not returned. James nibbled rather than ate, eating only bites out of his once relished ham sandwiches.

While James and Vivian enjoyed the gentle motion of the swing, Jason's wife, Lily, rocked in a Satterfield family heirloom, a chair crafted by Old Tom, James' grandfather, and smiled down at the youngest Satterfield. Bernard Thomas Satterfield, bearing names prominent in both his maternal and paternal family lines, was one month old. The child, promptly dubbed Buster by his father because one of his first independent acts had been to kick a glass nursing bottle from his crib to smash on the stone floor, was asleep in the portable bed next to Lily's chair, oblivious to the friendly argument conducted by his father Jason and Corney Goodenough who sat nearby on the porch steps.

"I tell you Jason," Corney waved his index finger to demonstrate his point, a gesture that Jason recalled vividly from his days as an acolyte at Corney's Alexandria Academy for Boys, "you are wasting your money."

Jason could think of nothing to say in reply. They had been discussing Jason's recent purchase of land at the great falls in the Potomac, a part of his investment for the future. Jason, now a family man, had substituted a material drive to accumulate wealth for his thirst for adventure. Now, he was content to build ships and sell them; since his marriage, he no longer contemplated foolish excursions to Martinique. His father and his friend Skinny Potts' experiences in the war had smothered the flame of desire to earn honor with Washington.

Skinny had returned to Alexandria in January, only weeks after the weakened and strangely silent James had arrived escorted by Uncle John and Vivian. Skinny reappeared almost the same enthusiastic young man he had been when he marched off with the militia to seek glory. He had not found what he sought, but he had lost an arm to an English ball. Skinny had not returned to the boat-yard; he could no longer wield the tools needed to shape the speedy lines of the larger replicas of the "Ghost," and James had compassionately given Speedy a job at the *Herald*. At first the position had been a sinecure designed to reward Skinny for his loss.

James had not believed Corney when the schoolmaster had suggested that Skinny, when he had attended the academy, had been surprising facile with the written word. James, for want of a better title, had dubbed Skinny his news collector. James recognized that he was recreating York Allen but did so sincerely not in jest. To every one's surprise, even his own, Skinny with one arm proved to be an adept news collector and writer. His weekly column, which focused on local personalities and events, had become one of the most popular recurring fixtures in the *Herald*.

"Corney," Jason finally replied. "One day we will dig a ditch around the rocks and open a water passage to the west."

"And if God intended that to happen, he would not have blocked the river with the great rocks in the first place," Corney replied.

"And when that happens," Jason persisted, "my land at the great falls will increase in value a hundred times."

"Hah," Corney sniffed. "But now it's worthless."

"That's why I'm buying now."

Vivian half listened to the argument as she lazily propelled the swing with her legs. The new leaves over the weekend had suddenly appeared to fill the empty spaces in the trees. The exploding Mother Nature relaxed Vivian. The azaleas and dogwood that made Fairfax an unbelievable delight were in full flower. The reds, whites, purples, pinks and even orange blossoms cascaded over every bush. Even the wild cherry and purple plum trees were at their peak. Vivian was not sure that she had ever seen the countryside with its avalanche of color so grand, but then, she thought that every spring. She felt James stir beside her and pressed her leg against his. He responded by taking her hand. Young Buster, still asleep, kicked his small legs in an involuntary jerk, and Vivian, noting that her husband smiled at the baby's movement, squeezed James' hand.

"I wonder what the Howe brothers have in mind for George this year?" James asked. As soon as he spoke, James regretted it. He had not intended to worry Vivian by disclosing the fact that he was still troubled by events in the north. He tried to avoid discussion of the distant war, but it still occupied his thoughts.

The Howe brothers with their army and fleet had wintered in New York. Washington with his diminished army had struggled through the snow at Morristown spending his days besieging Congress with pleas for assistance in rebuilding his army for 1977. Most of the militia had returned home in January, and the new drafts had yet to report. James knew this because Washington had said so in the long letter he had sent home with Martha last week. Martha Washington had wintered with her husband during the lean New Jersey winter, but when her husband began preparing for the new summer campaign, she had returned to Mount Vernon to keep friendly track of Lund Washington, the distant cousin who managed the plantation during George's extended absence.

"The same as last year, I assume," Vivian answered her husband.

She was delighted to see her husband showing interest in something, even if it was the war. Since his return, James had not been his usual inquisitive self, apparently finding it difficult to readapt to the slower pace of life in Alexandria. The boatyard had thrived under Jason's enthusiastic management, and it did not need him while the Herald with Corney as interim proprietor was more popular and more prosperous than it had ever been. Eastwind, because of the non-exportation ban was having difficulties, but under Vivian's close supervision had substituted grain for tobacco. She had the wheat ground to flour at Mount Vernon and Belvoir's mills and sold it in Alexandria for shipment north to Washington's army. Vivian was not making a profit, but she was breaking even. In any case, James was not a farmer—he had left the Short Hills as a young man for the world of ideas at William and Mary—and had no interest in the problems of the land.

"If I were the English," James speculated, "I would still try to link up with an army from Canada and split the colonies."

"That's an old strategy," Corney gave up on Jason and joined James and Vivian's discussion. "It was based on the mistaken idea that the citizens of the southern colonies were still loyal to the crown and would rise up against the rebels if given the opportunity."

"And that's an old argument," Vivian declared. She rose from the swing and pulled James to his feet. "Come with me husband for a stroll along the river."

"Ahh, Mom," Jason laughed. "You 're too old for lover's lane." The path along the river was popular with young couples in the springtime.

"Don't bet on it," Vivian waved her forefinger in mock remonstrance.

James meekly allowed his wife to pull him from the swing and off the porch. They strolled hand in hand along the lane towards Market Square.

Gentleman Johnny, as General John Burgoyne was known, had spent the winter in London lobbying for his personal plan to end the war in America. An author/soldier, Burgoyne had distinguished himself on the continent during the Seven Years War, the European counterpart to the French and Indian War, but he owed his status to good marriage. His wife, the daughter of the Earl of Derby, gave Gentleman Johnny access to the highest levels of English society, and like his superior in America, Admiral Lord Richard Howe, he made the most of it. Although his plan was no original, Burgoyne persuaded Lord Germaine, the Secretary of the Colonial Department, to approve it as the basis of English strategy for 1777. Burgoyne simply proposed a three pronged attack: he would lead an army from Canada south across Lake Champlain and capture Albany where he would link up with a Howe army from the south and a third but smaller force coming from the west along the Mohawk Valley. General Burgoyne's politicking delayed his return to the wars, but in late April, after obtaining Germaine's approval, he sailed for Canada via New York where he planned to coordinate his campaign with General Howe.

Unfortunately, Lord Germaine, a pliable and not very competent Minister who had already displayed his lack of military prowess, was not completely frank with Gentleman Johnny. He did not tell Burgoyne that he had also approved a plan submitted by the Howe brothers. Their family influence at George the Third's court proved too strong for Germaine to resist. Howe, while concurring with Burgoyne's planned drive south from Canada, proposed that he deploy his army for an attack on Philadelphia. Germaine, naively assuming Howe could take Philadelphia and return in time to meet Burgoyne at Albany, approved.

Gentleman Johnny arrived in New York on July 5th. Discovering that Germaine had also approved the Philadelphia plan and that Howe planned to carry his army to the battlefield in his brother's ships, Burgoyne argued strenuously but finally, tactfully, capitulated. He bade farewell to the stubborn Howes and continued his journey northward.

A buoyant James Satterfield arrived in Morristown in mid July. After six boring months in Alexandria, James had concluded that he would never be able to readjust to life at home as long as the united colonies' future remained to be decided on the battlefield. James had tried. After discovering to his chagrin that his family's interests were in good hands that did not need him, he had explored a return to local politics. To his dismay, he had relearned that George Mason was obsessed with his concept of a Bill of Rights for Virginia and for the united colonies. One hour had been enough to convince James that his old friend was clinging fiercely to the tail of a large problem. James still found Mason's discourses tedious. James had corresponded with his friend Tom Jefferson who had quit the Congress to cope with his wife's illness and pressing family problems, but he had not been able to share the young man's fascination with Virginia politics. Jefferson stood in line to replace Patrick Henry as Virginia's governor, but his problems had not interested James. His thoughts remained focused on New York, York Allen and his black hats, on the Howe brothers, and on Washington and his problems.

In June, a simple act of kindness resolved James' indecision. One morning a slave from Mount Vernon appeared with a large box and a short note. James broke the wax seal embossed with the initials "GW" and read the note first.

"Dear James,

"Believe I owe you one of these.

"Regards, Yr. Friend,

"George"

James had opened the box. Inside, wrapped carefully in thin, white paper, James had found what he had anticipated, a black tricorn hat identical to the one he had lost in New York when arrested at the Red Fox. James had studied the hat. It was brand new. He had put it on his head. It had fitted perfectly, but it was not quite as comfortable as his old one.

James had walked out on his porch and watched as the Mount Vernon slave, mounted on an old mule, slowly plodded in the direction of Mount Vernon. Washington's message had been brief, but James knew his friend well enough to understand it fully. Washington wanted James back. James had smiled as he turned and made his way to the barn to saddle his favorite horse. Once again, he had to ride to Eastwind and inform Vivian of his decision. James had the sense he had lived this moment before, and he had.

James had set his horse at a trot and was singing softly to himself when he passed the Alexandria town limits.

"Father and I went down to camp

"Along with Captain Gooding,

"And there we see the men and boys

"As thick as hasty pudding.

"...And there was Captain Washington,

"And gentlefolk about him.

"They say he's grown so tarnal proud

"He will not go without 'em."

There were hundreds of verses to the popular song, and James had heard most of them being sung by Washington's soldiers. James could not remember them all, but he liked one line best of all and kept repeating it.

"And Yankee Doodle had a horse

"And he named it Macaroni."

When James arrived at Morristown, he was surprised at the bustle. Young soldiers wearing their continental blues marched crisply as they practiced their drills. The victories at Trenton and Princeton had given Washington's army a new spirit, and the fresh recruits were greeted by veterans who had stories to tell. The rebel army had broken the tedium of its winter encampment by mounting raids against their opponents. While General Howe and his officers had enjoyed the pleasures of New York, the English soldiers had suffered a tedious winter in encampments haphazardly sited in New Jersey and the outskirts of Manhattan. Life had been difficult and the harassment of the rebels who attempted to deny the redcoats forage and food had been irritating. The English army waited for the Howes to map out their strategy for the 1777 fighting season, and the rebels waited for the English to move.

George Washington's priority information requirement was to learn what the Howes were planning.

Eric, who commanded the Black Hats in James' absence, was frustrated. York Allen and his informants had nothing to report.

James tied his horse that he had privately dubbed Macaroni in front of Washington's headquarters.

"I'll see to you shortly, Mac," James patted Macaroni on the nuzzle. James was too embarrassed to allow others to hear him call the animal by the now trite name of Macaroni and had settled on the shorter, more masculine appellation for public address.

James approached the two imposing sentries who guarded the entrance to headquarters and expected to be detained as usual. He knew he was still a stranger to the army.

To his surprise, the two soldiers stamped smartly to attention and presented their rifles at port arms.

"Welcome back, Mr. Satterfield, sir," the sentry on the right snapped.

James who had self-consciously been studying the ground as he approached jerked his head back and looked at the sentry who had spoken his name. The man appeared familiar. Suddenly, recognition flashed into James' mind. It was the large volunteer who had helped rescue James from the clutches of the English.

James stared. He did not know the man's name. They had separated after landing on the New Jersey shore without James ever having heard the names of his rescuers spoken. He had not thought to ask.

"It's Smoothers, sir. Sergeant Horace Smoothers, Sergeant thanks to you."

"I never knew," James stammered.

Later, James learned that the large sentry with the ridiculous name along with his three companions who had volunteered to join John had come from Washington's personal guard. All three had been promoted two ranks by the

General himself on their return. The four men now traveled with Washington wherever he went.

"I must thank you properly," James continued. "You and your companions. "If not for you... ." James let his voice trail off.

"It weren't us, sir," Smoother filled in for James' pause. "That brother of yours could have done it all by hisself. Will he be returning with you?"

"No, I'm sorry to say. John has returned to the mountains to control the Indians."

"I'm sure he does, sir. Control the Indians, sir. There won't be trouble in his mountains. If he were here, this war would soon be over."

James nodded his agreement.

"I must report to the general now," James excused himself, "but if later I could meet with you and the others, I would appreciate it."

"Certainly, sir." Smoother remained at attention while he talked. "It would be our pleasure, sir."

James, not knowing how to address the man's thick courtesy, continued through the doorway into the headquarters. It was like all the others occupied by Washington before it, a private mansion appropriated temporarily to meet the army's needs.

In the first room on the right, James found an officer wearing the sash of a staff aide sitting behind a desk guarding a closed door. James explained that he was a personal friend of Washington and desired to see the general. The aide smiled and directed James to a row of chairs that lined the wall facing the aide. All the chairs were filled with ranking officers, some generals. James, unwilling to create a scene by insisting that he see Washington immediately, went to a clear spot at the far wall where the chairs stopped. He smiled at the nattily dressed colonel who sat in the end chair, folded his arms and tried to make himself inconspicuous by leaning against the wall.

James had been in place only seconds when Sergeant Smoother stomped into the room. He winked at James and halted in front of the seated aide. Smoother leaned over and whispered something into the aide's ear. The young captain instantly jerked straight in his seat and stared with a startled look at James.

"Please excuse me Mr. Satterfield," the aide said as he rose to his feet. "I will immediately inform the General you are here." He started towards the door, then apparently remembered that James was standing while everyone else sat.

The aide paused and turned. "Please, sir, take this chair while you wait." The aide indicated the chair behind the desk where he had been sitting.

James, embarrassed to be singled out, turned to see if the others were listening. All were staring at him. They appeared puzzled, wondering who this Satterfield was; some had red faces indicating anger at the latecomer who had jumped to the head of the queue.

James shook his head to decline the aide's offer. Sergeant Smoother, now smiling in self-satisfaction, pivoted and stamped from the room.

The aide softly opened the closed door and slid inside. James heard him speak, but could not make out the words. Washington's voice boomed:

"Show him in. Gentlemen, if you will excuse me."

The door opened and three surprised generals filed out. James recognized the portly General Sullivan who had been present the first time James had visited Washington in his headquarters. Sullivan had been angered then by James' disrupting appearance and, judging by the look he cast in James' direction, he was again.

"Mr. Satterfield. The General will see you now," the aide announced.

The seated officers shuffled their feet signaling their irritation. James heard one of the generals speak to the man next to him.

"Who is this fellow Satterfield?"

Before James could hear the answer, the aide closed the door behind him. James carried his black tricorn in his hand.

"James," Washington spoke loudly. Washington hurried across the room and embraced his friend. After a brief, emotional hug, Washington stepped back.

"I'm so glad to see that you've recovered. Fully? I hope."

"Yes, George, thanks to you."

"Thanks to me?" Washington laughed. "No sir. Thanks to John. We both owe our lives to him now."

James appreciated Washington's words but suspected he was exaggerating. James knew John had accompanied Washington on his hazardous mission to deliver Governor Dinwiddie's demand to the French that they withdraw from Virginian land and that John had fought with Washington in the aftermath of Braddock's disaster, but he had never heard that John had saved Washington's life.

"John could not have done it without the assistance of Eric and the four volunteers. I see you have Smoother as one of your personal guards."

"Yes," Washington agreed circumspectly. "A good man." Washington did not explain that he had personally volunteered Smoothers and the other three key members of his guard for the rescue mission. "Couldn't have our chief of intelligence being hung, could we?" Washington's light words were out of character, giving James the feeling his friend was embarrassed about something.

James smiled but did not laugh. The fact that he had been within hours of mounting the scaffold was not something he considered a fit subject for humor.

"How long will you be with us?" Washington asked, changing the subject.

"I received your message," James replied, fingering his hat, the tricorn Washington had sent him as a gift summons. James was amazed at himself. His experience with the English had enhanced his self-confidence. George Washington's stature as commander-in-chief had previously intimidated him, but now James felt himself capable of dealing with Washington as an equal as he had previously in Fairfax County.

"I thought you might understand," Washington nodded approval. He guided James to two seats arranged in front of the fireplace. Since the windows were open and a hot July breeze heated the room, the fireplace was dark, but it remained the center of the room.

"I still need your help, James," Washington spoke quickly. He stood in front of the fireplace with his hands clasped behind him. James relaxed in the chair and listened as his friend spoke.

"I still don't know what the Howes are planning for this summer. I know that Johnny Burgoyne is preparing to march south from Canada. I assume he will attack Ticonderoga and press on towards Albany hoping to link up with Howe troops from New York, but General Howe is behaving strangely. Your Black Hats report that Howe's army is preparing for the field, but Black Dick's ships are taking on supplies. Do you think they might try to surprise me by moving on Philadelphia like they should have last winter?"

"I don't have a clue, George," James replied honestly. "Is Eric having difficulty with the New York net?" James wondered if Washington had summoned him back to take over the Black Hats again.

"No, No," Washington repeated himself. "Eric's doing a fine job. We just don't know yet what Howe has in mind. The man is unpredictable. Either he's not serious or he's stupid. He's spent the entire winter and spring enjoying himself with Mrs. Loring. I like going to the theater as much as the next man, but this is war." Washington paused, then continued. "Excuse me, James for venting my frustration on you. I have to maintain a pose for my staff and generals," Washington hesitated again. "No, to answer your question, no. Eric is doing a good job. He should continue to manage the Black Hats."

"Then what do you need me for?" James asked directly, surprising himself with his bluntness.

Washington caught James' tone and stared at him with irritation rimming his pale blue eyes. Then, to James' relief, Washington smiled.

"You talked with Sir Richard. Did he give you any intimation of his plans? "

"Me?" James could not keep the surprise out of his voice. "All Sir Richard said to me was that he was going to hang me."

"I thought so, James, but I had to ask." Washington took a seat opposite his friend. "Your office will be in there," he pointed at a closed door leading to an adjacent room.

"I thought you wanted your chief of intelligence to remain anonymous and not become identified with you or the army?" James said, referring to their previous relationship.

"I think the Howes and the entire English army now know who you are James, so I don't think you will be making any more anonymous visits behind the lines."

"But... ."

"I want you close at hand so I can keep an eye on you," Washington spoke solemnly. James did not catch the twinkle in his eye.

"But what can I do here? I'm still not a military man. Your staff will resent me. Why... ." James started to explain about the reaction of those waiting in the outer officer when James was rushed ahead of them into Washington's office.

"Do you want to wear a uniform?" Washington interrupted. "I could make you a colonel on my own authority, or I could ask Congress to make you a general. Heaven knows, I have enough of them around here. Silas Deane in Paris is promising high rank to any European officer who appears at his door."

"Never," James interrupted. "I do not want to wear a uniform, and I don't have a deep need for a title, but if I can help you and our country I will do whatever you ask."

"You know, James," Washington smiled to soften his words, "I think your experience has toughened you."

"Maybe it has always been there," James accepted Washington's words without taking offense. "I am after all John's twin brother. And he is the hardest man in these colonies. And the kindest and most loyal," James added.

"Among other things," Washington conceded.

"If I am no longer to be your chief of intelligence, and in truth I never really was that, what do you want me to do."

"I want you to put on your other hat," Washington pointed at the tricorn in James' hand. "Your new one."

"And that is," James laughed at Washington's duplicity. He had not realized his friend could be devious.

"When we first talked, I said I wanted you to be my political advisor."

James nodded, recalling the conversation.

"Personal adviser would be a more accurate description, James," Washington continued, "but for the benefit of my staff and generals I will call you Political Adviser. That way you will appear less threatening to them. Many are ambitious peacocks, you know."

"And as adviser, who all do I advise?"

"Me."

"When do I begin?"

"Go through that door," Washington indicated the door leading to the adjacent office, "and take charge of my relations with Congress. I 'm sure Mr. Reed or one of my aides can provide you with the files. Please begin with the one dealing with General Lee's abominable machinations. Why the man... ." Washington caught himself before he criticized his old visitor at Mount Vernon.

"I hear that he wants your job," James laughed.

"He's only one of many, as you will find out," George's thin lips tightened into a hard line. "Why if I thought that one of them, Gates, or Lee or...or...any of them could do it better, they could have it in a blink."

"But the honor, General," James spoke ironically.

"Honor, my God... ." Washington erupted before James' tone had registered. Catching himself, Washington laughed. "You will be good for me James,"

Washington smiled. "You will find a different Congress. Many of the fine leaders have already left."

"Including Tom Jefferson," James agreed.

"A real loss, and others, only to be replaced by second raters," Washington paused, "but we are fortunate we still have a few like John Adams making the sacrifice."

"Do you want me to return to Virginia and get myself elected to the Congress?" James was serious because he knew he could have one of Virginia's seven positions. "George Mason suggested... ."

"Bless his heart," Washington interrupted. "No. I need you here. You can expect to spend as much time as needed in Philadelphia, or wherever the politicians may be forced to run if Howe makes up his mind what to do. I want you to be my politician and free me to run the army."

"Agreed," James said. "How should I treat your military colleagues?"

"Our colleagues," Washington corrected. "However you wish. I will expect you to attend all of my military councils where we make the important decisions and any of my meetings that you want. I'm sure you will soon find them repetitious and boring, but I want you to know everything that is going on around here. I may ask you to help solve other special problems, military or whatever, at various times, so stay informed."

"Thank you George, I'll get to work."

"And that door will open any time you turn the handle. Use it. Don't rest on formality. You will be the one man who has total access to me."

"I promise, George," James turned to enter his new office. "And if I step over the line, tell me."

"Given the authority and access I have just delegated to you, I don't see how you can," Washington replied.

James disappeared through the connecting door, and Washington opened the door to his outer office.

"Captain, if I may have my next appointment," Washington spoke softly. He ignored the surprised glances of the waiting officers who peeked through the doorway attempting to learn what had happened to Satterfield.

Chapter 27
New York, New Jersey, Pennsylvania
Summer, Autumn 1776

Gentleman Johnny Burgoyne in the van of an army of 7,000 reached the bluffs overlooking Fort Ticonderoga on the western shore of Lake Champlain on the afternoon of July 4th. From his vantagepoint on the heights that the rebels had deemed impossible for cannon to attain, Burgoyne looked down on the rebels manning the isolated fort. He smiled to himself at the sight of his naval armada sailing and paddling down the lake. He assumed that General St. Clair, who commanded Ticonderoga, was as impressed by the demonstration of force as Gentleman Johnny himself. As the small armada led by the Indians in their birch-bark canoes that held as many as thirty braves each approached the outer reaches of the fort's cannon, Gentleman Johnny decided to announce his presence.

"Fire for range, then fire at will," he ordered, effectively turning control over to his colonel of artillery.

The colonel frowned. He looked at the single twelve pounder that constituted his full command on the bluff and swore under his breath. If given the time, he would have had a second twelve pounder in place by nightfall. He understood Johnny's order, however; they were on the verge of losing the advantage of surprise. Someone—the artillery colonel assumed it had been one of the undisciplined savages that Burgoyne had recruited—had lighted a cooking fire whose single column of smoke rose skyward. The colonel, recognizing that the possibility of surprise had been wrested from them by that simple act, turned to the captain who commanded the single cannon.

"Fire for range," he ordered.

The cannon boomed. The shot fell short, and the gun captain raised his elevation while his gun monkeys swabbed, poured their powder, and tamped in another ball.

Gentleman Johnny studied the fort through his long glass. When the first shot sounded, he saw the rebel heads turn. Johnny imagined the looks of panic and chagrin that must have clouded their faces. He felt General St. Clair's eyes focus on him, squinting with the shattering recognition that Burgoyne's cannon could now drop enfilading balls over Ticonderoga's walls.

The cannon crashed a second time. As Burgoyne watched, a guardtower on the fort's lakeside wall crumbled into rubble. The frightening shrieks from the savages in the lead canoes echoed across the lake. Inside the fort, St. Clair and his officers fought to still the panic, their own and that of their men.

The artillery colonel's second cannon arrived at nightfall. All the next day the two pieces dropped their balls on the helpless rebels.

On the evening of July 5th, one short day after the arrival of the English army, General St. Clair issued the order to withdraw. He took no solace in the fact that Gentleman Johnny had required twenty-four hours to recapture a fort that Greene and Arnold had seized in two.

Burgoyne rested his men, then followed the fleeing Americans southward. As his troops advanced, Burgoyne deployed his Indians as scouts. Although the menacing savages were a disrupting influence in camp, the presence of their war parties ahead of the army gave Gentleman Johnny a sense of security.

When General Howe had first ordered him to enlist the Iroquois and their allies in the English cause, Burgoyne had been dismayed. He had immediately recognized that the duplicitous Howe was attempting to substitute the savages for the English troops that Howe had diverted from the northern campaign to support his Philadelphia strategy. Gentleman Johnny did not trust the savages, knowing that they were fair weather fighters. They ambushed and ran, attacked defenseless settler cabins and looted and burned and ran, and they fled before organized fire of disciplined units without firing a shot themselves. After Ticonderoga, however, Burgoyne had listened to the assurances of Colonel Johnson, the King's appointed Chief of Indian Affairs, and had deployed the Indians. It did not take him long to learn he had erred.

South of Skenesborough, about fifteen miles from Fort Anne, a band of savages created a furor when they appeared in camp proudly displaying two fresh scalps. Investigation disclosed that one of the scalps had recently been worn by a young lady named Jane McCrea. One of Burgoyne's scouts named Wyandot Panther had brutally savaged and killed the unfortunate Miss McCrea. The fact that her father was a known Tory, an ardent loyalist, and that Miss McCrea was betrothed to one of Burgoyne's officers had not saved her. The incident was a minor one, but it highlighted Burgoyne's mistake in relying on the savages.

Before long, smoke plumes rose over the length and breadth of the Mohawk Valley; the braves of the Six Nations led by the bloodthirsty Mohawks unleashed their war parties on the frontier settlers with official English blessing.

Releasing the Indians was not Gentleman Johnny's only mistake. At Skenesborough, a prominent farmer named Skene advised him to pursue the retreating rebels by land eschewing the lake. It took Burgoyne twenty-three days to hack his way through twenty-four miles of thick forests. Farmer Skene had failed to confide that he was more interested in acquiring a cleared road south than he was in aiding an easy English victory.

Gentleman Johnny's slow moving army won costly victories as the rebels sniped from the woods and diminished Burgoyne's reserves. When the supply lines lengthened, shortages of powder and food developed. Assuming that these problems would be alleviated when he linked with an army from the south, Burgoyne pushed his luck.

The retreating General Schuyler was replaced. He had never pleased the New Englanders, and they used his northern defeats to maneuver in Congress and obtain his dismissal. In this endeavor the plotting politicians had been aided by General Horatio Gates who used his position as military commander in Philadelphia as a base for his intrigues. The fifty-year-old Gates had known Washington for over twenty years; he had served with Braddock and had been wounded in battle. Following that war, he had settled in western Virginia, building a home, Travelers Rest, not far from that of Charles Washington, George's brother.

When the revolution broke out, the ambitious Gates had ridden Washington's coattails to his major generalcy. A cautious man, he was known as Granny by his troops. Still ambitious and despite his former status as a professional soldier, Gates was more politician than fighter. His proximity to the Congress had inspired him to secretly seek Washington's title. Samuel Adams, more famous for his radical patriotism than his judgment, became Gate's mentor. Sam Adams had conspired for months to obtain the northern command for Gates, and Schuyler's difficulties gave him his opportunity. Soon, rumors circulated in Congress accusing the unpopular Schuyler, a wealthy New Yorker, of having sold Ticonderoga to the English. One wag even claimed that it had been "silver" bullets not lead that had driven the rebels southward.

Gates moved the main rebel defensive position from the mouth of the Mohawk to a plateau known as Bemis Heights. There, Colonel Thaddeus Kosciuzko, a Polish engineer, designed the defenses. By mid-September, Burgoyne's army, now weaker by two thousand men, approached. For two weeks the armies skirmished. On October 7th, the battle began. The British gave way and Burgoyne retreated to Saratoga. There, Gentleman Johnny decided to make his stand and wait for help from the south. None came before the Americans surrounded his position in the hills and demanded surrender. Now, outnumbered with his force reduced to less than five thousand, Burgoyne fought until his supplies ran out. Finally, on October fifteenth, Gentleman Johnny surrendered.

General Horatio Gates, Granny, was a hero.

On Monday, July 14th, at noon, York Allen sat at his desk in the small office of the New York *Dispatch* attempting to rewrite reports of the English victory at Fort Ticonderoga. For one of the few times in his life, the words did not come easily. He had all the information he needed; Ambrose Serle had given him copies of Bourgoyne's dispatches the previous day, but Allen's heart was not in the task; the news depressed him, and he had labored for over an hour to produce one paragraph. Fort Ticonderoga for Allen had been a symbol; its capture had been a major rebel victory, and Washington had used English guns acquired there to persuade General Howe to depart Boston, and now the English had taken it back. Allen, sitting in New York, recognized that all General Howe had to do was now drive north and meet the victorious General Burgoyne and the English would have split the colonies. Allen's head hurt. He dipped his quill in the inkpot and absently drew circles on the paper in front of him. He had just finished a complete row across the page when the front door burst open.

"Have you finished that report yet?" An excited Ambrose Serle demanded.

Serle's demeanor surprised York. Normally, the admiral's stolid secretary had all the personality of a three-day-old mackerel. York shoved his stringy, faded blond hair out of his eyes and stared at Serle without response. The man obviously had more bad news.

"Well, have you?" Serle demanded.

York hated working for the humorless man. He now acted as if the *Dispatch* were his own. Gaine, the proprietor, seldom visited the shop. York assumed the owner spent all of his time enjoying the payments he received from the English for having made the newspaper a blatant cheering section for the occupation army. If it were not for his secret life as a spy, Allen would have long ago fled through the lines.

"I'm working on it," York replied irritably. He made no secret of his dislike of the sour Englishman.

"Well, finish it. I've a new assignment for you. Something you've been begging for."

York knew instinctively that the new assignment would be something that would amuse Serle and make himself very unhappy. York had been reduced from his lofty peak as one of the city's most respected news collectors to servile scribe at a rubber stamp house organ.

Serle leaned against the counter in the front of the shop and studied the dispirited young man. He wondered if the plan he had in mind was a mistake or not. That very morning Lord Richard had summoned Serle to his cabin on the "Eagle" and alerted him to prepare to sail. Serle, like every tar in the fleet, had been waiting for an intimation of the commander-in-chief plans for the summer campaign. Even Serle, the admiral's very own private secretary, had grown uncomfortable with the Howe brothers' dilatory behavior. He suspected they could not make up their minds what to do. The truth was, as Serle knew from what he had overheard, the Howe brothers simply were in no hurry to commence the fighting. Even Lord Richard now recognized that his attempts to settle the disagreement with the colonists peaceably through compromise had fallen on deaf ears. The admiral had stopped making overtures, and his only alternative remained the battlefield. Now, the fleet was ready to board General Howe's army and to set sail. Lord Richard, who had been most insulting in his insistence that Serle swear an oath of secrecy, had confided that their objective was Philadelphia. Serle, who had only heard the previous day of Burgoyne's victory at

Ticonderoga,, wondered if that news had propelled the Howes' decision. Serle realized that jealousy of Gentleman Johnny's military victory might have forced the Howes to act.

"We are sailing tomorrow," Serle spoke softly.

His words caught York by surprise.

"You are sailing? With the fleet?"

"We are," Serle smiled enigmatically.

York leaned back in his chair and waited. Since he was nearing the end of his patience, he would listen to what the popish Englishman had to say then make up his own mind. If he did not like what he heard, he would quit the *Dispatch*. Then, if Eric and Washington did not approve of what he learned independent of Serle, possibly working for Rivington's *Gazette* or another newspaper, he would desert them too.

"We're sailing south with the army," Serle finally spoke after he decided he was not going to be able to provoke the excitable young man into another outburst.

"Have a good trip," York said sourly, turning sidewise in his chair and placing his feet on his worktable. He had heard that in some parts of the world it was an insult to turn the soles of your feet in the direction of another.

"I mean us, you and me," Serle laughed at Allen's churlishness. The colonists just had no sophistication.

York bolted straight up in his chair, jerking his feet to the floor under the table.

"Me?"

"Yes. To Philadelphia." As soon as the words left his mouth, Serle regretted having divulged Lord Howe's confidence. Serle had intended to keep their destination secret from York until they were safely at sea.

"What will be my function?" York demanded. "I'm not going to join the Loyalist Regiment." York referred to General Howe's latest pet project. After the Ministry had agreed to send only half the reinforcements he had requested, Howe had attempted to increase the size of his army by adding loyalist units and Indians.

"I know that. You will assist me writing reports of the battle for the *Dispatch's* readers."

"What time should I be at the pier?"

"Tomorrow morning at nine. Now, finish that story on Burgoyne's fine victory," Serle ordered.

James sat at his desk attempting to devise a plan for dealing with a demanding and uncooperative Congress when Captain Eric Grey burst into his office. Grey, who still wore his countryman clothes, had been promoted following James' rescue and his own assumption of James' former duties.

"We've got it," Eric spoke loudly, waving a piece of paper that James recognized immediately as an invisible writing report from one of their New York informants.

"Got what?" James growled impatiently. The problems with Congress frustrated him, and he was in no mood for guessing games.

"Serle told York Allen that the fleet is sailing with the army aboard for Philadelphia. General Howe is ignoring Burgoyne. I guess he thinks Gentleman Johnny is strong enough to fight his own battles, and Howe is going to capture our political center."

"I hope he catches all the delegates," James said only half jokingly.

"The General has been waiting for this information for a long time," Eric protested, assuming that James was not taking his report seriously. Eric knew it was a coup.

"I know," James softened his attitude. "Let's tell him immediately."

James, happy to set his own problems aside for the moment, rose and walked to the door that connected his office with that of Washington. He tapped lightly to warn Washington he was coming and opened the door. Washington sat in solitude at his desk studying the status reports on readiness for action that he insisted each of his commanders submit every morning.

"Yes, James," Washington smiled, happy at the interruption. Washington, like his army, was growing impatient at the Howes' delay.

"Captain Grey has some information that might interest you," James said.

"Come in, Eric," Washington invited the young officer who had politely waited at the doorway.

"Sir, I think we have the information you wanted," Eric waved the scorched paper in the air.

Washington, like James, immediately recognized that Eric was holding a secret writing report from New York. Washington, in silent response, held out his hand. He preferred, whenever possible, to receive his information on paper. He found that he retained what he read better than what he heard. To often, his officers bored him with details he did not want to hear, and his mind wandered.

Washington read the developed report quickly. "This is straight from Serle?" He asked.

"Yes sir. You'll note that Allen reports Serle ordered him to board the "Eagle" and sail with the fleet."

"That would have been yesterday." Washington's words formed a statement not a question. "So it will be Philadelphia," he mused. "That means he's abandoning Burgoyne. Gates will outnumber Gentleman Johnny, and we may defeat an English army."

"That's good news, sir," Eric blurted. James said nothing, waiting for Washington to continue.

"We must protect this information, of course," Washington said. "It will be no secret that the army has boarded Admiral Howe's ships, and they have sailed, but their destination will not be common knowledge. It will take them several days to get to their landing point. I wonder if they will land in Delaware or circle around into the Bay." Washington paused, and he and James exchanged worried glances. The two men were wondering if it were possible that the Howes might enter the bay and sail up the Potomac River to land in the vicinity of Alexandria.

"I don't think they will, George," James said, having anticipated Washington's thought. "They might like to burn Mount Vernon, but General Howe will want to capture Philadelphia as quickly as he can to take the edge off Burgoyne's successes."

"I think you're right James," Washington agreed. "I can't begin moving the army south until the Howes are sighted heading for Philadelphia. They will presume we are sitting here worried about their destination. We can get the army ready to march. The fleet sailing justifies that. And I think you had better take a quick trip to Philadelphia. We need to alert John Adams at least."

"Yes, sir," James said. He was delighted that finally the summer campaign was beginning. He was also proud that his Black Hats had provided the first information.

"Good work, Captain," Washington spoke formally. Both James and Eric recognized that this was high praise coming from the Commander-in-Chief who doled out commendations to others grudgingly.

Lord Howe's best intentions flagged, and the fleet did not sail until July 23rd. Despite the relatively short distance to be traversed, the Admiral dithered trying to make up his mind where to land. With 227 ships in the "Eagle's" wake waiting for a decision, Howe lingered off the New Jersey coast and reconsidered his plan. Given his brother's indecision, General William Howe began to doubt the wisdom of his plan to sail up the Delaware River to Philadelphia. General Howe cautiously decided to take the Chesapeake route, but he needed reasons to justify his action to subordinates and the Ministry.

Unwittingly, Washington gave General Howe what he needed. When the fleet was reported lingering off the New Jersey coast, Washington began to worry. Finally, he decided he could wait no longer and ordered part of his army to begin the tedious march southward. As soon as the troops broke camp for their journey, English spies reported the information. It was hurried by couriers to the Howes and ironically provided General Howe with his excuse to avoid the Delaware. He had no difficulty persuading his staff that Washington intended to take a blocking position at Wilmington or New Castle.

The fleet weighted anchor and sailed southward. General Howe studied his maps and concluded his new destination would let him land his army unopposed in a position that let him interdict the rebel supply lines that led to Carlisle and York. Sir William announced his decision to a shocked staff on the afternoon of July 30th. Those who knew the Chesapeake privately questioned the wisdom of the General's decision. Even a loyal bureaucrat like Ambrose Serle had his doubts.

"Here we are at the entrance of the Delaware," Serle complained to a wide-eyed York Allen. "In two days we can land at New Castle with Philadelphia only a short thirty miles away. Instead, we will sail for a month, torturing our army cramped in these wood prisons, and then land at a place called Head of Elk, sixty miles from our objective."

York carefully listened to Serle and made notes for reports he could not submit. He had not even dared bring his invisible ink with him and in any case had no means for sending his information to Washington. York was simultaneously in a spy's paradise and hell. He had complete access to all the enemy's plans and no way to share them with his superiors.

After two weeks of sailing southward, Lord Richard turned the "Eagle" with its two hundred and twenty-seven-vessel tail northward and entered the Chesapeake Bay. From Cape Henry the fleet moved easily past the Potomac, the Patuxent and Annapolis until they reached uncharted waters. There, they paused while the Admiral sent smaller vessels ahead to probe the passage. Not until August 25th did the "Eagle" and its convoy reach their destination, the Elk River. The army disembarked and began its march northward. At Head of Elk, General Howe again reconsidered his plans. Loyalists did not stream to join his army as he had been led to believe would happen.

Pennsylvania was not the hotbed of loyal citizens that Ambrose Serle with his many friends in the refugee community had described. Instead, spies reported that Washington and his rebel army waited twenty-five miles ahead at a place called Brandywine. General Howe decided to win the war on the battlefield. He accepted Washington's challenge and marched toward what he assumed would be a decisive victory.

York Allen, to his dismay, remained aboard "Eagle" with Serle and Black Dick and watched the English army disappear to the north. All of his notes and information were now worthless, and he was a virtual prisoner on board ship. He freely roamed the deck and one day even visited the cell where James had been held prisoner.

The fleet sailed back through the Chesapeake and then northward for the Delaware coast where they planned to do what they could to support Sir William's army.

On September 11th, General Howe found Washington where he expected, Brandywine Creek. Howe deployed General Knyphausen in the center as a blocking force and joined General Cornwallis in leading flanking movements to the west and north designed to envelope Washington and his fortifications. The rebels discovered his intent and turned to confront the flanking units. After a bitter struggle, the English carried the battle and sent the rebel army churning in retreat towards Philadelphia.

General Howe once again surprised his staff by deciding to pause and rest his army, giving the rebels the opportunity to escape.

Finally, Howe resumed his march. On September 26th, advance elements led by General Cornwallis marched victoriously into Philadelphia where they were greeted by cheering crowds.

As soon as his meeting with Washington and Eric ended, James raced to his boarding house, packed a saddlebag, and set off at a gallop for Philadelphia. While he rode, he thought of the Congress that he was hastening to warn. In two short years, the intellectual cream of the united colonies had forsaken it. Only six delegates who had been present when George Washington was selected from their midst to lead the colonial armies remained: John and Samuel Adams, John Hancock, Eliphalet Dyer, James Duane, Samuel Chase and Richard Henry Lee. The new members did not know General Washington personally and formed their opinions based on performance on the battlefield. Even James had to admit that those unfamiliar with the weaknesses of the colonial army and the no lose strategy it imposed on the commander would conclude that Washington's performance over the years had been less than scintillating. James recognized it was his job to correct the mistaken impressions, but it was difficult, particularly given the political machinations of ambitious officers like Lee, Conway and Gates, among others.

As he rode, James concluded that he could only rely on the discretion of those delegates that he knew and trusted, and given the Congress' reduced state, this meant John Adams, Richard Henry Lee and John Hancock. James wondered if he could have made a difference if he had followed a different route and had accepted George Mason's recommendation that he accept a seat in Congress himself. He concluded the answer was no, given the reduced quality of the delegates. This thought made James speculate about the regard that others might hold for him. Was he really considered to be of the second tier? The fact that friends had considered him a logical candidate to join the second raters at the diminished Congress raised that question. The thought combined with the news he was carrying depressed James.

John Adams, the portly New Englander who headed the Congress' Committee for Conducting the War was James' logical point of contact. After arriving in Philadelphia, James, following Washington's instructions, visited Adams' new Philadelphia home on Walnut Street between Second and Third. There, he discovered that he had just missed Adams who had gone off to visit his favorite barber, a man by the name of Burne. James found his prey, John Adams, sitting in Burne's chair with his faced wrapped in hot, white cloths joking with his Cockney friend. While James waited, Adams and Burne exchanged jests, and the barber scrapped the New Englander's face with a gleaming razor. Finally, Adams, a broad smile on his face, bade his friend farewell, beckoned to the waiting James, and departed. Outside, Adams turned right towards Carpenter's Hall and began to walk briskly. James, leading Macaroni, struggled to keep up.

"Well, James, what bad news brings you to Philadelphia this fine day?"

"It is bad news, John."

"What other kind is there?" Adams looked at the dusty and sweating James. James, tired of Adams' game, stopped, forcing Adams to halt with him.

"John," James said. "Howe is preparing to sail. South."

"For Philadelphia?"

"I can assure you and you alone that Howe plans to take Philadelphia within the month."

"Are you sure? What about the linkup with Burgoyne?"

"I can't answer your second question, but yes, I am sure that Howe plans to take Philadelphia."

"And what does our Commander intend to do about that?"

"He will move his army south as soon as Howe sails."

"And?"

"And take defensive positions between this city and Howe."

"And what should I do with this information?"

James paused and stared at Adams before responding. He recognized that the New Englander was merely attempting to obtain precise information in an efficient manner, but the man's abrupt tone irritated James.

"We must protect our sources," James did not attempt to conceal the asperity he felt. "You may brief those you trust, at least John Hancock and Richard Henry Lee, or those you know better than I, but we cannot speak publicly until Howe turns his fleet in this direction."

"And after I brief those fine gentlemen. What then? Are we to sit passively here and wait for General Howe to come for tea?"

Adams' insulting manner made James laugh. He assumed the doughty New Englander was recalling their most recent evacuation from the city and wanted to avoid the experience again if possible.

"Will Washington's army assume defensive positions between Philadelphia and the English or rally north of the city?" Adams asked sharply, irritated by James' apparent bemusement.

"Do you want my opinion?" James responded.

"Yes. "

"We will not be able to hold Philadelphia."

"And where does this Fabius of ours expect the Congress to go?"

"That's up to you and the Congress," James replied, "but to me Lancaster or York seem logical."

"Logical. Logical my fat backside," Adams steamed.

Adams hurried forward as fast as his short legs could carry him. James, encumbered by Macaroni, followed along behind. He occupied his mind with unkind thoughts about self-centered politicians. When they reached Carpenters Hall, James tied Macaroni at a stanchion outside and followed the still silent but angry Adams into the building. Adams led the way to the alcove off the main hall that served as office for the Military Department that Adams headed.

After they were settled in chairs in Adams' office, the New Englander began again.

"You know, James, I'm responsible for Washington having been selected commander-in-chief, and now it's my reputation that is on the line."

"How is that?" James asked.

"I understand George's problems and am doing what I can to assist. I know his army needs men, powder, rifles, cannons, clothing, food, wagons, horses, everything, but I'm not a magician. You know all that requires money, and the Congress has none. The colonies keep what they have to supply their militia. Where do I get money to purchase what Washington needs?" Without pausing for James to answer, the irate Adams continued. "Congress prints it. And what do you think that paper is worth?" Adams demanded. "Nothing, that's what its worth and that's what I get for it."

James allowed Adams to rant without comment. He understood the portly politician's problems, but James had his own. He had quickly learned that his new assignment dealt with problems that had no solutions.

"And what are we to do with the schemers?" Adams demanded, abruptly changing his tack.

"What schemers?" James asked, knowing full well the answer.

"Gates and Lee and these foreigners. I don't understand what we need these Germans and Frenchmen and English expatriates for. If they weren't successful in their own armies, what do we expect of them here?"

"I don't think General Washington is appointing them. Congress names the generals."

"Take this man Conway. Thanks to that fellow in Paris the man thinks he's a Brigadier General. He spends more time in Philadelphia demanding promotion than he does with the army. Can't you find something for him to do?"

James recognized that Adams was referring to Brigadier General Thomas Conway. A native Irishman, who had served in the French army, Conway had approached Silas Deane in Paris, offered his professional services and received promises of high rank. He had arrived in the colonies in May, been received by Washington and had been dispatched to Congress to seek his rewards. To Washington's surprise, Congress had appointed Conway a Brigadier General and sent him back to Washington. Washington had assigned Conway to command a regiment under General Sullivan but soon discovered that the unhappy Conway spent more time in Philadelphia campaigning for promotion than he did with the army.

"What has Conway done now?" James asked, having heard reports that Conway of late had severely criticized Washington's generalship.

"He's allied himself with those in the Congress who think Washington should be replaced, that's what," Adams sputtered.

"And who may that be?"

"James Lovell, Thomas Mifflin, your Richard Henry Lee and my very own cousin Samuel, that's who."

James was not surprised by any of the names except for that of his fellow Virginian, Richard Henry Lee.

"What are their chances?" James asked.

"Zero, none, at least not while I am here."

James recognized that John Adams was not taking a strong position out of altruism or his love and respect for Washington. Adams had nominated Washington for the appointment as Commander-in-Chief and was not about to admit publicly that he had been wrong.

"But we can't continue to lose every battle," Adams fumed. "Washington is not a deity, you know."

James did not attempt to persuade the angry politician of the wisdom of Washington's tactics. Adams knew the rationale and need behind Washington's battleplans as well as the Virginian himself did. James assumed that one of his functions was to serve as a buffer between the beleaguered general and the politicians and if this required him to passively listen as Adams and others vented their frustrations, he was determined to do so.

Chapter 28
Valley Forge, Philadelphia
Autumn, Winter 1777 / 1778

James, after delivering Washington's warning to John Adams, decided to pause in Philadelphia long enough to reacquaint himself with the delegates. The dour John Adams pretended to be Washington's friend, but his crusty demeanor left James with an uncomfortable feeling. Several of the more recent rumors had linked John Adams' name with that of his cousin Sam Adams as one of Washington's detractors. James recognized that the radical Sam Adams had lost considerable stature; he no longer ranked in eminence as one of the Revolution's foremost figures, but John Adams still had the respect of his peers, thus was the more dangerous of the two.

The first two Congresses had been dominated by conservatives who did not trust the fiery Massachusetts plotter, and Sam had deliberately attempted to cloak his radicalism. Samuel's lowered profile did not shield, however, his attempt to control the army from behind the scenes. As James understood Sam's views, he was motivated by a concern that the war might produce an American Caesar who would be tempted to establish a dictatorship, and this Adams was determined to prevent. It did not require a great amount of intelligence to conclude that Washington's increasing stature haunted Adams' vision of the future.

In James' opinion, Sam Adams, regardless of the potential impact on the war effort, deliberately encouraged rivalries among the senior generals in order to insure that no one of them became all powerful. One of Sam's instruments for congressional control of the army, the Board of War, had recently been promulgated. Sam planned to pack the Board with men subject to his influence and through them to control the incipient demigod Washington. James believed that John Adams, who shared a temporary dwelling with his cousin, was fully aware of Sam's machinations and by not restraining his relative tacitly approved his actions.

James had learned that General Horatio Gates was one of Sam Adams' favorite pawns. Sam had been primarily responsible for prodding Congress into appointing Gates to the Northern Command replacing General Schuyler, the wealthy New Yorker who had long been an Adams target. Several of James' military friends had confided that during Gates' tour as Philadelphia commander he had lobbied hard with Congress for his own advancement and while doing so had not been reluctant to hint that the army needed a new commander, a professional officer like himself.   ·

After taking his leave from John Adams, James found himself a room in a boarding house on Walnut Street not far from the residence that John Adams shared with his cousin. James, taking advantage of the proximity, again visited the Adams' house. He planned to invite Sam Adams to dinner in order to gauge for himself the truthfulness of many of the rumors. The Adams housekeeper displayed no surprise at James' reappearance, this time asking for the second Adams, and curtly dispatched him to the Sign of the Gored Bull where Sam frequently held court.

The ordinary was crowded with diners when James entered, and he had difficulty locating Sam who he had met once previously when he had stopped in Philadelphia on a return trip to Alexandria from Cambridge. Finally, he stopped a harried barmaid whose arms were filled with full mugs of brown ale and asked if Sam Adams was present. The barmaid, a stout, unattractive woman who James estimated to be about his own age did not speak. She merely nodded in the direction of a large table, one of the noisiest in the loud room, and hurried on her way. James belatedly recognized Sam sitting in the epicenter of a group of delegates, all of whom appeared to be talking at once, except for Sam who sat smiling and listening. Sam stood out in the group of well-dressed patriots who wore black suits, powdered wigs and freshly pressed shirts filled with ruffles. Sam, who made a religion of his disregard for money and things that it bought, wore a tattered brown jacket and a faded shirt that had seen too many harsh scrubbings. James had heard the story about how his fellow delegates to the first Continental Congress had raised a collection to buy Sam a wardrobe so that Massachusetts' preeminent patriot would not embarrass the colony. James assumed that the tattered brown suit was a relic from that initial attempt to dress the street organizer as a statesman.

James made his way around the table until he stood behind the silent Adams. James said nothing and waited until someone at the crowded table acknowledged his presence. After a long interval during which he was ignored, he decided self respect required him to speak. Just as he moved his hand to tap Adams' shoulder to demand the man's attention, Adams surprised him.

Adams pounded his almost empty mug on the rough table and called.

"Silence. Silence."

The heated conversation around the table subsided, and all stared obediently at Adams.

"Let me welcome to our humble table a colleague of our most esteemed commander-in-chief."

James detected the thin vein of sarcasm in Adams' stress on the words "humble" and "esteemed" but chose to ignore it.

"Mr. James Satterfield, Political Adviser to General Washington," Adams announced.

Several of the men applauded politely while others stared disapproval. At Adams' order, a space was made at his immediate left and a vacant chair produced. James sat down, wondering how in this bedlam he was going to engage Adams in the private conversation he desired. The portly barmaid appeared and deposited an armload of mugs on the table. One of the diners attempted to fondle her backside, but she wearily slapped his hand away and without a word retreated to the bar. Somehow, two mugs made their way to Adams and James. Adams raised his in silent toast and waited for James to respond. James did so and afterward set his mug on the table in front of him. To his surprise, the other men at the table returned to their noisy conversations and ignored James and Adams.

"Your visit is a surprise, James," Adams declared. James noticed an ironic twinkle in his eyes. "Did you bring us an urgent message from our fearless general. News of another defeat?"

"I delivered a report from the General to your cousin. I fear the news is not good."

"Tell me."

"I'm afraid I cannot here, sir." James glanced knowingly at the crowded table.

"Ah yes, fear of being overheard by our famous spy." Adams laughed snidely, as if appreciating his own humor.

James was fully aware that despite his tone Adams was not speaking loosely. James knew that the Adamses like Washington had been warned by correspondents in England that news of the Congress' most secret negotiations was reaching London. They had to conclude that one or more members of Congress were in English employ. Talk of the spies had spread, and speculation about their identities was a favorite topic among Philadelphia gossips. Sam Adams had been heard to say that Philip Livingston and John Jay were two of his candidates for the treacherous role. By speaking thusly, cynics noted unkindly, Sam blackened the names of two of his arch rivals while at the same time diminishing the impact of those who claimed that Adams himself was the spy.

"Tell me," Adams leaned close to James. "What does the great man think of the departure of our president? He knows that John Hancock is giving up his post and returning to Massachusetts?"

"He knows," James replied, "but I don't know what he thinks. I'm sure the General considers this a matter that concerns Mr. Hancock and the Congress not the army."

"Come now James. Be honest. Does he think the Congress should offer its official thanks to the president for his long service or not?"

James, who could not think of a reason why Washington should be concerned over such a petty matter, said nothing. He knew that such trivia often occupied the politicians.

"I'll let you in on a secret," Adams leaned closer to James and whispered. "I don't think Congress should. My colleagues and I," Adams nodded in the direction of the table, "do not think we should formally honor a man for simply doing his job. That's all Hancock has done."

Adams waited for James to respond to his ostensible confidence. When he did not. Adams continued:

"You know that Hancock aspired to the post your general holds?"

"Yes, and I also know he is a political enemy of yours in Massachusetts," James replied, his patience flagging.

"Now, now, James," Adams laughed with false amusement. "Is that any way for the commander-in-chief's political liaison to talk?"

"I understand that some of Washington's generals also aspire to replace him," James continued, determined to force Adams to comment.

"Why who could that be?" Adams asked. "You're not referring to Generals Lee and Gates are you?" Adams smiled insincerely as he waited for James' answer.

"Or even General Conway," James added, knowing that both Gates and Conway had been in touch with the scheming New Englander. "Rumor has it that even some of our delegates to Congress have been known to harbor such thoughts."

"I don't understand that," Adams observed, feigning seriousness. "Why our commander is so victorious, none should criticize him. It's not as if he is constantly retreating, is it?"

The man on Adams' left began to laugh. Too late, James recognized that Adams' colleagues had ceased their heated conversations to listen to James and Adams spar.

James immediately regretted having permitted Adams to entice him into a futile debate. To cover his dismay, he sipped from his mug and placed it heavily on the table.

"If you will excuse me, gentlemen," James said rising. "I have an important appointment."

"With the departing President Hancock, I assume," Adams laughed. "To offer the General's thanks for his loyal service." Adams could not resist a final barb.

James bowed and departed, regretting the impetuosity that had prompted him to seek out Adams.

In October, Burgoyne surrendered at Saratoga, and a complacent General Howe, who had left Gentleman Johnny to his own devices, settled down to enjoy the winter season in Philadelphia. General Washington retreated towards Chester on his way to Valley Forge, and the Congress moved from Lancaster to York, Pennsylvania. While the armies skirmished in the south, General Burgoyne's defeated troops prepared to march under parole to Boston where they had been promised free passage to England, never again to serve in North America. Washington, anticipating the annual departure of his militia troops, made plans to rebuild his army while General Gates, General Conway and disgruntled politicians caballed.

General Gates selected a favorite staff officer, Colonel James Wilkinson, to carry news of his victory at Saratoga south to Congress directly, arrogantly, bypassing his commander-in-chief. Unfortunately for Gates, Wilkinson, exuberant over his selection as the bearer of good news, paused first to celebrate with his sweetheart then indulged with an officer friend at a tavern. Exhilarated by drink and his own good fortune in serving a successful general, Wilkinson confided to the friend that he anticipated being the aide to the army's commander-in chief.

"To Washington?" The friend, an officer serving under General Lord Sterling who was one of the officers loyal to Washington, asked.

"No, to Gates. He will soon replace Washington," Wilkinson indiscreetly bragged.

Wilkinson then confided that he had recently read a letter written to General Gates by General Thomas Conway. The letter praised Gates highly and included words critical of Washington which Wilkinson quoted from memory:

"Heaven has determined to save your country, or a weak general and bad counselors would have ruined it."

The officer subsequently reported the incident to Lord Sterling who in turn wrote a letter to Washington. Sterling had heard that Conway had viciously described him as an incompetent drunkard and seized upon the opportunity to undercut his denigrator.

Washington received and read Lord Sterling's letter on the evening of November 8th. His first act was to summon James and give him the missive to read.

James was not surprised. His conversations in Philadelphia had convinced him that both Gates and Conway were attempting to promote their careers by snidely denigrating Washington. As pleased as he was by Gates' victory over Burgoyne at Saratoga, James had worried that it would create trouble for his friend. Already, Gates was demonstrating his independence by corresponding directly with Congress, ignoring the fact that Washington was his commander-in-chief and all reports should be submitted through him. The Congress, still smarting over having been driven to provincial York, Pennsylvania, from their comfortable lodgings in Philadelphia, had greeted the word of Gates' monumental victory with exhilaration. Lieutenant Colonel Wilkinson, the messenger who had carried the report of the battle to Congress, had arrived ten days after the news had reached Philadelphia, but Congress overlooked the fact he had delayed to celebrate with his girl friend and as a reward for bearing good news had promoted him two ranks to brevet Brigadier General without consulting Washington. When the new general finally got around to informing his commander-in-chief belatedly of the battle, he was given an icy reception.

General Conway's letter criticizing Washington was no surprise. After Conway's promotion to Brigadier General by Congress acting on Silas Deane's recommendations from Paris, Washington assigned him to a command under General Sullivan. Despite the fact that at the battle of Brandywine Creek General Sullivan repeated his performance on Long Island and again allowed himself to be outflanked costing Washington the battle, the subordinate General Conway had apparently behaved well.

During the period since Brandywine, Conway devoted his time to lobbying Congress for promotion to Major General. Conway made much of a report from the hapless General Sullivan that noted the following about Conway:

"His regulations in his brigade are much better than any in the army, and his knowledge of military matters in general far exceeds any officer we have."

Encouraged by Sam Adams, who in James' opinion had been merely attempting to place his rival John Hancock, the departing President of Congress, in a spot, Conway wrote a letter to Hancock. It began arrogantly:

"It is with infinite concern that I find myself slighted and forgot when you have offered rank to officers who cost you a great deal of money and have never rendered you the least service."

Conway concluded by listing seven reasons why he should be promoted to major general.

Conway's letter irritated Hancock and many members of Congress but pleased Sam Adams, James Lovell, Thomas Mifflin and Richard Henry Lee among others. John Adams remained silent on the issue, but secretly he admitted to his cousin and others that Conway was useful in keeping Washington in his place. John Adams remained fearful that Washington was becoming an American deity.

When James finished reading Lord Sterling's letter, he silently waited for his friend to comment. Washington stared at James, his face frozen hard with rage. He was as icily angry as James had ever seen him.

"I will handle this myself," Washington declared and sat at his desk. He grabbed his quill, jabbed it into the inkpot and wrote quickly to General Conway:

"Sir: A letter which I received last night contained the following paragraph.

"In a letter from General Conway to General Gates he says: Heaven has determined to save your country; or a weak general and bad counselors would have ruined it."

"I am sir your humble servant."

Gates also was informed of Washington's possession of the information. In reply, both Gates and Conway tried to dissemble. Conway denied that any letter of his contained such sentiments and praised Washington in his denial; Gates demanded to know who the spy on his staff was. John and Sam Adams vacationed in New England and said nothing publicly. In mid November Conway submitted his resignation to Washington, and the latter declined it, noting Congress had appointed him and Congress could accept the resignation. Gates, while patiently waiting for Congress to appoint him to replace Washington, blamed his staff aide Wilkinson for the disgraceful affair; Wilkinson, now a prideful Brigadier, challenged Gates to a duel. On the field behind the Episcopal Church in York, the two met. Before they could line up, Gates took his former aide aside for a conference. To Wilkinson's surprise, Gates burst into tears, called Wilkinson a dear friend and denied he had ever spoken against him. The two made up and called off the duel.

Congress in November busied itself passing the Articles of Confederation giving the united colonies a constitution and a new government. In its wisdom, it promoted Thomas Conway to Major General and appointed him Inspector General of the Army. Congress selected five men to serve on its newly created Board of War, the institution by which it intended to control Washington and the army. Among the five was General Horatio Gates who was designated President of the Board. In a final fit of independent enthusiasm, the Congress appointed a committee of its own to assess the winter campaign.

Washington, exercising the prerogatives of commander-in-chief, occupied himself with the problems of the army. To James he again delegated full responsibility for dealing with the politicians and their military pawns, but he could not resist gnawing at the bones.

"George," James began their evening postprandial discussion. "I understand Gates and Conway, but I don't trust the Adamses. And as far as Richard Henry Lee goes, I... ."

"...I don't understand Richard Henry at all." Washington finished James' sentence for him. Washington raised his glass of Madeira and studied its scarlet hues in the firelight.

James waited for Washington to continue his thought, but he did not.

"John Adams may pretend to be your friend George, but he has his own agenda," James continued.

"What politician doesn't?" Washington asked. "John wants what is best for the united colonies, and we cannot ask for more than that."

"But George," James protested. "He's devious."

"And the others are not?" George asked rhetorically. "Why are you surprised at Richard Henry? You think that because he is a friend from Virginia that he will act differently than the others?"

"Yes," James persisted. He remembered the Richard Henry Lee of his youth, a young man devoted to principle and honor.

"Has not Virginia turned on Richard Henry?" Washington asked.

"Only the politicians, in self defense. After all, Richard Henry threw down the gauntlet when he exposed their corruption."

"And now," Washington smiled, "they are trying to remove him from Congress. What did he expect?"

"But that is not your fault," James protested. "Why has he allied himself with your enemies?"

"He hasn't," Washington said. "He is merely trying to defend himself. He is still loyal to his principles."

"Is that why you still write to him?"

"Yes. "

"If you persist that Richard Henry is loyal, what do you think of Gates and Conway?"

"Gates is simply ambitious. Conway," Washington paused, "Conway is a foreigner poaching on our troubles."

"How should I deal with the congressional committee?" James asked, worried about the group that was due to arrive in the morning to investigate the army's plans for the winter.

"Truthfully," Washington laughed.

James made no attempt to hide his consternation. He stared at Washington with the doubt evident on his face. James sipped his Madeira and waited. He had learned from George the value of silence and was determined that George speak first.

"Show them the army. Let them see for themselves that our soldiers are barefooted, in rags, with no shelter for the winter. Let them talk with the soldiers and hear their complaints. The troops know who is responsible. How can they expect the army to attack Philadelphia in this condition?" Washington asked, not expecting an answer.

"Have you read the reports from the senior officers?" James asked. Washington had required each of his generals to submit in writing the words they planned to use with the visitors.

Washington smiled his response. He had not wanted to influence his generals' responses. He had simply wanted to know what they would say if he asked them a question before the committee.

"Then they will learn that the army believes the need is not for replacing you but to supply you," James said, finally understanding his friend's political strategy.

Washington nodded agreement. "This is a very fine Madeira, don't you think?"

James, who cared nothing about wine, nodded agreement.

The committee visited and returned to York convinced that Washington had no options. To attack Philadelphia with the army in its current condition was out of the question. Washington had to take his soldiers into winter quarters. By the time the committee reported its recommendations, word reached York that Washington had selected his winter encampment, a wooded region eighteen miles north of Philadelphia, Valley Forge.

Like a sputtering candle, the Conway Cabal consumed itself and finally died. Word of the affair spread, and the people accused the generals of attempting to depose the commander-in-chief in their pursuit of personal ambition. Sensing this reaction, the Machiavellian politicians abandoned their pawns and professed surprise as they turned to alternative tactics.

Conway, as Inspector, General visited Washington at his headquarters twice. Each time he was greeted with frigid reserve. Conway again resigned, and this time Congress accepted. Conway, frustrated, challenged General Cadwalader to a duel over an imagined slight. Wounded in the cheek but still alive, Conway sailed for home. Baron von Steuben, the German fraud who had diligently taught Washington's troops to drill in the misery of Valley Forge, was, at Washington's recommendation, made a major general and appointed Inspector General vice Conway. His limited command of English was considered by many, including James, an advantage.

While Washington's ragged army drilled and suffered in the snow at Valley Forge, General William Howe's army turned Philadelphia into a miniature London. Elizabeth Loring rejoined her lover, and the two presided over the balls, plays and parties. General Howe, after Burgoyne's defeat, decided to resign his post and return home. At his brother's urging, he kept his plans secret from his partying officers.

John Andre, still General Grey's aide, found his place in the English occupied Philadelphia. Blessed with social skills, he became one of the most popular young officers in a happy town. Becky Franks, the daughter of the British commissary of prisoners, became a frequent partner. Becky introduced Andre to the prominent loyalists and their families who entertained the enthusiastic British officers. Andre renewed his acquaintance with Peggy Shippen, the seventeen-year-old daughter of a former colonial judge. Through her, Andre met Peggy Chew, the daughter of a former Pennsylvania attorney general. The women led the charming Andre into the gay social whirl.

One of the influential Britishers that the ambitious young officer met was Ambrose Serle, Lord Richard's secretary who had accompanied his master on one of his many visits to playtime Philadelphia. Like Sir Richard, Ambrose Serle did not share General Howe's appreciation for the social whirl, but Andre was ambitious enough to take advantage of the opportunity to cultivate Serle who had access to the commander-in-chief himself. Andre in his effort to ingratiate himself with Serle was surprised to discover the dour Englishman accompanied by a New York newspaperman by the name of York Allen. Obviously uncomfortable in the presence of the disapproving Serle, Allen reciprocated Andre's overtures of friendship. Andre, who planned on pursuing his career in the colonies, recognized that contact with a newsman might prove useful while York for his own reasons appreciated Andre's offer of friendship.

From Serle, York learned of the deep disappointment of the Howe brothers. The latest dispatches from London blamed the Howes for Burgoyne's' defeat. The duplicitous Lord Germaine, the Colonial Secretary, criticized the general for failing to assist Burgoyne and chided Lord Richard for conducting a cautious war and ineptly deploying his fleet. On October 21st, the General in a fit of pique submitted his resignation. One month later, Lord Richard followed suit. When the Howes' resignations reached London, George III placed them on hold pending news of their latest campaigns. One thing was clear, however; the Howes had failed to meet the prime English objective for the 1777 campaign—the Howes how not destroyed the rebel army.

In January 1778, James visited the Congress in York. He did so as much to escape the misery of Valley Forge as he did to meet with delegates. Washington had succeeded in facing down his detractors and was now free to concentrate on rebuilding and resupplying his troops.

When he arrived in York, James, acting on Washington's advice, again sought out John Adams. When he visited General Daniel Roberdeau's home which John Adams shared with the General, a delegate from Pennsylvania, the general's wife, Elbridge Gerry and Samuel Adams, James was disappointed to learn that both Adamses were still visiting Massachusetts. Gerry confided that plans were afoot to appoint John Adams to replace Silas Deane as the third minister to the French court. James assumed that Washington would be disappointed to learn that the man he considered his strongest supporter would be leaving the Congress on diplomatic assignment. James was not so sure; he believed that Adams was of two minds about Washington and publicly took one position while privately encouraging his cousin's intrigues to replace the Virginian.

James' conversations with friends among the delegates proved one thing. The cabal had been soundly discredited and even Gates had muted his criticisms. James had difficulty believing that Conway had been the prime mover behind the conspiracy, but the real plotters had successfully concealed their involvement.

Finally, London accepted General Howe's resignation, though it asked Lord Richard to remain as commander-in-chief. Sir William was not disappointed; he had had his fill of the colonies and was prepared to return home. In May, Major John Andre, reflecting the admiration that the troops still held for their general, organized a an extravaganza to honor the departing army commander. Andre dubbed his celebration the Mischianza, a "variety of entertainments." Andre devised a medieval fair that was highlighted by a joust featuring two teams, one labeled the Knights of the Blended Rose and the other the Knights of the Burning Mountain. It was staged at Walnut Grove, the home of the exiled patriot Joseph Wharton. Some considered the affair childish, but Andre, his colleagues and Sir William Howe in particular reveled in the gaiety. The loyalist maidens dressed like fair ladies of yore and swooned before their impassioned suitors.

One week after the festival, on Sunday, May 24th, 1778, Sir William sailed for England. General Henry Clinton replaced him as army commander.

Three short years before, three English Major Generals had arrived in Boston to stiffen the resolve of the hapless General Gates. Of these three, Sir William had replaced his commander when he went home in disgrace only to face the same fate himself thirty-six months later. General John Burgoyne had surrendered his northern army at Saratoga and ended a captive of the rebels. The third, General Henry Clinton, now had his chance.

On Tuesday, May 26th, General Clinton summoned the foremost loyalist of Philadelphia, Mr. Joseph Galloway, a close friend of Ambrose Serle, and informed him that King George III had ordered the abandonment of Philadelphia a short nine months after its capture. After advising Galloway to instruct his loyalist friends to make their plans for the withdrawal, General Clinton confided his plans to march the army northward.

On April 30th, 1778, George Washington, still at Valley Forge, received word that France had recognized the independence of the united colonies. George showed as much excitement as James had ever witnessed when he declared:

"And now we will have supplies and the French fleet. The war has turned."

One week later, Captain Eric Grey delivered another invisible writing report from New York. This was the second received from York Allen since his return from Philadelphia.

"The English are withdrawing from Philadelphia!" Eric announced to the shocked commander and his political adviser.

York Allen had no idea why. Serle had simply confided that "His Majesty has ordered it. Something to do with the war in Europe."

Washington immediately concluded that British reinforcements were not forthcoming. With James' assistance, he calculated that General Clinton now had at most 16,000 troops at his disposal, 10,000 in Philadelphia, 4,000 in New York, and 2,000 in Rhode Island. With no reinforcements underway, common military sense dictated that the English reunite their divided army.

On June 28th, 1778, the British commenced their withdrawal from Philadelphia, and Washington deployed his troops to harass the complaining redcoats.

Washington assigned his second most senior major general, the former Connecticut druggist who had been wounded leading troops against Burgoyne in a key battle that cost the English Saratoga, as military commander of Philadelphia. Benedict Arnold had defiantly ignored the orders of General Gates and earned himself a court martial along with the rifle ball in the thigh. Since Washington's views of General Gates were colored by the Conway affair, Gates' heated charges against Arnold were ignored.

James, who kept his tongue silent on military matters, naturally formed opinions about the military officers. While he admitted to himself to being preferential towards Arnold because of the latter's stellar military record, wounds suffered in battle and his heated dispute with General Gates, James was of mixed mind about Arnold's appointment as military commander of the previously occupied city. Arnold's leg wound suffered at Saratoga was sufficient to keep him from commanding troops on the battlefield, his natural forte, and his new assignment offered him the opportunity to heal in congenial circumstances. Despite the fact he had been praised by the people who resided near Lake Champlain for his treatment of the civilian populace following his victory at Fort Ticonderoga, James worried about Arnold's autocratic nature. Beyond that was the nagging fact of Arnold's privateering career in the prewar era. Arnold made no secret of his material aspirations. James simply was not sure that Arnold's battlefield bravado equipped him to coexist in a city shared with the scheming delegates of Congress and the Pennsylvania Assembly.

General Arnold arrived in Philadelphia on June 19th, 1778, to assume command. Within the month, he moved into the John Penn house, which had served as General Howe's domicile during his Philadelphia residency. James, who visited Philadelphia in July to meet with the Congress, had been shocked to find Arnold traversing the city in a lavish coach-and-four accompanied by liveried servants. Even then, stories about Arnold's extravagance abounded. When the acid tongued Sam Adams asked James how the former druggist afforded such luxuries on the three hundred and thirty two depreciated paper dollars a month he earned as a major general, James had been unable to reply. Later, James asked the man who had succeeded John Hancock as President of Congress, Henry Laurens, the father of John Laurens, Washington's aide, if he was troubled by Arnold's life style. When Laurens dismissed the question with an offhand comment that many senior generals supplemented their meager incomes with personal investments, James decided to ignore his suspicions.

James returned from Philadelphia to pursue Washington's headquarters northward as the commander-in-chief dispatched units to harry the flank and rear of Clinton's redcoats on their journey through New Jersey to New York City. He finally found his chief just after the battle of Monmouth where Washington with considerable personal courage had turned a fleeing rebel army and led it to a victory of sorts. The English suffered more than twelve hundred casualties, roughly three times more losses than those inflicted on the pursuers. Washington's mood was not one of victory, however. General Lee had somehow confused his orders and panicked, joining his troops in a frightened charge to the rear. Washington had ordered Lee to attack the British rear guard; when the British wheeled to defend themselves, Lee had fled until he encountered an attacking Washington. When asked what he was doing, the confused Lee had difficulty understanding the commander's questions. Lee finally stammered that his intelligence was confusing, and he had chosen not to confront the British in such a situation. An angry Washington responded with a demonstration of temper that surprised even his closest aides. One later confided that Washington had sworn until the "leaves on the trees quivered." Another claimed that Washington dubbed Lee a poltroon. James suspected the young aides were guilty of exaggeration, but a court martial subsequently found Lee guilty and suspended him from command for a year. General Charles Lee, who had aspired to and conspired to attain Washington's post, had been found guilty for retreating when he should have attacked. James added Lee's name along with that of General Conway to his list of vanquished conspirators.

Clinton settled his army into New York; the French fleet arrived with Admiral d'Estaing as its commander, and Washington pondered the next English step. In October, Clinton went into premature winter quarters in New York, and Washington settled his troops at Danbury, West Point and Middlebrook. Washington established his headquarters in Middlebrook, New Jersey, and James dutifully followed along.

In mid-December 1778, James accompanied Washington to Philadelphia in response to a summons from the Congress to discuss plans for the 1779 campaign. James could have succinctly answered the queries—we will react to the British—but courtesy required that he not do so. Martha planned to meet Washington in Philadelphia for Christmas, and Vivian had written that she would do likewise. James was determined, therefore, that nothing upset these plans. On December 21st, James, Washington and the ever present escort departed Middlebrook.

James was disappointed to learn that fiery Laurens had resigned as President of Congress and had been replaced by John Jay. Rumors about General Arnold's cupidity continued to abound; to allegations of corruption and extravagant living had been added sly charges about the General's too kind treatment of the city's loyalists, particularly the young womenfolk who had so enjoyed the English occupation. By James' arrival, Arnold had begun his courtship of Margaret "Peggy" Shippen. Peggy,, now eighteen, blond and experienced in flirting with military men, had been a particular friend of Major John Andre, the aide who had organized General Howe's farewell extravaganza. Arnold ignored the fact that the attractive Peggy had been honored to be selected one of the medieval maids and defensively pointed out that her father had not allowed her to attend; Andre's prescribed gowns had been too scanty for Edward Shippen's taste. Peggy's father described himself as a "neutral" and had remained in Philadelphia during the occupation.

After the British departure, he stayed on in his native city, no doubt, James thought, because of the intervention of his cousin, Doctor William Shippen, the Chief of Washington's Medical Services Department. Rumor had it that Arnold, the thirty-seven year old widower who commanded the military in Philadelphia, was in love from the first moment he focused his slate gray eyes on Peggy. James, who found it difficult to forgive the Philadelphians who had made the English stay in their city so pleasant while the rebel army suffered in the Valley Forge cold, tried to avoid any social engagement attended by General Arnold and his Peggy.

Vivian was more forgiving. After hearing tales about the lovely Arnold paramour, she insisted that James take her to the New Years ball hosted by General

Arnold. James at first resisted out of principle but as soon as Vivian heard one Virginia delegate's wife quoting a friend of the vivacious Peggy, James knew he had lost.

"You can't believe how fond Peggy is of kissing. She gives old-fashioned smacks. Why General Arnold says he would give his fortune to have her for a schoolmistress to teach the young ladies how to kiss."

"And how do you imagine General Arnold knows that?" Vivian had asked archly.

The ball, held in General Arnold's lavish mansion, included over five hundred of Philadelphia's most prominent residents among its invitees. The lane leading to the immense home was decorated with candles. Given the long line of carriages carrying waiting guests, James was thankful that he and Vivian had accepted General Washington's invitation to share his and Martha's coach. Otherwise, James would have rented a small buggy and been forced to find a place to shelter it and a team by himself. Washington's status cleared the lane, and the coach glided to a stop at the front door. Servants assisted the General and Martha and James and Vivian as they dismounted. Despite the cold, the two front doors were thrown wide. Bright light from the many candles on a mirrored chandelier sparkled on the snow.

"How does he afford it?" Vivian whispered through a gloved hand in James ear. Vivian was accustomed to Virginia plantation luxury, but Arnold's city home took her breath away.

"Welcome General Washington," Arnold spoke from the front steps before James could respond to Vivian. James noted that their host's words left a frosty trail in the air. James assumed Arnold had been alerted to Washington's arrival because neither he nor Peggy who was serving as his hostess was dressed for the cold night air.

"And Martha. So pleased to see you again," Arnold spoke formally. James assumed Arnold had met Martha during one of her wintertime visits to the army's winter quarters.

James and Vivian waited politely behind George and Martha. As James watched, he saw Peggy shiver. Bravely, she stood beside Arnold. He was dressed in a finely tailored, blue dress uniform topped by his general's epaulets and a bright red sash. Peggy wore a thin, full gown made of a bright green satin that highlighted the color of her hair and vivid green eyes. Her shoulders were bare with a décolletage that revealed a full two thirds of her ample breasts. To James amazement, he could see the goose bumps form.

"Please, General," Washington spoke gruffly. "Don't let formality keep us in the cold. The women," he nodded at the scantily clad Peggy, "are risking frostbite."

Vivian squeezed James' arm in delight as Arnold briefly frowned before spinning and leading the guests into the house.

"I don't think that's how he planned to stage the welcome," Vivian whispered.

After surrendering their heavy coats to waiting servants, the Washingtons and Satterfields were led into a large ballroom. With Peggy and Arnold at their side, the Washingtons, followed by James and Vivian, paused while a formally clad black house servant announced their arrival to the already teeming crowd.

"General and Mrs. Washington," The servant declared in a deep baritone.

The crowd applauded politely and watched as Washington and Martha descended the two stairs to the ballroom floor.

Arnold shook James' hand, acknowledged Vivian and introduced Peggy.

Arnold turned and whispered to the waiting servant. The servant nodded, turned back to the ballroom and in a much more subdued voice announced:

"Mr. and Mrs. Satterfield of Alexandria, Virginia."

James and Vivian descended the stairs. Around them, the guests watched the Washingtons as they moved slowly into the admiring crowd.

"He hates it," James confided to Vivian.

She nodded acknowledgment of his words and took his arm as he led her to the right fringe of the crowd. A servant bearing a silver tray approached and offered them bright red punch in glistening cut glass goblets. James took two, handed one to Vivian, and raised his glass in a silent toast to his wife whose dark hair shimmered in the candlelight and drank. Vivian had never looked lovelier. Peggy might be twenty-five years younger, but in James' opinion she was far from his wife's class. As he stood admiring his wife, he heard a trill giggle behind him. He turned to see Peggy, still standing near the door, embracing a young couple who was obviously of the same age as the hostess. Peggy embraced the young man and kissed him deeply on the lips. The young girl on the man's arm smiled, but James noticed Arnold's deep frown.

"I think she does enjoy kissing," Vivian whispered.

James, resisting the impulse to stare, turned, and studied the room. It had four large fireplaces, one in each of the four walls, and the fires blazed as they consumed the four-foot logs. The walls, including a large staircase on the right that led to a long balcony, were decorated gaily in garlands of pine. Painted cones hung from the streams of green needles and gave the room a festive air. Candles winked in the central chandelier and from fixtures located every four feet along the walls. As imposing as the conspicuous use of candles was in this city still suffering from wartime shortages, the phenomenon that caught James' eye was a thirty foot spruce tree that stood exactly in the middle of the ball room. James had heard of the European custom of trimming Christmas trees, but this was the first time he had seen one in an American home. The tree was gaily decorated with bright colored ribbons, immense pinecones and candles.

"Do you think that the lovely Peggy acquired that custom from her Hessian friends?" A wry voice at James' elbow asked.

James turned and found Sam Adams standing at his side, also contemplating the tree.

"Good evening, Sam," James replied evenly, determined not to be provoked by the dour New Englander. "I'm surprised to see you here."

"That I would be invited?"

"No, that you would come. I thought you frowned on wasteful social extravagances." Adams' austere views were well known in Philadelphia.

"I had to come and see for myself. I've heard about our military commander's lifestyle. Where do you think he gets it?"

"Gets what?" James asked perversely, knowing what the austere New Englander was going to reply.

"The money," Sam Adams replied primly. "My friends tell me that Peggy is an extravagant puss. I'm told that General Howe's Mischianza, whatever on earth that is, was her idea."

"I don't have a clue," James replied, determined not to be drawn into a discussion of either Arnold's finances or his fiancée's background.

"Have you heard of the "Charming Nancy?" Adams asked.

"The charming Nancy? I can't say that I have," James answered truthfully. "Does Peggy have a competitor?" James thought it would be no surprise. Arnold had a reputation for being a ladies man.

"It's a sloop," Adams laughed. "Owned by three New York traders. I understand that somehow Shewell, the principal owner, obtained a pass and the "Charming Nancy" was allowed to sail with a full load of controlled goods."

James was aware that Congress had recently passed a law that decreed no goods were to be removed from Philadelphia until their ownership had been determined. The purpose, obviously, had been to prevent loyalists and the occupied army from smuggling patriot possessions from the city.

"Are you implying that Arnold issued the pass?"

Adams smiled in reply. "It bears looking into," he said, then slipped off to James' left.

James, once again alone in the crowd, resumed his survey of the room. Washington and Martha had seated themselves in one corner not far from one of the blazing fireplaces, and a line had formed of well-wishers waiting for their chance of passing a few words with the commander-in-chief. Noting the thin smile on George's face, James could tell that he was not enjoying the attention. As James glanced about the room, it occurred to him that the crowd had divided itself into groups. On one side stood the prominent Philadelphia residents who had remained in the city during the English occupation. They were aware of their reputation as either turncoat opportunists or loyalists and had apparently banded together for mutual support.

James wondered why they had accepted Arnold's invitation. He speculated that each was desirous of repairing relations with the victors in hopes of protecting his coveted property. In another corner the prominent Rebels seemed to have gathered. They included the delegates from the Congress, Pennsylvania colony officials and senior military officers. In a third corner stood a group of well-dressed merchants and city residents whose number included many well known Rebels who had vacated the city when Howe's army had arrived. Many wore angry faces, and James intercepted revengeful glances at the loyalists across the room. If they were angry, James did not blame them. Most had lost their homes and possessions to the ransacking loyalist mobs and looting English and Hessian troops.

In the center of the room, circling the spruce tree, young officers from Arnold's staff danced with laughing Philadelphia girls. James immediately decided the colorfully dressed girls with the bare shoulders and scarcely concealed bosoms were friends of Peggy. James chastised himself for wondering how many of them a few months ago were dancing and laughing with officers in red uniforms. James tried to convince himself that he did not blame them for seeking their pleasures; after all, most were in their mid to late teens and probably did not own a single political thought.

"James," a familiar voice called from close behind him and a firm hand gripped his shoulder. "I've been waiting for the mysterious Satterfield to appear. Is it true the English almost hung you?"

James immediately recognized the voice and irreverent tone. He spun and found himself looking directly into the mischievous gray eyes of George Denson, his old roommate from his William and Mary days. Denson had been the first person he had met on arrival at the small campus, and they had been close friends for two years.

"George," James spoke with genuine emotion. "When did you get here?" James had heard his friend had been appointed to the Virginia delegation to replace Richard Henry Lee who had finally fallen to his Virginian enemies still angry at his public attacks on their corruption.

"Yesterday," George replied. "And I am already immersed in the gay social whirl." Denson glanced in the direction of the dancing couples. "Do you have to wear a uniform to enjoy the company of the lovely ladies of Philadelphia?"

"And where is Marjorie?" James asked, referring to his friend's wife.

"Home caring for the boys," George replied. "And Vivian?"

"She's here, George, so you will have to be on your best behavior," James warned. He assumed that George still had a fond eye for the softer gender. Vivian and George's wife Marjorie had remained close friends from their days in Williamsburg after James' marriage and while he served as Dinwiddie's clerk.

"Will she be here long?" George asked, only half joking.

"She will return to Alexandria with Martha after the holidays, soon I expect."

"That being the case, I best convey my respects before she departs," George replied, smiling broadly.

The two friends collected fresh drinks from the silver tray of a circulating Arnold servant and retreated to two chairs in the corner of the room occupied by the dignitaries. George, James noted, had not changed. He took a glass of punch in each hand, winking at James as he did so. To James' relief, the presence of his old college friend solved James' social problem for the evening. The two spent an hour talking about old times, and James felt no compulsion to circulate and confer with various delegates from the Congress about military matters. As they talked, James realized that George might prove to be of considerable assistance in helping James fulfill his official duties.

"And what are you doing for our commander-in-chief?" George asked. "Are you still his chief spy?"

"Shh," James cautioned. "My title is Political Adviser."

"Still a behind the scenes politician," George referred to James' function while working for Dinwiddie.

"More or less," James agreed. "Right now, my main problem is liaising with Congress on behalf of the army."

"And you want me to take a place on the military committee and keep you informed," George immediately surmised James' intention.

"Would that bother you?"

"Why should it?" George asked blithely. "It's still our army isn't it."

"You will be a breath of fresh air in this Congress."

In response to George's quizzical expression, James explained the problems he had been having with the Congress.

"You want men and supplies to fight a war, and the delegates want to be politicians, appointing friends to high position and possibly making a little money on the side," George summarized James' lengthy exposition.

"You always could get to the heart of the matter," James laughed. "Will you help?"

"But of course," George laughed with the same carefree manner that had first attracted him to his friend many years previously. "And if I am not mistaken, the lovely Vivian approaches," George continued.

Vivian joined the two men, kissed George ardently on the lips, reminding James that she had always treated George like a brother, and dispatched James for a glass of punch. By the time he returned, his friend and Vivian were engaged in the same round of reminiscences that had occupied George and James. James handed his wife her punch and excused himself to pay his respects to the various dignitaries in attendance.

As he circulated through the room, he paused and chanced to overhear a brief conversation between two young ladies who obviously were from Peggy Shippen's social circle.

"I can see Peggy's hand in the planning for this extravaganza," the first girl observed.

"It's too bad her father has no money," the second girl replied. "Her paramour cannot afford this, you know. That's what daddy says."

"She thinks she is still spending John Andre's money for Howe's Mischianza."

James detected envy in the tone of both girls.

"Our Peggy has always known how to spend money."

"Wait until she learns that her general is a simple druggist from Connecticut. Can you imagine Peggy in New Haven?"

Both girls giggled in amusement at the thought.

"I understand her father is pressing her to marry General Arnold," the first girl continued. ·

"Her sisters, Polly and Sally are married, and Peggy is jealous."

"Her father has probably heard the rumors. Arnold will do anything for money. Daddy says Judge Shippen is an opportunist who thinks Arnold would make a good son-in-law who would open doors for him."

To James' regret, two young officers from Arnold's staff approached the two girls and escorted them to the dance floor. James gradually made his way about the room, pausing to listen to the conversation of the various groups. After a few polite words, he excused himself and moved on to the next. Many of the conversations focused on the extravagance of Arnold's home and speculation about the source of his funds. Noting a break in the line of well wishers waiting to be seen talking with Washington, James saw his friend nodding at him to approach. James hurried to Washington's side. Washington turned and in a low voice spoke:

"We best check on this fellow," Washington whispered. Washington glanced about him at the lavish setting.

"I understand his intended has high tastes," James paraphrased the conversation he had overheard between the girls.

"And Benedict has simple resources," Washington observed before turning to greet an approaching couple.

At midnight, Arnold gave an impassioned speech full of high praise for the army and General Washington and thanking his guests for attending. Arnold felt compelled to identify the name and rank of the invitees, and as he went along James began to fear that Arnold was intent on reading the entire guest list. Fortunately, after half an hour, Arnold stopped and the party resumed. Vivian appeared at James' side as the orchestra began a reel.

"You will be relieved to know that George, as guest of honor, feels compelled to leave soon so that others will not stay out of protocol."

"Lead the way," James replied with relief. He had been ready to depart since the moment he had arrived. Washington's meeting with the military committee of Congress to discuss strategy for 1779 was scheduled to begin at nine o'clock in the morning. Washington planned to return to his headquarters as soon as he could. James knew the commander-in-chief felt guilty celebrating while his troops suffered in the cold.

The interminable meetings with the military committee went exactly as James anticipated. Washington stressed that the lack of money, hence limited manpower and supplies, dictated a defensive strategy. The windy and at times astringent

comments of the delegates confirmed James' suspicions that the quality of the
Congress was deteriorating; this made the arrival of George Denson all the more
meaningful. Despite his supercilious air, George was an intelligent, highly motivated man. Following his graduation, he had read law at the offices of George
Wythe, one of Virginia's foremost practitioners. After five years, he had opened
his own office in Williamsburg and was now considered to be one of the colony's
most effective barristers. He did not have Patrick Henry's gift for oratory—what
man did—but his incisive knowledge of the law won far more cases than it lost.
James had suggested to Washington that George Denson would be a strong addition to the Military Committee, and the General had promised to speak with John
Jay and others about the matter. James assumed that "others" included the former President of the Congress, Henry Laurens, at whose house Washington and
Martha were guests.

The delegates from Pennsylvania and New York were most concerned about
the outrages being committed on their frontiers. When Howe declined to help
Clinton, the latter had in desperation turned for assistance to Colonel Guy
Johnson, the English Commissioner of Indian Affairs. As a consequence, the
Iroquois were making life a living hell for the frontier settlers. This complaint
struck a compassionate chord with General Washington whose early career had
been devoted to fighting the French and Indians in the west, and he promised to
consider a campaign to punish the savages. In turn, Washington argued for more
money to fund recruitment and reenlistment of regular army troops. Washington
also pressed for better allowances and half pay for life for his officer corps; the
military committee listened deferentially but promised little.

To Washington's dismay his consultations stretched on consuming all of the
month of January. The delay delighted James. For the first time since his return
to the army following his capture and escape, James was able to spend time with
Vivian. Washington was occupied with his meetings with Congress and the long
line of carriages that appeared outside the Laurens house during social hours.
James and Vivian entertained friends, including George Denson who suddenly
found himself assigned to the military committee. During the day, James met
with influential delegates in one on one sessions, and by the end of the month was
confident that Congress had a better understanding of the army's problems and
strategy.

On February 1st, Martha and Vivian departed on their return trip to Eastwind
and Mount Vernon. On February 2nd, James and Washington returned to
Middlebrook. Nothing of significance had happened during their absence.
Washington then devoted his days to pondering three questions: what could be
done to blunt the British attack in South Carolina; how could the army and its
new allies, primarily the French, work together; and what should be done to suppress the savage Indian attacks on the frontier. These military questions did not
involve James directly. Peripherally, however, he became concerned. Washington
offered command of a punitive expedition against the Iroquois to General Gates
who brusquely declined, apparently, James concluded, because killing Indians

was beneath the hero of Saratoga. Washington then selected General John Sullivan for the task, and that officer, anxious to atone for his past mistakes, eagerly accepted. Aware that James and his family had a direct interest in the west, primarily because of James' twin brother John, Washington shared much of his planning with James. One letter of instructions to Sullivan particularly impressed James. Washington wrote:

"...The expedition you are appointed to command is to be directed against the hostile Tribes of the Six Nations of Indians with their associates and adherents. The immediate objects are the total destruction and devastation of their settlements and the capture of as many prisoners of every age and sex as possible. It will be essential to ruin their crops now in the ground and prevent their planting more... ."

When James had finished reading the letter of instructions, he handed it back to the General and waited for the question he anticipated would follow.

"Do you think it is strong enough, James?"

"Just right, sir." James was relieved that this was not the question he had expected.

"Have you heard from John, lately?"

James took a deep breath before answering. This was the question he had feared.

"Just once. About three months ago. He reported the Indians along the Gauley River were few and quiet but friends to the north were suffering from roaming war parties. John's local militia was preparing to march north in the days after he wrote."

"Then, you think John might be back on the Gauley by now?"

"I don't know sir."

"I'm going to write John a letter and send it by special courier. If you wish to send along your own message, I'm sure he will be able to carry it for you."

"George," James paused. "Are you asking John to join General Sullivan?"

Washington studied his friend before replying.

"I know you would prefer that I don't," Washington began. "But I don't have a choice. Sullivan is a good man, but he doesn't know the savages. John does. I need John to serve as chief scout for the army."

"But John doesn't know New York," James protested.

"But he understands the Indians. Better than any white man alive. Better than Colonel Johnson."

Recognizing that Washington had already made up his mind, and knowing that he was unbudgeable when he had, James against his better judgment acquiesced.

"When does the courier depart?"

"Tomorrow morning."

"I will have my letter written."

Chapter 30
New York, Philadelphia
Spring/Summer 1779

James, much to his later regret, never investigated Sam Adams' New Years Eve hint that the "Charming Nancy" affair required scrutiny.

After obtaining a pass from Arnold, the "Charming Nancy's" captain had sailed for New York. Off the New Jersey coast, she had been captured by a privateer and taken to Egg harbor. There, an admiralty court ruled that "Charming Nancy" had been illegally seized. Before she could sail, however, a British squadron with Captain Andre on board attacked Egg Harbor, which was a notorious home of privateers, and destroyed several ships including "Nancy." Fortunately for Arnold and his co-investors, the cargo was saved, and Arnold again came to the rescue. As military commander, he dispatched twelve wagons belonging to the colony of Pennsylvania to retrieve the goods that he ruled was "in imminent danger of falling into enemy hands." Arnold intended to pay for the hire of the wagons and did not pretend that they were used for a public mission. The goods were retrieved and returned to Philadelphia where they were sold. At the end of January 1779, the wagon master called on Arnold to collect his fees. A dispute arose over the amount, and the wagon master did not get his pay. On February 9th, the Pennsylvania Council, which had been investigating Arnold's autocratic style and extravagant scale of living, published a list of charges against the military governor. Eight separate violations were filed including allegations over the impropriety of the "Charming Nancy" pass, the dispatch of publicly owned Pennsylvania wagons to retrieve the private cargo, the claim Arnold had arbitrarily closed shops so he could engage in private shopping, and the charge that he showed favoritism toward Tories.

Arnold traveled to Middlebrook and consulted with General Washington and James. Washington, who was privately dismayed at the imbroglio that one of his best fighting officers had created through indiscretion, advised Arnold to immediately demand a court martial to clear his name. The Congress considered the Pennsylvania charges, recognizing the political malice and jealousy involved in a situation where three autonomous powers shared responsibility i.e. the Pennsylvania Council, the Congress and the military governor. Congress in March ruled that only four of the eight charges were sufficient for trial by court martial. Arnold, requesting an early hearing, resigned his Philadelphia command.

On April 8th in the midst of this controversy General Arnold married Peggy Shippen.

Congress turned the charges over to the army for court martial proceedings. Washington set the date for May 1st, then subsequently postponed it until June or July. On May 5th, Arnold wrote an emotional letter to Washington asking that he be found guilty and hung or found innocent and restored to duty. The impassioned Arnold pleaded for justice. When Washington showed this letter to James and asked for his considered views, James replied that Arnold's passion was understandable. He pointed out that Arnold's income had been substantially reduced by his loss of the Philadelphia command at the very time he acquired a luxury-loving wife many years his junior. Washington sniffed disapproval but said nothing in response to James' snide comments.

The departure of the Howes and the evacuation from Philadelphia did not set well with the English army's officer corps. Most remained convinced they could have defeated the rebels on the field of battle if they were only given a chance. Captain John Andre shared these views, but the fun loving, ambitious, young officer was not one to mourn lost opportunities. Back in New York, he discovered a city with a social life comparable to London, on a smaller scale of course. Not long after the return to the northern city, General Grey, Andre's mentor, departed. To Andre's delight, General Henry Clinton, the army's new commander, selected the amiable young man who had planned the Howe Mischianza as his aide. Unlike many others, the flexible Andre soon acclimated himself to his dour new commander's personality.

Clinton was familiar with New York. His father, an admiral, had served as provincial governor of New York for ten years. Clinton's childhood had been spent among the colonists and in many ways his return to New York City was a journey home. Clinton was a morose, sensitive man who was quick to anger. Despite his rough relationships with peers and immediate subordinates, his abilities were beyond question. Since his personality made him a loner with few friends, it was only natural that the aloof, remote chief was susceptible to the charm and flattery of younger officers who posed no threat to him.

In this regard, Andre was the ideal aide. Andre, who perceived his future in terms of the rank of his sponsors, had achieved a major goal and worked to ingra-

tiate himself. He had an office next to his chief's at Number One Broadway.
Andre, because of his position at the elbow of power, soon found himself in frequent social demand. The prominent New York loyalists considered him far
more personable than his chief or the sour Ambrose Serle who had departed with
his Admiral. In turn, Andre with a handsome bachelor's fondness for female pul-
chritude found New York even more congenial than Philadelphia had been.
Andre helped relieve Clinton of the pressures of office by accompanying him on
afternoon rides and astutely losing to his superior many games of handball and
billiards. Andre worked long hours playing and laboring for the General, but he
enjoyed every minute of it. Before long his good cheer made him the point of contact for everyone, English or colonist, who had business with Clinton but did not
wish to go through the ordeal of dealing with the difficult general themselves.

In April 1779, Clinton rewarded his charming protégé by naming him his
Chief of Intelligence. Many in the command resented the appointment because
Andre as a mere captain was two grades below the billet rank of lieutenant
colonel. The assignment, which held the promise of early promotion, greatly
pleased Andre who ignored the charges of favoritism that graced the lips of jealous colleagues. As Chief of Intelligence, Andre possessed as much power as
Clinton wished to delegate and his aide desired to exercise. In theory, he was
responsibility for directing the collection of all intelligence on the rebel army and
for briefing his chief on the significant data. In reality, Andre's main task as intelligence chief was winnowing truth from fiction from the steady stream of reports
provided by refugees and defectors who crossed at will between the lines. A few
loyalist agents remained in place in Washington's army, and these reported via
intermediaries to Andre's office. In addition, he constantly sought to induce disgruntled rebel officers to consider crossing over to the English side. Andre, who
had begun his career in the colonies as a regimental intelligence officer, enjoyed
the game, particularly the latitude for individual action that his new post gave
him.

On the morning of May 10th, Andre was content as he sat alone in his office
at Number One Broadway. The General had had a late night and had yet to
appear, as was his wont on such occasions. Andre himself had enjoyed an
evening at the theater in the company of a delightful young lady who had attracted his attention. The windows were open and the curtains wafted in the soft
spring breeze. It was one of those peaceful moments in his life that Andre felt he
would remember forever. A young lieutenant appeared in the doorway, but the
day was so pleasant that Andre was not irritated by the interruption.

"Excuse me sir," the lieutenant apologized. He recognized Andre's distracted mood and had been reluctant to disturb it, but the waiting visitors had been
insistent.

"Two gentlemen are quite anxious to see you."

"And they are?" Andre asked gently. He did not recall having any scheduled
appointments.

"A Mr. Stansbury from Philadelphia and Reverend Odell."

"Joseph Stansbury?"

"Yes, sir. I believe that is his name."

"What do they want?"

"They would not say. Only that it was a confidential matter for your ears only. Shall I tell them you are busy?"

Andre remembered Stansbury. He had met the man in Philadelphia and knew a little more about him officially. Stansbury, who had been born in London, was a dedicated loyalist. He owned a china shop on Front Street, and Andre had purchased some tableware from him at what he learned later was an exorbitant price. Stansbury had been a favorite of the British officers, however, because of his favorable political views. Rumor had it that at one time Stansbury had been persecuted by the Sons of Liberty for having been heard singing "God Save the King" in the privacy of his home. Officially, quite by accident, Andre had learned that Stansbury was a part time informant and courier for the English. He occasionally carried messages from a man named Samuel Wallis who from his home on the Susquehanna kept the English informed about minor happenings on the frontier.

Andre knew less about the Reverend Jonathan Odell. The man was a clergyman physician who eked out a living as chaplain to the regiment of Pennsylvania Loyalists stationed in New York and as deputy chaplain to the Royal Fusiliers. Andre considered both men small fish and wondered what business they had with him. Being in a charitable mood, he directed the lieutenant to show them into his office.

"Good morning Reverend, Mr. Stansbury," Andre spoke without rising from his chair. He gestured for his guests to seat themselves in two chairs that Andre kept arranged in front of his desk.

"Captain Andre," the two men replied in unison, accepting Andre's offhanded gesture to seat themselves. Andre officiously waited for one of the two men to explain the purpose of the unscheduled visit. Andre, a busy man, had grown weary of being besieged by loyalists who sought to take advantage of a chance acquaintance to acquire official favors from the young officer who now stood at Clinton's side.

"It is good of you to see us without an appointment," Stansbury began haltingly.

Andre, who noted the tremor in the man's voice and the shaking hands, nodded encouragement for Stansbury to continue.

"I have a most unusual story to relate," Stansbury said. "As you may know, I have in the past performed small favors for His Majesty's Army."

Andre assumed that Stansbury referred to his role as courier for their frontier agent and replied before the nervous Stansbury could identify the man in front of his companion, Reverend Odell.

"Yes, and we are most appreciative, Mr. Stansbury."

"I have never made any secret of my political views," Stansbury began again. "I have had my troubles with the Sons of Liberty in Philadelphia. Since His Majesty's army chose to return to New York, my life has been difficult."

"I am very sorry to hear that Mr. Stansbury," Andre interrupted. "If there is any way I can be of assistance... ." Andre let his words hang, hoping to spur Stansbury to the point of his visit.

"Several days ago a most unusual thing happened," Stansbury continued. He paused and looked at Odell. "I have already discussed the matter with Reverend Odell, and he advised me to discuss the matter with you personally," Stansbury seemed to be apologizing for the other man's presence. "General Arnold, the military commander of the city who has on occasion accompanied his new wife, the former Miss Peggy Shippen, who you may know, on shopping visits to my shop on Front Street recently summoned me to visit him at his home, General Howe's old residence, you know."

Andre, who was having trouble following the man's jerky narrative had been about to interrupt Stansbury to urge him to quickly tell his story, abruptly sat straight in his chair. He of course fondly remembered the fun loving Peggy, but it was the mention of the former military governor of Philadelphia's name that caught his attention. Andre had recently read reports describing the circumstances of Arnold's pending court martial. As Chief of Intelligence, Andre was most interested in information about disgruntled American officers. As successful as he had been to date, the ambitious Andre recognized that his career would be guaranteed if he could obtain the cooperation of a ranking American officer. A man of Arnold's rank working for the English could assist in bringing the rebellion to a quick conclusion, and the horizon would be boundless for the man who achieved such a coup.

"General Arnold is a bitter man," Stansbury continued.

"He vehemently denounced the Congress, the French alliance and his political enemies." Stansbury paused to see if Andre accepted his story. "After swearing me to secrecy, General Arnold claimed that he from the very beginning has opposed the break from mother England and that he now recognizes it must be healed before both countries are destroyed in this bitter fratricide. He asked me to carry this message to General Clinton and to assure him that he, General Arnold, is now prepared to immediately join the English army and do whatever he can with his limited military abilities to end the struggle. Or...," again Stansbury paused, studied Andre's intent face, then continued when he saw he had the young man's full attention. "Or, do whatever is required to destroy the powers of the illegal congress and return the colonies to their proper state of fealty to the crown."

When he finished the last sentence, Stansbury took a deep breath, seized the arms of his chair with white fingers and waited for Andre to comment on his remarkable story. Stansbury was nervous because he knew full well what the message he had carried meant. Arnold was offering to defect to the English, and

Stansbury realized that as the messenger carrying the momentous news he had the opportunity to reap considerable personal gain.

Andre immediately recognized that Stansbury's tale offered the opportunity to fulfill his dream. He knew he could not make such a momentous decision on his own authority and had to discuss it promptly with General Clinton. First, however, he had to deal with Stansbury and Odell. Andre, while attempting to decide what to do, studied the two nervous men who squirmed in their chairs. Andre wished he had more reliable intermediaries but consoled himself with the knowledge that Stansbury was a tested factor. The man had at least proved himself to be a reliable courier.

"I have been following General Arnold's difficulties very closely," Andre began, stalling for time as he thought. "Your story has a strong ring of truth to it."

"I assure you sir, everything happened exactly as I related to you." Stansbury sat erect in his chair attempting to control his fear and to convey an impression of indignation at the very hint that his story was a fabrication.

"And I assure you, sir," Andre responded quickly to calm the nervous man, "I do not doubt you. I was merely speculating about General Arnold's motives. He is after all a very senior officer who has had his successes on the field of battle. We must consider the possibility of provocation, though I admit that Arnold's difficulties give his story the ring of truth."

"He has a new bride, much younger than he, who has a strong interest in wealth and material things," Stansbury attempted to justify Arnold's predicament

"I understand gentlemen. This is a subject that requires considerable thought. If you will excuse me.... If you could find it possible to return to meet with me at...say...three o'clock this afternoon, we can decide how to handle this interesting offer."

"Certainly, sir," Stansbury spoke for both himself and Odell. Stansbury recognized that the young officer wished to discuss the matter with his superior, General Clinton, and this is just what Stansbury had intended. Stansbury might be nervous, but he was shrewd enough to recognize that captains did not decide the course of wars. "We will return at three."

"And of course," Andre continued, "I need not caution you that this matter should not be discussed with another soul outside of this room."

"Understood, sir," Stansbury replied softly.

Andre stared hard at Reverend Odell.

"Of course, sir," Odell agreed in a meek, squeaky voice.

As soon as the two men departed his office, Andre rapped softly on the door that connected his office with that of General Clinton. Andre quickly reported the details of the visit and extemporized glibly his positive interpretation and reaction. Clinton enthusiastically agreed that the matter should be aggressively pursued and authorized Andre to accept Arnold's offer to remain in place. No men-

tion was to be made of the suggestion that he might cross over now and command a British unit.

"And to be sure there are no misunderstandings," Clinton cautioned, "I want
you to put everything in writing."

"Everything, sir?"

"Everything," Clinton emphasized. "We cannot have Arnold misunderstanding our agreement. This kind of a fellow is an opportunist who might later
claim commitments that were never made. Give this fellow Stansbury a letter to
Arnold. Tell him what we want, how we will communicate and what we will
give in return. Make it a clear-cut business arrangement so that there can be no
misunderstandings."

"Yes, sir. But... ."

"Just do as I say. I recognize the risks involved. The letter could fall into the
wrong hands, but I will take the responsibility for that."

"Yes, sir," Andre snapped, surprising himself by formally saluting before
spinning and marching back to his own office.

Clinton watched the back of his departing aide with some amusement. The
young officer reminded Clinton of himself at a comparable age. He was eager
and ambitious and still young and unformed.

Back in his office, Andre spent the next three hours drafting his letter for
Arnold. He was so intent that he failed to note he missed a dinner appointment.
His lieutenant interrupted once to remind Andre, but the general's aide's
response was so curt that the lieutenant departed without a word.

For his letter, Andre decided first to assign Arnold a pseudonym. Despite
Clinton's blithe assurances, Andre was determined to do as much as he could to
protect Arnold's identity against the possibility of the letter falling into the wrong
hands. He assigned Arnold the name "Monk." Andre promised that if any
important blow should be struck as a consequence of Monk's information and
actions his reward would be commensurate. On the other hand if Monk's assistance should lead to the seizing of a sizable body of men or the complete defeat
of the enemy the generosity of the benefactor would exceed any expectations. In
describing the kinds of information that would be appreciated, Andre included
the following: contents of dispatches from foreign abettors; originals of such dispatches including a description of channels through which they were sent; number and positions of troops; what reinforcements are expected and when; identities of commanders; identity of others who might be willing to cooperate; location of arsenals; instructions to interest self in prisoner exchanges.

Andre addressed in detail their means of communication. They were to use
cipher keyed to Blackstone's Commentaries. The messages would consist of
groups of three numbers. The first number would refer to the page of
Blackstone's Commentaries, the second to the line on the page, and the third to a
specific word in the line selected. In this matter Monk or Andre could select
words which would be used to compose the message. In addition, the ciphers
would be written in an invisible ink. At the top of the page, Monk was to write

either an "A" or a "F." The "A" would indicate that acid was to be used in developing the message and "F" would require fire (heat). On the opposite side of the paper from the message, an innocuous letter should be written talking about an old woman's health or some such uninteresting matter. Unable on the spur of the moment to devise a better system, Andre suggested that the letters be addressed to himself at one end and Peggy Arnold on the other. He suggested the letters be transmitted via flags of truce, exchanged officers, etc. with every messenger being ignorant of what they are charged with transporting.

After writing his letter, Andre cleared it with General Clinton. At three o'clock he met with Stansbury and Odell and completed his arrangements. On Andre's orders, Stansbury was taken that night to a sloop in the bay, placed aboard a whaler and returned to South Amboy where he could begin his journey back to Philadelphia.

That night Andre celebrated his victory. His career had taken a remarkable step upward.

Chapter 31
New Jersey, Pennsylvania, New York
Spring/Summer 1779

On the fifth of March the weary, mud splattered courier who had delivered General Washington's message to John Satterfield at his Gauley River home high in the Appalachians returned to Middlebrook. The gaunt, exhausted man who had completed the round trip in a little over six weeks, saluted James then stood erectly at attention in front of James' desk.

"That's not necessary, Richard," James called the man by his first name. "You know I'm not a military officer."

"I know, sir, but after the ordeal I just went through I felt some formality should mark its end."

"Then salute General Washington when you report," James smiled. "For me, relax."

"Thank you, sir," the young ensign took James at his word and slumped into a chair. "Six weeks, sir," he sighed. "It can't be done any faster."

"How do you like Gauley River?" James smiled at the man's relief to be back at headquarters.

"It's beautiful country, sir, but I prefer the valleys."

"I have never seen such mountains. Did you have trouble locating my brother?"

"I was lucky to find a guide at Lewisburg. An old mountain man who knew John. Without him, I would have never found the Gauley. I would have never found my way out of those mountains. I saw the biggest rattlesnakes I have ever seen in my life. At least ten feet long."

"And my brother?" James asked gently.

"I'm sorry, sir, but he was not there. I have a letter for you from Eli that tells the full story. A handsome lad, that Eli," the lieutenant sighed.

The tired officer wearily extracted a folded sheet of mud-stained paper from a leather pouch he wore suspended from his shoulder. James took the single sheet and opened it. It had been folded and refolded many times, and James recognized that it had been probably used to wrap small presents that John's family had given each other. James knew from personal experience that frontier families treasured pieces of paper, using and reusing them. Paper was rare in the west.

His nephew's letter was written in a clear and precise masculine script. The words were simple but properly spelled and exactly used. James was impressed because he knew that Eli, who had grown up on the Gauley, had to be self-taught with limited assistance from his father, John. Eli's mother, Nancy, a frontier child herself, was illiterate.

"Dear Uncle James,
"Please tell General Washington that dad and the militia are fighting Indians up in the Ohio River country near Fort Randolph. Some of Cornstalk's friends have been raiding the settlers to pay them back for the militia killing their chief during last year's troubles. Dad hopes to teach them a lesson and encourage them to go back north. When he left, he promised to be back for the spring planting. Please tell General Washington if he needs help before then I could come. Do not think I am trying to be bigger than dad. Nobody can do that, but Dad says that I am a better woodsman than he is so I am sure I can do the General's scouting for him. Dad kills Indians better than me, but I do it when I have to. If the general prefers dad I understand, but he will have to wait for a month.
"My regards to you and yours, especially Jason
"Your nephew
        Eli
"Ma sends her best to Aunt Vivian"

The letter's rustic simplicity brought a tear to James' eye. He self-consciously rubbed it away and looked at the young ensign.

"Please sir," he pleaded. "Don't ask me to go back and fetch Eli. That boy can do any job the General wants, but I can't climb those mountains again."

The man's sincerity was so heart felt that James had to smile.

"The general will have to make that decision," James said, "but I doubt it will be necessary. General Sullivan does not plan to march until May, and John will be here by then."

"Thank God," the young officer relaxed and leaned back in his chair, crossing his boots in front of him.

James watched a large clump of mud drop from the raised boot onto James' clean floor, but he said nothing. The young officer was so relieved to learn that he did not have to return to the Gauley that he was oblivious of his surroundings.

By late April the army began to assemble in Easton, Pennsylvania the units which General Sullivan needed to support his march into New York colony to punish the Iroquois Nation. Easton, located due east of New York City on the

Delaware river, appeared to be an excellent staging area for the push northward. Although General Sullivan himself did not arrive in Easton until May 7th, word of the rebel preparations had been reported by Seneca braves who had been mistakenly approached by colonial frontiersmen seeking Indians to serve as scouts for the rebel army. Of the six tribes of the Iroquois Nation—Mohawks, Oneidas, Onondagas, Cayugas, Senecas and Tuscaroras—only the Oneidas and Tascaroras had decided to side with the colonists. The Senecas and the Mohawks were the most warlike and strongest supporters of the English. The Seneca braves promptly reported the news of the American plans to the English commander at Niagara. The commander, General Haldimand, refused to believe the Indian reports and ordered that a reliable white person be dispatched to investigate.

Despite the limited English reaction, news of the American plans to invade the land of the Six Nations spread quickly. As soon as Joseph Brant, the war chief of the Mohawks, heard of the Seneca report, he gathered a war party together and hurried to the land of the Senecas to learn for himself about the threat. Joseph Thayendangea, or Joseph Brant as he was known, was a remarkable man. He was the grandson of a Mohawk chief and the younger brother of Mary Brant, a Mohawk maiden who Sir William Johnson, the English Commissioner of Indian Affairs, had selected as a second wife. Sir William had migrated to the colonies as a young man to manage the Mohawk Valley estates of his uncle, an English admiral. He learned the customs and the language of the Mohawks and earned the respect of the Indians while gaining a substantial reputation as an expert on Indian affairs. He died in 1774 and his nephew, Guy Johnson, succeeded Sir William as Commissioner. Mary Brant, Sir William's Mohawk widow and Joseph Brant's sister, lived long after her husband had died and continued to play an influential role in Mohawk affairs as a consequence of her relationship with the highly respected Sir William.

After the outbreak of the revolutionary war, Guy Johnson was summoned "home" to London to discuss the role the Indians might play on England's behalf. He took with him Joseph Brant, who after his mission schooling, had fought with the English in the French and Indian War earning an honorific title of colonel. Johnson and Brant returned to the colonies in time for Brant to distinguish himself fighting against the Americans in the Battle of Long Island. Shortly thereafter, he infiltrated through the American lines and returned to his native tribe. During many raids on the homes of frontier settlers, Joseph Brant distinguished himself as the cruelest and most bloodthirsty savage to ever lead a Mohawk war party.

Brant, representing the Mohawks, met with his Seneca brothers at the southern end of the long lake that bears the Seneca name. Joining them was Captain Walter Butler, son of the Mohawk Valley Loyalist Ranger chief Major John Butler. Captain Walter Butler and his scruffy frontier rangers dressed in deerskins and except for their lighter color were virtually indistinguishable from the Indian allies.

Some of the younger Seneca and Mohawk braves advocated the immediate dispatch of war parties to confront the gathering rebel troops in the south before they could reach Iroquois land. Brant and Butler, who had participated in the battles in the north between Burgoyne and the rebels, counseled caution. Like the English general, they recommended preparation and the collection of information. As a consequence, several small parties were dispatched southward, and Brand and the other chieftains returned home to mobilize their braves to repel the anticipated invasion.

In mid-April James was sitting in his office with the windows thrown wide enjoying the cool, northern spring breeze which was only slightly warmed by the weak sun and contemplating whether another visit to Philadelphia would help prod the dithering Congress to pass the legislation required to procure much needed supplies when he heard the hallway door leading to the outer office slam shut.

"Mr. Satterfield," the nervous voice of the general's on duty aide spoke loudly. "I thought you were in your office."

James heard the scrape of the aide's chair as he jumped to his feet.

"Are you planning on a trip?"

James, curious, listened, but whoever had banged the door did not respond to the aide's question.

"Are those your frontier deerskins?" The aide asked.

Sudden understanding flashed across James' face in the form of a broad smile. He leaped to his feet and hurried to the open doorway. When James suddenly appeared, the aide turned, stared and began to stammer.

"But Mr. Satterfield... ." Before finishing his thought, the young lieutenant turned and faced a familiar figure dressed in grimy deerskin trousers and a long, fringed hunting shirt.

James leaned in the doorway and smiled at his twin brother. John, silent, smiled back. The aide, still confused, looked from one brother to the other. Except for dress and the long frontier hair of the newcomer, the two men were identical.

"Lieutenant, may I introduce my brother, John Satterfield, from the Gauley River," James finally broke the silence.

"Lieutenant," John smiled, offering his hand to the still confused aide.

"Sir, Mr. Satterfield, Sir," the aide stammered. He was immediately conscious of the calluses and strength of the second Satterfield.

John dropped the aide's hand and strode towards his brother. They embraced, totally forgetting the now silent lieutenant. Finally, James turned and led his brother into his office, closing the door softly behind him.

"You're looking pale, James," John spoke first.

"I spend all my time in this office worrying about politicians," James replied. "How's the family, Nancy, Eli, Becky, Romp?"

"All fine. Eli wanted to come along, but I felt his place was with Nancy and the young'uns. Time for spring planting."

"Did you stop at Eastwind?"

"Overnight. Vivian sends her best. I might have a letter in my saddlebag if I haven't lost it."

"And Alexandria?" James suddenly felt a longing to see his family.

"Jason, Lily and Buster are fine. The little guy reminds me of Romp," John referred to his own youngest son.

"How did Jason look?" James asked. He was still concerned that his son might succumb to a sudden urge to join the army.

He knew Jason felt guilty about remaining behind while his friends and father fought for their country.

"Don't worry," John replied, having immediately sensed his brother's concern. "Jason is busy building boats, buying land, caring for Buster who's a handful. He's too smart to get involved in this foolishness."

"Unlike his father and uncle," James observed wryly.

"Now that you bring it up, tell me what's troubling George," John said, referring to his urgent summons.

"This summer's campaign will concentrate on the Iroquois Nation, if the English let us."

"About time," John agreed, nodding his head in approval. "The poor settlers are having a bloody time with the savages. I just got back from Fort Pitt. Mohawk and Seneca war parties are roaming as far south as the Monongehela. Thanks to the English, they have better rifles and all the powder they need."

"Because of the war in Europe," James unconsciously revealed his expertise, "the English are trying to make up for lack of reinforcements from home by using Indians and Tories."

"What does George want with me?" John asked. "I don't know the Iroquois country."

"I think he needs someone who knows Indians that he can trust," James answered. "I'll let him tell you. I don't get involved in military matters."

John studied his brother soberly. "Best keep it that way, brother." John knew that James was not by nature a warrior. "As I recall, your last effort almost got you hanged."

James frowned as his brother's words brought to mind his close call in New York. "Thanks to the Howe brothers," he spoke bitterly. "Come, John, let's tell George you're here."

James patted his brother fondly on the back as he passed him and led the way to the inner door that opened on Washington's inner office. James tapped lightly and pushed the door open.

John followed, grinning broadly. He genuinely liked the sober Washington with whom he had shared several tense experiences in western Pennsylvania as a young man.

Washington, who was meeting with two of his generals, looked up impatiently when the door opened. As soon as he saw John, he broke into a broad smile, rare for him, and rose.

"John," Washington spoke with warmth that surprised the grim faced generals.

"George," John responded. The two men embraced.

The two generals stared with open mouths at the deerskin-clad frontiersman. To their surprise, except for the long hair tied in back with a black ribbon, he was the exact image of the general's political aide, James Satterfield. The generals had heard the stories of the Satterfield twin's existence and frontier escapades, but they had frankly discounted the stories as western exaggerations.

"Gentlemen, may I present Mr. John Satterfield who is going to solve some problems for us. John, General Sullivan and General Clinton."

John, who did not receive newspapers on the Gauley River and did not follow the war in the east and north closely, had not heard of either man. He glanced at the short, pudgy Sullivan and nodded. The second man, Clinton, was taller and presented a more formidable appearance.

"Gentlemen," Washington spoke to the two generals before either had a chance to speak. "If you will please excuse us, I need to confer with Mr. Satterfield. I have not had a chance to brief him on our plans."

James, who had stood a few paces to the rear, noted a flash of irritation cross Sullivan's face. James sympathized with the general who was to lead the campaign against the Indians. He was being dismissed so that Washington could confer with a mountain man who Washington had selected as his chief scout without any consultation with him.

"Certainly, sir," Sullivan replied and followed a silent Clinton from the room.

James recognized that Sullivan, who had a reputation for being a vain and ambitious man, was fighting to control his temper. James assumed that Sullivan recognized he should do nothing to jeopardize his chances for a new command, particularly following his most recent failures.

"Thank you for coming, John," George said as he led the Satterfields to the chairs aligned in front of the unlighted fireplace.

"If I had been a week later getting home," John observed, "I would be doing the spring planting, and Eli would be here."

"I understand your son has grown into a fine woodsman," Washington observed. James had shared Eli's letter containing the young man's frank, poignant self-appraisal with Washington.

"Better than me," John observed honestly without any evidence of undue pride. "But I understand you might need something more than mountain skills." John focused his clear green eyes on Washington and waited for his old friend to explain without further small talk.

"Last year Burgoyne and the English turned the Iroquois loose on the frontiers."

"So I hear," John spoke laconically.

"Life in the Mohawk Valley has been a hell," Washington continued.

"Six Nation war parties are raiding far to the south," John said.

"And we intend to teach them a lesson."

"I hope so, and not the reverse," John spoke seriously.

"That's why I want you to assist us," Washington said.

"Where? You have to hit the Iroquois at home, burn their crops, villages, kill their warriors, their squaws, their children," John said coldly. "Otherwise, they will simply run and return when you've left."

"I think I've already learned that lesson from you,"Washington said, not unkindly.

John nodded and waited for Washington to continue.

"I plan to send an army up the Susquehanna to the Chemung and into the lake country... ." Washington began.

"The Senecas," John nodded.

"Another army will come from the Mohawk Valley down the Susquehanna and join up with the first army at Tioga."

"The Mohawks," John agreed. "And the west?"

"A third army, much smaller, will rally at Fort Pitt then follow the Allegheny northward to the Genesee country."

"That should do it, if your armies are any good as Indian fighters." John studied Washington, and James knew both men were recalling their experiences when a professional English army under General Braddock had been devastated by a much smaller French and Indian irregular force.

"I hope I have learned from my past mistakes, John." Washington studied his old friend. Time had narrowed the two-year age difference between them, but Washington still felt the strength that flowed from the rugged mountain man. Washington was commander-in-chief and accustomed to subservience from all around him, but something about John still made him feel like a novice.

"I'm sure, George," John fixed his hard green eyes on Washington. "But I don't intend to risk another Braddock."

"Nor I," Washington agreed. "General Sullivan, who you just met, will command the force that moves up the Susquehanna."

John nodded with disinterest.

"I assume you want me to scout for the army gathering at Fort Pitt." John spoke matter-of-factly. Washington knew that John was personally familiar with the country north of Fort Pitt. He and Washington had carried a message from Governor Dinwiddie north to the French commander on Lake Erie some twenty-five years before.

"No, John, I need you on the Susquehanna," Washington replied, catching John by surprise.

"I don't know that country," John said flatly.

"Our main effort will be against the Senecas, and that is where we must succeed," Washington explained. "That is where I need someone who knows Indians and who I can trust."

"What about your General Sullivan?" John asked noncommittally.

Washington paused before answering.

"He is a serious officer," Washington began slowly. "He is one of my most experienced generals. He is cautious and will take no chances."

"Can he fight?" John asked.

James, who had been listening closely, wondered how Washington would answer. Sullivan was experienced, but he had been badly outflanked and out-generaled in two major battles, costing the rebel army high casualties.

"He has made mistakes and suffered major defeats," Washington admitted. "But I believe he has learned from them. He did not know his terrain, did not listen to advice from others, and was badly outflanked and surprised. He promises it will not happen again."

To James' surprise John nodded approval. "Does he know Indians?"

"No. He is from New Hampshire."

James assumed this response would elicit a flat refusal from John, but instead his brother nodded again.

"You do need help," John said.

A silence settled over the room as the three men occupied themselves with their own thoughts. John impassively studied his friend Washington who stared straight ahead. Finally, John spoke.

"I don't know the Susquehanna or the Seneca country," John said. "Do I have time for a private scouting trip?"

James, who knew Washington was pressing for the army to form and move promptly, assumed Washington would answer negatively.

"Yes, John," Washington said. "How long will you need?"

"As long as it takes," John responded. After a few seconds, he smiled and added: "I'll need a month."

"Washington nodded approval, not disturbed by John's curtness. James suddenly realized that the two men had traveled alone through dangerous country and knew each other well. Washington tolerated far more from John than he would any other man.

"Sullivan, as I said, John, will be cautious. Like any general he will try to accumulate more men and supplies than he needs. He will do everything he can to guarantee success this time. If he is ready to move before you return, which I strongly doubt, I will order him to wait."

"We should reach the Seneca homelands in August just before their crops are ready for harvest. We can burn the corn and maize in the fields. And they will not be able to replant this growing season."

"And burn their villages," Washington added.

"That should be easy," John agreed. "If we are careful and avoid ambush, the Indians will not stand and fight. They'll run in order to live to raid another day."

"But this time we will be in their homeland."

"Where we can burn their fields and destroy their villages instead of letting them burn our settler cabins and run."

"And this winter," James entered the conversation, grasping the strategic significance of the maneuver, "the Indians will gather at the English forts at Niagara and in Canada with their starving tribes and demand food and supplies. The English will be pressed to supply them and will discover they have a burden instead of reinforcements for their diminishing army."

"And the French fleet," Washington smiled, "can blockade New York and harass the English ships delivering supplies."

James nodded, acknowledging a favorite Washington theory—control of the sea is the key to victory.

"I will burn the fields and villages and kill as many savages as I can," John promised. "But I will leave the strategy to you two. Now, I will do my scouting."

"Do you want a patrol to go with you. Carefully selected men?" Washington asked.

"No," John answered. "I'll travel alone. I might pick up an Oneida or Onondaga that knows the land to guide me at Easton or Wyoming ... depends on what's available."

"I'm not sure you can trust one," James interrupted, suddenly worried for his brother. He knew that some of the braves of the lesser Iroquois tribes had sworn fealty to the colonists, but he did not trust them, particularly when it came to his brother traveling alone with one.

"Trust one?" John laughed good-naturedly at his brother's comment. "James, the word trust does not enter my vocabulary when dealing with savages. I may use one as a guide, but I promise you I will return, alone."

James did not ask what his brother meant by the remark.

Washington looked soberly at John and nodded agreement.

Chapter 32
Pennsylvania, New York
Summer 1779

The summer campaign season began for James in what had become a customary pattern, that of waiting for the English to decide where and when the armies would feint and skirmish. James for one had decided the armies would never fight a fixed battle that would determine the outcome of the rebellion; in his skepticism he feared the war would continue until the English declared victory and went home leaving the colonies to their independence.

At the end of May, Washington sent Sullivan his final instructions; they did not differ from those issued when Washington had settled command for the expedition on his second choice. In early June General Henry Clinton forcibly demonstrated his intentions. He landed troops at King's Ferry, which linked Stoney Point on the Hudson's west bank with Verplankt's Point on the east. The fact the English were now twelve miles from the American strongpoint at West Point provoked Washington and his army to hasten northward.

To Washington's delight, Clinton emulated his predecessor, Sir William Howe; he paused to regroup his army and fortify the land already taken, and in doing so sacrificed the opportunity for an easy victory over his objective, West Point. Having given his opponents the opportunity to get their breath, Clinton waited while Washington paced at his new headquarters near the tavern in Smith's Clove. Frustrated over his inability to learn Clinton's intentions, Washington issued orders through James to Captain Eric Grey and his New York informants to intensify their efforts.

Clinton signaled his indecision by withdrawing his supporting fleet from Stoney Point to New York Harbor. Washington retaliated in early July by retaking Stoney Point and preparing an assault across the river at Verplankt's Point. To his dismay, Washington discovered that the intense fortifications prepared by Clinton's forces had been dug with a clear opening to the river on the assumption that the English would control the waterway and the enemy would come from the land. Deciding that Stoney Point for him was indefensible, Washington withdrew.

Meanwhile, to the south and east General Sullivan prepared for his Iroquois campaign with an attention to detail that made it one of the most carefully planned efforts of the war. In early May, General John Sullivan arrived in Easton, Pennsylvania to take command of his assembling army. The rebel strategy called for Brigadier General Clinton to lead his brigade of fifteen hundred men from Otsego Lake southward along the Susquehanna River to Tioga where the Susquehanna joined the Chemung; there, he would linkup with Sullivan coming from the southeast. Sullivan occupied himself at Easton for a month and a half assembling his men and stockpiling supplies. Finally, on June 23rd Sullivan ordered his army to leave its Delaware River base and to march to the west to Wyoming on the Susquehanna, which would serve as their jumping off place for beginning their northern sweep.

Sullivan's careful preparations gave John Satterfield the time he needed to complete his scouting trip north into Iroquois country in advance of the overladen army. After his brief visit with Washington and James, John had traded his two tired horses for a fresh pair at Washington's headquarters' stables and galloped alone westward to Easton and then northward to Wyoming. There, he consulted the advance elements of Sullivan's army and carefully assessed the small group of Oneidas and Onondagas who had been selected to serve as the army's scouts. Having confronted the warlike Mohawks and Senecas on more occasions than he liked to recall, John was not impressed. After two days of carefully circulating through the Indian encampment, which was located outside of the army's strongpoint as a defensive measure—the army trusted the scouts on whom it intended to rely for their protection from surprise no more than John did—John selected an older Oneida brave to accompany him.

The Oneida's age was difficult to determine, and the brave himself could not count his years with certainty. His name, Many Summers, had been adopted in his later years when he could no longer live up to the name of his youth, Swift Foot. John realized that Many Summers had traveled far in his lifetime, and this is what led John to select him. Many Summers claimed to have wandered for decades from the Iroquois lake country to his adopted home in the Carolinas; he no longer considered himself a brave and carried no firearm, limiting himself to the knife and tomahawk that he used to sustain his daily life. John planned that his companion would have one task, to lead him into Iroquois country. Once there, John would have no further use for his guide and would make his own way back. Since he would avoid fights, his companion need not be a brave; since he would travel only one direction, he need only be able to move for three weeks. The old Indian's sparse frame had covered many miles, and John estimated it could bear another two hundred, especially when much of the travel would be by canoe upriver.

In addition to his native Oneida, Many Summers claimed to speak the language of the neighboring Senecas as well as English. Since the Indian's English vocabulary was limited to about fifty words, John hoped he underestimated his ability to converse with his Seneca brothers. Knowing that Indians always over appraised their prowess, John was skeptical. In his view, Many Summers was the best of a bad lot.

On a clear May morning about a week before Sullivan's arrival in Easton, John and Many Summers slipped into the light bark canoe that John had commandeered and pushed into the Susquehanna. Many Summers at John's nod took the squaw position in the front of the canoe. James, more comfortable where he could control the canoe, watch his companion and study the shorelines, kneeled in the stern. To John's relief, he noted that Many Summers, despite his age, still paddled with a firm stroke. John traveled light. On the floor of the canoe rested his long rifle and a small pack. A powder horn was draped over his shoulder on a rawhide thong, and he wore his knife and his tomahawk suspended from a belt that circled his deerskin-hunting shirt at the waist.

John planned to follow the Susquehanna northward to the point where it joined the Chemung at Tioga. From there he would paddle the Chemung through hostile Indian hunting grounds to Newtown. There, he would beach the canoe and skulk through the forest avoiding as many villages and war parties as he could. Many Summers had assured him that a two day walk would take him from the Chemung to the long lake that rested in the heart of Seneca country, his objective. One of the reasons he had selected Many Summers was the Indian's assurance that he was still welcome in the villages of his Seneca brothers. John hoped to avoid contact with Indians during his brief scouting trip; he recognized that any hostile action on his part would only alert the Iroquois to the plans of the army they certainly knew was assembling to their south. If he could, James planned to masquerade as a loyalist member of Butler's Rangers returning with his Indian companion from a scouting trip to the south to learn what the Americans were preparing. John knew the suspicious Seneca would disbelieve his story and that any chance meeting with one of Butler's loyalist rangers would immediately expose him, but he had little choice. John did not know how much he could rely on Many Summers, but like most Indians the old man promised much. John was experienced enough to expect little.

The river was full, crowded with the waters from the winter snows melting high in the mountains, and the current was strong. An experienced canoeist, John kept his light craft as close to the shore as the river permitted, avoiding the strength of the racing water. The bark canoe skipped over the shimmering surface as John and Many Summers stroked.

At Tioga, John crossed to the western bank of the surging river and followed the Chemung northward. John noticed two figures on the distant east bank carefully watching the canoe's progress but ignored them. They did not wave, only studied the racing canoe. John assumed from their dress that they were settlers carefully assessing the threat posed by the Indian and white man who studiously appeared to be avoiding contact.

The Chemung, freed from the stronger, surging Susquehanna waters, was still full. Much narrower, now that it was alone, the river wended its way through thick forests. On each side tall oaks, maples, sycamores and pines stretched skyward while bending their shadows over the slate gray and white of the rushing waters. John did not see another human on the banks of the winding river as he and Many Summers traversed the river.

The old Indian paddled without complaint; he was no longer swift, but his thin arms still stretched with uncomplaining sinews of taut muscle.

Game was plentiful. Twice John and Many Summers surprised fishing brown bears standing on rocks at the river's edge with large paws poised to snatch unsuspecting bass and rainbow trout. Deer were plentiful, and tall elk watched the passing canoe with wide, distrustful eyes. Nights, John and Many Summers camped at the river's edge. The Indian expertly speared large succulent trout and cooked them over smokeless fires that were quickly extinguished as soon as the meal suspended on a small branch held by forked twigs was done. John, even though he was sure their passage had been noted and announced from village to village as they progressed upriver, wanted to move as quickly and quietly as possible.

After ten days, Many Summers grunted to indicate they had reached the river bend near the Indian village known as Newtown. John and Many Summers, both silent men, no longer attempted to communicate with words. John, anxious to travel as quietly as possible, discouraged conversation. When needed, a quick hand movement, a look, a blink of the eyes or a nod of the head sufficed. Neither man had spoken directly to the other for the past three days, and John was becoming pleased with his choice of companions. At first he had feared he had encumbered himself with another garrulous Indian who one day would endanger them both with his attempts to ingratiate himself with the white man, but Many Summers had quickly gotten John's message. Now, the old Indian consoled himself with his thoughts and memories as he paddled.

John guided the canoe to the east bank. As they neared the gravelly shore, Many Summers stopped paddling and studied the land as they silently approached. Both John and Many Summers listened. John knew that Many Summers sensed something. John himself felt another presence watching their approach. He thought about returning to the river but decided against it. They were now deep in Seneca country, and John knew that as long as they were on the river they would be watched. On the water in a canoe there was no place to hide. John had hoped to be able to land, hide the canoe and proceed on foot, but he knew if they were being observed any attempt to conceal movement would be interpreted as hostile, and he decided to test Many Summers' ability to project their story that John was a returning Butler scout.

The canoe crunched onto the pebbled shore, and Many Summers stiffly stepped ashore. He tugged at the canoe's prow then faded into the protective cover of the tree line. John stepped into the water, waded alongside the canoe until he reached the bow, then leaned over and with one hand picked up the front of the light craft and pulled it onto the shore. He stopped at the tree line and made no attempt to conceal the canoe. He turned, retrieved his pack and rifle, then quietly blended into the trees to join Many Summers. One glance from the old Indian's tired, bloodshot eyes told him they were being watched by more than one. John nodded at Many Summers, indicating he should proceed inland. The shoreline at this point consisted of a flat, forested bed that led to a series of low rises that quickly led into steep, mountain foothills. John was anxious to obtain the security of the high land where he and his companion could disappear into the obscurity of the forest. Here, they were trapped on the flat land between the hills and the river with limited options of movement.

They had gone no more than ten paces when Many Summers paused, almost imperceptibly, and glanced at John. He nodded. He had sensed them. A faint hint of wood smoke and grease wafted on the wind, an odor too thin to come from the fire itself. Experience told John it emanated from greasy deerskins. John's sharp hearing detected movement to his right. They were caught between a semi circle of braves and the riverbank. Recognizing that resistance under the circumstances was impossible, John decided to brazen it out. He paused, rested the stock of his long rifle on the ground with the barrel pointing unthreateningly to the sky, and spoke in a loud, incautious voice, trying to appear as a man who did not care if he were heard or not.

"Many Summers," John called. "How far to your Seneca brothers' village?"

"Near," Many Summers answered, in Seneca, immediately grasping John's intent. He made a sharp, chopping motion to the northeast, indicating the direction to the village.

"Lead the way," John ordered gruffly as he raised his rifle and draped its rawhide sling over his shoulder. "We'll rest overnight, then I'll head north to Mohawk territory. Butler will be anxious to hear our news." John gratuitously referred to Captain Gus Butler who now commanded the bloodthirsty frontier Tories who called themselves Butler's Rangers. The Butlers along with Joseph Brant, the Mohawk war chief, led the Iroquois for the English.

Many Summers turned and continued inland several yards until he found a path that paralleled the river bank.

"Path, here," he grunted for the benefit of the still hidden stalkers.

John pushed through a patch of briars and joined Many Summers on the path. Leaves rustled behind him. Suddenly, ten Seneca braves, wearing bright red and white war paint on their bodies and faces, surrounded them. All carried shiny, long rifles and wore bright knives and tomahawks dangling from their waists. John correctly assumed that the braves had recently visited Niagara or another English fort on the lakes and had been showered with presents.

John raised his right hand in greeting and snarled gruffly at Many Summers.

"Tell the savages who we are." John acted belligerently, like a member of the coarse Butler Rangers.

Many Summers spoke in the guttural Seneca language. The surrounding braves stood with their rifles pointed at John and his Oneida companion, but they listened intently as Many Summers talked. The tallest brave barked a few words at Many Summers and pointed down the river in the direction from which John and his companion had come. John assumed he was asking where they had been because Many Summers turned, also pointed to the south, and emitted another string of barks and grunts.

When Many Summers finished, he paused and glared at the young man. He then issued what was obviously an order. Many Summers turned to John and in English explained.

"I told him to take us to his village."

"Did you tell him we have to find Captain Butler?" John asked, using their agreed upon story.

"Yes. They know we scout army, have news."

"Welcome. Me speak English," the taller brave spoke.

He had apparently accepted their story. "Come," he ordered, turning to lead the way north along the path.

John pushed ahead of Many Summers and followed the brave. Many Summers and the others spread out single file and began trotting along behind. The leading Indian ran at half speed. The only sound the file of men made was the soft pad of their moccasins as they whispered along the well-worn path.

They trotted for about an hour covering approximately ten miles. Despite the fact that the Seneca braves were all twenty to thirty years younger than John and Many Summers, neither had difficulty keeping up. Both, hardened to the frontier, could have kept up the pace all day. John marveled at the countryside. The path led from the forest to broad meadows that stretched on each side of the river. The rich, black loam, which had been deposited along the banks over the centuries, seemed to John to be peering skyward pleading for seed and plow.

After several miles, the river turned gradually from its northern path to the northwest and then to the west into the setting sun. The banks widened to a large valley rimmed to the south, east and west by high foothills. Suddenly, cultivated fields of corn spread to the north and west. John estimated the stalks stood at least ten feet high. Already, long green cobs had formed. The tassels were thin and white. John estimated the corn would be ready in for harvest in another five to six weeks. The lead Indian slowed to a walk. He glanced over his shoulder and smiled proudly as he watched John stare at the corn. He clenched his fist and wrapped his knuckles against his bare, bony chest. John recognized that he was declaring ownership of the corn and nodded approval.

The cornfield suddenly gave way to long rows of waist high bean plants. In the distance John saw three squaws gathering the fat green bean pods. The valley was long and flat and stretched to the north and west. The Indian village consisted of four Iroquois longhouses surrounded by a picket palisade that marked it as a relic from older days. John knew the Iroquois, confident in the power of the Six Nations in the heart of their homeland, no longer felt a need for the protective fencing. The long structures housed several families each. They were about fifteen feet wide and forty feet long and were built on stout, forked poles that supported a roof lashed to the crossed infrastructure. The outside was lined with peeled poles covered by long strips of tree bark that had been harvested in the spring when the material was soft and pliable. John estimated the village and surrounding fields supported some two hundred Indians, at least half of whom would be males of a fighting age.

Barking dogs alerted the village to the return of the war party with the two strangers. The women and children gathered around John and stared and chattered. They were accustomed to the presence of white frontiersmen but still considered them an oddity to be studied and denigrated. The tall Seneca who had led the war party began talking in a loud voice. John hoped he had accepted Many Summers' story and was explaining it to the village elders who had gathered to learn the news.

"He explains you scout Butler," Many Summers whispered. "Elders not like and want know why Oneida do you instead Mohawk. Me tell me know south waters."

The conversation between the elders and the braves sounded harsh and threatening to John, but he knew they were discussing his story. Most Indian languages consisted of sharp barks and grunts that struck the white man as unpleasant. Finally, a decision was made. The young buck turned, smiled and gestured for John to follow the old man who seemed to be the primary chief.

"They want smoke, talk, know what see," Many Summers explained.

The Indians escorted John to the center of the village and sat around him in front of one of the longhouses. The afternoon passed slowly as in broken English John explained that the white man was gathering an army in the south. They seemed relieved when John dissembled by reporting he had learned they planned to march west and not north into Seneca country. John learned that Joseph Brant and Gus Butler had recently met at the southern end of Seneca Lake with representatives of the Iroquois nations and had made plans to gather an army composed of Iroquois and Rangers to resist any American incursions from the south. John immediately declared his intention to travel north to meet with Butler and Brant and to report his findings.

After a tedious night in the village, John and Many Summers said good-by to the elders and began their journey north. It was only with difficulty that they succeeded in dissuading the Senecas from sending a warparty to escort them through Seneca land. Many Summers assured them he knew the way well from his youth. It was only John's suggestion that the young warriors establish an ambush to the south to intercept any Americans that might have picked up their trail that let them escape on their own.

John and Many Summers trotted along the trail that led north from the Chemung to the lake country for several hours before they were confident they were free from their Seneca hosts. Breathing a sigh of relief, John led his companion from the trail into the thick forest that filled the wide valley. He did not want to acquire any more Seneca companions. He knew that a chance visitor from the north at any moment could give lie to their weak story of scouting for

Butler and thus preferred the security of the deep woods even though it meant they had to travel slower. John planned to go as far as the lake of the Senecas, make his way up the east side then cross over to its companion body of water, Cayuga, scout the Seneca villages along both lakes, then return quickly to the south and rejoin Sullivan just as he finished preparations for the march north-wards. John knew Sullivan would be interested to learn that the Iroquois and their allies already were alerted to Sullivan's plans and were preparing to raise and army to confront him.

John and Many Summers moved quickly but cautiously through the foothills that rimmed the valley northward. They kept below the ridge lines where the horizon would have outlined their bodies against the sky, thus were forced at many points to make their way carefully around sharp cliffs and rock falls. Twice they observed Seneca war parties following the path below them heading towards the Chemung. Each time John and his companion exchanged glances congratulating each other for having decided to avoid the enticement of the path.

South of the lake, not far from a large waterfall, many Summers pointed out a village where, he claimed, resided an old white woman, the squaw widow of a famous Seneca chieftain. Many Summers claimed the woman was known throughout the Iroquois Nation for her cruel treatment of white prisoners. After three days, they reached the long lake of the Senecas. It was the largest inland lake that John had seen. North of the Seneca village on the lake's southernmost end, John and Many Summers cautiously made their way to the lakeshore. John tested the crystal clear blue water. Despite the summer heat, the water was ice cold. John immediately abandoned his plan to bathe in the lake. He splashed some of the frigid water on his face, nodded at the knowing smile on Many Summers' usually impassive face, and pointed northward.

Seneca villages with their telltale longhouses dotted the lakeshore. Many Summers assured John the lake abounded with tasty trout and bass, but he did not pause to test his guide's story. Each of the villages was surrounded by lush gardens of tall corn and heavily laden bean bushes. John assured himself that Sullivan would have no difficulty fulfilling two of his army's objectives, destroy-ing Seneca villages and burning their crops.

After another two days of travel, John still had not reached the northern end of the lake of the Senecas. John asked Many Summers how much further. The Indian indicated they were half way leading John to estimate that the lake must be about forty miles long. Deciding that time was closing on him, he reluctantly turned eastward and made his way to Cayuga. The second lake, also lined with Indian villages, was much smaller than the first. John, deciding that not much more was to be gained from following lake waters, turned southward towards the Chemung. From a bluff overlooking the southern terminus of Cayuga, John stud-ied a large Indian village. While he watched, he saw a group of white men arrive from the northeast. They were dressed in buckskin and led by a tall white man with a long hooked nose.

"Rangers," Many Summers opined.

John assumed the confident man was Gus Butler. John decided he had to get a closer look. Over Many Summers' objections, John slowly descended from his vantagepoint on the hill high over the lake waters. After two hours, John and his companion reached a small hill about three hundred yards from the village at the end of the lake. A glance at the sun indicated that they had about two hours before sunset. While they watched, the villagers gathered wood and built a large campfire. To John's surprise, they gathered skins and hides from the floors of their long houses and arranged them in a semicircle around the fire they had built at the lake shore. Usually, the Indians were content to sit on the ground as they had at the Seneca village on the Chemung.

"Important chief come," Many Summers opined. "We go," he suggested, tugging at John's arm as he lay beside him concealed under the limbs of a huge overhanging pine.

"Soon," John replied, to his companion's obvious dismay.

"Very dangerous," Many Summers warned, his tired brown eyes squinting with warning.

John shook his head negatively and studied the village. The sun setting in the west bounced long red beams across the lake waters as the squaws gathered around the fire and began preparations for a feast. Smaller cooking fires were lighted, and smoke curled skyward. John felt his empty stomach muscles contract, calling for food, but John ignored the familiar sensation. Then, motion to the left of the village caught his eye. A war party led by a tall Indian appeared. In the declining light John's sharp eyes distinguished the man's distinctive features. He had a coppery skin several shades lighter than the average Indian. His long brown, not black, hair, was straight, gathered by a rawhide tie into a long mane behind his massive head. His face was dominated by a broad, sharp nose that ran in a straight line from a perfect triangle in front to his forehead. Cruel frown lines marked the wide mouth.

"Thayendangea," Many Summers gasped. "Joseph Brant, Mohawk," he explained needlessly.

The mention of the Indian name "Thayendangea" was sufficient to alert John to the man's identity. He was the half-breed war chief of the Mohawks. Despite his white father and mission education, Joseph Brant's cruelty and propensity for torture distinguished him in a land renown for its inhumanity to others. Studying the man, John remembered the story of Jane McCrea. Despite the fact her father was a loyalist and her fiancé a young Tory captain, she had been captured by marauding Mohawks. When two young braves had begun arguing over who owned the captive, Joseph Brant had calmly walked over, decapitated her with one blow of his heavy tomahawk, sliced off her fine blond hair and suspended it from his belt. He then cut off her nose and ears and tossed them to the ground for the arguing braves to share.

John stared at the war chief and felt the evil that emanated from the man. He had previously discounted the story as a typical frontier exaggeration, but seeing Brant in person persuaded him otherwise. Brant was flanked by two older

Indians who caught John's attention. John would have expected Brant to be attended by Mohawk bucks, but his two closest companions were neither Mohawk nor young. John studied them closely. For some reason the two mean looking Indians were familiar; one had a long scar that curved from his left temple in front of the ear to a spot in the center of the man's chin. The wound had been jagged, as if gouged with a sharp stone or ripped on a nail; it was not a smooth knife cut.

"Massawomee," Many Summers whispered.

The very mention of the name brought memories to John's mind. The Massawomee had occupied the Allegheny land in Pennsylvania and Virginia between the Ohio and the Blue Ridge before roaming Algonquin hunting parties and the intruding white settlers had driven them westward towards the plains. One of John's bitterest savage foes as a young man had been Massawomee. Red Eye, the foul savage who had murdered John's grandmother, who had stolen James' knife, and who had been in turn killed by John following one of his western journeys with George Washington, had been Massawomee. The thought of Red Eye immediately reminded John why the two braves with Joseph Brant looked familiar. The two evil looking men, Red Knife and Three Scalps, were Red Eye's sons. Three Scalps, the one with the savage scar, had been so named because he had won three scalps by age ten, the youngest brave in his tribe to be so honored. Red Knife had earned his fitting name by following in his brother's and his father's footsteps at an early age, staining his knife with the blood of careless settlers.

Both Three Scalps and Red Knife had been sleeping in the tent when John had killed their father. He had struck silently but the discovery of his absence and their father's body in the morning had certainly left no doubt who had been responsible. John had often wondered what had happened to Red Eye's offspring. He had fully expected to one-day assist them in joining their father in his pagan hell, but until this moment had never encountered them again. Obviously they had joined a roving Mohawk war party and now held special status at Joseph Brant's side. John fingered his long rifle and was tempted. He would have one shot, and he wondered who he should take first. Joseph Brant or Three Scalps or Red Knife. Red Eye's two sons were equally deserving, but John studied Joseph Brant. The Mohawk war chief posed the greatest threat. John slowly began drawing his long rifle into position. Before he could raise it and take aim, he felt a tug on his sleeve.

Many Summers looked pleadingly at John and shook his head negatively. He knew John could kill the Mohawk chief but that would bring three hundred braves down upon them.

"Not now," Many Summers cautioned.

John looked at Many Summers then back at Joseph Brant. The man with the wide sharp nose stood facing him, no more than two hundred yards away. John again fingered the trigger and studied his target. It would be so easy, but he knew that Many Summers was right. John was confident he could elude the Mohawks, even in their own woods, and he did not care what happened to Many Summers, but he owed it to Washington and his army not to precipitously ignite the Iroquois. The killing of the Mohawk chief at a council of war would prematurely unleash red passions before Sullivan's army was in position. John decided to let Sullivan and his army plod its way into Iroquois land. If the savages resisted, as it appeared they planned, John knew he would have another chance, and then he would kill all three.

When John relaxed his grip on his long rifle, Many Summers exhaled a long sigh of relief. He did not care what happened to the hard white man with the flashing green eyes, but he intended to see another winter at his camp in the south surrounded by his sons and their sons. Many Summers looked at the sky. The sun had set and a dark gray dusk had settled over the forest. Now was the time to retreat. Many Summers turned and began silently to creep away from the Iroquois council fire. He heard no noise behind him but knew that the white man followed.

From May 7th to June 18th, General John Sullivan patiently assembled his army and collected his supplies; he was determined that this time he would be victorious and replace the patronizing smirks on the faces of his fellow generals with supplicating smiles of envy. He concerned himself with every detail. His supply trains carried 4,285 horseshoes, insurance that not one wagon would be halted for lack of an iron shoe, 254 spades and 385 shovels; General Sullivan's fortifications would be dug; and 100 candlesticks, presumably to light his officers' messes.

Sullivan pressed his harried staff to overlook no detail; if a supply sergeant discovered one barrel of spoiled meat, fifty replacement barrels were ordered. When finally the compounds at Easton could hold not another nail, General Sullivan issued the long awaited order to march from Easton on the Delaware to Wyoming on the Susquehanna. Traveling at the rate of ten miles a day, the overladen army struggled to reach Wyoming by the twenty-third. There, more supplies waited. General Sullivan on arrival inspected not his soldiers but his logistics. He had not visited the terrain he intended to conquer, but he reasoned that his army, equipped with adequate powder and food, could vanquish any defense the savages and their allies might muster. Sullivan decided: that some of the cattle were too feeble to walk; that the supply of shoes was inadequate; that the bread was moldy and the meat stiff with maggots; he complained to Congress and to General Washington. Washington, offended that even the sullied General Sullivan saw fit to bypass the commander-in-chief, lost his patience and reprimanded Sullivan for wanting too much. He counseled his cautious general to march while the crops were still in the fields and while a modicum of surprise remained.

John, traveling fast with the sinewy Many Summers at his side, arrived at Wyoming in time to watch Sullivan's army celebrate the Fourth of July with a sloppy parade and a thirteen-gun salute. Despite his intention to return alone,

John had tolerated his companion's persistence. Day after day the ageless Indian had silently followed John. If he had lagged, made a single mark that flagged their passage, John would have killed him without hesitation. If Many Summers sensed this threat, he had not shown it. He accompanied John with a stubbornness and a devotion that John had not witnessed since his old trail companion, Wolf, the rugged canine of John's youth, had died of age.

Upon arrival, John reported to General Sullivan. Although one might have expected that John's news that the Iroquois knew of the army's existence and that Joseph Brant and the Tory Rangers were preparing to greet it would have prodded the pudgy general into action; it did not. Instead, he ordered more supplies. Not until July 31st did Sullivan give the order to march for Tioga and the rendezvous with Brigadier General James Clinton who planned to convey his northern army to the juncture by boat.

Some days, delayed by heavy rain and rough terrain, Sullivan's army covered only five miles. On August 9th, advance elements encountered a deserted Indian village. After pausing to burn the thirty long houses, the army resumed its trek. John, discouraged by Sullivan's turtle-like pace, broke contact and proceeded for Tioga with Many Summers doggedly at his heels. The countryside between the army's vanguard and Tioga was deserted; even the animals had heard the noisy advance and had cleared a way. At Tioga, John and Many Summers rested at the point where the Susquehanna and the Chemung meet. Since only the fat trout remained unaware of the army's approach, John and Many Summers feasted on the rainbow and speckled browns, which the Indian adroitly speared with a sharpened branch.

Three days later, Sullivan's weary vanguard arrived. The march through difficult terrain had been a hard one; the army lost several soldiers to heat exhaustion and one while cooling himself in the quick waters of the Susquehanna. When the general himself arrived, he surveyed the spot where the rivers met and ordered the construction of a fort and palisade. While he waited for Brigadier General James Clinton and his force from the Mohawk Valley to appear, he built his forward base.

General Sullivan had ordered Clinton to depart Otsego Lake on August 9th. While he waited at the lake, which is the mouth of the Susquehanna, Clinton decided to try a proposal suggested by one of his young engineers. He directed that his idle troops build a dam across the lake outlet that fed the river. The engineer theorized that after the army's supplies were loaded on the boats that would carry them down river to Tioga, the dam could be broken, and the accumulated water would rush down the rocky bed sweeping any obstructions before it while the loaded boats sped on the artificial tide to the rendezvous. That was the theory, and Clinton, a practical man, was skeptical, but he gave the imaginative engineer his head.

On August 9th, the boats were loaded. While the some fifteen hundred rugged troops who were to march alongside watched, the dam was broken. The water surged southward and to everyone's surprise did exactly what the engineer had predicted. It smashed fallen tree trunks that clogged the bed and the water rushed between the banks. The sudden flood, which had no ostensible source, frightened the Indians who lived in villages along the river and flooded their fields. The Indians fled, and the river saved Clinton's men time by destroying the Indian crops. The boats with the cheering crewmen rushed downstream. When the waters reached Tioga, they lapped at the base of the palisade that surrounded Sullivan's new fort while his army watched the passing flood with amazement. When Clinton's boats arrived and the jubilant troops repeated the story of their feat, Sullivan's army cheered.

John watched and shook his head in amazement at the boyish enthusiasm of the men who waited to kill Indians.

Clinton's troops arrived at Tioga on August 19th. Sullivan's band serenaded the tired but fierce looking soldiers while the generals saluted before retiring to Sullivan's headquarters to confer. The army, now assembled, included some 4,500 men and officers. On August 26th, after posting a garrison at the fort to receive and forward any additional supplies that might be sent from the south, Sullivan ordered his army to ford the Chemung and commence its northward march. Three "friendly" braves, claiming to be Oneidas, appeared and offered to serve as scouts. Sullivan personally accepted the volunteers, praising his luck.

"Senecas," Many Summers muttered.

Without a word, John turned and entered the wood line. Traveling fast, John and Many Summers left the army and its new scouts behind. John assumed that by placing himself between the army and the Iroquois on the upper reaches of the Chemung he would soon meet the three "Oneida scouts" on their return trip north racing to report to Joseph Brant. It would be easier to dispose of them then than to wait to argue with Sullivan about his naiveté in hiring them in the first place. Two days later they ambushed the "Oneida scouts" as they trotted northward.

John estimated it would take the army three days to cross the difficult country between Fort Sullivan, as the new structure at Tioga had been dubbed, and the Indian village at Newtown, a distance of some twelve miles. After giving the matter much thought, John concluded that if he were Joseph Brant he would attempt to ambush the army some place in the area near where John and Many Summers had abandoned their birch canoe on their first scouting trip. If the army marched along the eastern shore of the river, where the going was easier, the spot where the valley squeezed between the river bed and the sharp foothills would funnel the invaders into a killing field. Surprise would be important, so the Indians would lull the army into relaxation by deserting the area between Tioga and Newtown. Then, on this southern tier of Iroquois land, their ambush could slaughter the invaders and turn them away from the rich lands with their ripening crops. Joseph Brant knew as well as the Americans that the Iroquois would need the land's fruit if they were to survive the harsh northern winter. This had been an eternal truth for Brant's people for centuries.

Sullivan exercised all of his painfully acquired military skill in deploying his troops. He assigned Brigadier General Edward Hand, "Scotch Willie," and his brigade to march in front, Brigadier General William Maxwell and his brigade to his left flank, and Brigadier General Enoch Poor to his right. Clinton and his men guarded the rear with Colonel Thomas Proctor and his artillery in the much coveted, protected center. As John had anticipated, the army covered only four miles the first day.

While the army camped and rested tired feet and muscles after its first day of march, John and his companion studied the Chemung Valley at Newtown from an escarpment on a high foothill overlooking the river. Below them, they could see the campfires of a large Indian force. Unbeknownst to them, Colonel Butler with ranger reinforcements had joined his son and Joseph Brant to assess the situation. Iroquois scouts reported accurately on Sullivan's army's advance. They estimated the invaders to number at least three thousand troops. Indian spies had learned the names of some of the commanders, and Butler recognized that all were seasoned leaders. He concluded with dismay that Washington had assigned some of his best commanders and most experienced troops to assist the hapless Sullivan. The Indians had not detected a militia unit among them. This indeed was bad news. At one of the council campfires that John and Many Summers watched, Colonel Butler conveyed his views to his Indian allies. In addition to the Mohawk War Chief, Joseph Brant, Black Snake, Sayenqueraghta, Red Jacket, Little Billy and others listened along with Butler's son Walter and other rangers as Major Butler spoke.

"General Haldimand at Niagara does not believe the Americans have sent such a large force," Butler began honestly.

"Then let him fight them," Joseph Brant growled. He owed much to the English, but his first loyalty was to his tribe.

"But they are in our lands and are burning our crops," one of the Delaware who lived near Newtown complained.

"Our scouts report they are too strong," Butler continued.

"But we must fight them," the Delaware insisted. The Senecas whose land lay in the army's path muttered.

"I agree," Butler persisted, "but they are too strong for us to battle. We must attack their heels from the rocks and trees as they march, fight as we know how, and nibble until they grow tired."

"Meanwhile, they destroy our crops and burn our villages," Red Jacket said sourly. Blacksnake and other Senecas growled agreement.

Major Butler soberly studied his companions. His rangers, when combined with those of his son, numbered about two hundred, all tough, experienced, well armed frontiersmen. The rangers had discreetly counted the Indians; Butler estimated that all the tribes represented had no more than six hundred braves at Newtown, Chuknut the Indians called it. To them, this was a sizable force, but Butler knew they could not confront the much larger American army head on. This posed a dilemma. For the first time the Indians were fighting on and for their own land; they were accustomed to striking settler homes on the white man's turf, hitting and running. Their strength came from stealth and surprise, but Washington had accepted the challenge. If the Indians adopted their usual tactics, they would leave their crops and villages to be destroyed by the invaders. This was what the Iroquois war chiefs had difficulty accepting.

The discussion went on for hours, and finally Major Butler realized he had lost the argument. When the Senecas and Delawares repeated their insistence on a fixed battle with the Americans, Major Butler agreed. One of the local Delaware immediately described a spot that was ideal for ambush and the Seneca concurred. Major Butler promised to meet them at dawn to survey the site and to deploy their forces.

The next morning, as John and his companion watched, Major Butler, his son and several rangers, Joseph Brant, Red Jacket, Blacksnake and other Iroquois chieftains surveyed a ridgeline below their hiding place. The ridge, which was about a half mile long, overlooked a plain that ended in a narrow pass at the edge of the river. Looking south, John concluded the Indians were selecting their ambush site and had done well. Sullivan's forces would be squeezed between the river and the foothills at this point. Sullivan's weary soldiers would undoubtedly take the path of least resistance and would be drawn with their heavy supply wagons and artillery to the Chemung's edge where the Indians on the ridge could decimate them at will, if surprised.

As John watched, the Indians, assisted by the Rangers, began doing something John had never seen savages try before.

They cut logs and constructed ambuscades to block the army's path. They appeared to be planning the use of a blocking force to trap the army in the ambush area. Usually, Indians relied on nature, trees and rocks, for temporary fortifications, but under the direction of the rangers were this time preparing for an extended fixed battle. John, aware of the army's slow movement, calculated he had time to study the Indian preparations before sounding the alert. All day, he watched. The Indians and rangers worked hard and quickly. After building their log barriers, they cut saplings and shrubs, which they placed in front to conceal them from the enemy.

Major Butler and Joseph Brant met alone and decided on the deployment of their forces. A large force of Mohawk and Senecas, the most war minded tribes of the Six Nations, were assigned to the ridgeline on the left. They would wait quietly until the Americans entered the trap and encountered the blocking force. At the appropriate moment, they would reveal themselves and charge down the hill shrieking their blood curdling war cries and panic the Americans caught between the river, the blocking force and the red tide from the hill. Joseph Brant with his most trusted braves and about sixty rangers under a white captain commanded the ambuscades. They were to repel the initial defensive attack of the American vanguard long enough for the army to stack upon itself and prepare for their surprised slaughter from the hill. Major Butler joined the Indians on the hill and named his son to command the remaining rangers who were to serve as a reserve waiting to reinforcement any point in the Indian line that weakened.

Late in the afternoon, the Indians completed their preparations and manned their positions. As John and his companion silently watched, Many Summers shook his head in disapproval. The Iroquois were violating every tenet of warfare that he had been taught as a young man. They were going to try and fight a white man's battle, and Many Summers knew they would lose. He nodded his head in silent approval of his own choice. He had selected well. The white man's army would win the battle.

As dusk fell, the Indians and rangers withdrew from their ambush positions. They gathered along the riverbank and soon many campfires dotted the horizons and sent long smoke trails skyward. As they prepared their food, they arrogantly signaled their presence to any watchers.

Finally, John decided the time had come to withdraw and alert General Sullivan and his army. John directed Many Summers to remain in place and to continue to watch. John planned to return after making his report and ordered the Indian to miss nothing.

John traveled quickly along the ridgeline, avoiding the river paths. From a distance he observed the flicker of Indian campfires and circled the advance war parties cautiously. He arrived at Sullivan's camp some four rugged miles from the ambush site at daybreak. He surprised a sleepy guard and obtained directions to the general's tent. John quickly described the Indian plans for the anxious general, helped himself to several strips of jerky then retreated to the forest. Behind him, Sullivan hastily summoned his senior officers to council and related John's report of ambush.

The army required two hours to break camp. Aware that they were surrounded by Indian scouts, they made no secret of their preparations. Finally, at ten o'clock General Hand's advance party resumed its march. The troops, now briefed on the Indian presence and the awaiting ambush, proceeded cautiously. The army's other elements assumed their usual positions with Sullivan, his headquarters staff and the artillery snugly tucked in the protected center. Caution impeded progress, and at nightfall the army halted, this time about one mile down river from the ambush site. Sullivan was tempted to send out scouts to verify John's information, but decided this might alert the Indians that they had lost surprise. After much consultation, Sullivan accepted his generals' advice—rely on Washington's favorite frontiersman. If the battle were lost, they would have a convenient scapegoat.

Below Newtown, the Indians waited behind their barricades and on the hill. The day was hot, and the Indian tempers cooled with the boredom. Their scouts reported on the slow progress of the American army, but that did not stem their impatience. Late in the afternoon, the leaves on the saplings and bushes that had so artfully concealed their ambuscades began to dry and curl in the spiteful heat of the burning day. Finally, the sun set, the American army camped, and the Indians retreated to their campfires. John and his companion patiently watched.

During the day, John had briefly glimpsed Joseph Brant; the man's sharp spined nose was impossible to miss. John waited for Brant's two personal bodyguards, the Massawomie sons of Red Eye, Red Knife and Three Scalps, to appear, but he watched in vain. John was sure that if Brant commanded the ambush, the Massawomie would not be far from his side, and John vowed to complete his revenge on Red Eye's seed during the coming battle.

By daybreak, the Indians were back in ambush. The army, aware of the enemy's proximity, hastened its preparations and set off in its usual formation by nine o'clock. As an added precaution, Sullivan deployed teams of Morgan's frontier scouts with their murderous long rifles in the van. Before long, the Virginians encountered several Indian scouts and exchanged fire with them. The Indians retreated. Within an hour, Morgan's scouts spotted the mottled leaves of the Indian fortifications. The dry and curled leaves marked the ambush point as clearly as if it had been lined with flags. The scouts and General Hand paused to wait for the main forces to move into position. Here and there, Indians emerged from their fortifications, stayed exposed long enough to attract fire from the long rifles, then darted back into hiding. John, watching from his concealed vantage point, assumed the Indians were trying to entice the army to chase them, giving the ambushers the opportunity to spring their trap.

Sullivan cautiously moved his force into position. He set up a blocking force to his left along the river and in his center with the artillery sited about three hundred yards from the Indian fortifications. To his right, along the ridgeline, Sullivan deployed both Poor's and Clinton's brigades. With Poor in the lead, these two forces were ordered to flank the enemy's left where the Rangers and a few English soldiers were concealed along the ridge hoping to provide the killing fire after the Indians halted the Americans to their front. After waiting for the flanking brigades to move into position, about three o'clock Sullivan ordered the artillery to open fire.

John with Many Summers at his side watched as the two sides deployed. Before a shot was fired, he decided the outcome of the battle was foreordained by the American superiority, its tactical movements and the natural inclinations of the enemy. John, determined to fulfill his personal mission, glanced at Many Summers, raised a hand to signal him to remain in place, then rose and moved swiftly to the northwest, deliberately circling the rear of the Indian defense lines. He assumed the Indians would not hold their positions and as soon as they came under heavy fire would retreat.

The crash of the artillery startled the waiting Iroquois. When the balls began to land to their rear, they immediately assumed they had been flanked and the Americans had them surrounded. A few blindly fired their new rifles from their hiding places, but most turned and charged to their rear through the fearsome exploding balls. On the ridge, Major Butler and his Rangers watched the panicking Indians and cursed. General Poor's flanking brigade had encountered difficult terrain and was not yet in place. As soon as the artillery had commenced, Poor ordered his men to attack. Major Butler was meeting in a hastily summoned battlefield conference with his son, Captain Butler, Joseph Brant, the Mohawk war chief, and several of his lieutenants to decide how to stem the Indian retreat when Poor's brigade burst from the woods on the Ranger's left rear.

"This battle's lost," Butler declared. "Let's get out of here and rally at the lake," he ordered, referring to the southern end of Cayuga where John had witnessed the pre-battle conference.

Without a word, Joseph Brant whirled and began trotting down the hill to the northwest. His faithful Massawomie bodyguards, Red Knife and Three Scalps immediately joined him. Before they reached the lower woodline, about twenty fierce Mohawk braves rallied about them.

John watched from the Indian rear as Brant and his braves split from Butler and his Rangers. With Butler in the lead, the Rangers formed ranks and defiantly quick marched past John's hiding place and disappeared to the north. John ignored the rangers and his exposed position in the midst of the crumbling Indian lines and watched Brant and his party as it quickly crossed through the lines of fleeing Indians who were trotting up the path toward the Seneca village some ten miles upriver.

John, at first puzzled by Brant's diagonal route, suddenly realized the group's objective. They were heading towards the Chemung. Brant knew that Sullivan's army was afoot and had wisely concealed canoes on the riverbank for use if needed for retreat or more optimistically a flanking movement.

John, deciding that he could move more quickly by assuming the pose of a separated Butler ranger, stood erect and began trotting downhill in the direction of the path along the river that he and Many Summers had traversed with the Seneca war party on their original scout of the area. John's route crossed that of several fleeing braves. He ignored them and they him. It was obviously every man for himself. Nevertheless, John remained fully alert. He tried to track the progress of Brant's party, remain on guard for an unanticipated Indian attack against the lone white man, and at the same time quickly reach the path which he intended to follow along the river to a point where he could intercept Brant.

It took John ten minutes to reach the path. He paused briefly and watched as individual Indians trotted past, each intent on his own survival. The running braves concentrated on their escape and did not pause to study the lone ranger who stood by the trail. John hesitated only long enough to locate the Mohawk chief and his small band. They had reached the river, were now in the canoes and paddling vigorously upstream. John waited for a Seneca brave to pass. To John's surprise, the brave grunted recognition. It was one of the braves from the Chemung village where John and his companion had spent their first night in Seneca territory. The brave obviously assumed that John too was retreating from battle. John fell in line behind the Seneca and began running. He had covered only a few paces when he heard the sound of another person darting through the underbrush on his right. John stopped and turned aiming his rifle at the sound. Many Summers, who had ignored John's signal to wait, appeared, brushed past John's rifle and began trotting along the path after the fleeing Seneca. Without a word, John followed Many Summers. John had given the Indian his chance; now, he would use him to deflect any unwanted questions about his presence among the fleeing Iroquois.

Behind him, Sullivan's jubilant army consolidated its victory. The excited American troops occupied the Indian fortifications and searched the battlefield for Indian dead and wounded to scalp and loot. Sullivan ordered his brigades to halt in place and establish defensive positions. A cautious man, he was determined to rest his troops and regroup his force before continuing his march. The enemy had broken and run, and Sullivan wanted to savor his first major victory. Initial reports indicated that casualties had been light. Three men had been killed, all in the flanking force, and several wounded. Sullivan had no idea how many Indians had been killed; he suspected that most had fled before confronting his army's fire, but he ordered his aide to survey the enemy dead.

Many Summers did not know what his white companion had in mind, but he had his suspicions. He had watched while John tracked Joseph Brant and his Massawomee companions retreat to the river. He recalled the look of hatred on John's face and how close he had come to firing at Brant while they watched the council fires at Cayuga. Many Summers assumed his companion intended to take advantage of the confusion of retreat to ambush Brant. The idea did not trouble him. Many Summers had long stopped caring how the white man and war leaders of the Iroquois killed each other. Many Summers did not consider the Mohawk half son of the white man a fitting leader for his tribe, the Oneidas, but realized they had no choice but follow whoever the war loving Mohawks chose.

John followed many Summers along the trail for about an hour to a spot not far from the Seneca village on the Chemung. There, John halted and stepped off the trail and made his way to the river. There was no sign of Brant and his canoes in either direction. Many Summers, who had also stopped when he noticed the absence of the sound of John's padding moccasins, joined John at the river. In the distance, John could see the Seneca village. Confusion reigned. Many of the fleeing Indians did not pause; they continued north and west. John watched as squaws and children hurried about gathering what possessions they could before joining the trek towards the lake country.

"Senecas fear white man. Leave village," Many Summers grunted.

John nodded and turned away from the village to study the river again. It was still empty. John signaled that Many Summers should remain and hurried to the riverbank. Without pause, he leaped from the high incline to the rocky edge that skirted the water. He jumped into the water and began wading towards the opposite shore about fifty feet away. The water rose to his knees, his waist, and then his shoulders. John held his rifle and powder horn high over his head. The current was strong and pushed him downstream as he crossed. Within minutes he was on the opposite shore. He climbed the bank, noted he had reached a point where the river angled eastwards and that he had a clear view of the approach from the south. He lowered himself into the high grass on the slope above the water and disappeared from sight.

While he waited, John emptied the powder and ball from his rifle. He replaced it with fresh powder from his horn, dropped the ball back down the barrel, inserted a wad and rammed the charge home with the rod that he carried attached to the underside of his rifle. He cocked the gun, test sighted on a tree on the opposite bank and then studied the river.

He heard the working Indians before he saw the canoes. The sounds of paddles striking water and of men grunting as they worked alerted him seconds before the small fleet of canoes rounded the river bend. Then, the first canoe appeared. Red Knife and Three Scalps led the way. The second canoe had a fierce looking Mohawk in the bow and Joseph Brant in the stern. Behind them, at least ten canoes followed; all moving swiftly.

John estimated he would have two maybe three shots before the Indians reacted effectively. He could reload his rifle in thirty seconds. He planned on two reloads before the braves beached their canoes on one shore or the other. He estimated the Massawomie would come directly at him, and Brant would turn to the far shore for safety. The others, he could not predict. After the third shot, John knew he had to run. Twenty Mohawk braves were too many for one man to handle. For that reason, he had selected the southern shore. He doubted that even angry Mohawks would pursue him back in the direction of Sullivan's army.

If Brant had been in the lead canoe, John would have targeted him first, but he was in the second canoe, some ten yards behind Red Knife and Three Scalps. John aimed at Three Scalps who sat in the stern. John knew Red Knife in the bow would have difficulty controlling the canoe alone in the panic that followed John's first shot. He placed his sight directly on the ridge of the ragged scar that marked Three Scalps' face. John regretted that Red Eye's oldest son would never know who had killed him. John would have preferred to save the two Massawomies for his knife, but he instinctively knew he had to take his opportunity when it presented itself. He considered himself lucky to have found these two old enemies again.

John waited until the canoe was about forty yards from his place of concealment. He took a deep breath, held it, then squeezed the trigger. The hammer fell on the pan, the powder ignited with a loud clap and a puff of smoke rose divulging John's hiding place.

The side of Three Scalps' head exploded, splattering bone, blood and tissue for several feet in the direction of the opposite bank. The headless torso momentary sat erect in the back of the canoe before slowly toppling into the bloody water.

The canoe careened toward the left, and Red Knife found himself facing the bank over which hung the small cloud of white smoke from John's rifle. Red Knife had been in the midst of a deep paddle stroke on the opposite side of the canoe when John had fired and the momentum of his push had swung the canoe wildly out of control the moment the ball drove Red Knife's brother's lifeless body into the water.

John did not pause to study the scene below him. He poured powder methodically into the pan, added more into the barrel of the rifle, dropped in the ball and the wad and tamped them home. When he turned back towards the river, he saw Red Knife glaring directly at him no more than twenty yards away. The Indian had dropped his paddle and was raising his rifle towards John's patch of weeds. John calmly sighted the tip of Red Knife's beaked nose, took a deep breath and squeezed the trigger.

Again, the long rifle barked, a white cloud rose, and this time Red Knife's face disintegrated. John paused long enough to survey the river in front of him. Red Knife had been blown backward into his canoe which was drifting drift southward with the current. The second canoe, John's new target, had already turned and was only yards from the opposite bank. John swore. He recognized he would not have time to reload his rifle before Joseph Brant found refuge in the tree line. John glanced at the following canoes. The first two immediately behind Brant had turned toward John, and the Mohawk braves were paddling fiercely to reach the bank to attack the ambush. Some of the following canoes had turned towards Brant and the last four were already beaching some forty yards from John. John grasped his empty rifle, leaped to his feet and crouched as he ran south towards Sullivan's army.

Following the battle at Newtown, Sullivan delayed while his men destroyed the few longhouses they found in the vicinity and burned fields of corn then resumed his march. The Indians, having tasted battlefield conflict, fled in advance of Sullivan's pursuing army. At the village on the Chemung some ten miles from Newtown where John and Many Summers had paused, Sullivan again waited while his troops burned the long houses and destroyed the vast flat fields of crops. Here, Sullivan sent a scout force west along the Chemung to a place the Indians called Big Flats. There, the troops again encountered deserted long houses and rich fields of maize, tobacco and corn. General Sullivan led his main force northwards determined to pursue the retreating Indians into the heart of the their lake country. Sullivan's troops, flushed with victory, anxiously looked forward to further encounters, but they had to content themselves with the empty long houses, ripe fields and occasional small war parties.

John, after reporting to Sullivan at Newtown, separated from the army and traveled northward alone. He reluctantly admitted to himself that he would like to rejoin Many Summers who he had left behind after his personal ambush of Brant on the Chemung. He and the old Indian had never talked much, but John felt a sense of loss as he recrossed the southern New York foothills. He never again encountered Many Summers and subsequently often wondered what had happened to the helpful old man.

Recognizing that Sullivan could anticipate an easy campaign, John dedicated himself to one personal objective: he planned to track down Joseph Brant and kill him before he could rally his warriors and take revenge on defenseless settlers for his loss of face at Newtown. John recognized that as long as Brant lived, life for settlers in the Mohawk Valley would be a constant purgatory.

By September 7th, Sullivan's army reached the northern end of the long lake of the Senecas. At Kanadesaga (Geneva), Sullivan paused long enough to dispatch a detachment of four hundred men eastward towards a second lake, Cayuga. Their instructions were simple: destroy all villages and crops in their path and make their way east then south back to Chemung to rejoin the main army. Sullivan by then realized the Iroquois were determined to avoid battlefield confrontation, and Sullivan was equally resolved to destroy everything in his path that might ease the winter of starvation and discomfort that faced the Indians of central New York following his visit.

John, unable to locate Joseph Brant, conferred with Sullivan at Kanadesaga. The two men concluded that Brant had led his Mohawks back to the northeast to his tribe's heartland in the Mohawk Valley. Sullivan's orders called for him to march westward and take Niagara if he could. Since his supplies were running thin and his men operating on half rations, Sullivan realized Niagara was beyond his reach. Sullivan decided, however, to continue marching. Couriers had reported that Washington had already informed Congress that his campaign was a success, and Sullivan was determined to make the most of his opportunity.

On September 9th, the army turned towards Canandaigua. Four days later the army reached the westernmost of the so-called finger lakes, Conesus. There, Sullivan again paused while his troops rested and destroyed still more crops. Having decided to establish Genesee as his westernmost goal, Sullivan consulted John about the need for scouting the area immediately ahead. John, having obtained Sullivan's permission to back scout the area of the army's planned return march, including a brief sojourn into Mohawk territory to search for Joseph Brant, suggested a small army scout party. John doubted that many Indians waited to confront the armed force; they had already evacuated everything in its path. Sullivan agreed and chose Lieutenant Thomas Boyd of Morgan's Rangers to lead a group of three soldiers and two Oneidas to scout in advance of the army.

Boyd, an experienced frontiersman, was an ambitious young man, eager for glory. For some reason unknown to John and his commanding officers, the rash young man increased the size of his scout team to a force of over twenty men. Experienced scouts knew that four men could navigate the wilderness undetected, but larger bodies invited attention. Boyd should have kept his group limited to four or increased it to several hundred, a unit that could defend itself if detected. Instead, he unwisely commanded a unit that could neither rely on stealth nor fight its way clear of difficulty.

Unbeknownst to Sullivan, John and Lieutenant Boyd, John Butler, Joseph Brant and several Iroquois leaders planned to ambush Sullivan en route to Genessee and revenge themselves for their humiliating defeat at Newtown. Some five hundred Indians under their command set up their ambush and waited on the edge of a large swamp. Lieutenant Boyd and his oversized scout party stumbled into their vicinity. Their path led them through a small village where they discovered two of Brant's braves. Boyd's men fired first and killed one of the Indians; the other escaped and retreated into the forest to alert Butler and Brant's warriors of the scout team's presence. Boyd ordered four of his men to return to the main body of the army to report they had encountered two braves who could have been Iroquois scouts. Not long after they left Boyd, the four men spotted two more Indians in the woods. After hurried consultation, two of the men hurried on to alert Sullivan, and two returned to warn Boyd. Upon receipt of the news, the eager Boyd wanted to give chase, but the Oneida scout advised that the Iroquois might be trying to lure them into a trap. After much discussion, Boyd accepted the advice and decided discretion required they rejoin the army. They were within two miles of Sullivan's vanguard when they stumbled into the main ambush prepared by Brant and Butler.

Boyd's force stood no chance. Although his flankers escaped, the Lieutenant, several others and the Oneida guide were captured immediately. The angry Indians whose carefully laid ambush had been exposed killed all but Boyd and a man named Michael Parker. The soldiers were scalped and their dead bodies savagely mutilated. Major Butler intervened to save Boyd and Parker, both of whom he wished to interrogate. After briefly questioning Boyd, Butler sent him and Parker under Ranger guard to Genesee Castle where he intended to hold them until he could move them on to Niagara as living proof for the English general that an American army was north of the lake country.

En route, the angry Indians who accompanied them overpowered the rangers and took control of Parker and Boyd. The two hapless men lived long enough to undergo the most excruciating torture. The Indians beat them with tomahawks and ripped their clothes from their bodies. They then slashed and striped the naked, screaming men before methodically cutting off their ears, noses and fingers before turning their attention to their genitals. Boyd's stomach was cut open and his intestines pulled from his body and stuffed into his mouth to still his irritating screams for mercy. When this did not suffice to quiet him, they poked sharp sticks into each of his eyes then cut off his head. Strangely, they did not remove the dead men's' scalps. One savage explained to a ranger that the victims were treated thusly as sacrifices to the Iroquois God of War who needed atonement for the failures of his braves.

Butler, Brant, the Rangers and the braves withdrew from their ambush and retreated northward.

The next day Sullivan's advance guard discovered Boyd and Parker's bodies. The parts were buried with full military honors.

Sullivan continued to the Genesee River. After consulting his senior officers and appraising the condition of his men and supplies, Sullivan ordered the army to turn. He had halted sixty-six miles from his objective, Fort Niagara.

On September 15th, the army began to retrace it steps. At Cayuga, John rejoined the army after his fruitless search in the east and learned to his extreme chagrin and dismay that he had missed his prey. For once, he had erred, and the unlucky scout team had paid with their suffering.

John Butler and Joseph Brant retreated to Fort Niagara.

On September 24th, Sullivan's army paused about ten miles north of the Chemung. They slaughtered fifty of their packhorses. Later, some claimed the horses had been too weak to continue; others, with greater honesty, admitted the troops had needed food. Some of the soldiers placed the heads of the horses on each side of the trail forming a grotesque corridor lined with glassy eyed sentries who silently and accusingly monitored the army's long file as it continued southward. The later village of Horseheads thusly acquired its odd name.

The army reached Tioga on September 30th, Wyoming on October 7th, and Easton on October 15th. John terminated his military service at this point, purchased two horses and began his journey home, interrupted only by a brief stop in New Jersey to report to George Washington and his brother James.

Chapter 34
Pennsylvania, New Jersey, New York
Winter, 1779-80, Spring/Summer 1780

On December 23rd, 1779, General Benedict Arnold sat on a hard, straight chair behind a bare table in Norris' Tavern in Morristown and sourly contemplated the thirteen colonels, lieutenant colonels and brigadiers who composed his court martial. Major General Robert Howe of North Carolina presided. Despite his appeals to Washington pleading for a speedy trial, the proceeding had been postponed while the army responded to perceived threats from the English to break out of their bastion in New York. Finally, after both armies had settled down in winter quarters, Arnold faced his accusers on the eight charges trumped up by jealous Pennsylvania authorities.

While General Howe droned on with his lengthy briefing of the court, Arnold thought back on the months that had passed since he had relinquished his command of Philadelphia. In May, Arnold, piqued by anger at colonial authorities and dismayed by expenses being incurred by his new wife Peggy despite the fact he had no income, had dispatched the fool Stansbury with Arnold's overture to the English. He had reasoned that if the rebels did not respect the fighting spirit that Arnold had to offer the English would. General Clinton's aide's initial response, transmitted in a letter carried by Stansbury, had been promising. Arnold had immediately sat down and following Andre's detailed instructions had laboriously drafted a return letter in cipher using Bailey's Dictionary, twenty-first edition, and invisible ink. The arduous process had taken six hours. Arnold could still remember verbatim the first sentence:

"Our Friend Stansbury acquaints me that the proposals made by him in my name are agreeable to Sir Henry Clinton and that Sir Henry engages to answer my warmest Expectations for any services rendered."

Arnold had then attempted to whet the English appetite with a few tidbits of information about Washington and his army's plans for the summer.

Thoughts of that auspicious beginning made Arnold's nervous stomach growl. He glared straight-ahead trying to act as if nothing had happened. He ignored the tense looks that the junior members of the court cast in his direction as General Howe rambled on reading each charge word by tedious word.

Arnold's mind again wandered back to his approach to the English. The promising start had wavered into frustration. First, Stansbury and the other idiots who had been selected to convey the messages between Arnold and Andre, Clinton's aide, had allowed the invisible ink of one letter to become smeared by an inadvertent soaking. Then, the English, obviously distrusting Arnold's motives, had decided to quibble. They had wanted to learn precisely what they were buying before they would make the firm commitments on reward that Arnold needed. They apparently had been put off by the fact that Arnold had resigned his Philadelphia commission and faced court martial.

Suspecting that the English would not meet his demands until he cleared his name, Arnold had pressed Washington for a speedy trial, and all he had gotten in return for two serious battle wounds and hard service was a six month delay. Despite the uncertainty, Arnold informed the English of Washington's plan to send Sullivan to punish the Iroquois. At the end of July Andre had the courtesy to thank him for his information but then demanded a report on West Point. The one satisfying point conveyed in Andre's curt letter had been the suggestion that the two meet. Arnold had already reached that conclusion himself. Unfortunately, he had had to wait for the court martial nonsense to resolve itself. Then, he surmised, with his name cleared and a new command in hand, the English would stumble over their boots in their enthusiasm to meet his every demand.

Arnold in irritation glared at his opposition, John Laurance. The Judge Advocate General of the Army was himself directing Arnold's prosecution. In defiance, Arnold had decided to represent himself. The prosecution planned to call seven witnesses including Arnold's aide, David Franks, Washington's scut man, Alexander Hamilton, John Mitchell, the army's deputy quartermaster general, and his clerk.

Finally, General Howe completed his instructions and turned the proceedings over to John Laurance, the prosecutor. Laurance, an efficient man, confined his attention to four charges that the Congress had directed be considered by the court. Arnold listened with dispassion as the witnesses testified. He had no intention of limiting his defense to only four of eight charges. He was determined to clear his name. The trial droned tediously on. The court sat on the twenty-third and twenty-fourth then adjourned for Christmas. On the twenty-eighth they began again, worked for three days, then to the frustrated Arnold's despair, adjourned to celebrate the New Year. Arnold privately cursed all involved. He denounced the fools who had made him wait for almost a year before they selected the December holidays to torture him with the nagging complaints of his enemies and their lackeys.

Then, the court did not reconvene. The army could not free its deputy quartermaster general to testify because of the press of his duties. Arnold could not imagine what they might be. Finally, Arnold appealed directly to Washington, and he ordered Mitchell to appear. On January 20th, the deputy quartermaster testified. The next day, Arnold presented his defense against all eight charges, ignoring the fact that he was only being tried for four. He began passionately:

"When the present necessary war against Great Britain commenced I was in easy circumstances and enjoyed a fair prospect of improving them. I was happy in domestic connections and blessed with a rising family who claimed my care and attention. The liberties of my country were in danger. The voice of my country called upon all her faithful sons to join her in her defense. With cheerfulness I obeyed the call. I sacrificed domestic ease and happiness to the service of my country, and in her service I have sacrificed a great part of a handsome fortune. I was one of the first that appeared in the field; and from that time to the present hour have not abandoned her service... ."

Arnold claimed he had issued the "Charming Nancy" pass solely to save the cargo for the people of the united colonies. He found laughable the charge that he had closed Philadelphia shops to citizens solely so he could shop himself. He described the charge that he had imposed menial duties on Pennsylvania soldiers as a ploy to alienate the militia from him. He denied he had arbitrarily abused power and did not deny that public wagons had been sent to transport private property, but he insisted he had always intended to pay the state for their use. To the Pennsylvania charge that he was disrespectful, Arnold asserted that no one had more respect for civilian authority that he himself. He found the charge that he favored Tories too ludicrous to consider but comment he did:

"... conscious of my own innocence and the unworthy methods taken to injure me, I can with boldness say to my persecutors in general, and to the chief of them in particular that in the hour of danger when the affairs of America wore a gloomy aspect, when our illustrious General was retreating through New Jersey with a handful of men, I did not propose to my associates basely to quit the General and sacrifice the cause of my country to my personal safety by going over to the enemy and making my peace."

The court president presented his summation on January 22nd, then adjourned for four days. The final verdict found Arnold guilty on two charges: he should not have issued the pass to the "Charming Nancy," and he had been imprudent and behaved improperly when he sent public wagons to collect privately owned goods whether he had intended to subsequently pay for their use or not. On these two charges, the court sentenced him to receive a reprimand from the Commander-in-Chief.

Three months later, on April 6th, General Washington issued the reprimand in the daily orders. Washington succinctly stated he would have been happier if the occasion called for him to commend Arnold who had done so much for his country; instead, Washington noted, he was obligated to declare that he considers General Arnold's conduct in the matter of the pass to have been reprehensible and in the affair of the wagons imprudent.

Although angered by the court's decision and Washington's mild reprimand, Arnold decided his personal plans, primarily the furtherance of his negotiations with the English, required him to obtain another command. Through intermediaries and directly Arnold petitioned Washington. The sympathetic commander-in-chief who still considered Arnold one of his best fighting generals assessed his options. Meanwhile, Arnold tried to reopen his negotiations with Clinton. Unfortunately for the dispirited officer, Clinton, accompanied by his Chief of Intelligence, John Andre, now a major and the army's Adjutant General, had departed for the Carolinas where the English hoped to make a southern strategy a major focus of their 1780 summer campaign.

Arnold's new appeal was received by Lieutenant General Wilhelm von Knyphausen who commanded in New York during Clinton's absence. Arnold repeated his offer to assume an American command and promised that in doing so he would respond to English instructions in return for the security he had previously requested. In addition Arnold asked for the immediate transmittal of a small amount of "ready money." When he received this communication in late May, Knyphausen responded that he did not have the authority to reply but promised to communicate the matter to Sir Henry's attention at the first opportunity. In the meantime, he authorized the reimbursement of any "trifling charges" that might develop. In reporting to Clinton, Knyphausen summarized the state of negotiations: Arnold has agreed to take a "treacherous" command in the American army in return for the following: reimbursement for the loss of his private fortune, 5,000 pounds sterling; the debt due him by the community, 5,000 pounds sterling; to be provided with command of a newly raised battalion; and to be supplied with money from time to time as circumstances require.

In June Arnold visited Washington at Morristown then continued on to his home in Connecticut. On June 20th, he informed the English that he expected to be given command of West Point. On his return trip from Connecticut, Arnold visited West Point, which was then commanded by General Robert Howe who had distinguished himself as a brigade commander during Sullivan's campaign against the Iroquois. Howe graciously allowed Arnold to inspect the post. Arnold later reported to the English that he had been greatly disappointed by what he had found; the Point had only 1,500 troops, less than half the number required to man the fortifications, and in possession of provisions adequate for less than ten days. From Howe he learned that "two or three" individuals the English had hired as spies to report on West Point were actually controlled by the Americans. Arnold did not find this tale of double agents as amusing as Howe did. Arnold later asked the English for 1,125 pounds to defray the costs of the trip.

Clinton and Andre arrived back in New York on June 17th. Both men were buoyed by the capture of Charleston, South Carolina, an English victory that both men believed would end the rebellion in the Carolinas. Clinton, the English Commander-in-Chief, was now prepared to concentrate on achieving a comparable English sweep in the north. A victory there would in Clinton's estimation end the rebellion. Recent reports had indicated that Washington's army was in a mutinous mood. Prospects looked good; Arnold's offer to betray West Point seemed to promise the chance for an easy victory that would give Clinton what he wanted. The one cloud on the horizon appeared in a report from Arnold. Washington expected the French fleet to arrive shortly off Newport. This worried Clinton; the French ships could alter the balance and take away from the English their one decided advantage, control of the seas. Without supplies and reinforcements from home, not to mention tactical flexibility granted by sail mobility, Clinton could be isolated and defeated. This prospect whetted his desire for the early victory that Arnold seemed to offer.

In July, an impatient Arnold, now back in Philadelphia and waiting for a response to his recent request for confirmation of his demands, penned another letter. This time he demanded ten thousand pounds for his debts and ten thousand for his effort. He also requested a personal conference with Andre. He put his demands in cipher and concealed them in invisible ink and dispatched his message to New York with a nervous Stansbury. The next day, July 12th, Arnold wrote a second message. He had forgotten to include the phrase "I expect soon to command West Point" and to demand immediate expense money of two hundred guineas.

The day after he dispatched his second letter, Arnold received a letter from Clinton. Unfortunately, it had been written before the receipt of Arnold's July letters containing demands for specific sums. Clinton thanked Arnold for his recent information, expressed hope that he obtained the West Point command and promised that they could work out matters to their mutual satisfaction. The response irritated the frustrated Arnold; Clinton made no mention of specific sums. He decided a meeting with Andre was imperative. Communicating by cipher in messages that frequently went astray was totally unsatisfactory not to mention risky. Arnold was no novice; he knew he had many enemies and that it would take only one intercepted letter to seal his fate.

Arnold's letters reached Andre in New York on July 23rd. He responded immediately. He promised that if West Point fell into English hands in response to Arnold's actions, the English would pay Arnold twenty thousand pounds. He hedged in promising an annuity but assured Arnold he would be paid for expenses. He wrote that two hundred pounds had been advanced to Stansbury for Arnold's use and advised that an additional three hundred had been set aside in Arnold's account. He agreed that he and Arnold should meet.

Andre's response satisfied Arnold. He decided to concentrate on obtaining his appointment as commander of West Point and then he would exact a higher price for his betrayal from the English.

In New York, Andre began to worry. After the first excitement over Arnold's offer to betray his country, Andre's handling of the potential spy had become routine. He had been bored with the tedious negotiations by cipher and unreliable courier and had begun to suspect that the discredited officer who faced court martial would become nothing more than a demanding problem. Arnold's January hand slapping by the court martial and renewed prospects for reinstatement in commanded rekindled Andre's interest. His involvement in the Carolina campaign interrupted his concentration on New York centered espionage operations, but his July return and Arnold's report that his appointment as commander of the key rebel defense bastion at West Point stimulated Andre's passion for the operation. The increased interest combined with the series of letters from Arnold enhanced General Clinton's concern about Arnold's security. When General Clinton fretted, Andre worried.

Deciding that he had to do something to improve both the quality and the security of his courier system to Arnold, Andre began to consider his options. Stansbury, Odell, Peggy Arnold and possibly others already were privy to Arnold's planned treachery. Andre did not worry about the British officers who of necessity had been informed of the negotiations, but uncontrolled Americans posed problems. Several days passed, and Andre failed to identify any new means of communication.

He could meet with Arnold once, but the passage through enemy lines would be risky and could not be relied upon for regular transmittal of information. If the principles could not meet, written messages in cipher and invisible ink would have to suffice, but the movement of the letters remained a problem. Andre needed to find a new courier, more than one if possible. Stansbury and Odell had outlived their usefulness. Both men had been identified as English sycophants and were probably suspected by the rebels as English agents. If Arnold were compromised by one of these two men, London and General Clinton would hold Andre responsible and his promising career would be blighted. He would lose his titles and be assigned to a menial position with one of the regiments.

York Allen was seated at his customary corner seat in the Red Fox and was addressing his second mug of dark ale when John Andre appeared at the room entrance and peered into the gloom. The dinnertime crowd was unusually sparse; York attributed it to the intense August heat. Even the Tories from Virginia and points south were complaining that home was never like this. York tended to believe their memories were short, but he had to agree that the dog days of August in the city were stifling. Even the harbor refused to cooperate; the cooling sea breeze that usually appeared in the late afternoon had occupied itself elsewhere for the past week.

York waved a languid hand at his English friend. Catching the gesture, Andre nodded and worked his way through the tables towards York's corner. As he watched the amiable English officer pause to speak to an acquaintance, Allen mused for what had to be the hundredth time about the difference between John Andre and old Sir Richard Howe's aide, Ambrose Serle. York had grown to despise the sour, conceited Serle. He thought Serle should have been a churchman; he had spent as much time talking about the deity as any preacher. When the Howe brothers had departed and taken Serle with them, York had been relieved. Despite his worry about what would happen to the *Gazette* when Serle, the newspaper's chief sponsor, the editor if the truth were told, departed, York had cheered when the event actually occurred. If need be, he had been prepared to cross through the lines and take his rightful place at James Satterfield's side. York had reckoned he knew more about the spy business now than his chief sponsor.

Despite the fact that Gaines, the paper's ostensible owner, had not reappeared and Serle had not introduced his replacement, Allen had kept the paper operating in the months of indecision, as York had called them. Without the monthly English subsidy, the *Gazette* did not earn enough for York to pay himself a salary, but revenues from sales to anxious Tories who had continued to assume the newspaper was still the official English voice had kept it afloat. York had not minded; he enjoyed working as a newspaperman, collecting news and deciding what would appear in the paper. He had hated being Serle's flunky. If it had not been for his second job as Washington's spy, he would have fled New York without a flicker of remorse.

"York," Andre spoke warmly, sincerely conveying his delight at finding his friend at the Red Fox. Andre, an extrovert, patted York affectionately on the back. "Mind if I join you?" He asked, sitting himself heavily opposite Allen.

"Major," Allen welcomed the Englishman, trying to tint his inflection with a light sarcasm.

To Allen's surprise, John Andre, then a captain and a newly appointed aide to General Clinton, had appeared at the *Gazette* about two months after Serle's departure. He had reintroduced himself—the two had previously met in Philadelphia—and had explained that he had been selected to replace Serle as the military's control for the newspaper. York Allen had immediately assumed he had acquired a new boss, but the passage of time had proved him wrong. Andre, personable where Serle had been unpleasant, had been more interested in resuming the young men about town relationship that he had enjoyed briefly with York in Philadelphia than he had been in managing the newspaper.

He had left that job completely up to York. Andre had restarted the monthly subsidy and to brief York on the desired propaganda lines as well as planting an occasional fabricated story, but other than that he had not interfered. York did not like the reputation he had acquired as the English lap dog, but he had long previously persuaded himself he could live with the derogatory sobriquet for a while. He continued to believe that when the war ended Washington would divulge York's undercover service and publicly reward him with the medals the young man thought he rightly deserved.

"How did things go last night?" Andre asked, referring to the young lady York had escorted home from the Tory party the two young men had attended.

"Not so well," York answered. He had not been really interested. The girl had been young, barely sixteen, and preoccupied with her social background, Virginia aristocracy. She had let the handsome New Yorker escort her home, but she had no intention of dipping below her class. "She cut me at the door," York confessed.

"I thought so," Andre commiserated. At the time, he had thought York was squandering his limited charm. "These New York girls are nothing like the Philadelphia stock."

"Virginia Tories, either," York agreed.

Life in Philadelphia had been different. He assumed the excitement of the early war years had infected the Philadelphia girls. He still remembered the Shippen sisters, Peggy Chew and all their friends. Even the girls from patriot families had joined the gay festivities that had engulfed the young English officers of the occupying army. New York was different. The patriot girls had fled town with their parents, and the Tories were worried. After two years of futilely cultivating the English military conquerors, the Tories no longer expected a decisive end to the war that would let them return to reclaim their abandoned homes and to share the spoils of winning. Life in New York these days was sad. The pretty girls concentrated on the young English officers, obviously hoping to marry escape for themselves and their families.

"I hear the French fleet is heading for Newport," Andre changed the subject in that facile way he was prone to do.

"You would know better than I," York replied. He wanted to sip his ale and not discuss the war. That was work, and he wanted to relax. Sometimes he felt guilty about his relationship with Andre. York knew if he worked at it he could elicit much more information about English plans than he did, but he considered Andre a friend. Sometimes, he even forgot that John was now Chief of Intelligence for the English army in North America. When the thought did cross his mind, York was struck by the irony. He, a small time news collector for a minor New York newspaper, was a paid informant for the Chief of Intelligence for the American Army, James Satterfield, and at the same time was an employee and friend of the Chief of English Intelligence. He wondered if there was another person in the world in such a distinctive position.

"Clinton's worried," Andre confided.

York was not surprised by his friend's indiscretion. He considered York a loyal English citizen as well as friend and confidant. He frequently shared office gossip with York. Fortunately for Andre, he did a better job keeping his intelligence secrets to himself.

"Then Washington must be happy," York observed indifferently. An acute political observer despite his cynically indifferent exterior, York recognized that the arrival of a substantial French fleet could affect the outcome of the war.

"I have a problem," Andre changed directions abruptly again. His friend's apparent indifference to the fate of the rebel cause persuaded him to make a decision he had been pondering for several days. "Do you think you can help me out with a slight matter?"

"Sure," York said. "Female or monetary?" York recognized Andre's serious tone but decided to feign indifference.

"Female," Andre dissembled with a smile. "One of my old Philadelphia girl friends. She's married now, but we're still in touch."

"Do I know her?" York asked. The story sounded plausible. Andre had been one of the most popular and sought after English officers in Philadelphia. A handsome bachelor in his twenties with excellent prospects, Andre had attracted the fun loving young ladies like a clover field attracted bees. York had been delighted to share Andre's prosperity.

"Maybe, but don't ask," Andre laughed. "Her husband is a rebel officer without a sense of humor."

"Then why bother?" York asked seriously. "New York still has its opportunities. They just require a little more work."

"She's special. Don't worry. All I want to do is have her letters delivered to the *Gazette*. Like letters to the newspaper or something."

"That's no problem," York flicked his hand indifferently. "Two ales," he called to the passing barmaid. Since York and Andre were regulars, she nodded wearily, brushed an errant strand of hair from her forehead, and called to her husband, the owner of the Red Fox. "Draw two."

York was instantly alert. He had been in the spy business long enough to sense when someone was trying to use him. He did not resent Andre's casual sounding request. York used the young English officer whenever he could. It sounded like Andre was trying to set up a means for communicating with an English spy. Despite Andre's light attempt to dissemble, York suspected the English might have an officer in Washington's military in their employ. The news would be worth a report to Washington. Inwardly he smiled at the thought of James and Eric reading his message and groaning at the impossibility of identifying the English spy. It had to be someone of importance or Andre would not be handling the matter himself.

"I thought you would be reasonable," Andre laughed. "You can expect to receive an envelope in the next week or two."

"Who will bring it? How will I recognize it?"

"I don't know. A traveler. A refugee. A trader traveling under a flag of truce. Maybe a Tory relative. She will just take advantage of any opportunity."

"Is she nearby?"

"Not close. Maybe Philadelphia. Don't ask."

"How will I recognize the envelope?"

"She will seal it with purple wax and stamp it with the letter 'P.'"

"'P'? Could it be Peggy... ."

"Don't ask." John's face lost its good humor. "If you can't do what I ask, we'll forget it."

York raised his hands in feigned surrender and smiled. "All right. I won't ask."

"What's the special?" Andre asked, changing the subject abruptly.

"Boiled shoe," York laughed.

"Marinated in horseradish sauce?"

"My favorite," York smiled.

"Two specials," Andre called to the barmaid.

"And two more ales," York echoed.

Chapter 35
New Jersey, New York
Summer/Autumn, 1780

James sat in his headquarters office in Morristown and frowned dispiritedly at the pesky green fly that refused to land anywhere but on the hand that James was using as he tried to write his weekly letter to Vivian. James waved half-heartedly at the fly and tried to think of something to say. During the four years he had been separated from his wife, James calculated he had already described in infuriating detail every facet of his depressingly repetitive life. James missed Vivian and his family. They knew that. Vivian, who had spent the winter with James, had returned to Eastwind three and one half months ago. James estimated that she would return in late November after the army had again retreated to winter quarters. Half way, he wrote on the paper, meaning half way to Vivian's return. Certainly Vivian would not misunderstand his meaning. James had no idea when his "service in the needs of his country" would end; he knew Vivian would not think that. James missed Vivian, but he knew he was irrevocably losing something that he could never retrieve, Jason's young manhood and his grandson Buster's childhood. James had visited Alexandria three times since Buster's birth, and he had spent most of his time "mooning over that child," as Vivian disapprovingly put it. James could not help himself. Buster represented the next generation of Satterfields, the fourth since James' grandfather, Old Tom, had moved the family to the Short Hills of Loudoun.

"I wonder if Jason has ever taken Buster to the Short Hills?" James asked himself. The thought took hold, and James began to write, inspired to record even more advice for Vivian to pass along to Jason.

A brief knock on the open door interrupted James' concentration, and he looked up, unable to stifle the flash of irritation.

Major Eric Gray waited patiently in the doorway for James' invitation to enter. The young man had aged in his four years of service. Worry lines had appeared on his forehead to offset the still refreshing grin that the young man wore. James remembered when the maturing man, then a green ensign, had first appeared on the doorstep of the *Gazette* with his summons from Washington.

"May I enter? Sir?" Gray, despite their long association, still deferred to James. Now, he tempered his courtesy with a sardonic tint of humor, not dissimilar to that used by Vivian.

"Certainly," James replied, irritably flicking futilely at the fat green fly as he spoke. The insect had attempted to take advantage of James' momentary pause to explore the hand that held the quill. "Must you continue to wear that silly hat?" James asked, referring to the worn, black tricorn that Gray affected. James still wore his, but that was different. His was a replacement for one that had been given to him by Vivian when he had so indiscreetly begun his military career. He wondered, as he had many times before, if Eric and the others were mocking him by wearing identical hats.

"I have a message from New York that I think you must see," Eric replied, ignoring James' question about the hat as he always did.

"That doesn't surprise me," James declared. He could not count the number of times this very scene had been repeated. He held out his hand and waited for Eric to produce the developed report with the telltale brown lines of numbers that had been etched in invisible ink.

The green fly hovered, waiting for another opportunity.

"We have a spy in our midst," Eric said, handing the sheet of paper to James.

"Who doesn't?" James asked rhetorically, instinctively swatting at the fly with the message.

"Breeding flies?" Eric asked.

James ignored the silly question and quickly scanned the report. He began with the last number. "495." James recognized York Allen's identifying number. The professionalism that had developed over the years to mask their espionage operations continued to amaze him. They had been so amateurish when they had begun. James read the deciphered text quickly while his mind wandered. A sign of advancing age, he scolded himself. York Allen's words suddenly caught his full attention.

"Senior American officer is English spy."

"Who is it?" James asked Eric as soon as he finished those words.

"Read on," Eric replied. "He doesn't know."

"Andre has asked me to retrieve letters from old Philadelphia girl friend whose name is 'P'" Allen wrote.

"P... .?" James mouthed the words. "What in the hell does that mean?"

"He thinks maybe Peggy," Eric explained.

"Peggy who?" James demanded.

"Don't holler at me," Eric smiled good-naturedly. "He doesn't know. Of course Andre would not tell him. He let slip the fact that she is from Philadelphia and would seal her letters with purple wax and a 'P' cache."

"Peggy," James mused before reading further. He hated the deciphered messages with their barely legible script. Eric insisted on handling the decryption himself, and his writing was impossible.   "Andre was in Philadelphia with Howe."

"And he spent much time with the girls."

"Peggy Loring. Peggy Chew," James mused. "How many girls named Peggy are there in Philadelphia?" He asked rhetorically.

"Who are now married to senior American officers."

"Peggy Lor... ." James blurted before catching himself. "Don't say it," he snapped at Eric. "Don't say it."

"I wasn't saying it. You were," Eric laughed, recognizing that James had reached the same quick conclusion he had. General Benedict Arnold, one of Washington's favorites, had just been appointed commander of West Point, and he was married to a Philadelphia girl, the former Peggy Loring.

James irritably swatted again at the persistent fly and returned to the text. Allen expected to receive within the week his first message from the alleged girl friend who was in his opinion a British spy. James noted the young newsman had no proof, only his interpretation of chance remarks made by Clinton's Chief of Intelligence. James' first reaction was to ignore the report, but he immediately contradicted himself and concluded he could not. York Allen's previous information from Andre had checked out, and Allen's instincts had been proven correct time and again over the past four years.

"He doesn't have any solid information.. .." James began, thinking aloud.

"But he will soon. Once York gets on the trail... ."

"...He doesn't stop until he finds out what he wants to know," James finished Eric's thought. The two had worked so closely over the years they could almost read each other's minds. "If someone like... like that general..." James could not bring himself to speak Arnold's name.

"...Who commands a key fort and is in English pay. We could have a major problem," Eric again completed the thought.

"Some officers are very displeased with their treatment by the army and Congress..." James began again.

"...Some have even had to suffer through courts-martial that maligned their reputations," Eric observed.

"Do you want to discuss this matter with General Washington?" James asked. He was not anxious to deliver another disappointment to his friend; so many had fallen on the General's shoulders of late.

"I think it best if you do," Eric countered. Nobody liked to be the bearer of bad news.

"Come," James ordered. "We both will."

By mid-August Benedict Arnold had assumed command of West Point. The path to this post which both he and the English had coveted for him had been rocky. Despite the fact that in July he had assured Andre that West Point was his, he had almost lost it at the last minute. Arnold had visited Washington's head-quarters on the first of August and had been crestfallen to learn that the general orders for that day had announced that General Arnold would command the army's left wing during the pending action. He had been flattered that Washington had thought so much of his fighting abilities to assign him to such a key position, but the English wanted him to betray West Point. Arnold had visit-ed Washington and had embarrassed himself by having to plead for a lesser assignment by claiming that his still festering leg wound prevented his accept-ance of the more active assignment. A disappointed Washington had not hid his dismay over the fact that this fighting officer preferred a passive role, but he had finally acceded to Arnold's plea. On August 3rd, Arnold's orders were changed, and he had hurried to take command of West Point before Washington had a third thought.

On arrival Arnold had decided to take the Robinson House for his quarters. Colonel Beverley Robinson, son of an acting governor of Virginia and brother of a colonial treasurer, had been a childhood friend of George Washington. Following service in Canada in 1746, Robinson had married the daughter of a wealthy and prominent New Yorker. George Washington himself had once pur-sued his wife. After marriage, Robinson had contented himself with managing his wife's fortune and settling into New York's gentry. In the mid 1770's, Robinson had quietly sided with the Crown. He had lived serenely at his New York estate on the banks of the Hudson until 1777, when circumstances forced him to demonstrate his loyalties; he took refuge in New York City where he raised a regiment called the "Loyal Americans" who he later led into battle against his former friends and neighbors. The loyalist regiment composed of colonialists considered turncoats by the rebels was most profoundly hated by Washington's troops.

The Robinson House was located on the east bank of the Hudson opposite West Point. Arnold liked the house for its very isolation. Set on the mountain-side with only trees for neighbors, the house would be safe from English guns when the attack on West Point materialized. Peggy and her new child could live there without fear, whatever happened.

Now that he had attained his objective, Arnold waited anxiously for Peggy to join him. He knew she had left Philadelphia over a week previously, and he had sent detailed instructions to guide her journey. All he could do now was immerse himself in duty and wait for her arrival. Arnold was not bored; he had much to do. He had already summoned his staff. Major Franks who had been his aide in Philadelphia had joined him at the Point and had written to Lieutenant Colonel Varick at Hackensack advising him of the general's desire that Varick serve as his secretary. Franks was already busy acquiring the household furniture and sup-plies that Peggy would require to establish their temporary home.

On August 24th Arnold had finally received Clinton's reply to his July letters which clearly spelled out Arnold's demands. The message had taken so long because it had to take a circuitous route passing through Peggy's hands in

Philadelphia. When it finally reached Arnold, he had sighed with relief. All now appeared in order. The British had not accepted his demand for an annual stipend to follow his defection, but Arnold had no doubt that a brief meeting with Andre would solve this problem. All he had to do was arrange this meeting, obtain the needed English concessions then plan the betrayal of the fort on which rebel control of the Hudson depended.

George Washington did not know what to make of York Allen's report about possible betrayal by a senior officer of his army. He found the speculation about the officer's identity tenuous, but at the same time he could not ignore it. West Point was too important to his army's control of the Hudson. To lose it would revive the old Howe strategy designed to divide the colonies by linking up with British forces in Canada. Washington recognized that such a strategic loss in the north following the devastating blow in the Carolinas could spell defeat for the colonial cause. The war had dragged on for so long that Congress and the army's hold on the public resolve was already weak at best.

During August, Clinton's preparations in New York seemed to signal an imminent Hudson campaign. Something had happened, however, that distracted the English commander, possibly the arrival of the French in Rhode Island, and he had relaxed his preparations. Recognizing the need to closely coordinate plans with the French, Washington scheduled a conference with Count Rochambeau in Hartford to develop the plans for a joint American/French assault against the English army in Yorktown.

James, with Washington's blessing, gave Major Gray his orders for conducting his investigation of Arnold. James by explicit direction of the commander-in-chief was a member of the party who was to accompany Washington to the conference with the French, and Gray would have to guide the Arnold investigation in his absence.

"We have two officers whose judgment you trust at West Point doing nothing more than observe Arnold." James intended his statement as a question.

"Yes, sir," Eric responded, "and I have dispatched Sergeant Smoothers and three trustworthy men from the Black Hats to West Point."

Eric's use of the phrase "Black Hats" as brief way to describe the men and officers of the company whose only duty was to support the army's intelligence collection activities no longer irritated James. It was as easy a way to discreetly refer to the secret unit as any other. James fondly recalled Smoothers as the tall sentry from Washington's personal guard who with three others had assisted John in effecting James' rescue from the gallows in New York.

"To do what?"

"To form a reserve independent of Arnold's command who can do whatever is necessary," Eric replied.

"And is there any news from New York?" James asked needlessly, knowing that he would have heard if there had been.

"No, sir. York has received only that one letter for Andre, and he has reported it was as Andre anticipated. Addressed to Andre in a female handwriting and sealed with purple wax stamped with a large 'P.'"

"And he did not open it?" James knew York had not, could not, or Andre would have immediately discovered the action.

"No sir," Eric answered, humoring James, knowing that his friend was simply using the dialogue to assure himself that all was in order.

"So, we don't know what was in the letter."

Eric did not reply to the statement.

"And York will report as soon as another letter arrives."

"Yes, sir, and we don't know who delivered the first letter," Eric anticipated James would return to the question.

"But we will learn who delivers the next."

"Yes, sir."

"How?"

"Allen will personally follow the messenger."

"Isn't there some better way?"

"No sir."

James took a deep breath and silently studied his companion. James now agreed with Eric and Allen. Something was afoot, and it involved Benedict Arnold. James was afraid it involved the betrayal of West Point, but he could not prove it. Since receiving the first report from Allen, they had closely watched Arnold. The man had done nothing that an experienced commander taking over West Point would not have done. The one thing that piqued James' interest was the man's persistent efforts to identify the two double agents on Arnold's staff who ostensibly spied for the English under James' control. James wished that Major General Robert Howe, Arnold's predecessor as commander at West Point, had not been so assiduous in briefing his successor. Having failed to learn the identity of the two spies from Howe, Arnold had gently probed his staff, unsuccessfully, James hoped.

"And if significant news arrives from New York or West Point in my absence, what will you do?" James asked.

"I will dispatch a courier to find you wherever you and the General are," Eric replied. "And then I will personally go to West Point and take whatever action is required."

James nodded approval. He recognized that Eric had just extemporized the idea to personally go to West Point, and it bothered James, but he could not tie Eric's hands. He had to trust him to act in his absence.

Recognizing that they had talked the matter to death, Eric shook his friend's hand and bid him farewell. Following Eric's departure, James rose and turned to join Washington and walk to the stables to collect their mounts for their journey to Hartford. James still hated these hurried trips, but he had no choice. Washington, a skilled horseman, always pressed the pace and seemed to enjoy James' discomfort.

James looked around his office one last time. The green fly that had nagged James persistently for the past month landed boldly on the desk as if to challenge James. James turned, pretending to leave the fly free to savor his victory, then at the last second spun and slapped at the fly. To his surprise he captured the agile creature in his closed fist. Now that he had him, James did not know what to do with him. The fly had been a major irritation, but James did not want to kill him. Always kind hearted, sometimes against his own best interests, James walked to the window and stuck his hand out into the August heat. He opened his fist. The startled fly sat in his hand and studied James. Apparently satisfied that no further threat lingered, the fly arrogantly flapped his wings and headed in the direction of the stables where James had always suspected the fly resided.

On Monday morning, September 4th, 1780, an attractive English lady in her mid-thirties appeared at the offices of the *Gazette* and identified herself as Mary McCarthy, the wife of an English officer stationed in New York. Explaining that she had the previous day arrived from Canada, she handed York Allen an envelope addressed to Mr. John Anderson. Mrs. McCarthy had acquired the letter in West Point and had promised to deliver it to the *Gazette* in return for a pass through the American lines. Without another word, the lady turned and hurried away. Since York expected the mysterious messages for his friend to be addressed to Andre personally, he had dropped the letter delivered by Mrs. McCarthy indifferently on his desk. The newspaper frequently received angry correspondence criticizing its support of the English from behind the rebel lines. An hour passed before York returned his attention to the letter. He casually turned the envelope over preparing to open the flap when he discovered the large purple wax seal embossed with the flamboyant letter "P" on the back. With regret, Allen acknowledged to himself that his lethargic indifference had prevented him from following the courier as James had instructed.

Two hours later, John Andre visited the newspaper, ostensibly to pass the time of day with his friend. York had noted without comment that since arranging for use of the *Gazette* as a letter collector, Andre's appearances had grown more frequent. York handed the letter to his friend with the purple wax seal facing upwards.

"I assume this is yours," York said.

Noting the seal, Andre eagerly grabbed the envelope. He turned it over, noted the name on the front, "John Anderson," looked at York as if expecting a comment, but said nothing.

York's stare was his reply.

"Thank you, York," was Andre's only explanation. He spun on his heels and hurried away.

Peggy Arnold departed Philadelphia on September 6th. On Sunday, September 10th, General Benedict Arnold boarded his personal barge at West Point. With no explanation beyond a casual wave of his hand to his aide who stood on the riverbank, Arnold ordered the eight enlisted rowers to proceed downstream. Major Franks assumed that his uncommunicative superior planned to meet Mrs. Arnold somewhere to the south.

Arnold spent the night at the home of Joshua Hett Smith. Smith, whose brother had been a royalist Chief Justice of New York, lived in a country home on the west bank of the Hudson near Haverstraw. An ardent rebel, Smith had cultivated a close personal relationship with General Robert Howe, Arnold's predecessor as commander of West Point, and Howe had introduced the two men. On the morning of Monday, September 11th, Arnold boarded his waiting barge and continued southward in the direction of the landing at Dobbs Ferry.

At about the same time that Arnold set out from Smith's house, the English armed sloop "Vulture" set out from its station at Spuyten Duyvil near Kingsbridge. On board were Major John Andre and his companion, Colonel Beverley Robinson, the loyalist Virginian cum New Yorker whose home opposite West Point Arnold had appropriated as his personal residence. Andre had cleverly decided to use the unwitting Robinson as a beard to cover his meeting with Arnold. Robinson could always claim with justification that he had arranged the meeting to discuss the disposal of certain personal items he had left behind.

Captain Andrew Sutherland, the "Vulture's" commander, regularly patrolled the Hudson waters his craft now crossed. A cautious man, he had earlier dispatched three gunboats in advance of the "Vulture" to make sure that his prominent passengers were not venturing into dangerous waters. Rebel craft frequently appeared off Dobbs Ferry to harass the English patrols. Sutherland did not consider it necessary to alert his guests to these precautions.

When Arnold's barge injudiciously attempted to approach the landing at Dobbs Ferry, one of the Captain Sutherland's gunboats spotted it and opened fire. At Arnold's shouted command, Arnold's rowers immediately reversed direction and beat their way to the western shore where they took refuge under the protective guns of a rebel blockhouse.

Unaware of this development, Andre ordered Sutherland to anchor "Vulture" off the Dobbs Ferry landing. There, Andre passed several hours oblivious to the fact that Arnold was doing the same one mile away on the opposite shore. When dusk fell, Andre ordered the "Vulture" to return to Kingsbridge. Arnold, never having sighted the English sloop, directed his tired and puzzled oarsmen to return to the Point.

On September 14th a drained and emotional Peggy Arnold arrived at West Point to be greeted by her genuinely pleased husband.

On the morning of September 16th another envelope bearing the now familiar blob of purple wax and the letter "P" was delivered by a stranger to the offices
of the New York *Gazette*. To York Allen's dismay, the messenger appeared while
he was absent running a menial errand. The printers had run out of ink, and
Allen had had to scurry about the city searching for a new supply.

As soon as he discovered the letter on his desk, York Allen rushed off to deliver it to Major Andre at his office in General Clinton's headquarters. Again, an
appreciative and obviously nervous Andre had thanked his friend for his assistance and then had disappeared without opening the message in York's presence.
This time Andre had simply said good-by and rushed to his superior's office.

The now dejected Allen returned to the *Gazette* convinced that he would
never identify the English spy. When he approached his desk at the back of the
shop, Allen was stunned by the sight of another envelope bearing the purple wax
and embossed "P" prominently resting in the center of his papers.

"Where did that come from?" Allen shouted.

"What?" The printer who was working in the back of the shop spreading the
black ink on his press bed responded.

"That." York pointed at the intruding envelope.

"What?" The surly printer repeated himself. He was too busy with his own
problems to worry about the young news collector who was always shouting
about something.

"This," York grabbed the offending envelope and waved it at the printer.

"Oh, that. Some guy left it for you about half an hour ago. Looks like it's
from one of your girl friends." The indifferent printer continued to spread gobs
of ink over the large metal plate.

"What did he look like?" York demanded angrily.

"Who?"

"The person who delivered this."

"Who knows." The printer shrugged his shoulders, turning his back to York
signaling that the conversation had ended.

York waved the envelope in the air. A single sheet of paper slid loosely
inside. Not knowing what else to do, the frustrated newsman hurried back to the
English military headquarters intent on confronting his friend and demanding to
know what was going on.

York, a familiar visitor to the military installation, nodded to the sentries and
made his way to Andre's office. An aide stopped him at the door.

"The major's with the general," the young English lieutenant who did not
like any American growled.

"Get him," York ordered. "I have an important message for him."

"Sit down," the aide countered. "Nobody disturbs him when he is with the
general."

York glared at the rude young officer but did as he was told.

Inside, Andre and Clinton were still discussing Arnold's latest message.

"I knew something had happened," Andre said, relieved that the failure to meet with Arnold had not resulted from something he had done. "He says he was at Dobb's Ferry but one of our gunboats fired on him."

"I can read, John," Clinton remonstrated with his Chief of Intelligence. Sometimes the eager young man got on his nerves. "I see he wants to meet with you on the twentieth at midnight. What do you think of that?"

"I'll go," Andre enthused. "It's too important not to."

"Take Colonel Robinson with you," Clinton ordered.

"I don't think his story about discussing family possessions will hold up for a midnight meeting," Andre tried to keep his voice even. It did not do to argue with the general. Andre did not want to be encumbered with the presence of the unwitting Robinson.

"Take him," Clinton ordered. He would have preferred to have Robinson undertake the mission alone. He did not want to lose his useful young assistant and could not have cared less about the loyalist. He would let the rebels have him if things did not work out.

"And stay on neutral territory. I don't want you going through the lines."

"But... ." Andre began,, knowing he would go wherever he had to go to meet with Arnold. He was too close to achieving his major coup to back off.

"And wear your uniform. I won't be embarrassed by having you hanged as a spy," Clinton ordered. It was always easier to explain to London why he had not done something than it was to justify having been stupid.

"Yes, sir," Andre retreated, recognizing that his superior was in no mood to be crossed.

Clinton tossed Arnold's message to the corner of his desk and picked up another piece of paper. His gesture indicated to Andre that he had been dismissed. Andre retrieved the message and quietly left the room.

"Mr. Allen is here," the lieutenant who guarded his door called. He had obviously heard Andre close the door that connected his office with that of the commander-in-chief.

"Again." Andre tried to sound cheerful. He folded Arnold's letter and put it into his pocket. "Send him in."

"John, what's going on?" Allen demanded, waving the purple wax sealed letter as he entered the room. "I found this waiting when I got back to the office. I'm not in the courier business. What does this woman want?"

Andre studied his friend. The genuine surprise etched across his face.

"I don't understand," he said sincerely, holding out his hand for the envelope York carried.

"Neither do I. Explain," York demanded.

"I'm sorry, York," Andre said. "I'll make it up to you. I promise there will not be many more of these."

York did not know what else to say. He stood in front of his friend's desk and watched as Andre collapsed into his chair. He placed the offending letter on the desk in front of him and stared at it.

"Aren't you going to open it?" York asked, trying to sound considerate. He knew he had pushed the tough guy tone as far as he could. Andre did not allow himself to be pressed.

"Later," Andre dismissed the matter.

The two friends discussed plans for later in the week then parted. As soon as York left the room, Andre rose, closed the connecting door to the outer officer and returned to his desk. He broke the wax seal and took out Arnold's second message of the day, anxious to learn what else had gone wrong. Andre spread the single sheet on his desk and took a bottle of acid from a drawer. With a piece of cotton he carefully swabbed the back of the paper. Immediately several rows of numbers appeared. Andre opened another drawer and took out a worn copy of Blackstone's "Commentaries." He quickly deciphered the numbers. The message was brief:

"General Washington will be at King's Ferry Sunday Evening next on his way to Hartford where he is to meet the French admiral and general. He will lodge at Peak's Kill."

Andre studied the paper, stunned. That was all Arnold had written. He had committed the final act of betrayal. Clearly Arnold was alerting the English so they could capture or kill the American commander.

Before rushing to inform General Clinton, Andre paused to fix the dates firmly in his mind. It was Saturday, September 16th. Arnold had written his message on the 15th; he said Washington would be at King's Ferry on Sunday evening, presumably tomorrow. Arnold's first message had set his meeting with Andre for the night of September 20th. Andre wondered if they had time to make plans to intercept Washington.

Andre tapped lightly on Clinton's door and entered. Clinton sat at his desk studying a document. He glared at his assistant.

"John, I'm not going to argue the matter. I've decided."

"I've a second message from Arnold," Andre explained. Obviously Clinton had thought he wished to continue their previous discussion.

Andre offered the deciphered text of Arnold's latest message. Clinton grabbed it irritably from his hand and read quickly.

"Washington," he muttered. He turned and studied Andre thoughtfully. "King's Ferry. Do we have time?"

Andre, who had already made up his mind not to let anything interfere with his meeting with Arnold, not even the opportunity to capture the American commander, studied his superior. He knew he had to choose his words carefully if he was to conceal his own plans. He knew that if the English captured Washington, he stood the very real possibility of losing the opportunity to win the war with his own stratagem of personally leading Arnold to betray West Point. Washington's capture would so dismay the Americans they would probably capitulate making the surrender of West Point unnecessary.

"We would be rushing, but I think we could do it," Andre spoke tentatively.

Clinton, who never liked to give his assistant the chance to have the last word, blustered: "And if we rush and bollix the opportunity, what will London say?"

"I don't know, sir. We could... ." Andre hesitated deliberately.

"Could what? What man? What?"

"If Washington is going to Hartford, he obviously will have to return. We could obtain the needed information from Arnold on Wednesday then plan our ambush carefully."

Clinton studied his young assistant while he carefully assessed his words. Andre was obvious. He wanted to earn the credit for both the capture of Washington and the betrayal of West Point. A double coup would certainly end the war, and Clinton the commander-in-chief could return to London a hero, successful where the Howe brothers and all others had failed. Under those circumstances, he could share a little of the honor with Andre. On the other hand, if he rushed and they botched the capture of Washington... .Clinton did not need to finish that thought.

"What do you recommend?"

"I...I... ." Andre hesitated because he knew his future rested on his answer. "I would wait. Arnold's information could be wrong. We need time to plan and to confirm it. "

"Confirm it," Clinton seized on the words. "Can we?"

"Yes sir. I can have spies at King's Point. If Washington appears as Arnold predicts, we will know we can trust the man. Then, we can plan an ambush for Washington's return."

"Very well," Clinton made up his mind. "The responsibility is yours. If anything goes wrong... ." Clinton threatened.

"I understand, sir." Andre clicked his heels as he jerked to attention and saluted Clinton. He fought to avoid smiling.

Clinton acknowledged his assistant's emotional salute with a nod of his head.

"Very well," Clinton repeated himself. "Keep me informed."

Andre spun on his heel and marched to the connecting door. He had many plans to make.

Andre spent the rest of the day consulting with his assistants. He summoned Colonel Livingston and informed him to keep Tuesday the 19th free. He also ordered the confused Livingston to instruct Captain Sutherland to have the "Vulture" and her crew to stand by for a special mission. That night, Andre joined York Allen for their usual Saturday night on the town. A weary Andre relaxed and let Allen ply him with brandy. Unaccustomed to the harder drink, Andre let slip that he would be unavailable on Tuesday and Wednesday.

"I've got a special mission for the General," Andre confided, his voice slurred by the brandy.

Allen tried to entice Andre into revealing more, but the usually tight-lipped intelligence chief realized he had said more than he should have and refused to further discuss the matter.

Early Sunday morning, York walked with his strangely excited companion to Andre's home not far from Clinton's headquarters. After the door had closed on the near intoxicated Andre, an equally nervous York Allen rushed to the fisherman's shack of his uncle. He roused the sleeping man from a deep stupor and insisted that he be delivered immediately to the New Jersey shore.

On Monday, September 18th, a bone tired York Allen arrived at Washington's Morristown headquarters. He was dismayed to learn that both Washington and James were absent. The arrogant lieutenant colonel who was serving as duty officer found the insistent civilian irritating. He had called for the sentries and was about to order that the demanding young man who refused to identify himself be forcibly removed from the army headquarters when the visitor ripped his black tricorn from his head and slapped the colonel's desk.

"Then I must see Major Gray," the man shouted.

The colonel reacted with anger to the young man's arrogance in slapping his desk with the hat. The colonel stared at the hat, then suddenly he realized what was happening. The hat was identical to that worn by Mr. Satterfield, Major Gray and the rest of the spies. The insistent youth was one of them.

"Why didn't you say so," the colonel controlled his anger and tried to smile. "The major is in Mr. Satterfield's office. I will tell him you are here." He turned with a nod to the sentries to watch the visitor and proceeded down a long empty hallway.

Allen tried to stifle his frustration and waited anxiously for the colonel to return.

Chapter 37
New Jersey, New York
September, 1780

On Sunday the 17th, General Arnold and Peggy entertained several officers and aides from West Point at the Robinson home. Arnold surprised his guests with his good humor. While they were at the dining table, a messenger arrived carrying a letter for the General from the Loyalist Colonel, Beverley Robinson, in whose expropriated home they were now seated. Arnold quickly read the note that had been handed to him by a servant and smiled.

"It seems our absent host," Arnold paused before continuing, "Colonel Robinson, is currently on board an English sloop which is anchored at Tellers Point and desires to consult with me about some of his treasured possessions." Arnold pointed indifferently at a painting on the wall, which depicted a smiling Governor Robinson, the colonel's father.

"Certainly, sir, you would not consider such a request." The colonel on Arnold's right blurted.

"Of course not Colonel Lamb," Arnold replied, folding the note and shoving it into his pocket. Arnold turned to the waiting servant. "I have no reply."

The next morning Arnold prepared a private message for Robinson and sent it with a house servant to be delivered to the English sloop "Vulture." Arnold did not trouble to seal the envelope. The text of his letter politely declined to meet with Colonel Robinson. Included on the back in invisible ink was an enciphered message for Andre that stated:

"I shall send a person to Dobbs Ferry to the "Vulture" Wednesday night the 20th instant and furnish him with a boat and a flag of truce. You may depend on his secrecy and honor and that your business of whatever nature shall be kept a profound secret."

Major Eric Gray was surprised and did not know whether to be dismayed or pleased at York Allen's sudden appearance. Whatever he felt did not matter because he soon was confused by the excited newsman's report. Two things were clear: Major John Andre had received two apparently urgent messages from his rebel spy, and they had triggered a meeting set for Wednesday that was important enough for Andre to risk approaching American lines. When York finished his story, he sat and expectantly waited for praise and further instructions. Eric, suddenly faced with responsibility for decision, did not know what to say.

"Well, what are you going to do about it?" The impulsive York demanded.

Eric studied the young man who was about the same age as himself and was struck by his own calmness. The four years he had spent with James and the Black Hats had surprisingly matured him. He found himself reacting just as he imagined James would have in the same situation. He smiled calmly at the disbelieving Allen, rose to his feet, retrieved his dusty, worn tricorn from its usual position of honor on his desk, placed it on his head and moved towards the door.

"Where are you going?" Allen asked, unable to keep the excitement from raising the pitch of his voice.

"To West Point, of course."

"Benedict Arnold," Allen gushed, surprised. He had not been privy to James and Eric's suspicions. "Of course. Peggy Loring."

York Allen jumped to his feet and jammed his own black hat on his head. "I'm going with you."

"No you're not," Eric paused at the door and held out his hand to press York Allen's chest. "We need you in New York in case we miss Andre this trip."

"But...but... ." Allen sputtered. He knew Gray was right. "I've earned the chance to watch the capture," York insisted, stepping back from Eric's restraining hand.

"You have, but you're still going back to New York before you're missed," Eric persisted. He was pleased to note that York had stepped back from his restraining hand instead of attempting to brush it away. The move indicated he respected Eric's control.

"I guess you're right," York reluctantly agreed.

Eric reached out and vigorously shook York's hand. "Thank you, York," he spoke softly. "You've done an excellent job. You may have saved the Revolution." Eric was not sure if he had overspoken, but the young newsman seemed pleased with the words.

Eric rushed from the headquarters building and went directly to the nearby structure that housed the Black Hats' support company. He located a senior sergeant, ordered him to have ten men, fully armed, prepared to ride in half an hour. The sergeant, accustomed to spur of the moment demands, saluted, turned and shouted up the stairs to the second floor.

Exactly one half hour later, Eric and ten soldiers, including the sergeant, galloped out of Morristown and headed north. Eric did not know where he going, except to West Point, and he had no idea what he was going to do there. Several hours later, north of New York City in the midst of the neutral territory, Eric reined up his horse. He called the sergeant to his side, spoke quickly as he briefed him on Allen's report, then ordered him to ride immediately for Hartford to alert Mr. Satterfield and the commander-in-chief.

On Tuesday morning, the 19th, Arnold met with Joshua Smith, the same Smith who owned a home on Haverstraw Bay that Arnold had previously visited, and gave him a pass:

"Permission is given to Joshua Smith, Esquire, a gentleman Mr. John Anderson who is with him, and his two servants to pass and repass the guards near Kings Ferry at all times."

On Wednesday, September 20th, Major John Andre boarded the sloop "Vulture" at Dobbs Ferry at seven in the evening.

Late that same day, Joshua Smith approached a waterman named Samuel Cahoon, who tenant-farmed a parcel of Smith's estate, and ordered the man to take him in his boat to a sloop anchored in the bay. Cahoon, knowing the boat was an enemy warship, refused. Smith explained that he was on a mission for General Arnold, but Cahoon still refused to assist. After much argument, Cahoon agreed to meet the next day with General Arnold and in person receive his orders.

On board "Vulture" an anxious Andre spent a disappointed night. By daybreak it was apparent that General Arnold's man was not going to appear. Andre pondered his options. He could return to New York and face Clinton's wrath, or he could devise a story for Captain Sutherland and Colonel Robinson and linger a second night. A determined Andre chose the latter option knowing that by doing so he might anger General Clinton even more. He reasoned that if Arnold finally appeared, his superior's mood would rapidly alter. He pretended to have acquired a severe cold and accepted Colonel Robinson's well-intentioned advice to rest on board "Vulture" before returning to New York.

General Arnold met with Samuel Cahoon the boatman late Thursday afternoon and counseled him to assist Mr. Smith that night. After much discussion, the less than enthusiastic Cahoon agreed. Arnold's threat to arrest Cahoon if he refused to respond to his country's need was persuasive.

Late Wednesday afternoon Major Eric Gray and his small party of Black Hats arrived at Haverstraw. While the sergeant arranged fresh mounts, Eric stretched his legs and walked through the small village. On impulse, he decided to check with the guard detachment assigned to control traffic on the road.

After identifying himself as a member of Washington's staff en route to West Point where he planned to meet the commander-in-chief returning from Hartford, Eric asked the rough sergeant for news of happenings in the area.

"All's quiet," the man answered. "Except... ." he began but did not finish.

The answer was what Eric had expected. He had simply been making conversation. He waved and turned towards the door when something about the man's last word caught his attention.

"Except?" He asked.

"Oh, nothing."

"What nothing?"

"Well, General Arnold passed through about an hour ago. On his way to Josh Smith's house to spend the night."

Eric, surprised, silently considered the portent of the man's words.

"And there was that tall sergeant with three riders who came along behind."

"Tall sergeant? What was his name."

"Didn't say."

"Could it have been Smoothers?" James had sent Sergeant Smoothers and three others to West Point to keep a watch on Arnold.

"Can't say," the guard grew irritated. "Said that didn't I?"

Where is this Smith's house?"

"Down the road a piece."

"I need one of your men to show me the way."

"Not sure I can do that."

Eric walked to the door and called to his sergeant who had halted Eric's small troop outside the guard shack with their fresh mounts.

"Sergeant. Send me three husky men."

Eric turned and glared at the unhelpful guard. The man smiled at the dusty major, turned and spit a load of tobacco juice in the corner and watched as three large men crowded through the door with rifles at ready.

"Well, major," the guard said. "Just so happens I might be able to help you myself."

The guard led Eric and his troops to the lane that led to Smith's house.

"Up there a piece," the guard declared before wheeling his horse about and riding through Eric's troops who lined each side of the road.

Eric watched as the man disappeared in the direction of town. He turned and studied the lane that led to the Smith house. He was unsure what to do next. While he pondered his problem, his troopers waited. Suddenly, a familiar voice called from the woods to his right.

"Major. Major Gray. Be that you?"

Eric whirled his horse about to face the tree line.

"Who's that? Show yourself," Eric ordered.

A tall figure wearing a black tricorn over his blue uniform appeared. He deliberately pointed the muzzle of his long rifle towards the ground.

"It's me. Sergeant Smoothers."

Eric, recognizing the man James had dispatched to watch Arnold, dismounted. He quickly conferred with the laconic sergeant. Smoothers reported he and his men, now concealed in the woods, had followed Arnold down from West Point earlier in the day. Arnold was holed up in the house on the bluff overlooking the river with the man known as Joshua Smith. As best as Smoothers had been able to learn, Smith was a friend of the general. Eric briefed Smoothers on York's report noting that he suspected that Andre planned to meet with Arnold that night. With Smoother's assistance, Eric deployed his men around the Smith house.

After about an hour, General Arnold emerged from the Smith House, mounted his horse and rode north towards West Point. Smoothers, whose orders were to track Arnold, regrouped his men and with Eric's blessing followed along behind the galloping general. Eric, suspecting that Smith was somehow involved in setting up the meeting scheduled for midnight, continued to watch the Smith house. Just as dark descended, Smith emerged and rode a short distance to a tenant house near the river. Eric and three of his troopers followed at a discreet distance. They watched as Smith and another man they later identified as Cahoon seemed to argue. Cahoon persistently shook his head. Smith pointed at a long boat beached along the riverbank and gesticulated wildly. Cahoon continued to shake his head. After about an hour of persistent argument, Smith mounted his horse and returned home. Eric sent two of his troopers after Smith and waited to watch Cahoon. Since the man owned a boat and lived on the river, and since York suspected Andre would be coming by sloop up the river, Eric decided Cahoon was key. To his dismay, about fifteen minutes after Smith's departure, Cahoon closed the doors to his small house and retired for the night.

Eric and his troopers spent an uncomfortable night with their backs propped against the trees. The experience reminded Eric of his days waiting for York Allen on the New Jersey coast.

About midnight on Thursday the 21st, Smith and Cahoon boarded the latter's long boat, muffled the oars in sheepskins, and rowed several miles down the Hudson to Haverstraw Bay. They approached the darkened "Vulture." Cahoon waited in his boat while Smith boarded the larger vessel. After several minutes, Smith returned, accompanied by a second man wearing a bulky blue cape. The two joined Cahoon in his boat, and Smith ordered Cahoon to row to shore.

After beaching the boat, Smith and the unidentified second man, Andre, walked inland.

"General Arnold will meet us nearby at Old Trough Road. He will have a spare horse, and the two of you will ride to my house for your meeting."

Andre, who wore his uniform underneath the cape, was nervous, but he was excited by Smith's words. He was about to meet the man with whom he had corresponded for over sixteen months. Their negotiations of treachery were about to reach a conclusion.

Andre followed Smith up a steep incline to an evergreen forest. Smith shoved through the outer trees and led Andre to a clearing. The full moon illuminated the forest in a soft gray light. The air was cool, but Andre sweated under the weight of his uniform and cape. He was would have liked to take the cape off but did not dare. He did not know how much Smith knew about his identity. Clinton had ordered Andre to wear his uniform, and he had, but he did not want to advertise the fact. Clinton had also ordered him not to cross the lines, but Andre had no idea where he was. For all he knew he could be on enemy territory. Once he had boarded the long boat, he had lost control and had fallen completely into Arnold's hands.

Andre stared at the outline of the thick, lumpish man who emerged from the shadows where he had waited for them. He took one limping step forward as Andre approached and held out his hand. Andre found the man's grip soft and damp.

"Where is Colonel Robinson?" Arnold demanded. "He was supposed to come too," Arnold seemed to complain.

Andre explained he had come alone because Colonel Robinson was unaware of the true nature of his mission. "Surely, you agree that is best," Andre said, trying to remain polite despite Arnold's churlishness.

"Are you authorized to speak for General Clinton? Arnold demanded, ignoring Andre's question.

Andre turned and stared at Smith, his silent answer obvious.

Arnold dismissed the anxious Smith and ordered him to return to the boat as planned.

"I speak for General Clinton. I am Major John Andre, Chief of Intelligence for His Majesty's forces."

Arnold nodded.

"We must be perfectly clear," Arnold continued gruffly. "I will be paid twenty thousand pounds for turning over West Point and its three thousand troops to General Clinton's army. And, because I am abandoning my home and all my property, I must also be given an additional ten thousand pounds."

"Agreed," Andre responded. Clinton had advised Andre to offer less, but he decided the circumstances were not conducive to bargaining. He stood alone in a dark forest, probably behind enemy lines, talking with a rebel general.

Arnold began briefing Andre on the fortifications that would be found at West Point. Arnold limped and paced as he talked, and Andre listened, wondering how on earth he was going to remember all the details. He had not planned on standing in the dark and listening to Arnold drone on and on. Finally, Smith reappeared and cautioned Arnold that they should move on to his house. Arnold glared at the man, nodded, then gestured for Andre to follow. Andre had no choice. He had lost all semblance of control of his fate. He had to depend on the odd American traitor.

Arnold led the way uphill through the pine forest. Branches kept lashing back from Arnold's abrupt passage striking Andre in the face. Finally, they reached a trail. A black servant waited for them, guarding three horses. Andre, Arnold and the servant mounted the horses. The servant led the way to what Andre presumed would be Smith's house. That was where they had said they were taking him. Andre began to sincerely regret his impulsive actions that had placed him in this helpless trap.

They passed near a village that Arnold identified as Haverstraw. A sentry stopped them, frightening Andre, but as soon as Arnold disclosed his face, the sentry saluted and waved the riders on. Andre did not look back but assumed the guard stared after them, wondering what the general was doing afoot in the blackness of night.

Andre noticed that the track led past darkened farmhouses. He hoped they would soon reach their destination. The first traces of dawn streaked the skyline to Andre's right. Finally, the servant turned on a lane and led Arnold and Andre up a steep rise. When they cleared the forest line, Andre caught his first view of Smith's house, a rough two story dwelling that appeared to look out over the river far below.

Andre handed the reins to the black servant and followed Arnold into the empty house. If Smith had a family, he had apparently moved them elsewhere during Andre's visit. Arnold led Andre up the stairs and into a large bedroom overlooking the river. Andre was startled to see bright flashes of light in the distance.

"Gunfire. Teller's Point," the uncommunicative Arnold grunted.

"Vulture?" Andre gasped with a start.

Arnold did not answer.

The cannon fire Andre had observed indeed involved "Vulture." As instruct-ed, Captain Sutherland had anchored off Teller's Point following Major Andre's curious late night departure. The night had passed slowly, and at dawn, rebel gunners began to harass the English sloop that had so arrogantly anchored off their shore at the outer range of a new six pounder that had been put in place over the weekend. "Vulture" returned the fire. After one of the rebel balls struck the sloop's foremast and a flying splinter pierced the captain's neck, he ordered his crew to take his vessel downstream. He did not intend to risk his vessel and crew for the sake of one fool hearty English soldier, general's aide or not.

Late Thursday night, Eric's patience was rewarded. He and his men watched as Smith and Cahoon pushed the long boat into the river and rowed southward. Sergeant Smoothers trailed Arnold to Smith's house and then to his midnight meeting in the pine forest with Andre. When Andre and Arnold returned at dawn to Smith's house, Eric, his men, and Smoother with his troopers jubilantly watched in silence.

Success presented Eric with a problem, and he struggled to determine what James would do under the circumstances. He could surround the Smith house, break in and capture Arnold and the stranger who had appeared in the boat with Smith and Cahoon. Eric assumed the man was his prey, Major John Andre, James' English counterpart, but he was not sure. Smoothers had reported the story of Arnold's letter from Beverley Robinson requesting a meeting to discuss his family house. Smoothers suggested the stranger could be Robinson, not Andre. If Eric and the Black Hats crashed into the Smith house and found Robinson not Andre, they would alert Arnold to their suspicions and he might succeed in deflecting their charges with the Robinson story. Arnold could admit to an indiscretion and would probably escape with another reprimand.

On the other hand, if the stranger were Andre, the Black Hats would have captured both the traitor and the enemy's Chief of Intelligence delivering a mas-sive blow to the English.

Eric knew he had to make a decision based on inadequate information. Deciding that suspicions were not enough, he opted to wait. The men would eventually separate. Smoothers could follow Arnold back to West Point, and Eric could capture the stranger alone on his way back to English lines. Then, without the distracting presence of Arnold, they could identify the stranger.

Washington was meeting with Rocheambeau for his last planning session on Friday morning when Eric's messenger reached Hartford. He found James waiting at the local military headquarters and breathlessly relayed Eric's message. James immediately recognized its portent. He ordered Washington's staff to prepare for an immediate departure. At noon, the doors to the large room where the commander-in-chief was debating with the French his plans for a decisive attack on Yorktown opened; James immediately crowded into the room, took Washington by the arm, and repeated the message:

"Andre met with Arnold yesterday." James had assumed the meeting had come off as scheduled.

Washington turned pale, agreed with James they should depart for West Point immediately, then rejoined the French admiral to express his apologies for having to cancel plans for a celebratory dinner.

"Military necessity," was the only explanation Washington offered.

Rochambeau, eyelids drooping, watched Washington depart. To the French, form and protocol were more important than substance.

On the "Vulture" Colonel Robinson became involved in a shouting match on the quarter-deck.

"You cannot abandon Andre. He is in hostile territory," Robinson declared.

"I will not put my ship or my crew in harm's way for one man," Captain Sutherland replied heatedly.

"But he is the general's key aide," Robinson insisted.

"Then he should not have unwisely risked his life and this ship by landing in hostile territory," Sutherland stubbornly replied. "In any case he can make his way by land back to safety," Sutherland snapped, turning his back on his passenger indicating the conversation was at an end.

Chapter 38
New York
September 1780

Despite his concern about the apparent departure of "Vulture" and worry about his return to New York, Andre forced himself to concentrate on making the most of his meeting with Arnold. In response to Andre's questions, many of which required Arnold to repeat material he had already covered during their conversation in the pine woods, Arnold grew increasingly irritable. Finally, he produced a series of maps and diagrams and shoved them across the table to his anxious interrogator. One glance convinced Andre that Arnold had prepared them to use at their meeting, and they covered most of the material that Arnold had so hastily disclosed.

"May I keep these?" Andre asked, without giving a thought to how badly they would incriminate him if captured. Andre still assumed that somehow he would reboard "Venture" for a safe sail to New York under the protection of English cannon.

"Certainly," Arnold agreed quickly. He had already obtained the commitments from Andre that he had sought and was now anxious to return to West Point.

The black servant who had guided them to the Smith house prepared and silently served breakfast. Andre, whose stomach continued to churn nervously, ate quickly, concentrating on his many questions and Arnold's quick answers rather than the food.

At ten o'clock, Arnold announced that he had to return to his headquarters.

"Mr. Smith will arrange for your return to New York."

Andre assumed Arnold meant return to "Vulture" and did not question the statement. Andre, weary from lack of sleep, had already concluded that the documents in Arnold's own handwriting and the information already provided constituted as much as Andre could digest at this meeting.

Eric and his troopers watched from their hiding places in the woods as Arnold mounted his horse, which the black servant had led from the stables in the rear of the house. Arnold, alone, departed in the direction of West Point. After a hurried conference with Eric, Sergeant Smoothers and his three companions waited a few minutes then set off to follow Arnold. To the best of Eric's knowledge, Andre and the black servant were now alone in the house. Eric now had his opportunity to seize the Englishman alone. Not knowing if Arnold planned to return, Eric decided to wait and in doing so missed his opportunity.

Inside the house, Andre retreated to the bedroom where he could watch the harbor for "Vulture"s return and study Arnold's documents while he waited for Smith who was to accompany him back to safety. Andre assumed they would wait for nightfall then Smith and his companion would take him in the long boat back to "Vulture."

About one o'clock Joshua Smith returned to his home. When Smith informed Andre that the plan now called for them to wait for dark and then proceed to the English lines by horseback, Andre reacted heatedly, insisting that he be returned to his boat. Smith settled the argument with a question.

"What boat?"

Andre who had been pacing strode to his bedroom window. Smith was right. The harbor was empty. Smith and Andre waited impatiently in nervous silence until sunset. Time and again Andre fingered and studied the passes that Arnold had signed and left behind. Finally, unable to stand the tension of inaction, Andre issued an order:

"Let's go."

While Smith arranged for their horses to be saddled, Andre retreated to his bedroom. There, he folded Arnold's maps and diagrams in neat squares and placed them in his boots where they fit comfortably between Andre's stockings and the boot soles. Andre had just pulled his boots back on when Smith entered the room. Smith carried a worn claret colored coat.

"You can't travel in that one," Smith indicated Andre's bright scarlet uniform jacket. "Take this one."

"I can't," Andre replied without confidence. He knew it would be dangerous to try to cross rebel held lines in a British officer's uniform. On the other hand, if captured out of uniform, he knew he would be summarily hung as a spy.

"Then you will travel on you own. General Arnold said you were to wear a disguise." Smith held up the tattered coat. "It's an old one of mine. Take it."

Andre, torn by indecision, studied the civilian coat. Finally, with reluctance he took off his scarlet uniform coat and replaced it with Smith's old coat. It was too large but would do. Smith took Andre's scarlet coat and folded it carefully. Andre watched with concern as Smith stuffed it into a bureau drawer.

Eric waited as Smith and Andre mounted their horses, then departed in a canter down the lane. At the intersection with the road, the two men turned south. On their right, the trailing edge of the sun sank below the horizon. Eric decided to follow the two men a short distance before seizing them. He wanted to first identify their direction and make sure they were not again meeting with Arnold.

Arnold spent the day at his West Point Headquarters. Late in the afternoon, he crossed the Hudson in his barge and dined alone with Peggy. Arnold was in a buoyantly infectious mood despite the strangely sour looks he had encountered at headquarters following his return from Smith's farm.

Unknown to Arnold, his aide Major Franks and his secretary, Varick, had had a tense conversation that morning. Neither man liked Joshua Smith, and both suspected his motives. Franks, displeased that his commander had again visited the Smith farm, had voiced his concerns to Varick.

"The general is an avaricious man," Franks had commented disloyally. "I had hoped he learned his lesson in Philadelphia." Franks referred to the court martial which was a subject of common gossip at West Point.

Franks and Varick's discussion disclosed that both men feared that Arnold was concocting with Smith some kind of smuggling venture involving trade with New York. Rumor at the Point had already accused Arnold of hoarding supplies in the storerooms at Robinson House. The two men terminated their talk by agreeing that they could not serve a corrupt commander. Franks, who was the closest to Mrs. Arnold, having first met her in Philadelphia, promised to discuss their concerns with her at the earliest opportunity.

Washington and James departed Hartford late on Thursday afternoon. They rode hard for two hours until darkness forced them to overnight at an ordinary some twenty miles from the conference site. They rose at daybreak on Friday and resumed their gallop. Several hours were lost in mid day when James' horse lost a shoe, and they had difficulty locating an adequate replacement. As insurance,

Washington and James each purchased backup mounts. Late in the afternoon, a local farmer divulged that British patrols were scattered in the area ahead, possibly alerted to Washington's passage by spies in Hartford. Washington's party, dismayed by the possibility of lost time, turned northward at James' insistence. Washington's security was paramount.

Wearing his blue cloak, Andre impatiently followed his guide Smith. To Andre's irritation, Smith found it necessary to pause and pass the time of day with every local rider they met. A smoldering Andre silently waited while Smith chatted. Smith without asking Andre's permission stopped at an ordinary in Stony Point for a drink with some rebel officers. Andre's uncomfortable charade seemed to amuse Smith who for some reason had taken a dislike to his taciturn companion. Andre recognized that Smith had less than average intelligence and worried that his overconfidence might betray him.

Andre planned to ride all night to reach White Plains. He had no intention of lingering any longer in rebel territory than necessary. Smith had already begun talking about his obligation to retrieve his family on the return trip home and had indicated he thought his mission with Andre a burden. This did not discomfit Andre. The sooner he was free of Smith, the happier Andre would be. Each passing mile saw Andre's normal assurance return little by little.

In the distance, Andre saw the dim flickering lights of a village.

"What's that?" He called to Smith.

"Crompound, about eight miles from Verplankt," Smith replied.

At the outskirts of the village, three guards emerged from the woods and halted them. As a dismayed Andre watched, one of the guards, an officer of some sort, approached Smith and demanded to know who he was and where they were going at this time of night. Smith confidently replied they were on a mission for General Arnold. He showed the officer their passes. The man studied them by lamplight then stared skeptically at the silent Andre. The officer asked how far they planned to travel.

"A far piece," Smith replied enigmatically.

The officer to Andre appeared to take a dislike to Smith.

"I must warn you that loyalist bandits are operating tonight on the road south," the officer cautioned.

A long discussion ensued with the officer insisting that Smith and his companion spend the night in the village. He even identified a house where they might find lodging. The officer frequently used the word "cowboys" to describe the loyalist outlaws. Finally, Smith agreed and led the way to the house recommended by the officer. Andre followed, worried and a little frightened by the delay, but convinced he had no choice. To insist on moving on would have only enhanced the suspicions of the rebel officer.

Smith and Andre spent an uncomfortable night in the bed they shared. Andre resented the fact that Smith had not even removed his boots. At daybreak, declining to pause for breakfast, Andre insisted they continue southward.

Eric and his troop watched Smith's long conversation with the guards from a distance. Eric waited until Smith and Andre had entered the village house and then approached the rebel guard. Eric identified himself as an aide to General Washington returning with his troop to Morristown. He asked the guard officer about his conversation with Smith and Andre and was delighted to learn the two had decided to halt their journey before proceeding south. Eric assigned two of his men to observe the house where Smith and Andre were staying then led his troop a short distance south where they camped in the woods just off the road.

Smith and Andre rode hard after they left Crompound Saturday morning the 23rd of September. Andre pushed past Smith and forced the pace. After about an hour's ride, Andre began to relax. Each mile between him and the suspicious guard officer improved his disposition. He had lain awake the entire night listening for sounds that might indicate the guards had decided to arrest the strangers. They paused at an isolated farmhouse and purchased breakfast from a willing farm wife. About seven miles south of Crompound village, Smith decided the time had come for him to turn back. He explained that he was unfamiliar with the remaining fifteen miles to White Plains and noted he was no longer of use as a guide. Andre delighted at the prospect of being free of Smith, agreed. He suspected Smith was worried about the prospect of encountering loyalist marauders. Andre, confident of his ability to explain his status as an English officer, was delighted.

Eric and his band concealed themselves in the woods and waited for Smith to pass on his return journey northward. Eric assigned two men to track Smith. He continued to pursue Andre. Recognizing that Andre was approaching the security of neutral ground, he decided to overtake his prey and place him into custody. This proved more difficult to implement than decide. Buoyed by his nearness to safety, Andre rode hard. It was all Eric and his Black Hats could do to keep pace about a mile behind the galloping Englishman.

Taking the advice of a farmer boy who warned that bandits were operating ahead, Andre took the road to Tarrytown. About ten o'clock at a bridge just north of Tarrytown, three men bearing arms halted the galloping Andre. While they were examining his pass, Eric and his troops appeared. While a surprised Andre watched, the rebel soldiers surrounded the three guards and the worried Englishman. Eric identified himself, accepted the word of the three Westchester men that they were members of the patriot guard, and announced that the stranger was an English officer who was now his prisoner.

The three guards led Eric and his prisoner surrounded by the Black Hats cross-country to North Castle where the American army maintained an outpost. Upon arrival, Eric, using his rank and superior force, commandeered the building. To the dismay of a militia sergeant, he and the three guards were ordered outside. Eric posted two of his men at the door and retreated inside with Andre.

"Identify yourself," Eric demanded, uttering his first direct words to Andre.

"I am an officer in His Majesty's Service," Andre replied proudly. He recognized that he had been captured by rebel forces and was determined to ensure they understood he was not masquerading as a civilian. He regretted having bowed to Smith's advice and changed coats.

"You do not look like one," Eric challenged. "You must be a spy."

"I insist I am an English officer on an official mission for General Clinton."

"And what may that be?" Eric smiled.

Andre did not reply, not knowing what to say.

"Show me your papers," Eric insisted.

Andre had a gold watch in his pocket, a few continental dollars he had borrowed from Smith, and Arnold's papers in his boot.

"I do not have any," Andre replied honestly.

"Except for this pass from General Arnold," Eric said accusingly. "Where did you get that?"

Andre's silence again answered the question.

"I recognize the circumstances appear strange," Andre admitted. He quickly decided that his only hope for escape from this rebel officer might be bribery. He had heard many were corrupt. "If you help me, I give you my word that you may keep my horse, my watch and...one hundred guineas."

"Show me the guineas," Eric challenged.

Andre did not respond.

"Empty your pockets," Eric ordered.

Reluctantly, Andre laid his gold watch and the handful of continentals on the table in front of him.

Eric studied the meager hoard and laughed. "Is that all?"

"That's all I have with me," Andre said honestly. "But I give you my word that General Clinton will pay one hundred guineas for my release."

"For a spy," Eric again accused.

"No," Andre persisted. "For an English officer on a mission for his King."

"Your name," Eric insisted.

Andre stood silent.

"Take off your boots," Eric ordered. Couriers frequently concealed documents in their boots.

Andre did not move.

"All right," Eric smiled. He was enjoying himself. He knew who Andre was and who he had met. Andre did not know what Eric knew.

Eric strode to the door and called out. "Two men. Inside, quickly."

"We will help you," Eric spoke softly, turning back to Andre.

The Englishman shrugged, sat on a chair and pulled off his boots. He stared forlornly at the white trimmed leather of the boots that he had had custom made by a bootsmith in New York.

Andre set the boots on the floor in front of his chair. Eric nodded to one of the soldiers who had entered at his command. The soldier looked into the dusty boot and smiled.

"What do we have here?"

Andre watched silently as the soldier extracted the documents that Andre had so carefully folded. The soldier handed the parcel to Eric. Eric sat behind the table and unfolded the smudged papers. He carefully pressed them flat on the table and began to study them.

"Yes. What do we have here," Eric smiled at the soldier and Andre. "These are sketches of the fortifications at West Point. Where did we get these, my friend."

Andre stared at the floor. He recognized that if the rebel officer were smart enough to recognize the plans that he would know how to deal with Andre.

"Major John Andre, Chief of Intelligence for His Majesty's North American Army, you are under arrest for committing espionage." Eric could not think of a more formal charge on the spur of the moment.

The smiling officer's words shocked Andre. The man knew exactly who he was. Either Smith or Arnold had betrayed him. He recognized that he had failed. Clinton would be embarrassed, the rebels would keep West Point, and the war would continue. Andre wondered if he could negotiate for his life.

"And you will be hung just like poor Nathan Hale."

The American officer's words battered Andre like a club. Determined to honor himself despite his failure, Andre stood at attention in his stocking feet and declared:

"You are correct. I am Major John Andre, an aide to General Clinton, on an official mission for my superior. I deny I am a spy."

"And what are these?" Eric held up the papers.

"Those were given to me by General Arnold. I visited him at his official invitation under his flag of truce. Those papers are the property of His Imperial Majesty."

"I commend you for your honesty, Major Andre," Eric laughed. "Now, where is this flag of truce?"

"It was issued orally by General Arnold. You may ask him." Andre forced himself to reply dispassionately, treating his captor as an equal. "You can see my pass issued by General Arnold."

"And your uniform?" Eric smiled. Is claret the official color these days for His Majesty's officers?"

Andre shrugged his cape from his shoulders and let it fall to the floor. He looked at Smith's worn coat.

"This coat was forced upon me by Mr. Smith at General Arnold's recommendation. Otherwise, my uniform is intact. See for yourself." Andre pulled his arms from Smith's coat and threw it on the table. He stood proudly in his uniform shirt, trousers and stocking feet. "I am now in uniform."

"Some spies try to have it both ways," Eric replied acidly. "Please sit down Major Andre, I have some questions that I want answered."

Eric, knowing he had Andre in hand, decided to obtain as many details as he could from the English spy while he was still on edge from his capture. Eric recognized that Andre had decided his only possible salvation lay in placing full responsibility on General Arnold for his presence behind American lines in disguise. Eric intended to let the man convict himself. To Eric, capturing Andre was more important than Arnold at the moment. Sergeant Smoothers had Arnold under observation. Arnold, unaware that Andre had been seized, would behave normally. Rather than facing the bluster of a lying, treasonous American general himself, Eric preferred to arm himself with whatever information he could acquire from Andre and then let James and Washington confront Arnold. He anticipated that Washington and James had received his message and were now riding hard for West Point.

While Eric talked with Andre inside the commandeered guard post, the angry militia sergeant conferred with the militia officer who had first detained Andre at the bridge. Neither had ever heard of Major Eric Gray or the Black Hats and wondered if they were actually on Washington's staff. Both resented being shunted aside.

"Who is the prisoner?" The sergeant asked one of the Black Hats.

"An English spy. Don't worry about it. Major Gray will handle him."

The sergeant returned to the militia officer's side.

"They claim he's an English spy," he muttered out of the side of his mouth.

"And they will claim all the credit. Me and my boys caught him at the bridge," the officer said angrily.

"Then we better do something about it," the sergeant agreed.

"What?" The officer, a local butcher, asked.

"We don't know who they are. Let's check with West Point. General Arnold won't like Washington's boys poaching on his turf.

"By golly you're right. Who should go?"

"I will," the sergeant decided. "I'll tell them you sent me." The sergeant began forming his story in his mind. Somehow he would get the credit and the reward for capturing the English spy.

"Go," the officer agreed. He had just slaughtered a large boar and was not anxious to undertake a hard ride to West Point. The sergeant was a local farm boy, and the butcher was confident he could outmaneuver him for the credit when Arnold's boys showed up to take charge of the spy.

The sergeant casually strolled towards the barn at the far side of the guard post where he kept his horse.

"I better get back to the bridge and keep an eye on things," the sergeant extemporized for the benefit of the strangers.

"Vulture" with Robinson and Captain Sutherland still on board returned to Teller's Point on Friday evening. After being driven southward by the rebel shelling, the two men had calmed down and had agreed they had not expected Andre to return Thursday night. Therefore, they had not reported Andre's absence to Clinton and had returned to await the absent aide. They passed a disappointed night, retreated southward and returned a third time Saturday after dark. On Sunday, the 24th of September, after waiting another long and fruitless night, Colonel Robinson directed that "Vulture" return him to Kingsbridge. He retrieved his mount and rushed to New York City. The duty officer at headquarters had no knowledge of the General's whereabouts, and the harried Robinson left a hurriedly drafted message:

"It is with the greatest concern that I must now acquaint Your Excellency that we have not heard the least account of Major Andre since he left the ship. I hope to have your Excellency's further instructions what to do. I shall do everything in my power to come at some knowledge of Major Andre."

The anxious sergeant from the Tarrytown militia reached West Point late Sunday afternoon. He sought out the duty officer and informed him he had an urgent message for General Arnold. The duty major, who had just settled down to his evening's ale, had a curt response:

"Give it to me."

"I must speak directly with the General," the sergeant insisted, not willing to surrender his news to another.

"Who is it from?"

"I cannot say." The sergeant was not about to be bullied by a fat duty officer.

"Then you can wait."

"Until when?"

"Tomorrow morning." The major sipped his first mug of the day.

Despite his fervent pleas, the sergeant was not able to persuade the major who was content in his knowledge that Arnold was at home in the Robinson House across the river and would not want to have his weekend disturbed by a scruffy militia sergeant. The sergeant finally surrendered to the fat major's obstinacy and retreated to a nearby ordinary where he soothed his irritation with several mugs of his own.

At nightfall on Sunday James and Washington, riding mounts exhausted by the mountainous back trails they had been forced to traverse, halted at Fishkill still two hours south of the Robinson House on the western side of the Hudson.

At the Robinson House, General Arnold and Peggy presided over a table that counted Colonel Lamb, Major Franks and Lieutenant Colonel Varick as the only guests. Franks and Varick were in bad humor. Although neither man admitted it, both were disturbed by the late afternoon visit of Joshua Smith who the General had met privately behind the closed doors of his library. Neither Franks nor Varick knew the purpose of the visit—Smith had reported the news that John Anderson (Andre's alias) had safely cleared the American outposts--and both men had been irritated that the General had met yet again with Smith. The two men quibbled throughout the meal, surprising both the general and his wife with the intensity of their feelings. Neither suspected that both men were in reality angry with the general. Mrs. Arnold, concerned about her husband's increasing irritation at having his Sunday meal so disturbed, finally asked both men to quit their petty arguing. Later, Arnold in the privacy of his library sharply reprimanded Franks before dismissing him.

On Monday morning the militia sergeant obtained a ride across the river to the Robinson House on a skiff that was carrying provisions for the general's dinner. About nine o'clock two surprise visitors from the south arrived, Colonel Alexander Hamilton and another aide had set forth at sunrise from Fishkill to alert General Arnold that he could expect General Washington and Mr. Satterfield to arrive sometime during the morning. Arnold personally welcomed the Washington aides and sat them down to breakfast with him. He apologized for his wife's absence; she was still asleep in her chamber. A servant served the hungry men from a platter heaped with fried eggs, country ham, sausages and griddlecakes that were a particular favorite of Arnold. The servant filled the General's plate last and backed from the room. Arnold, who particularly liked breakfast, had just taken his fork in hand when his aide, Major Franks, entered the room.

"I'm sorry, general, but a special messenger has just arrived from the south." Arnold, like Hamilton, assumed that Franks referred to another courier from Washington.

"Show him in," Arnold ordered, pleased at the opportunity to demonstrate to Washington's aides his own responsiveness to the commander-in-chief.

Not comprehending the misunderstanding, Franks frowned his disapproval. He did not consider the dusty militia sergeant a fitting person to enter the general's breakfast room.

"Show him in, Franks," Arnold repeated his order, making no effort to hide his displeasure at Franks' hesitation.

Franks pivoted and hurried from the room. Seconds later he reappeared followed by the dirty militia sergeant in his makeshift uniform. Arnold stared at the odd messenger then glanced at Hamilton who looked as confused as Arnold by the man's appearance.

"Give me the message," Arnold ordered, now anxious to be free of the disreputable man. Arnold made a mental note to find out if he were from his own command and correct the oversight if necessary.

The sergeant, who was hesitant to speak now that he had finally attained admittance to the general's august presence, was glad he had written a few words on paper the previous night to be used if aides refused to let him see the commander.

"Here it be, general," the sergeant smiled, displaying several brown and broken front teeth. He held out a ragged piece of dirty paper.

Arnold snatched it from the man's hand and opened it, repelled by the dirt.

"We catched the spy."

The words staggered Arnold. He blanched and almost dropped the paper. He needed know no more. Aware of the necessity of maintaining a front of normality, he nodded.

"Very well, sergeant. Please wait outside. I will handle this."

Relieved to be dismissed, the sergeant hurried from the room. Arnold crumpled the message and shoved it into his pocket. He turned to Colonel Hamilton.

"Colonel. A minor matter. I should dispose of it before General Washington arrives. If you would please continue with your breakfast, I will rejoin you shortly."

Arnold rose and strode briskly from the room. Hamilton looked at his companion who shrugged his shoulders to indicate his puzzlement, shook his own head negatively to agree and turned back to his heaping plate. Both men were hungry from three hard days on the road. Without a word, they began to eat.

Arnold rushed upstairs to his wife's room. He had just begun in an excited voice to explain they had been found out, that Andre had been captured, when someone knocked on the door.

"Yes," Arnold shouted.

"One of General Washington's riders has arrived," the Robinson House servant announced. "The General is nigh."

"Christ " Arnold swore. He bent over his wife's bed, embraced her and almost shouted. "Stall. I will send for you."

With those words Arnold raced from the room, hurried down the stairs, out the front door.

On the porch, he passed Major Franks.

"Greet General Washington on my behalf. Tell him I had business at the Point and will see him shortly."

General Arnold in a most undignified fashion ran towards the waterfront where his barge waited. Major Franks watched in befuddlement. Arnold leaped into the boat.

"Quickly, down river," he ordered."

The eight oarsmen, accustomed to the general's sudden quirks, rushed to obey. Within minutes they were in the current and paddling vigorously southward.

Before Major Franks had a chance to wonder about the general's odd choice of directions, he heard the hoofbeats of several horses approaching from the south.

"It must be General Washington," Hamilton, who had appeared at his side, observed.

Franks' slack mouth revealed his confusion. He noticed the motley militia sergeant standing at the foot of the porch waiting.

"Don't stand there, man," Franks called. "Go out back to the stables and wait. We'll send for you when we need you." Franks knew that Arnold would be furious if the unsoldierly man were present when the fastidious Washington arrived.

Washington, accompanied by James and five guards, the maximum escort the general would accept, arrived. Franks noted the horses panting and sweating and wondered why the general had ridden so hard. Hamilton saluted Washington and nodded at James.

"Is everything in order?" Washington asked.

His question struck Major Franks as strange. Washington looked at Hamilton who in turn stared at Franks.

"Welcome General Washington. Mrs. Arnold is in her room. I will inform her of your arrival. General Arnold expresses his regrets. He has just been summoned to the Point on pressing business. He asks that you have breakfast and expects to join you shortly." Franks hoped that he had fulfilled his orders. One of an aide's duties was to cover for his general.

Washington glared at Hamilton. In self-defense he nodded agreement with Franks. Washington seemed to struggle to control his irritation. James who sat on a horse, which stood behind the general's mount, stared anxiously in the direction of the river. He was about to speak when he noticed Sergeant Smoother appear around the corner of the house. Smoother, who had been in the rear of the house trying to make himself inconspicuous, had not witnessed Arnold's abrupt departure. He nodded at James and smiled. James relaxed. James dismounted.

"I don't know about you general, but I'm starved."

Washington looked at his friend quizzically, then relaxed.

"Very well, James." Washington raised his eyes to Major Franks on the porch. "We accept General Arnold's hospitality Major. Please lead the way."

Within an hour, the barge, riding on the strong current and propelled by the muscle of eight experienced rowers, rounded Teller's Point.

"Head straight to that sloop," Arnold ordered.

The general's command surprised the oarsmen. The flag over the anchored vessel was English.

"Don't worry," Arnold assured them. "We are meeting under a flag to discuss certain approved matters for General Washington."

On board "Vulture" Captain Sutherland and Colonel Robinson watched as the long boat approached. General Clinton had ordered them back to Teller's Point for one more day of waiting against the possibility that Major Andre might unexpectedly appear.

"That's General Arnold," Colonel Robinson whispered, unable to keep his astonishment muted.

The long boat pulled alongside "Vulture." English seamen leaned over the rail and trained their rifles on the boat's crew. Arnold made his way on board the sloop, turned, saluted and dismissed his barge. The confused oarsmen allowed their boat to drift with the current. They watched as Arnold appeared to confer with two Englishmen, then disappeared from sight. The sloop pulled anchor, raised sails and headed south. The astonished oarsmen turned their craft and began the tedious pull back to the Point.

Washington impatiently breakfasted with his aides. When neither Arnold nor his wife appeared, he decided to proceed across the river to West Point to join the fort commander there. He cast a summoning look at Hamilton and James, and both scurried to follow him to the riverfront.

While Washington had breakfasted, Peggy Arnold had busied herself behind locked doors in the bedroom she shared with her husband. Arnold had not had time to issue instructions, but she had not hesitated. Peggy devoted the entire hour to stuffing letters and notes into the burning fireplace.

When Washington and his party arrived at West Point, they proceeded immediately to Arnold's headquarters. They greeted the duty officer's report that General Arnold was still at Robinson House with dismay and concern. Washington seated himself at Arnold's desk, summoned the senior officers and immediately issued orders designed to secure the fort against any untoward developments. James hurried back to the riverfront. He arrived just in time to meet a second barge from the Robinson House. It carried a distraught Sergeant Smoothers. He was accompanied by one of the more disgusting appearing militia sergeants James had ever seen. Smoothers reported what he had learned. The militia sergeant had been present when a tall major wearing a black tricorn accompanied by a troop of ten men had arrested an English spy. The man had reported this information to Arnold at Robinson House just minutes before Washington's arrival. Arnold had fled to his barge and disappeared downstream.

James and Smoothers hurried to headquarters and reported to Washington. Eric had apparently captured Andre, but Arnold, thanks to the sergeant's inept warning, had escaped to the south. Washington, relieved that West Point had been saved, did not take the time to relish the capture of the spy nor denounce the flight of the traitor. He concentrated on assuming command of West Point, leaving James to worry about the fleeing Arnold and Eric and his prisoner.

A guard was posted at the Robinson House. By mid afternoon a doctor was summoned by Major Franks to treat a distraught Mrs. Arnold who appeared to be suffering some kind of nervous breakdown. She seemed to be alternating extreme hysteria with frightening moments of clear lucidity during which she lamented the loss of her husband and speculated about her future. Franks could not tell whether she was playacting or not. He asked the doctor who only replied:

"Who knows? If she's not stage acting, she's in serious emotional straits and needs more assistance than I can give her."

Chapter 40
October 2, 1780
Tappan, New York

James sat in his newly acquired office in Washington's temporary headquarters in Tappan, New York, and sadly contemplated the open window. In the distance he could see Mabie's Tavern where Major John Andre had been held since he had been moved from his makeshift prison at the Robinson House. Responsibility for the prisoner's care had been turned over to the army's Provost Marshal, but James still felt a strong sense of obligation. The Black Hats had unveiled the conspiracy, and the Black Hats had apprehended Andre. James knew all credit belonged to York Allen and Eric Gray, but the responsibility was his.

The damp leaves of the oaks and maples and sycamores and elms shimmered in the mid-morning sunlight. The brilliant colors had begun to fade, and the first of the falling, brown, withered leaves, nature's harbingers of winter's approach, rustled in the light breeze. James studied the outlines of Mabie's Tavern and thought of the prisoner. James had difficulty sharing the popularly held view that Andre had earned the punishment meted out by the court-martial. The court, personally selected by Washington, had been composed of the army's finest. Nathaniel Greene presided. Lord Sterling, Lafayette, Baron de Steuben, St. Clair and Robert Howe, along with eight eminent brigadiers, had served, and they had taken two days to reach their verdict.

"...that Major Andre, Adjutant General to the British army, ought to be considered as a spy from the enemy; and that, agreeable to the law and the usage of nations, it is their opinion he ought to suffer death."

Washington in the next day's general orders had approved the sentence and set the execution for five o'clock in the afternoon on October lst. A formal appeal from General Clinton, which was duly accepted and denied, resulted in a postponement until noon on October 2nd.

The pounding of hammers interrupted James' contemplation. He turned, briefly studied the gallows and the workmen who were making last minute repairs, then swung away and stared at the wall.

James had spent much of the past week talking with Andre. Against his predilections, James had found himself attracted by the young man's charm and courage. In the face of adversity, Major Andre had stood tall. He had stoically presented his own case to the court-martial, and he had accepted their verdict. He had written letters to his family and to General Clinton; despite his contrary inclination, James had read the letters; they represented duty. Andre had expressed his love and concern for family and regret for any negative impact his actions might harbor for General Clinton's future. Andre reminded James of himself and John in their youth, and of his son Jason. He remembered his own experiences following his capture in New York. He had not faced a court-martial, but he had heard Admiral Sir Richard Lord Howe casually order that James be hung as a spy. If it had not been for his brother John, Eric Gray, York Allen, Sergeant Smoothers and the three Black Hats, James would have suffered the same fate that now awaited Andre.

The thought made James wonder why spies were summarily hung. Andre, like James, like Hale, like others, was simply an officer doing his country's bidding, unquestioningly obeying orders. They stole secrets; they listened when others were indiscreet; some of what they did could be construed as corrupting others, but they did not fire cannon or rifle balls or wield bayonets, all of which did considerable harm to others. Andre was an intelligent, charming, hard working young man who was sincerely dedicated to his country, his king and his army. If there was a villain, James knew it was Arnold who had deliberately and with malice betrayed his country for gold.

Andre had not corrupted an innocent patriot; Arnold had sought out the English; yet, Andre found the gallows, and Arnold lived in luxury in New York, undoubtedly demanding that the English fulfill their commitments. James anticipated that the English would pay, and pay, and he knew that Peggy who was every bit as guilty as her husband would one day join him to enjoy their dirty gains while Andre's bones rotted in American soil.

James shook his head in frustration, hoping the abrupt movement would unscramble his thoughts. He kept asking himself: Why Andre? Why not Arnold?

James had no answer. James continued to study the blank walls with unseeing eyes. The room felt like a prison. James had not marched to war; he had not sensed the excitement in the beat of the drums or the screams of the fifes. He had tried to avoid the conflict, despite his rational understanding of the patriot cause; events and his friendship for Washington had inevitably drawn him into the vortex. He felt no pride in the fact he wore mufti not uniform; he recognized that to do so would be false. He could have had a title, but he had declined, though he recognized he was bound tighter to Washington and service than any militiaman or regular. They at least returned home when they chose or when their enlistments expired. James wondered why he had no finite term. Like Washington, his sense of honor and duty bound him to service as long as the war lasted. James could sense that the English were stumbling; he could not say it aloud, but he doubted the English resolve would hold past another year. And then, James could not even allow himself to think it; then,...and then... .

A knock on his door interrupted his reverie, his old man's questioning dream filled with whys and what ifs.

"Sorry to disturb you, James."

Lieutenant Colonel Eric Gray stood in the doorway, immaculately clad in a new blue uniform decorated with gold buttons, epaulets and the sash denoting that the wearer was a person of importance, one of Washington's aides. James drew pleasure from the fact Eric still was a little out of uniform; he wore his black tricorn. James looked at Eric and remembered the brash young ensign who had delivered Washington's summons to duty. Neither man had then recognized that their futures were to be so closely entwined. Eric had prospered, rising from ensign to lieutenant to captain to major and now to lieutenant colonel.

James was conscious of the fact he remained simply Mr. Satterfield. Eric deserves the reward, James thought, unable to recall a single instance when Eric had faltered, had questioned an order, had hesitated to act. His actions in James' absence had resulted in Andre's capture. James was as proud of Eric as he would have been if he had been his own son. James felt a sense of paternal responsibility. He knew Eric had tried to imitate James; the black hat had begun as a simple joke, but it had quickly become a symbol, Eric's way of declaring that James was his master. Some claimed that Eric had allowed Arnold to escape and did not deserve reward, but not in James' hearing.

James wondered if he had been responsible for Eric having allowed Arnold to flee. James remembered the green fly. He had held it in his hand and could have crushed it, but in a moment of compassion had allowed the insect flight. James suspected that Eric's decisions may have been deliberate; he could have anticipated the militia sergeant's actions; he should have known Arnold would run as soon as he learned of the capture of the English spy, but he did not give the orders that would have kept the sergeant in Tarrytown, and James knew Eric had behaved just as James would have.

"Yes, Eric."

"If you want to have a last few minutes with Andre..."

"Yes. Thank you."

Eric, like James, like most continental soldiers who had come in contact with Andre, respected the young man and was saddened by the prospect of his inevitable end.

James rose, placed his worn black tricorn on his head, and walked slowly towards the door. Eric stepped aside and allowed James to lead the way.

Outside, the streets were filled with sightseers. All had come to see the English spy hung. Farm youths darted about shouting in their intrusive, newly acquired foghorn voices. Farmwomen sniffed on handkerchiefs while their husbands shared the rapidly moving jugs. James noted that a wagon had been backed into place under the rope. Andre did not rate a hinged trap door. The rope, dangling from an improvised A shaped frame constructed of rough hewn timbers, hung over the rear of the wagon where Andre would stand. A farmer, James assumed he was the owner of the wagon, waited patiently on the wagon's front bench holding the reins to two husky but placid farm horses.

James nodded to the sentries and entered Mabie's Tavern. Followed by Eric, James ignored the filled main room. The chatter subsided when the stern faced James appeared. The guards swung open the storeroom where Andre waited. Eric and James entered, and the guard slammed the heavy door shut behind them.   Andre looked up expectantly, and James realized he still hoped for clemency. James sadly shook his head from side to side. The false anticipation slipped from Andre's face as he sank to his makeshift cot.

"Did you have breakfast?" James asked, not knowing what else to say.

"From General Washington's very own table, I am told," Andre responded.

A heavy silence settled on the room. James noticed that Andre was dressed in a clean uniform. He had heard that Clinton had personally ordered that one be sent from New York. Andre had been offered a Bible and a chance to meet with a preacher, but, unlike Nathan Hale, Andre had declined both. He was quoted as having said that in death he would not require the assistance of crutches he had not used in life.

James sat on the cot next to Andre and affectionately patted the young man's knee. Eric, who in a sense was responsible for Andre's presence in the gloomy room, leaned against the door.

"John, I'm sorry," Eric broke the silence.

"No, Eric," Andre spoke the name softly, "you did your duty as I did mine. No regrets."

James noted that the young man struggled to maintain his composure. He had been told that one of the guards when serving Andre his breakfast had broken into tears. "Leave me until you can show yourself more manly," Andre had quietly remonstrated.

A tap sounded on the door. It opened, and Captain John Hughes and Ensign Samuel Bowman appeared.

"I am ready at any moment, gentlemen, to wait on you." Captain Hughes stood at attention as he spoke.

James nodded, and the two men withdrew.

Andre and James stood.

"John. Is there anything I can do?" James asked, his voice breaking. James knew the sense of hopelessness that the young man felt. He remembered the moment he had been dragged from his cell on Lord Howe's flagship and escorted roughly to the boat that was to take him to the gallows. The crude jailer had spit on his shoe as he passed, a sign that he considered James beneath contempt.

"No thank you, James. I have been treated fairly, and you and Eric have been kind."

James embraced Andre and stepped back. Eric, fighting to control his emotions, stepped forward, clasped Andre briefly in his arms then retreated and saluted.

"If you are ready, major."

Andre nodded. Eric led the way through the tavern's public room to the outside. Two guards appeared on each side of Andre. To the roll of drums, the guards and Andre marched through the parted crowd to the waiting wagon. James and Eric followed.

When he sighted the makeshift gallows, Andre paused briefly before continuing.

"Gentlemen, I am disappointed," Andre spoke softly.

James knew that Andre's request to die by firing squad had been denied by Washington himself.

"I am reconciled to my death but not to the mode," Andre said to no one in particular.

The crowd grew quiet. All watched as the procession marched in step to the wagon. Andre stared at the cart bearing a black coffin that stood to one side. He started to speak, then caught himself. When he reached the wagon, Andre stopped and turned to face the crowd. His pale face revealed no sign of emotion. James stepped forward and shook Andre's hand. His action had been involuntary. He heard the crowd's negative gasp; they had come to see a spy hanged, not honored, but James ignored them. Eric, following James' example, also shook Andre's hand. This time the crowd silently watched. James noted that Andre's foot had found a small stone and he was rubbing his foot back and forth over it, almost as if he were privately trying to feel the earth for the last time.

James nodded to the hangman waiting in the wagon. He reached down and helped Andre up into the bed. For some reason the hangman had smeared his face with soot. He led Andre to the waiting rope and raised his hands to lift the noose over Andre's head. Andre reached up and guided the rope into place. Andre looked at James.

"It will be but a momentary pang," Andre said softly, speaking only loud enough for James, Eric and the hangman to hear.

Captain Hughes stepped forward:

"Major Andre," he said loudly. "If you have anything you wish to say more, you have the opportunity."

Andre looked at Hughes and replied in an audible voice.

"I have nothing more than this. That I would have you gentlemen bear me witness that I die like a brave man."

Captain Hughes ordered Andre's hands tied and a blindfold put in place. He nodded to the hangman. He took his seat beside the waiting farmer at the front of the wagon, grasped the reins, cracked the whip, and the wagon jerked forward. Andre's neck cracked when the rope took his weight. His body writhed. James and Eric stood at attention and watched until all movement stopped. James turned and retreated through the silent crowd.

Eric and James returned immediately to headquarters where they reported to Washington that his orders had been carried out. Washington nodded and said nothing. James and Eric sat themselves in the chairs arranged in front of Washington's table. Washington stood and faced the window. A heavy silence filled the room. All three men turned inward, each wondering how much longer the dreadful war would continue.

About the Author

A graduate of West Virginia University, Robert L. Skidmore spent thirty-five years in the foreign service of the United States government. Now long retired, he devotes himself to two lifelong passions, historical research and writing, both of which allow him to play with his computers.

Printed in the United States
1941

9 781588 270016